I0614546

BUT NOT
FOR ME

J.S. COOK

Dreamspinner Press

Published by
Dreamspinner Press
5032 Capital Circle SW
Ste 2, PMB# 279
Tallahassee, FL 32305-7886
USA
http://www.dreamspinnerpress.com/

This is a work of fiction. Names, characters, places, and incidents either are the product of the author's imagination or are used fictitiously, and any resemblance to actual persons, living or dead, business establishments, events, or locales is entirely coincidental.

But Not For Me
Copyright © 2013 by J.S. Cook

Cover Art by Aaron Anderson
aaronbydesign55@gmail.com

All rights reserved. No part of this book may be reproduced or transmitted in any form or by any means, electronic or mechanical, including photocopying, recording, or by any information storage and retrieval system without the written permission of the Publisher, except where permitted by law. To request permission and all other inquiries, contact Dreamspinner Press, 5032 Capital Circle SW, Ste 2, PMB# 279, Tallahassee, FL 32305-7886, USA.
http://www.dreamspinnerpress.com/

ISBN: 978-1-62380-416-9
Digital ISBN: 978-1-62380-417-6

Printed in the United States of America
First Edition
March 2013

To Jennifer Stillman LaClaire:
You're aces, kid.

They're writing songs of love, but not for me....

George and Ira Gershwin
"But Not For Me"
1930

CHAPTER
ONE

"THERE he is." Nino leaned back in the seat and jerked his chin at a tall, thin figure ascending the steps of the Public National Bank.

"You sure, Nino?"

One of the young men was already reaching down to the floor of the car to retrieve a violin case. He kept his eyes on the figure on the steps as he snapped the chopper together with practiced ease and mounted a drum magazine. "You sure that's him? You don't wanna make a mistake."

"I ain't makin' a mistake!" Nino snarled. "Now go on! Do as you're told!"

A series of deafening reverberations shook the interior of the vehicle. The man on the steps danced like a marionette before falling facedown against a pillar.

Nino grinned. One less mug was one less mug. "That'll teach him." The big Packard pulled away from the curb and disappeared into the milling traffic of the late-night street. "Yeah." He sat back and lit a fresh cigar. "That'll teach him to mess with Nino."

THE phone woke him early the next morning, shrilling just inches from his ear and jarring him from an unsettling dream of night and endless city streets. He rolled over, a stocky, dark-haired young man in silk pajamas, and grabbed the phone just before the ringing stopped.

"What?" The voice that spoke was a flat, rather nasal voice, a New York voice, born on the Lower East Side among tenements and corner stores, cigars and street cars and laundry hanging from the fire escapes and iron balconies of innumerable overcrowded, low-rent apartment buildings. "Whoszis?"

"Hey, Nino, you up?" His brother Tony was younger by three years but infinitely simpler in temperament and disposition. His one claim to fame was his ability to back Nino to the wall, no matter what. "It's Ma. She ain't so good."

"Whatta ya mean? She was fine the last time I seen her." He grabbed the alarm clock and held it close to his eyes; like the rest of the Moretti family, Nino was slightly near-sighted, a fact he refused to admit. At thirty-eight, he was quickly approaching the age when spectacles would be necessary for any ordinary man. Not Nino, though; not The Little Prince.

"The doctor says it won't be long. Maybe you better come home, Nino. Come and see her before it's too late."

A click, and the line went dead. Nino lay back for a minute, screwing his fists into his eyes. What day was it? Yeah, Saturday… or early Sunday, something like that. If he was still living at home, he'd be getting up in a few hours, going to Mass with Tony and his mother, but Nino didn't do that anymore. He hadn't been inside a church since Louie the Goat was bumped off, and then only so the other mugs could see him and know who was supposed to get the credit. The news that The Little Prince had shown up at the funeral lit up the Lower East Side for weeks. It took a lot of guts to stand there in church, but that was Nino.

He nudged the palooka beside him—a compact, blue-eyed youth with a mop of ginger hair—with his elbow. "Hey, you. Get up."

"Awww, Nino, come on…." The other man winked at him. "You said last night we was for keeps."

"Ain't nothing for keeps around here, mug." Nino stuck one foot in his back and shoved. "Go on! Get out!"

The young man made a face. "You don't love me no more?"

"I never loved ya to begin with. Get your clothes on." Nino rolled onto his back and contemplated the ceiling while the palooka got dressed. "What's your name?" he asked. Somehow they'd never gotten around to names; Nino had picked him up in a club just after midnight and spent five minutes slipping him the tongue and a C-note before inviting the boy home on impulse. It wasn't something he usually did; for reasons of personal safety, Nino preferred to take his pleasures elsewhere. It wasn't good business to take somebody home. You never knew who was working for who and what kind of heat they were packing. Marco Dinetti got it the same way—stabbed in the eye by some Village gunsel working for Lili Wacker's mob. By the time his boys found him, he'd been dead a week and blue flies had set up housekeeping in his skull.

"Don't you remember?" Nino's latest conquest pouted. "It's Charlie." He slipped into his coat. "Am I gonna see you again, Nino?"

"Don't lay no bets on it... wait a minute." Nino reached for his wallet and gave the guy another C-note. "Here. Go as far as it'll take ya, mug." He waved as the other man went out the door. "Yeah, see ya."

Nino went into the bathroom and ran the shower hot. There had been a lot of drinking the night before and a lot of whoopee, and he felt like half the Brooklyn Navy Yard was rattling around inside his head and banging on his brains in two-four time. He stripped off his pajamas and stood under the shower for twenty minutes, then soaped up good, shaved away the shadow of his dark beard, and rinsed off cold. Once the coffee got going, he swallowed a cup with two aspirins and dressed: dark suit, dark tie, black shoes. He slipped a sleek black handgun into his shoulder holster and checked the knot of his tie in the mirror.

He looked like hell.

TONY was waiting when Nino arrived with Danny Murphy. Danny and Nino had grown up together, stealing from freight cars and chasing each other through the streets, raising Cain wherever they could. Danny, an amateur boxer of some note, had been known to help Nino out of a scrape or two in his time. Murphy wasn't very big but was real handy with his fists—maybe too handy. Some guys whispered that Danny Murphy was crazy, trying to get himself killed, starting fights with anybody who came near him and taking down guys twice his size just for something to do. Danny grew up just as poor as Nino—the youngest of fifteen loud, redheaded kids in a tiny apartment on the Lower East Side, right above a fruit store. Danny even walked like a guy spoiling for a fight—balanced on the balls of his feet with his fists sorta swinging by his sides, ready to deck somebody in the kisser. Danny's big blue eyes and gentle mouth belonged on a matinee idol, but anybody who thought Danny Murphy was soft was a real dumbbell.

"How's it goin', Tony?" Danny faked a punch at Tony's jaw.

"Yeah, keep them flippers where I can see 'em, mick." Tony stepped back and crashed into the cupboard. Put one foot wrong in Nino's ma's old place and the whole joint shuddered like a hophead on a Saturday night.

"You wanna keep the noise down?" Nino stepped in between them. "Ma's sick, okay? Or ain't I being clear enough for you two mugs?"

"Sorry, Nino, I didn't mean nothing." Danny shrugged his hands back down where they belonged. "No disrespect to your ma, you know me."

"Yeah, I know you." Nino found some coffee in the usual place and dug the percolator out from under the sink. It was pretty dusty, but so was everything else. "Hey, how long has Ma been under the weather, huh?" He glared at Tony. "You don't call me, you don't get no word to me? Whatta ya think this is, huh?" The anger was there inside of him, boiling just under the surface of his skin, and the blood beat in the back of his eyes and in his fingertips.

"Don't be like that, Nino." Tony shrugged like the big gorilla he was, all brawn and no brains. "You know I didn't mean nothing. I was talking to Big Jake and Arnie the Dope and nobody knew where you was."

"Big Jake?" Nino sneered at him. "Arnie the Dope? You know where to find me. You just didn't have the guts—"

"You go on, Nino." Danny took the percolator out of his hands and ran it under the tap. "I'll make some coffee. You go on in." He nodded toward the back bedroom. "It's oke. I can handle this big mug. He gives me any trouble, I'll put him out like a light bulb."

The room was dark, all the window curtains drawn. Nino's mother was a faint figure lying in her bed, pale and silent. There was a queer sort of smell in the room, like blood and vomit mixed; he tried to hold his breath and not breathe it in too much. Nino had no stomach for that sort of thing. "Ma? It's me, Nino."

"Nino?" Her voice still sounded the same as it always had: melodic and a little bit tired. "Come here, *caro*. Let me see you."

It was bad. There was an odor of pus and blood in the room and the smell permeated everything. "Right here, Ma. I'm right here." He sat on the side of her bed and embraced her, and tried not to cry. It was no good to cry. Ma had been sick like this for months and never told anybody; even though Nino had money for the doctor, she wouldn't go, wouldn't take anything from him.

Maybe Ma don't want your blood money. Tony's take on the whole thing was not exactly comforting.

It ain't blood money. I earned this with my own two hands, see.

Yeah, we all know how you earn your money, Nino.

You ain't never been too proud to take it.

"I want you to be good boys, okay?" She reached for him, held his wrist. "You and Tony look after each other, huh?"

"Aw, Ma, don't be talking like that. You're gonna be just fine. I'll get a different doctor. Doc Yoplanski don't know nothing. He ain't so smart." His bottom lip trembled; he struggled not to cry. Not now. Now it was too late.

She held on to his wrist. "Be good to your brother. Tony ain't got your smarts, you know that. Look after him."

His face suffused with blood; Nino stood up. "I gotta go."

He walked right out, past Tony and the coffee pot, right out onto Broome Street like he was touched in the head and didn't stop until Danny's hand fell on his shoulder.

"Don't be coming down all hard on Tony," Danny said. "You know he ain't…." He took a breath. "You know he don't like lookin' for you in them places."

"She ain't good, Danny." Nino went back, sat down on the stoop, and laid his pounding head in his hands. "She ain't so good."

"We'll get a good doctor for her, you and me. We'll get a great doctor and he'll get her fixed up in no time, huh? That's what we'll do, me and you. We'll do it, Nino. We can do something for Ma, can't we?"

But they couldn't. Nino was in Dutch, but good. And in a week or two, she was gone: cancer. He would never forget the smell, the blood-and-vomit smell in her room the day he went to see her. And at the funeral, carrying his mother's coffin, he thought about his old man and how he beat on her almost every day—beat on her and beat his brother Ray, beat him 'til he died—and it did something to Nino, killed something inside of him. After the funeral he went back to their old apartment with Danny and with Tony and opened a bottle and proceeded to drown his sorrows in the traditional manner. By midnight, he was well and truly stewed; Danny, who rarely took a drink, brought him home, stripped him naked, and rolled him into bed.

"Nino, I'm leaving the phone here by you, alright? You promise me you'll call me if you need to? You're gonna be jake." Danny leaned down and patted Nino's cheek. "You listenin' to me, Nino?"

"Why dontcha stay?" Nino curled up on his side, head swimming, the skin of his face tight with the salt from his tears. "What's the matter with you? Why can't you stay here? What's your big hurry, anyway?" He grabbed a handful of Danny's coat and held on. "Why're ya in sucha big rush, huh? Can't stand to be here with me?"

Danny tried unsuccessfully to extricate himself from Nino's grip. "Awww, don't start that again!"

"Danny, come on. Ain't we always drunk outta the same bottle, huh?"

Danny gazed down at him, and something moved in his expression. He shrugged out of his jacket. "Alright, quit your yappin'." He pulled a chair and sat beside Nino's bed. "I'll sit here 'til you fall asleep." Nino made as if to say something, but Danny was quicker: "We've had this argument before. No."

Nino made a face. "Yeah, but—"

"You know why."

STANLEY ZADWADZKI was some kind of clerk, only nobody was really sure which kind or what he did. Technically one might classify him as a bookkeeper, if one were inclined to be generous, but really he did all the little jobs around the office nobody else cared about or wanted to do. His pay varied, depending on what he happened to be doing and how generous the boss—Big Frank O'Hara—was feeling. Stanley had no set lunch hour, got no regularly scheduled breaks for coffee or a cigarette, and he belonged to nothing remotely resembling a labor union. Everybody—from the big boss all the way down to the wiseacres who brought the newspapers in—made it a point to pick on Stanley, mostly because he was smaller than the rest but partly because he didn't or couldn't fight back. It was alright with Big Frank to trip Stanley up if he was coming past a row of desks with a tray full of dirty coffee cups—and if it was half-past quitting time on some sunny afternoon, the guy who dropped a flask of something wet on Stanley's double entries in the ledger was the biggest hero of them all. Even Phyllis, the leggy redhead who worked Reception and who swore up and down Stanley was a nice guy and maybe they ought to stop picking on him, wasn't above bumping him with the filing drawers or stepping on his wingtips with her stiletto heels.

Stanley wiped his mouth in his handkerchief, suddenly nervous. "I was just... I was having my lunch, I don't think—"

"Boss wants to see ya." The goon shrugged. "He don't like to be kept waiting by no pencil-pusher. You know that."

"Al-alright." He laid the sandwich down and wiped his sweating palms in his pants. Big Frank wanted to see him. That was never good.

Stanley came from a little town in Kansas, some place not much more than a wide spot in the road, with a few cows and some fields full of corn and a few willow trees bending and swaying in the summer breeze. Stanley's parents had loved him once, but that was a long time ago and they were both dead now, and with them went the memories of that little town, and the pretty white church where he'd spent Sundays, and the little school, and the swings in the park. It was all gone, and Stanley was in New York now and had been ever since he'd come East on a train one wet Monday morning with nothing to his name except a cardboard suitcase with a change of clothes and five dollars in change. He'd cried from Kansas to Virginia, stopping to change trains at Union Station in Washington, DC, and then he'd wept silently from DC to New York, his forehead pressed against the window. A large man with a Siamese cat in a carrier had sat next to him when Stanley changed trains at Union Station; the large man fell asleep and the cat yowled in its carrier and Stanley was miserable. When he finally got off the train in New York City, he was still miserable and still alone, and the only place he could afford was a third-rate flophouse with a hand-painted sign advertising "BEDS: FIFTEEN CENTS." He paid the fifteen cents and climbed the stairs and somehow never left. His landlady, Mrs. Reilly, cooked his meals and did his laundry with something less than Christian charity, but it was cheap, and besides, he couldn't think of anywhere better to go. He had no friends.

He'd found the job with Big Frank when a guy in Tiny's Bar mentioned Big Frank was looking for a bookkeeper, some smart guy with an education and a good head on his shoulders. What Big Frank got was Stan the Rube, or as the backroom boys liked to call him, Stan the Stupe, short for stupid. It wasn't too long before Stanley realized what working for Big Frank meant—Big Frank wasn't just another honest businessman—but by then it was too late: once in, never out. So he stayed and did Big Frank's books and the boys all called him Stan the Stupe.

Big Frank liked to call him something else, and it wasn't long before Stanley realized what that meant, and he wept secretly with shame and was glad his mother and father were dead. The rest of the boys knew and teased him: "Hey, gunsel, how's tricks?" The rest of the boys teased him because they knew what it meant when Big Frank called for him, when Big Frank sent one of his gorillas to find Stanley and bring him to the office. Big Frank's office was in a private part of the business, set behind a fake wall. You had to press a button to get into it, and you didn't get out until Big Frank was ready to let you out. The first time Stanley went to Big Frank's office, he'd stood there with his mouth open until Big Frank yelled at him, told him to get his stupid rube ass in the door and not waste time. That day—those moments—effectively crushed the last of his innocence. When he was finally let out again, he was bruised and bloodied and it felt like someone had torn his insides out.

He wondered if a man could die from it. He wanted to ask someone—a doctor—but he was too ashamed. He had dreams about something very different, dreams he hardly dared to think about, dreams of someone kind and gentle laying him down on a soft feather bed and touching him and kissing him, bringing him slowly and effortlessly to a shattering peak and letting him drift down slowly, softly.

He had been with Big Frank for five years now and he knew Big Frank owned him, body and soul. There was nothing Stanley could do about it. There was nothing anyone could do about it. Big Frank owned this territory and nobody had better not say anything about it. Or else. That was what Big Frank said, and he drew his finger across his throat and laughed. "Ain't nobody takes what's mine," he said. He stroked Stanley's cheek the day he said it, and kissed him and said Stanley was his favorite out of all the boys he'd ever had.

Big Frank often gave Stanley little jobs to do. Whenever there was an important party, Big Frank took Stanley with him, made Stanley stand beside him and light his cigarettes, flick the dust off his shoulders and his shoes. "He's a clever gunsel," Big Frank would often say. "Does everything I tell him to." And he would tweak Stanley's cheek. "Ain't that right, kid?"

Stanley waited now while Jimmy Two-Shots Brown opened the hidden door for him. He had that name because he once took out half a dozen cops with only two shots left in his revolver. Jimmy was about six feet six and weighed maybe a hundred and fifteen pounds, soaking wet and carrying books. His two front teeth were missing and he'd left the tip of his nose somewhere in the Bowery, but he was smart and Big Frank trusted him, and that was all that mattered.

"Go on in, gunsel. The old man's waiting for ya."

"A-are you sure it's me? I m-mean, I was just doing the books and I think—I mean, I'm sure he—"

"Go on in!" Jimmy Two-Shots shoved him through the door into Big Frank's office. Big Frank was with his tailor and this made Stanley glad—somebody else meant Big Frank didn't expect to be serviced, didn't want Stanley down on his knees in front of him or worse.

Big Frank was easily as tall as Jimmy Two-Shots but three times as heavy. His huge gut stuck out in front of him like the prow of a tug, and his enormous buttocks quivered when he walked. His eyes were pale and bulbous and set flat in his bloated face, and his big lips were pink and greasy-looking. He favored a lot of jewelry and all of it was real, from his diamond pinky rings to the emerald stickpin shimmering in his cravat. Big Frank liked aftershave lotion too, but not that bay-rum garbage the rest of the boys used; Big Frank's cologne came from France in tiny little bottles and smelled like lots and lots of money, and the pomade Big Frank wore in his hair was made from ingredients that smelled like his cologne, and Big Frank only wore the very best clothes.

Big Frank started out as a fabric cutter in some garment district slop shop when he was eight years old, and stole and lied and cheated his way up until the Volstead Act made the sale and possession of alcoholic beverages illegal, and then he branched out into a little liquor on the side. Big Frank ran numbers and he ran girls; he owned a string of fancy nightclubs where patrons could drink and dance and screw the dames from the floorshow in special rooms upstairs.

Big Frank liked living large and he didn't care who knew it. His organization ran like the proverbial well-oiled machine—except in this case it was oiled with sex and booze and maybe a Cadillac of good-quality cocaine on the side, if that's what Frank's guys wanted. There were only two other bosses in the entire city with as much pull as Big Frank, and one of them was Joey Texas, whom everybody said was almost washed up except he'd found himself a brand new torpedo.

"Some little greaseball named Nino," Jimmy Two-Shots said. "They call him The Little Prince." Rumor had it Nino Moretti had his eye on Joey's territory, and it was only a matter of time before he drilled Joey and took over the works. Yeah, Nino was the big six, alright.

"You want—you wanted—uh, Jimmy said—" Stanley ran a hand through his hair, which was dark blond and very soft and never stayed put. No matter how much he combed and brushed and pomaded, there were always one or two strands springing loose to tickle his pale forehead. "You wanted me."

"Yeah, there's a big shindig Saturday night and you're going." Big Frank shoved the tailor away and got down off the stool. "I need you with me. You got it?"

"Of course, boss." Stanley let himself exhale. A party. It was just a party. "You know me. I'll be there."

"Vinnie here is gonna give you one of Jimmy's old suits to wear. Gotta have a monkey suit to go to one of these things. I don't want you looking like no hick, you hear me?"

Big Frank wanted him to go because Big Frank wanted to show off his power and his wealth, which meant all of Big Frank's mob would be there, and all the other bosses—including Joey Texas.

Yeah, Big Frank wanted Stan to go because Big Frank wanted a flunky—somebody to dust off his shoes and wipe his chair down. "Thank you, s-sir. I'd be happy to go, if you think it's alright. I wouldn't want it to interfere with my work, you know I'd rather—"

"Shut up!" Frank lifted a decanter off the desk and poured for himself. "You talk too much! I want any lip from you, I'll undo my pants."

The tailor was looking at him strangely, and Stanley felt a hot flush color his cheeks. "Yes, sir."

Big Frank jerked his chin toward Stanley. "He gives really good blow, this one." He grinned at the tailor, who grinned back in a knowing manner. "You wanna try him some time? I shit you not. This boy can really blow the pipe."

Stanley wanted to claw a hole in the floor and crawl inside, but he forced himself to stay silent. He'd learned the hard way going up against Big Frank O'Hara was a mug's game, one Stanley always lost.

"The Silver Arrow, nine o'clock Saturday night. You be there. Jimmy and some of the boys'll be by your place to pick you up." Big Frank waddled over and caressed Stanley's cheek. "Just to make sure you won't be late. It's nice to have an escort."

NINO was waiting when the delivery boy came up with his suit; he peeled a twenty off the roll and handed it to the kid. "That's what I like about this place," he said. "They always deliver on time." He shut the door behind the kid and glanced over at Danny Murphy, who was sitting in Nino's easy chair cleaning his nails. "You gonna sit there like a bump or you gonna help me?"

"Dwawwww!" Danny made an exaggerated face. "Does the itto boy need help getting dwessed?" He folded away his pocketknife and got up. "Alright, gorgeous, let's see what Santa brought." He unzipped the suit bag and whistled appreciatively. "Holy Mother of God," he exclaimed. "Ain't you gonna cause the hoo-ha tonight!"

"Yeah," Nino said. "I figure if I got it, I ought to show it off." He shrugged out of his dressing gown, revealing his silk boxers and imported sock garters. "I'll show Big Frank's mugs who's the biggy around here." He regarded himself critically in the mirror, craning his neck to see over Danny's shoulder. "You think this suit makes me look short?"

Danny raised an eyebrow. "No." He plucked Nino's diamond shirt studs off the dresser and inserted them carefully into the boiled shirtfront. "Maybe you ain't the tallest guy around, but you got plenty going for you."

"Yeah?" Nino smoothed his thick, black hair with his hand. "You think so?" Nino's face was too broad to be considered classically handsome, but there was something attractive in his lively dark eyes with their thick, luxurious lashes, his wide, sensual mouth, and the dramatic sweep of his winged black brows. His suits were cut to make his shoulders look broader than they actually were, and his tailor knew how to tuck and drape his shirts and trousers to make him seem taller, his figure more elegant. He resembled the movie actor Edward G. Robinson and was highly conscious of it and vain; he favored pinstriped suits and silk shirts and dark fedora hats.

"I think so," Danny replied. He stood back to admire his handiwork. "You're gonna be fightin' off the nookie tonight! Hoo boy!"

"I'll leave the janes to you," Nino said. "Women ain't my department." He ran a critical finger under his collar. "This thing is choking me," he said. "I'd like to get my hands on the guy who invented this thing. Tell me, why do we gotta get all rigged out like this for? I ain't meeting the president. This place is just another one of Frank's dirty speakos."

"All the more reason," Danny replied. "Let those mugs know you are one very pricey article."

"Alright," Nino sighed. "Let's get it over with." He cast a final glance at himself and sneered. "Nookie," he muttered. "Nuts to that."

"IT DOESN'T fit." Despair: Stanley gazed at himself in the full-length mirror fastened to the back of his bedroom door. The suit was too large and hung on his slender frame as if it had been made for a much bigger man, which it had. The sleeves weren't too bad and the trousers had been hemmed by Big Frank's tailor, so at least Stanley wouldn't be tripping over himself, but he looked ridiculous—a boy playing in a man's clothes. He had gone to some significant trouble to be ready for tonight: showering, shaving away his light blond beard, and combing enough pomade into his hair so it ought to stay put for more than its usual half hour. He had even steeled himself to the idea of appearing yet again in public as Big Frank's catamite and flunky, and was almost looking forward to the evening because there would be music and dancing, and Stanley loved music above almost everything else. He'd go almost anywhere, provided there was a dance band. And there would be food—Big Frank paid him next to nothing, and Stanley was almost always hungry.

But this—this was horrible, almost certainly calculated to further humiliate him because humiliation was Big Frank's stock-in-trade. He delighted in belittling those around him, as if his own powerful ego couldn't bear even the smallest of challenges. "I can't go looking like this." The more Stanley looked, the worse it got; he looked like a puppet or a child, a clown. Everyone would be looking at him, looking and laughing, wondering what Stan the Stupe had done this time that Big Frank needed to punish him. *Hey lookee here, boys! Stan the Stupe musta spilled Big Frank's coffee...!*

The radio was playing in the background:

> *They're writing songs of love, but not for me*
> *A lucky star's above, but not for me*

Nobody cared about Stan the Stupe. Nobody cared about Stan the country bumpkin, the rube, the stooge from some Kansas hick town half a mile past the end of nowhere. Nobody cared if he lived or died, and if he washed up on the Jersey shore tomorrow, it wouldn't matter a damn to Big Frank or any of his hoods. Just another greenhorn who couldn't take it. Just another wide-eyed farm boy too far out of his league.

But he loved this song, and he dreamt of love like that—late at night, alone in his bed, he imagined someone cared about him... someone really gave a damn.

"You are an idiot." He swiped at his face angrily. He would go. It wasn't like he had a choice.

"AHHHH, Sam, how's tricks?" Nino Moretti, resplendent in a handsome cutaway coat, reached past Danny to shake Sam the Butcher's meaty hand. "Have a cigar?" Nino's thick, wavy black hair was combed back over his head and glistened with its own cold, blue light. His dark eyes, twin pools of black water, surveyed the room and its occupants dismissively.

"Thanks, Nino, that's white of ya." Sam leaned in while Nino offered him a light, nodded at Danny. "Big crowd come to see Frank, huh? Everybody loves Frank." Sam was as broad as he was tall, with a huge barrel chest and a luxuriant growth of thick, black hair on his knuckles and in his nostrils. His wide shoulders made him look like he had no neck, which was Sam's other nickname, "No-Neck."

"Yeahhhh." Nino, contemptuous, drawled the word out to its longest possible extension. "What's he been telling you boys lately?"

Sam bristled. "Now look here, Nino—"

"Aw, stick it in your eye!" Nino puffed on his cigar, his wide mouth distorted by a sneer. "Big Frank don't frighten me! He couldn't frighten a stable full of choirboys and you know it!"

"It ain't good business to be talking that way, Nino," Sam said. "You better watch what you're sayin'. Something might happen to ya."

"Like what?" Danny stepped sideways a little so he was between Nino and Sam. "Don't be getting ideas, Sammy. Your head might burst." The Irishman grinned, a flash of white teeth. "Big Frank wouldn't like the mess."

"That ain't funny," Sam huffed.

Danny hunched up his shoulders and stuck out his head. "Dat ain't funny," he mimicked. "You're dazzling me with your wit, here."

"Yeah, well…." Sam eyed them both. "Youse guys better watch it." He turned away, headed toward the buffet table where the caterers had laid out a diverse sampling of cold meats, cheeses, smoked fish, and the like.

Danny waved him off. "Aw, watch your mother."

"You trying to get us kicked out or something?" Nino glared at Danny, who appeared to be enjoying his own joke far too much. "Don't be riding him. We're here to keep an eye on things, maybe do a little business." He looked Danny up and down. Like Nino, Danny was dressed to the nines, but where Nino favored dark clothing, Danny's outfit was a pale dove gray, with a dark tie and shoes buffed to a blinding shine. His hair was combed back from his temples in waves, and he'd even had a manicure. "And keep away from Big Frank's dames. I don't want you getting dizzy with some jane, see?"

"You worry too much." Danny gazed around the room. "Here comes Big Frank. I'm so excited I think I might wet myself."

Nino stubbed out his cigar in a potted plant. "He's even fatter than he was last week," he said. "It's a wonder his heart's still beating. Hey, maybe—"

They're writing songs of love, but not for me

A lucky star's above, but not for me

Nino couldn't breathe.

Eyes... pale-blue eyes... that face... that long-limbed boy, moving effortlessly in his too-big suit, his body drifting... in the space between heartbeats, something slammed into Nino's chest like a freight train.

Danny's face swam into his vision. "You okay?" He followed Nino's gaze, trying to understand what it was his friend had seen. "You look like you seen a ghost. You sick or something?"

"Who's the kid?" It came out as a tortured croak. He couldn't take his eyes off the young man by Big Frank's side. If he did, the boy would disappear and Nino would never find him again, not ever, and he would be... he'd die. He'd just—no, better not to think about it. "That kid with Big Frank. Who is he?"

"Aw, that's Stan the Stupe. He's Big Frank's gunsel, you know." Danny shrugged. "So I hear. Some country boy. He's been with Big Frank for four, five years now. I'm surprised you ain't seen him before."

"Don't you think I'd remember?" Nino snapped. His heart was slamming into his ribcage. "If I'd seen him, I'd remember him. You think I'm stupid?"

"Yeah, I do," Danny said. "Cuz you're mouthing off to me, and you seem to forget I ain't one of these regular dopes you can push around."

"What's his name?" Nino whispered.

"Uh... Stanley Zadwa—something Polish, I dunno." Danny grinned. "You like him? When you take over Big Frank's territory, maybe the kid'll come over to your bed."

Nino turned on him savagely. "That ain't funny! Don't you never let me hear you say nothing like that, never no more, you hear?"

Danny held up his hands in mock surrender. "Okay, I'm jake. Sorry I said anything."

The kid and Big Frank were standing by the buffet table, the kid staring at the food hungrily. Big Frank was talking to Rick and Blackie, two of his Brooklyn guys. They ran a backroom distillery for Frank's organization and took a little off the top for themselves. Someday they'd get caught, and Big Frank would have somebody take them for a ride and they'd wash up on the Jersey shore. As Nino watched, the kid edged around behind Big Frank and reached for one of the sandwich trays.

That did it. Big Frank whirled around and brought his fist down on the kid's arm. "What'd I tell you? Don't be eating when I'm doing business, okay? What's the matter with you?"

He was like a kicked dog, Nino thought—just like a kicked dog nobody wanted, that nobody cared about or loved, just a poor dumb animal to be abused whenever Big Frank felt like it.

"I'm hungry." His voice was quiet, dignified, with a flat Midwestern twang. "I haven't eaten all day."

"You'll eat when I tell you to eat!" Big Frank's fist made contact with the point of Stanley's chin, throwing him backward. The kid stumbled and cannoned into a row of chairs and slammed into the floor. He lay there, stunned, and raised a shaking hand to his bloodied mouth.

Nino's blood roared in his ears. "That rotten bastard!" He started forward but was momentarily stayed by Danny.

"Nino, it ain't none of your business, okay?" Danny held Nino by the upper arms, shook him gently. "He's Big Frank's problem. He ain't your problem."

Nino shrugged him off. "Let go of me!" He watched himself as if from somewhere outside his body; he charged forward, got between Big Frank and the kid.

The crowd parted for him, reformed a tight little circle around him and Frank. "What's your problem, little man?"

"Don't hit that kid again." Nino slipped one hand into his coat, fingers closing around a set of brass knuckles. "Ain't none of us packing a rod in here tonight, but you touch him again and I'll beat you to death."

"Oh, big guy, huh?" Jimmy Two-Shots charged toward Nino, but Danny stepped in neatly, dropped him with a single punch. The tight circle around Nino and Frank wavered and shifted; Big Frank was suddenly in heated conference with one of his lieutenants.

"Anybody else want to try it?" Danny's fists hung at his sides. "'Cause I brought plenty for everybody."

Nino reached for Stanley. "Can you stand up?" he asked. "Or do you need some help?"

"I'm okay." Stanley flinched away from Nino's touch, climbed shakily to his feet. "Leave me alone. You shouldn't touch me. Frank will be mad. I don't want to make him mad." He reminded Nino of himself, of Nino's own apprenticeship to Joey Texas, his early years clawing his way up from the streets.

"Listen to me." Nino made his decision. "You ain't Big Frank's no more. You're coming home with me, see? I'm gonna take care of you." He raised his voice for Danny, who came hurrying over.

"Nino, we better get outta here. These boys ain't none too pleased and I think some of Big Frank's goons are carrying heaters." He glanced at Stanley. "I hope you're worth it, kid."

"Come on, kid." Nino helped him up. "We gotta breeze."

"Wait a minute!" Stanley stepped back. "You guys have got me wrong. I c-can't just—I mean, Frank—"

"Nino is offering you his hospitality," Danny said. "You are gonna go with Nino because Nino stood up for you." He closed one hand around Stanley's elbow. "You don't want to shame Nino by refusing his hospitality." He squeezed Stanley's arm—gently, but with intent. "Right?"

"Leave the kid alone," Nino said, "You don't gotta scare him."

Big Frank broke away from his lieutenant and started forward.

"Alright," Stanley said, "I'm going. I'm going."

"Car's waiting," Danny said. He swung Stanley around so the younger man was in front of him. "Got her warmed up and everything." A gun had appeared in Danny's other hand, seemingly out of nowhere.

"Don't none of you boys get any fancy ideas, now. Me and Nino, we're leaving and we're taking this kid with us for insurance."

He hustled them out to the curb, where a dark sedan was waiting with Danny's brother Michael at the wheel. Michael looked like a taller, thinner version of Danny. His face was pale and gaunt, with the flesh bitten away under the cheekbones; his nose had been broken numerous times and had never healed properly.

"Okay, Mikey." Danny climbed into the front with Michael and Nino helped Stanley into the back seat.

"I just would like to know one thing," Stanley said. His pale eyes gleamed in the dark.

Goddammit, Nino thought, *he's too goddamn beautiful. Nothing should be so beautiful... nothing that beautiful could survive, not in this world anyway.* "What?" Nino deliberately sat apart from him to give the kid a little breathing room. "What is it?"

"Why me? I'm nobody. I haven't done anything to you. Why do you want to kill me?"

"Kill you?" Of course—the kid thought they were taking him for a ride! Nino laughed gently. This kid was delicate. Not yellow—he had plenty of guts, Nino could see it right away. But delicate in that God only knew what Big Frank had been doing to him for the past however many years. He'd been kicked around, had horrible things done to him. "You got me all wrong," Nino said. "I'm taking you away from Big Frank for good. He ain't never gonna hurt you no more, see."

The kid—Stanley—stared at him. "But he'll kill you," he whispered. He turned around in his seat, glanced back at the club now vanishing swiftly into darkness behind him. "You gotta let me out! Big Frank will kill you for this! I can't be part of it, I can't let you—"

Nino laid a hand on his shoulder, pressed him back into his seat. "Let us worry about Big Frank. Okay?"

"I don't know who you are," Stanley said. He was shivering, probably from cold but more likely from fear. "I left my hat in the club. I haven't got another hat." His mouth was still bleeding but it had slowed to a trickle. A dark bruise stained the pale skin of his face.

"I'll get you another hat. I'll get you all the hats you want, okay?" Nino had a sudden, inexplicable urge to cry. "It's okay. You can have anything you want." He forced himself to breathe; it felt like a sob. "Anything. Anything you want."

Stanley straightened his back against the seat. "Why should you want to help me?" he asked. "I'm not your problem."

"Big Frank ain't no friend of mine, see." Nino lit a cigarette, offering one to Stanley, who shook his head. "I see him beating on you, I think it's good business to step in and say something about it."

"Do a lot of that, do you?" Stanley looked him up and down—slowly, taking his time, his gaze sliding over Nino's clothes, his jewelry, his face. "Saying things about things?"

"Yeah," Nino replied. "Yeah, I guess I do. But you can relax now, kid. I rescued you." He sat back and puffed on his cigarette. He couldn't figure this kid out.

"What makes you think I wanted to be rescued?" Stanley asked.

Nino frowned. "Say, kid, you screwy or something? Why wouldn't you want to be rescued? You like Big Frank beating on you?"

"I didn't say that." Stanley slumped back into the shadows. "I didn't say anything at all."

"YOU sure you'll be okay?" Danny leaned out of the car. "Cuz I can stick around." He grinned at Nino and the kid. "You're in good hands, kid. Nino here owns most of the Lower East Side. He'll take care of ya."

"Naw, you go on, I'll be okay," Nino replied. "I'll call ya if there's any trouble."

"We'll wait 'til ya get inside, hey, Mikey?" Danny conferred briefly with his brother inside the car. He hung over the door, his upper body out the window.

"Come on, kid. I don't think Big Frank's gonna come after us, but we better get in, just in case some of his boys get ideas." Nino ushered Stanley up the steps, one hand held across the boy's lower back, hovering but not quite touching him. The kid was skittish; Nino didn't want to scare him off. "Right up here. The elevator's nice. It's part of the reason why I like this building." Stanley was silent as they rode the cage up to the fifth floor. "Yeah, it's nice here," Nino said. "Nice building. It's got a lotta class."

"Mr. Moretti, what is it you plan to do with me? I would like to know." Stanley drew himself up, dignified and tragic. "Are you holding a rod on me now?"

"Why would I be holding a rod on you?" Nino asked. "You ain't giving me no cause."

Stanley arched one pale eyebrow. "Aren't you afraid I'll run away?"

The elevator bumped to a stop. Stanley followed Nino down the hall and waited while Nino put the key in the door. "I just wanna keep Big Frank away from you... make sure he don't hurt you no more. You're useful to him. I take you away from him, it's good for me. You know, good for business." He pushed the door open, motioning for Stanley to enter. "Come on in, kid, make yourself at home."

Nino's apartment was understated but tasteful: a main room with the requisite couch and chairs, several nice lamps, and, occupying a place of prominence along one wall, a large cabinet radio set.

"Do you like music, Mr. Moretti?" Stanley drifted to the radio but didn't allow himself to touch it. He'd never seen a radio as nice: floor model, in a nice walnut cabinet, with an intricate geometric pattern on the grille cloth. It sure was fancy.

"Yeah, I sure do." Nino shrugged out of his coat, stowing it and his hat away. "Listen, enough with the Mr. Moretti stuff, okay? Call me Nino." He went into the kitchen, a smaller room just off the sitting area, and opened the icebox. "You must be hungry. You want something to eat? Let me fix you a sandwich or something. Glass of milk?"

"You don't need to go to any trouble." Stanley hovered in the middle of the floor, uncertain whether he should stay or go. It was even money, he figured, as to who would kill him first, Nino or Big Frank. He had no reason to trust Nino, except....

"Here you go." Nino laid a plate of sandwiches on the coffee table and a glass of milk, and a slice of chocolate cake. "I can't take no credit for the eats. Everything's from the deli around the corner, but they're real good. The superintendent's wife made the cake, and she's a real nice lady."

"I don't want to be any trouble. You've been so kind to me." Stanley sat down on the couch and gazed at the food longingly.

"Well, don't just look at it," Nino said. "Go on, dig in." He wavered, shifting from one foot to the other. "I'll leave you alone." The bruise on Stanley's face had shaded to a dark purple mottled with red; it covered part of his bottom lip and stretched around the side of his jaw. "I'll get you some ice for your face, after you're done eating."

He went into his bedroom and shut the door, shucked his clothes, and put on a pair of silk pajamas and a dressing gown. He took the gun out of his shoulder holster and tucked it under his pillow. He doubted Big Frank would send anybody after him tonight, but it wasn't beyond possibility. Big Frank had to be pretty sore now because Nino had taken away his toy, and he wasn't likely to let something like that pass without comment.

Nino smiled wryly. Usually Big Frank's "comments" had guns behind them. He gazed at himself in the mirror above his dresser. "You sure you know what you're doing, Nino?" What had possessed him to rescue the kid, anyway? This kid was nobody, nothing to him. Maybe he was getting soft... which meant what, exactly?

He didn't know. He had no idea. For the first time in a great many years, Nino had no clue, and he wasn't sure he liked the feeling. Perhaps it was a mistake—maybe Big Frank deliberately put the kid in Nino's way to trap him... yeah, dangle the pretty candy....

Dangerous. It was real dangerous. But he couldn't just leave the kid there. He couldn't leave him there and let Big Frank beat on him like—

Get away from that window!

What'd I tell you? You lookin' for something out that window?

The old man, yeah... the old man had a bad temper, for sure... and it was always Ray he went for, never Tony or Nino, even though they were plenty worse than Ray, were always making trouble, little snot-nosed brats. It was Ray he went for, even when Ray was only looking out the window... he liked looking out the window because he never went to school, never went outside to play with the other kids; Ma would never let him. The other kids would pick on him, throw rocks at him, hit him 'til he bled.

Yeah, hit him 'til he bled, like the old man did. Until one day when he hit Ray so hard—

Nino blinked. "Yeah, you're getting soft, alright." He tightened the belt of his dressing gown and sneered at himself in the mirror. Maybe it wasn't such a hot idea, bringing the kid here. He wasn't like the other men Nino knew, the torpedoes and the trouble boys that hung around the speakos and the clubs, or the painted, pin-curled fags looking for trade on late-night sidewalks. Nino knew them all by name, the pansies who'd take money for a blow, wearing out their knees for easy change, maybe an extra fin in their pockets come the weekend. No matter what he'd been doing for Big Frank, this kid was no smack-off.

He wasn't what Nino usually went for, not at all. That thought alone was enough to give Nino serious pause.

Stanley was still eating when Nino came back. The plate that had held the sandwiches now sported nothing but a faint smear of mayonnaise and some crumbs. Likewise, the glass of milk was empty, and the kid was working on the cake.

He'd cut it up into small individual sections, each approximately the same size and shape, and had set the icing to one side.

"Don't like the icing, huh?" Nino grinned.

"Oh, no," Stanley said quietly. "I always save the icing for last. It's my favorite part."

He saves the icing for last. Mother of God.

Nino held out the ice bag. "I brought you some ice. You want to put some on your face. It's pretty bruised, there. I got an extra bedroom; it's all ready for you when you want to go to bed."

Stanley took the ice bag from him. "Thank you. This is really very nice of you. I appreciate it."

Nino sized him up. "Not too much you're scared of, is there?" He gestured at the kid's face. "I mean, you took it on the chin from Big Frank and you didn't even whimper."

Stanley licked chocolate frosting off his fingers. "I'm used to people hitting me," he said.

It went through Nino like a blade of ice. "Don't you ever—" He sat down. "Kid, don't let people hit you."

Stanley peered at him curiously. "Why?"

"Because I don't like seeing people get beat on, what can't defend themselves." Nino took a breath. His hands were trembling. It was too much, being close to the kid like this, looking into those guileless blue eyes. He knew what Big Frank saw in Stanley, what anybody with half a brain and a beating heart would see in Stanley—his innocence and his beauty. "Look, kid, I'm gonna go in and get you some pajamas there, and some towels and stuff if you wanna take a bath or whatever, I dunno. I got plenty of books, if you wanna read, or listen to the radio."

He stepped into the spare bedroom and laid a pair of his own pajamas out on the foot of the bed, along with a stack of fresh towels and some other things the kid might want.

I'm used to people hitting me.

Why?

If Danny could see him now, he would probably laugh. Nino "Spats" Moretti—The Little Prince himself—finally caught. No more lonely nights. No more cheap palookas sleeping in his bed. "Yeah, you're getting ahead of yourself," he whispered. He half expected Stanley to be gone when he went back into the living room.

Stanley was sound asleep on the sofa, the ice bag pressed against his cheek.

Nino took a spare blanket and covered him up.

CHAPTER
TWO

STANLEY was up and dressed—after a fashion—when Nino rolled out of bed late the next afternoon. Nino had slept horribly, tormented by his usual nightmares of pursuit and ambush. He stood under the hot shower for a solid fifteen minutes, trying to clear the cobwebs from his brain. It would do no good to walk into Lucky O'Mannion's private office looking anything less than ready.

Lucky had been one of Black-Arm Willie's boys before Willie's health went south and he retired to Florida to grow oranges and play shuffleboard. When Willie left, most of his old territory automatically defaulted to Lucky, who ruled it with the usual iron fist. Lucky didn't bother fighting with wise guys who tried to take what was his, and he didn't bother calling out the button men.

He was a real hands-on sort of guy—if you pissed him off, he'd come to wherever you were and blow your brains all over the wall. But Lucky and Nino had grown up together, so there was a kind of understanding between them. Lately Lucky had been making noises about some small-time Bronx mob that seemed about ready to bust in on his territory; he wanted a meeting with Nino so they could discuss business.

Stanley drew back from the table. "I made some breakfast. I hope that's okay."

Nino grunted. "Kid, do whatever you want to do." He sat down at the table and poured himself a cup of coffee. "Did you sleep?" he asked.

"Yes, sir. I did." He had fallen into a deep, dreamless well without feeling, dreams, or memory. "Will you have some toast?" He handed the plate across to Nino.

"You don't hafta wait on me." Nino sipped his coffee and made an impressed noise. "Huh. This is good. Who taught you to make coffee, your ma?"

Stanley nodded. "Yes, sir. My mother made wonderful coffee."

Nino peered at his outfit. "Yeah... we gotta get you some clothes."

"I don't want to put you to any trouble." Stanley stirred a spoon of sugar into his coffee. "Besides, I haven't got any money on me. I don't—he doesn't let me—well, sir, what I mean is—"

"No cash and you don't wanna risk going to the bank—is that it?"

Stanley nodded miserably. "They'll be looking for me," he said. "Eventually they'll find me." Harry "Bugs" Mitchell had tried to run away from Big Frank O'Hara. Big Frank's boys found him in a speakeasy over in Jersey and made an example of him. They caught him in the crapper and put two dozen holes in him before he could pull up his pants. Stanley didn't want to die that way.

"You don't need to worry about them. You hear me?" Nino buttered a piece of toast. "Ain't nobody gonna hurt you no more. I told you last night. I meant it." He narrowed his eyes. "You don't think Nino can take care of you? Is that it?" Nino stabbed the air with a thumb. "Nino takes care of his own, see? I told you I'd take care of you and I will!" He unfolded the newspaper and laid it on the table beside his elbow. "I'll get you some clothes." He glanced at Stanley, sized him up. "I guess you're about Danny's size. Danny should do nicely." He laid his toast on the plate. "I don't want you going anywhere just yet, without protection. It ain't safe. You okay to stay inside today?"

"Of course. Yes, sir, I'll stay inside." Stanley swallowed hard. "If—if you don't mind. I realize this is temporary."

Nino sighed. "Enough 'sir' stuff. You ain't beholden to me. I ain't your old man."

Stanley nodded. "Of course." He flushed bright red but forced himself to stumble on. "I just meant... I know things have to be paid for."

Nino laid down his cup and fixed Stanley with a gaze. "I don't wanna hafta say this again: you don't owe me nothing. You ain't gotta pay for nothing, you got it?"

Stanley dropped his head and nodded, suddenly very close to tears. "Yes, sir," he whispered.

"What'd I tell ya about 'sir' stuff?"

"I'm sorry, I keep forgetting, I keep—"

And he was sobbing.

Nino reached out for him, laid a hand on his shoulder. The boy leapt away from him, crashed into the opposite wall, and clung to the curtains, trembling like a startled alley cat.

He thinks you're going to hurt him.

Nino remembered how Ray used to be after Pop was done beating on him, and he dropped to the floor and made his movements small and slow, deliberate. He crept close to where Stanley was but kept enough distance between them so the boy would feel comfortable. He sat on the floor, his hands in plain sight, and waited. After a moment, Stanley slid to the floor and sat down, watching Nino with the wariness of a wild animal.

"I'll be just fine on my own if you need to go out," he said. His diction was flawless, clear and perfect; the mask was back in place.

"Anything you need me to get you before I go? You want some magazines? Books?"

"I'd like some wood. And a knife." He tucked his hands into his armpits, his eyes never leaving Nino. "Is it alright if I take a shower?"

Nino blinked. "You can do anything you like. You can eat or drink anything you like. Just... keep away from the windows, and don't let nobody in if you don't know them." He climbed to his feet slowly, tugged down the hem of his jacket. "I get it," he said after a moment. "You think I'm like Big Frank."

Stanley raised his chin. "Aren't you?" It was defiant—he was testing the waters.

"Nope." He held out a hand. "Help you up?"

"I can get up on my own, thank you." He stood up and straightened his clothes. He wouldn't come near Nino.

"I got some soft wood, whatcha call it? Pine. Is that okay?" He located a couple of pieces of scrap wood in a storage space behind the couch; his landlady had used it to prop open the door in hot weather. "Whatcha doin', anyway?"

"I like to carve. If that's alright."

"It's alright." Nino gave him a .22 automatic. "This here's my spare piece. It's loaded and I want you to keep it handy, you hear me? Stay away from them windows. Frank's boys ain't stupid. They ain't gonna come bustin' in here in broad daylight. That'd have the cops down on 'em in a minute—but I'll feel better knowing you got some protection." He gestured at the gun. "You know how to use that?"

Stanley turned the gun over in his hand, caressed the trigger with his long fingers, and Nino shivered. Beautiful... the kid was too beautiful. It wasn't right.

"Yeah," Stanley said quietly, "I know how to use it."

Nino hovered for a moment. "Okay," he said at last. "Okay."

"NINO, come on in! We've been waiting for ya!" Lucky O'Mannion was, as his name suggested, of Irish heritage—a tall man with thick, dark hair and dark eyes that might have come from an Old Masters painting, but which probably came from the Moorish blood on his mother's side. His ruddy complexion hinted at a fondness for drink, and his liking for fine cigars rivaled Nino's own. His office was located on the top floor of a bank building, a deliberate piece of subterfuge designed to instill confidence in those who came to do business with him. Like Nino, Lucky had "inherited" a large territory that included everything from a thriving bootleg business to several thousand penny-ante numbers rackets, which together brought in millions, and like Nino, he operated under the guise of legitimate business—in this case, a fruit importers' protective association.

"You're looking very prosperous, my friend."

"Hey… you sayin' I'm fat?" Nino pretended to be offended, then laughed and took the cigar Lucky offered. He took his usual seat at Lucky's right elbow and accepted a cup of strong coffee.

"Heard you gave Big Frank some trouble, Nino. That the truth?" Lucky laughed, his hands held up in a gesture of surrender when Nino frowned at him. "I'm not saying he didn't deserve it. The guy is scum and we both know it. So—you take his favorite gunsel away?"

"He ain't a gunsel," Nino snarled. "Get that through your thick head. He's nobody's gunsel!"

"I was just saying," Lucky replied, "don't get yourself all hot under the collar." He canted a look at Nino. "When are you gonna find yourself some nice moll and settle down, huh? Some of the boys were saying—"

"Were saying what?" Nino stood up, braced his hands on the desk. "Saying what, Lucky? Huh? Somebody been shooting his mouth off? Maybe my rod oughta do some talking, huh?"

Lucky shook his head. "You got it bad," he said.

Nino's hand lashed out and grabbed his necktie, tightening it around Lucky's throat until the Irishman's eyes bulged. "You don't talk about him," he hissed. "You don't say nothing about him. He ain't nobody's business but mine. You got that?"

Lucky nodded.

"And don't try pressing any buttons, see. I brought backup." Nino released him; Lucky tried to massage some feeling back into his windpipe.

"You're a real piece of work, Nino." Lucky adjusted his necktie.

"Rumors?" Nino's whole body quivered with indignation. "What rumors?"

Lucky shrugged. "Some of the boys were talking. Said they saw you coming out of Lili Wacker's place over on Canal Street the other night with a sailor on your arm."

"That ain't nothing but bushwa!" Nino snarled, his face burning. "You know me! I ain't like that!"

"I never said you were." Lucky moved back out of Nino's reach. "But some of the boys, you know… they see you walking arm-in-arm with a sailor—"

"I wasn't walking with no sailor, you got that?"

How much for a blow? I'll give you a C-note if you come home with me. Yeah, it's jake. I got a place near here.

"Jake with me, Nino." Lucky adjusted his cufflinks a little too obviously. "Only some of the guys, they say you're trolling for trade." He frowned. "Not my call."

"You got a problem in the Bronx," Nino said, ignoring Lucky's play for information. "So tell me."

"Lili Wacker," Lucky said. "And it ain't just the Bronx, see? She's been trying to stick her nose into my territory. I told her before to keep out of it, but you know Lili, she don't listen."

Nino sneered. "Yeah, just like every other bulldagger. They think they can handle it. Somebody oughta shove the dame back in a skirt where she belongs." He leaned over the map Lucky had unrolled. "She got a new place over on Ludlow, calls it Guys and Dolls."

"That ain't my problem," Lucky said. "My problem is she's buying up properties I had my eye on, see?" He traced a rough rectangle on the map. "This here warehouse and what used to be Dicky Styler's old place. I was gonna move some of my stuff in there. She came in right under my nose and bought the works! Word is, she's getting bankrolled, and whoever's behind her is in the money for sure."

"She's running girls outta her places and cutting into my profits," Nino said. He chewed on the end of his cigar. "Yeah. This ain't good. You sent her a message?"

"Yeah." Lucky sat down heavily behind the desk. "Yeah, I sent her a message, alright. I tried it the old-fashioned way—" This would have taken the form of personal intimidation, Nino knew: two or three of Lucky's biggest, toughest guys would show up at Lili's place of business and put the squeeze on her. If she had any brains at all, she'd fold, but Nino knew Lili: once she got the bit between her teeth, she was harder to stop than a team of goddamn mules. "And I tried putting the word out." He showed Nino a newspaper clipping, a section cut from the agony column: *THE LADY PROTESTS TOO MUCH AND THEN THE LADY VANISHES.*

"Mm," Nino said, "that's as clear as it gets."

"You think so?" Lucky rolled his eyes. "She showed up here yesterday, barking about how I was libeling her! She even brought along her scumbag lawyer."

"Libel?" Nino made an irritated noise deep in his throat. "That dame is daffy. She needs to be taught a lesson."

"Then I can count on your help?"

Nino thought about it. "Yeah. I got a score to settle with her myself. I wouldn't mind getting a whack at her."

"Whatcha got in mind?" Lucky asked.

Nino laughed, but there was nothing pleasant in it. "Yeah. I'll teach that dame to play in her own backyard."

"So, IS he gonna do business with us?" Danny Murphy held the car door open for Nino, slid in beside him. "Or did you have to do some talking?"

"He's gonna do business," Nino said. "He needs us. The Bronx is a mess, and so is Lucky's territory, thanks to Lili Wacker. It's his own fault. He can't hold onto nothing, Lucky. If Willie hears about this, he'll come outta retirement. You can bet on it. What time is it?" He fished his watch out and peered at it.

"Still need glasses," Danny said. "When are you gonna give in and go see somebody?"

"I don't need glasses." Nino stowed his watch back into his waistcoat pocket. "Say, you wanna do me a favor?"

Danny was instantly suspicious. "What kind of favor?"

"I want you to come to Templeman's with me."

Danny squinted at him. "You want me to go shopping with you. What for?"

"For, ah, for Zadwadzki… for Stanley."

"You buying his clothes now?"

Nino frowned. "He ain't got nothing—not even so much as a coat."

Danny chuckled. "Good thing summer's coming, ain't it? I don't get it—whatcha need me for?"

"You're bout the same size as he is. I figure I'll just buy a bunch of stuff and get it delivered."

"Uh-huh."

"Don't gimme 'uh-huh'."

"Uh-huh." Nino knew Danny couldn't resist. "You got it bad, Nino. This ain't like you at all. You goin' screwy or something? Usually you just pick 'em up and drop 'em like a hot potato."

"He ain't like that." Nino recalled Stanley's frightened face, his almost abject terror that he'd angered Nino by making breakfast for them. "He's about as tough as wet paper. He needs somebody looking out for him."

Danny nodded. "And that somebody is you."

Nino shrugged. "Why not?" He leaned forward and tapped on the driver's shoulder. "Take us to Templeman's, will you, Al?"

"So now you're shopping for him." Danny leaned over and patted Nino's cheek familiarly. "But he don't mean nothin'."

"That's right."

Danny regarded him for a moment. "You ever been in love, Nino?" He lit a cigarette. "Besides me, I mean." He handed the cigarette to Nino and lit another for himself.

"I ain't in love. This is business. The kid used to do Big Frank's books. He's got a head on his shoulders. He could take care of the numbers part of it for me, get things in line. You know how much of a mess things are. I ain't got no head for figures and neither do you."

Danny sat back against the seat and shook his head. "You keep tellin' yourself that, Nino. You keep tellin' yourself that."

THE staff at Templeman's Department Store knew Nino from the early days—indeed, they devoted two or sometimes even three salesmen to meeting Mr. Moretti's shopping needs, to fetching and carrying samples from the shop floor, to offering on-the-spot alterations, and to making certain Mr. Moretti would be disposed to part with the greatest possible amount of dough. The manager, Mr. Elliot, spied Nino and Danny and rushed over from his perch behind the reception counter to greet them. He laid down the wig stand he had been fondling and clasped his hands together in rapture.

"Mr. Nino, it's so good to see you and Mr. Danny! It's been simply ages!" He grinned and ushered them into the elevator. "We have some new items just arrived and you simply must have a look at them. Trust me—they are glorious!" He put a hand to his breast and rolled his eyes heavenward, as if the mere idea of new merchandise was too much for his delicate constitution.

"Mr. Nino is shopping for a friend today," Danny said. It was a credit to Danny's innate common sense that he curbed his mirth. "Mr. Nino would very much like your help in choosing some things for the gentleman."

"Yeah, and we want 'em delivered, see." The elevator stopped and Nino pushed his way out, headed directly for the menswear section. Nino was an indifferent shopper—to Mr. Elliot's endless horror, he never took the time to go through the racks systematically, but attacked the merchandise in classic berserker fashion. "We need suits and trousers, some of them shirts with the French cuffs, oh and cufflinks and a… yeah, he needs a decent watch—"

"Third floor, jewelry!" Mr. Elliot clapped his hands and dispatched Mr. Stephen and Mr. John to the third floor with strict orders to return with a selection of watches suitable for a gentleman of Nino's wealth and style.

Nino hardly stopped to draw breath: "—morning coat, evening tails, opera cloak, gloves, walking stick, hats, oh yeah, and, uh—" Nino colored delicately, looking to Danny for assistance.

"He needs underwear and socks," Danny said. "And I ain't trying 'em on, neither."

Mr. Elliot raised one elegant brow. "I beg your pardon?"

"Danny here's gonna be the mannequin, see." Nino plopped down into a chair and lit a cigar. "Yeah, he's about the same size."

Mr. Elliot nodded. "You will be... standing in for the gentleman?"

"Yeah, but only for tryin' on the clothes, so don't be gettin' any ideas, there." Danny glanced around. "Which way's the dressing room?"

For the next hour, Danny tried on a seemingly endless array of suits, shirts, waistcoats, neckties, trousers, evening wear, boots, and shoes. He would allow Mr. Elliot or one of Mr. Elliot's assistants to outfit him inside the relative privacy of the dressing room before coming out to do a short walk and a turn in front of Nino, who gave the outfit either his yes or his no. Handsome as Danny was, he attracted no end of attention, and before long there was an eager semicircle of wide-eyed admirers gathered around him.

"Pretty fancy," a young woman said. "Does he come in any other sizes?"

"Gimme your phone number," Danny said, "and I'll show you all the sizes I got, sister." The crowd hooted its appreciation, but Danny wasn't as gracious with all spectators: an effete older man who had the effrontery to ogle got shouted at, with the promise Danny would, if necessary, "shove yer eyeballs back into your head!"

"And the jewelry," Mr. Elliot said. Mr. Stephen and Mr. John laid out a dazzling assortment of watches and chains, cufflinks, shirt studs, and diamond pinky rings. Nino picked it over critically, selected what he liked, and sent the rest back. He gave Mr. Elliot the address and instructed them to deliver the whole works to his address right away, to Mr. Zadwadzki. He had to spell the name three times before the clerk got it right; a delivery driver was immediately dispatched with his pile of boxes.

"You sure you ain't soft on this guy, Nino?" Danny held the car door for Nino and climbed in after him. "What's with spending all the mazuma?"

"He ain't got nothin'," Nino replied. "I'm doin' the guy a favor." He checked his watch. "We're going out to dinner tonight, me and you."

"Izzat right?" Danny lit a cigarette. "Me and you and Junior, huh?"

Nino ignored him, his gaze on the passing scenery outside the car. "I can't figure him, Danny. He was Big Frank's gunsel, his...." Nino huffed out a sigh. "A kid like that! I mean, come on! He ain't like you and me. Lay a finger on him and he folds up."

"He put up with everything Big Frank could dish out—for years," Danny said quietly. "He's a lot tougher than you think."

"You know what he asked me for when I went out today?" Nino fished in his pocket for his cigarette case. "Wood. A piece of wood and a knife."

"He planning on bumping himself off?" Danny rolled the window of the car down. It was a beautiful spring day, the scent of flowers in the air; the sidewalks were full of people walking with their coats open, smiling and laughing.

"Naw—said he likes carving stuff. Making things. You should see him. He ain't got no nerve left." Nino drew on his cigarette. "But he ain't yellow. That's one thing he ain't." He pulled out his watch and squinted at it. "Listen, can you go on over there for a while? I got some business uptown."

"You ain't got no business without me," Danny said. "Next thing you'll have a bullet in you. And I ain't lettin' that happen, Nino." Over the years, Danny had functioned as Nino's shadow and his strong right arm. Nobody got close to Nino without Danny's say-so, and anybody dumb enough to take a potshot found himself fitted for a Chicago overcoat or swimming the East River in a pair of cement shoes.

"Naw, I'm going to see Ma Keller." Nino patted his arm. "I'll be oke. I want you to go over there and see if he's doing alright."

"Whatcha going to see Ma Keller for? You got a sudden hankering for strawberries or something?"

Ma Keller owned a fruit store—a front, really, for all sorts of underworld activity, much of it in Nino's domain. If you wanted information, you got it from Ma Keller, who knew everything that went on in Nino's part of the city. Ma Keller made a nice pile of dough passing on information and occasionally providing a safe house for unwary bootleggers stupid enough or careless enough or brazen enough to attract the attention of the local police. More to the point, she liked

Nino, looked on him as a son, and he reciprocated her regard by bringing her the one thing she appreciated more than money—a fine cigar.

"I wanna get the goods on Stanley... find out his history. Maybe him and Big Frank go back a long ways, I dunno."

"Didn't you ask him?"

"No." Nino couldn't imagine asking Stanley anything about Big Frank. Just the mention of Big Frank's name would probably be enough to give the kid nightmares for weeks. "I didn't want to scare the kid off."

Danny gazed at him. "And you want me to babysit while you go digging in the dirt?"

"Yeah." Nino narrowed his eyes. "That a problem?"

Danny leaned forward and tapped the driver on the shoulder. "Right here's fine, Al." The car slid alongside the curb and he hopped out. "You owe me, Nino."

Nino gave him a beatific smile. "Don't I know it." He shook the Irishman's hand. "I'll meet you back at my place in an hour."

STANLEY liked to carve, and what he carved were tiny wooden horses. There had been horses where he grew up—horses and fields of tall corn, and the big sky as far as you could see. He liked to carve because carving kept his hands busy, which sort of kept his mind from roaming all over the place and gibbering with fright. He wasn't a coward—he had seen more in his thirty years than most men twice his age—but his years under Big Frank's thrall had broken something in him. He had long ago decided never to trust again. Even when people were nice, it only lasted a little while. Before long, they wanted you to do things for them, and if you didn't do exactly as they asked, they got angry and took it out on you. Sometimes they did the job themselves or maybe they turned you over to their goons and let them beat you up until you threw up and passed out. It was never nice. It was always ugly and it was painful and it was something Stanley had learned to get through by whatever means necessary, until the next time.

There was always a next time.

And while he waited, living under the pall of Big Frank's threats, under his power and his influence, Stanley made his own plans. They weren't sophisticated plans, not like the ones Big Frank made. As far as schemes went, these were the simplest of the simple, but what made them powerful was that Stanley owned them, and because he owned them, he imbued them with as much emotional energy as he could muster. Lying in his bed at night, his body broken and sore from Frank's ill-use, he pored over these plans, breathed new life into them, imagined them as clearly as he possibly could.

Sometimes he even prayed. He remembered all the prayers his mother had taught him, and he prayed them all over again. From his memory he pulled the Bible passages he remembered, and he whispered them again and again. In his desire for vengeance he was merciful, just, and pure—to stamp Big Frank out of existence would be a mercy. It would be absolutely just, and justice was its own sort of purity. He amazed himself with his ability to rationalize such things. He felt no guilt.

Nino Moretti was an unexpected element. Stanley had heard about him—the whole city was abuzz with constant talk of Joey Texas and his torpedo, the man they called The Little Prince. Stanley had heard stories about Nino, how he started out with Joey's mob and then got too big for his britches. Joey took exception to it, and there was a showdown between them one day in the garage where Joey sent his fleet of taxicabs for servicing. Word had it Joey showed up with almost his entire mob, while Nino came with only Danny and Danny's brother Mike; between the three of them, they routed Joey Texas and took his boys away from them, pressed every last one into service in what had rapidly become Nino's organization.

But there were other rumors, too, and Stanley had long been privy to conversations in Big Frank's presence, rough talk among the boys and dirty jokes that always, somehow, featured Nino. Some of Big Frank's boys made swishy gestures and said Nino was a *finocchio* and laughed. He had expected a punk with too much jewelry, flashy suits and lots of loud talk, and perhaps Nino really was that way with other people. Nino wasn't that way with Stanley, but Stanley had only known him for less than a day and people could change. Why did Nino want him? What did Nino want him for? Was Nino planning to use him, somehow, to get back at Big Frank? If so, then Stanley would go along with it. Having gotten free of Big Frank's clutches, Stanley would do just about anything to see Big Frank destroyed. If that was Nino's plan, then it was surely divine intervention that had landed Stanley in Nino's lap, so to speak. Nothing would make Stanley happier than to see Big Frank crushed and broken, as he had broken Stanley. Yeah, it would be good, maybe, to put a bullet in Big Frank, to see him beg and plead for mercy, maybe grovel on his knees, the way Stanley had so often groveled in the past.

Please, Boss, don't do it. I'm still sore from last time. Please don't make me.

But for now he carved horses and listened to the radio and stayed away from the windows. He was content to do as he was told, and he was curious, as well, to see what Nino intended. Perhaps Nino would make the same mistake Big Frank had, or perhaps Nino would be a bit more subtle and try to get at Stanley through his feelings.

They all tried something. No one could be trusted, not really.

Stanley remembered sitting on his mother's porch in the summertime, watching the trains pull into the dusty landscape and back out, bearing their cargoes of wheat and corn. On hot days they'd drink lemonade and wait for Pa to come home, whistling his way down the street with his briefcase, his tie already loosened, his hat crushed on the back of his head. There was school in the mornings and church on Sundays and swimming in the creek in the summertime, diving deep down where trout hid in black pools, and surfacing with the sun in his eyes.

Stanley wasn't like the other boys. He never had a childhood sweetheart, never walked girls home from school, never took anybody to the harvest dance. He had never kissed anyone, never been kissed; he had never given his body willingly to another. He read a lot and got good grades, and after graduating he went to night school in nearby Trenton and learned how to manipulate huge sums and delicate numbers. He had a natural aptitude for figures and could calculate in his head what others labored over with pen and paper. It was only natural that he go East to the big city, to try and make a decent life for himself. He packed his few things; he made sandwiches to eat on the train.

He met Big Frank and his life ended.

The doorbell rang, jarring him from his reverie. He laid aside the piece he was carving and peered through the security lens that Nino had installed in his door. He saw Danny Murphy standing there, bouncing on the balls of his feet. Stanley took the chain off and ushered Danny in.

"Hey there, kid, how's it going?" Danny stopped short at the sight of Nino's dining table, draped in old newspaper and covered in wood shavings. "Yeah, Nino told me you like carving stuff. Whatcha makin', a toothpick?"

Stanley rushed to the table and wrapped the unfinished sculpture in a piece of newspaper. "It's nothing…. I… I like working with my hands."

"That's good, kid. It's good to have a hobby. Listen, Nino asked me to come over and see how you were doing. He's taking you out to supper tonight, just the three of us." Danny went into the kitchen and spooned some coffee into the percolator. "You'll like that. Nino knows all the best places in town to eat, and there ain't nobody gonna give Nino the brush-off, know what I mean?" He came out and sat down in the easy chair. "So, you comfortable? You like it here? Nino's treating you good?"

"He's been very kind to me," Stanley said. He wiped his hands on his pants. "I could never hope to repay his kindness."

"Yeah, that's Nino." Danny leveled a gaze at Stanley. "Uh, kid, look—how much you know about Nino, anyway?"

Stanley wondered if Danny could be trusted. Best not to venture there. "I don't know anything about him, except what I've heard…. Bits and pieces, in passing."

Danny nodded. "Mmm. Yeah, I want to tell you, uh, don't believe everything you hear, okay?" He shrugged and tugged at his cuffs. "People talk about Nino because he's not always running around with some new dame every week. They might say things to ya, make you think certain things about Nino."

Stanley raised his eyebrows. "What sorts of things?"

"Oh, you know...." Danny became acutely interested in a loose thread hanging from a cushion. "That he's... you know, different."

"Did you chew that over before you spat it out?" Stanley unwrapped a stick of gum and shoved it into his mouth. "According to certain people in the know, so am I." There was venom in it.

"Naw, kid, don't go puttin' yourself down." Danny did his shrugging thing again and tugged on his cuffs. "You ain't so soft."

"What about you?" Stanley asked facetiously. "Have you and Nino been more than friends?"

Danny was saved from answering—literally—by the bell. He opened the door to the Templeman's delivery man, laden down with boxes and parcels. "He wants you," Danny said, motioning to Stanley. "Ya gotta sign something."

One of Stanley's hands crept to his throat. "I didn't—I didn't order anything," he said.

"I just need Mr. Zadwadzki to sign this form," the deliveryman said. "These things is already paid for." He held out the clipboard. "Go on, son, just sign your name. You can do that, can't you? Everybody can sign his name."

Stanley took the pen and scratched his signature; then he and Danny carried the parcels into the sitting room. "I hope this stuff fits, kid." Danny eyed the parcels with more than a hint of irritation. "He made me try stuff on to see if it would fit you." He smiled. "Things I do for that guy, huh?" He nodded at the packages. "Better get started, kid—there's everything in there."

"He bought me clothes?" Stanley blinked at Danny. "Why would he buy me clothes?"

Danny got up and came to stand beside Stanley, who wavered in front of his parcels as if secretly fearing they would vanish in a puff of smoke. "Something you might not know about Nino: if he likes you, he likes you all the way. No back doors." The Irishman's gaze said Stanley had better not betray Nino's kindness if he knew what was good for him.

"What's in here? I don't...." Stanley lingered over an especially large box wrapped in brown paper and tied with string.

"Why dontcha work up to it, huh? Start with one, open that one first." Danny pulled out his watch, glanced at it. "Take as much time as you need, kid. I gotta go."

"Yes, but—you shouldn't have to go on my account. I wouldn't want you to feel—"

"You ain't makin' me feel nothing. There's this dame I want to see. Nino will be home soon. I'll see ya tonight."

And just like that, Danny Murphy was gone, leaving nothing behind him but the smell of fresh coffee. It occurred to Stanley that perhaps he ought to insist Danny stay, but even after several years among the mobs of New York, he still wasn't certain of all the rules and regulations, the complex social conventions that were very nearly a rule of law. Maybe he was supposed to let Danny go. Maybe insisting that Danny stay would be a breach of protocol, even as hospitality dictated otherwise. It was so confusing... just like this huge pile of boxes.

Why dontcha work up to it? Start with one, open that one first.

It was good advice, very sensible advice. He'd do that.

"NINO, you never come see me anymore! What's the matter with you? Don't you love me?" Ma Keller was a large woman somewhere between forty and seventy, with a shock of bright-red hair she wore piled on top of her head and secured with about a dozen jeweled clips. It was rumored the clips had been a gift from a wandering Russian Gypsy who traded away his children for them, but Ma Keller had been known to embroider the truth, and her legend was such that she had attained nearly mythic status in the neighborhood. Her fruit store was the point of entry for any new swell who wanted an in with the mobs, and nothing got past Ma. If you didn't know it, she knew it, and if you did know it, you probably heard it from her.

At any given time there were a dozen kids hanging around outside the front door, but these weren't the usual street urchins. Ma employed the boys as runners and as couriers, useful because they carried anything and everything: drugs, booze, money, and information. The boys all knew Nino by name, and they tipped their hats respectfully to him as he passed by. "Hey, Mr. Nino!" The smallest of the group, a ragged little black-haired boy, sketched an exaggerated bow in front of Nino. "You goin' in to see Ma?"

"No, I'm goin' in to buy strawberries," Nino said. He stood back and looked the boys over. "Why ain't you kids in school, huh? Ya gotta get an education." He dug in his pockets and tossed them a handful of change as he went in the door. "Here. Go as far as it'll take ya."

Ma favored flowered cotton dresses accented with half a dozen silk scarves; silver bangles slid up and down her arms and punctuated her speech with their incessant staccato clanging. She rushed to embrace Nino like a long-lost son.

"Aw, you know how it is, Ma—all the time tied up with business." Nino reached into his pocket and handed her a half-dozen cigars. "Here, I brought ya a little somethin'."

"You don't need to bring me gifts," Ma said, smiling coyly. She tucked the cigars into the bodice of her dress. "What can I do for you, Nino? Will you drink a cup of coffee with an old woman?"

"Sure," Nino agreed. He followed her into the back of her store where a miniature sitting room waited, complete with couches and a radio, all of it very elegantly furnished. He accepted a cup of coffee from Ma and sat down.

"How is your new little friend?"

Nino raised his eyebrows. "Oh, you're good," he said. "Who told you?"

Ma Keller laughed. "Last night, Big Frank blew in here like stink—he was real upset at you, Nino." She waved her arms and her bangles clinked. "He said he was gonna show you something."

"Yeah?" Nino sneered. "Is that so? Maybe if he had brains enough to get outta his own way." He puffed on his cigar. "Let him come and show me something. I'm ready for him."

"He said you took one of his guys away—little accountant, used to do the books. He said his guys were gonna take you out of the picture." She pushed a plate of cookies across the table, but Nino refused.

"I'm watching my figure," Nino said. "I like to look good." He ran a hand over the front of his waistcoat, patted his flat belly. It was a mark of Nino's vanity that he kept himself neat and trim and never ventured out without his trademark spats. His gloves were tight-fitting, of the finest leather, and cut to hide his squarish, rather ordinary hands; his shoes shone with an unnatural brightness.

"That's what I'm wondering," Nino said, "about this accountant of Big Frank's. How much do you know about him?"

Ma dimpled—or tried to. It was the sort of look that went well with a hotsy baby vamp; on a face-stretcher like Ma, it just looked grotesque. "What's it worth to you?"

"I just gave you half a dozen heaters! Them things cost me a dollar apiece!" Nino's face flamed. "Now see here, if all you got is nothin', then I'll just breeze. No point in me wastin' your time—"

"Aw, sit down, Nino!" Ma pushed at him playfully; it was like being tapped by a grizzly bear. Nino fell helpless against the sofa. "I'll tell you everything you wanna know." She tilted a glance at him. "What's so important about this boy?"

"None of your business."

"You like him?"

Nino's face darkened. "That ain't nothin' but a filthy rumor! I'll have you know—"

"Nino, Nino, calm yourself." Ma waved her bangles at him. "I can tell you everything you want to know—if you want to know it. I mean, if you really want to know."

"I do." He glared at her. "Why are you beatin' around the bush?"

"You can't unhear what you heard, Nino. You know that." She topped up his coffee. "You sure?"

It had to be something really bad, he reasoned, for her to be giving out warnings. "Talk," he said, and "I'm sure."

"The boy is a genius with the numbers. Big Frank told me and I have no reason to disbelieve him."

"Right." Nino made a rude noise. "Because Big Frank is such an honest mug."

Ma spread her hands. "He says the boy is a genius with numbers. He can do things with tax that would make your head spin."

"Yeah, I bet." Nino twirled his pinky ring around his finger, thinking about acquaintances of his, other mob bosses who had tried to beat the taxman and had failed. Nino wasn't dumb enough to keep his money were the government could find it. "What else?"

"His parents are dead. No relatives at all. The boy is all alone in the world."

"So what?" Nino squinted. "I'm starting to think I wasted my cigar money…."

"He comes from a little place in Kansas, he has no family. He is a genius with numbers. Why do you think Big Frank is so angry that you take this boy?"

Nino ignored the question. "What else was he to Frank, huh? There's more. You ain't telling me something."

"He was Big Frank's fag." She chuckled. "You know that word, Nino, eh? He was Big Frank's gunsel, his gaycat."

"Aw, that's bushwa!" Nino cried. "Nothing but rumors." He was lying through his teeth; both he and Ma knew it. There were no real secrets in the underworld—everybody knew your peccadilloes, if you had them. Everybody knew who you were banging, who you had rubbed out, who you planned to bump off, and where the bodies were buried.

"You know Jimmy Two-Shots? You ever heard of him?" Ma Keller stirred more sugar into her coffee.

"Yeah, I know Jimmy. He's a no-good hoodlum. I dunno why Big Frank keeps him around. His best days were over ten years ago." It was typical of Big Frank to get attached to his toys, but he was always terrified one of his boys would betray him, so he made a practice of taking them for long, quiet rides in the country as soon as they had lost their usefulness. It mystified Nino: why was Jimmy still around?

Usually Frank saw to it the useless ones got fitted for a wooden overcoat, but not Jimmy—which meant Jimmy wasn't as useless as everybody thought.

"Jimmy saw them, him and Big Frank, in Big Frank's office. Big Frank had him bent over the desk and he was giving him the business." Clearly Ma relished giving Nino this news; her eyes sparkled and her mouth pursed as if she were tasting a particularly succulent morsel. "Big Frank was giving it to him, and the boy was crying…. He was begging Big Frank to stop, but you know Big Frank."

The blood pounded in Nino's head; his eyes felt hot. He crushed out his cigar in a nearby ashtray and rose to go. "He's nobody's gunsel," he said. He was too warm; his necktie was choking him. "You been lied to, Ma."

"Yeah?" She cackled. "Is that why your face is so red now, Nino?"

"I ain't got nothin' to say to you." He stuffed a fifty-dollar bill into her hand and stumbled out of the shop, his pulse booming in his ears. For several long moments Nino stood on the sidewalk, breathing in the warm air and the regular rhythm of the city until the nausea passed. Two women in summer frocks passed by; he lifted his hat to them and smiled, feeling he was somehow enacting an elaborate pantomime. The sun was shining and it was a beautiful day, but he felt sick inside, as though tainted by a crime he was forced to witness but which he was powerless to prevent. It reminded him of Ray, of being made to stand by while his old man beat Ray to a pulp. It wasn't fair. It wasn't right that others should suffer just because they weren't quite strong enough to defend themselves.

THERE were more suits than Stanley had ever seen: suits for day wear, suits for evening wear, even a swallow-tailed morning coat with a silk cravat. There were shoes: black shoes and brown shoes and tan shoes for day wear and black-and-white spectator shoes, wingtips and oxfords and even a pair of ankle boots in buttery-soft brown leather. He was especially affected by the socks and drawers: literal heaps of fine silk boxer shorts in white and cream and pale blue and oyster, pair after pair after pair of fine hose in every conceivable pattern. He was beside himself, overwhelmed with Nino's largesse, unable to conceive of such patent material wealth.

The jewelry made him cry. He closed the boxes and backed away. He sat down and dropped his head and cried. That was how Nino found him: crying by himself in the midst of his new clothes.

"Hey, kid, what's the matter?" Nino tossed his hat onto the back of a chair and rushed toward Stanley. "Somebody say something to you? Was it Danny? Did Danny say something to you?"

Stanley gestured at the pile of clothing, the unopened boxes of jewelry. "I can't—it's too much. I—I don't expect—I mean, why would you—" Overwrought, he clenched his fists, a shudder running through his slender body. "Why would you—" It tore itself out of him, anguished, desperate: "Why would anyone? Do you think that I'm for sale?"

"No, kid...." Nino slipped out of his coat. "No, that's not it at all. I know about... someone told me about... about Big Frank." He loosened the knot of his tie, took off his tiepin. "I talked to Ma Keller. She knows everything about everybody." He took off his jacket. "I wasn't... I wasn't digging dirt, but I wanted to know. I needed to know." He cast an anguished look at Stanley. "Nobody should ever have to go through that.... Nobody." Nino flung his folded waistcoat on top of his jacket and took his gun out of his holster, stowing it in a drawer. "I ain't trying to buy you, kid. But you got nothing. And I know what that's like. I know what it's like to have nothing, to be nothing, to look into your future and see nothing." He rubbed his forehead. "I wouldn't wish that on anybody. I certainly wouldn't wish it on you." He sighed, and Stanley detected something wistful in it. "I'm sorry." Nino took a breath. "I didn't mean nothing by it. I ain't tryin' to—I ain't trying to buy you."

"What did she tell you?" Stanley scrubbed a hand across his face, ashamed of his tears.

"Enough," Nino whispered. "Enough so that I want to find that rotten son of a bitch and finish him off."

Stanley shook his head, eyes pressed shut. "It wouldn't help," he said quietly. He took a shuddering breath. "I'm sorry," he said. "I behaved very badly. You've been so kind to me."

"It was the drawers that did it. Be honest. Them silk drawers there, they got to ya, huh? A nice pair of shorts does that to me sometimes too."

"I'm sorry," he said again. "I think perhaps I was slightly overwhelmed."

Nino reached out, let his hand drop back to his side. "Can I take you out for dinner?"

The silence stretched between them—a vast, unbreachable gulf. "Alright," Stanley said. He nodded. "Alright," he said again. He cast his gaze over the enormous pile of clothes. "I'll go get dressed." He gathered his new clothes and went into the spare bedroom. He would put one of his wooden horses in the pocket of his pants: a touchstone, something to remind him of how things used to be.

NINO showered and shaved with the care of a nervous bridegroom. He applied cologne and dressed in a somber dark suit with a gray waistcoat and a blue silk cravat. *You're an idiot.* He indulged in his old habit of talking to himself, silently, in the mirror. *You shoulda known better. You overwhelmed the kid. What the hell is the matter with you?* He brushed his thick black hair straight back over his head and applied a thin sheen of pomade. He buffed his nails and inserted onyx cufflinks in his sleeves and a diamond stickpin in his tie. He examined himself critically, sneering at his own reflection, vaguely ashamed his gesture of goodwill had been so misunderstood. Clearly what was called for in this instance was tact, diplomacy, and gentleness—the things Danny Murphy was good at, not Nino. If Danny Murphy were in love with—

Nino watched himself pale visibly in the mirror. One hand went to the knot of his tie; he swallowed hard. *Yeah. Now you're being honest.* "Aw, nuts to that." The kid—Stanley—was cute. He was winsome and innocent and cute and Nino was doing him a favor, rescuing him from Big Frank. That was it. There was nothing more to it. He was in a position to help the kid and that was what he was doing. Was there anything wrong with it? No. Anybody with an ounce of compassion would do the same.

Yeah, The Little Prince. The definition of compassion. And that was just it—what was the matter with him? Why was he acting this way all of a sudden? One quick look at the kid and he was head over heels? Was that it? He was The Little Prince, he was the big six—what was wrong with him?

They're writing songs of love, but not for me

A lucky star's above, but not for me

He was in trouble but good. There had been crushes, and pretty boys had often come to stay the night, but Nino "Spats" Moretti had never, ever been in love.

Except...

It ain't gonna be that way with us, Nino. I don't go for other men. It ain't nothin' personal. It just ain't my thing.

Nino was nineteen years old and here was Danny Murphy, letting him down gently, letting him down and trying not to break his heart, if such a thing was even possible. And Nino, to his eternal shame, had cried, even though he swore up and down he wasn't—he had something in his eye, the cigarette smoke was bothering him. He shook Danny's hand and thanked him for being honest with him, for being man enough to say it, to tell him the truth, but something inside of him died that night. He made a promise to himself: he'd never be dumb enough to fall in love with anyone ever again. That way lay nothing but pain, and he'd had enough of pain, thanks. He'd had enough of the world's guff, putting up with the crap it could do to a man, taking it on the chin and carrying on. He hadn't fought his way up from the gutter to lay himself bare like that. Nino was nobody's fool.

You don't know nothin'. You ain't even tried. Maybe if you tried it, you might like it. A foolish, futile argument, an argument beneath him, but he had felt something when he leaned in to kiss Danny Murphy that hot summer night. And Danny had let Nino kiss him, even kissed him back for several long, heart-stoppingly delicious moments, then pushed Nino away.

It ain't my thing, Nino. No hard feelings, okay? We jake, you and me?

Yeah, Danny. Hard to talk with his heart breaking. Hard to say anything at all. *Yeah, we're jake.* He still loved Danny, and Danny loved him—Danny would always love him—but it was different between them now. Danny couldn't or wouldn't ever give him what he most wanted, and maybe he might get that from someone else, but never from Danny. The Irishman had made that understood. And so Nino would never fall in love again, never let himself feel that way about anybody because, when all was said and done, it simply wasn't worth it.

THE dove-gray suit, a crisp white shirt, diamond cufflinks, a silk tie, black wingtips. Stanley Zadwadzki examined himself critically in the mirror as he patted aftershave lotion into his pale cheeks. A hot shower had loosened up his tense muscles; his body felt more fluid under his suit. He shifted his feet and shivered as silk boxer shorts brushed the sensitive places on his body. He was beginning to see the appeal, beginning to understand why guys like Danny and Nino dropped the extra dough for things that felt so good. He had never considered himself a hedonist—indeed, it had never occurred to him to indulge in the sensual pleasures—in a suit that fit like it had been tailored for him personally, in silk drawers that (here he blushed a little) caressed his backside and his thighs like hidden hands. The Stanley who returned his gaze from the mirror was a different Stanley than the one who had spent nearly five years in painful thrall to Big Frank and his goons. He wasn't ready to hope, not just yet, and maybe Nino wasn't much different from Big Frank. Maybe Nino was playing with him like a cat toying with a mouse—and it was more than Stanley's sanity was worth to allow himself to hope.

He stepped out of the bedroom and nearly ran into Nino, who had just come out of his own room. "Hey, kid, you ready?"

"I—I suppose—I mean." He was stuttering again, but perhaps it could be forgiven. Nino was…

… Nino was *gorgeous*.

And staring at him. "Something wrong?" The gangster lifted an eyebrow. "You jake, kid?"

"You look wonderful." It slipped out before he could pull it back. He tensed. Now Nino would get angry.

But Nino didn't get angry; he smiled. "You think so?" He glanced down at himself. "Guess I clean up okay."

"No, it's m-much m-more than that." Stanley reached out, stopping short of touching the dark fabric of Nino's coat. "You look like a movie star."

Nino laughed, clearly pleased. "Well, that's good enough for me." He took stock of Stanley, sucked in his breath. "Wow. You're really hitting on all six, kid." He took the fabric of Stanley's lapel between thumb and finger and caressed it. "You like this suit, huh? It fit okay?"

"It's perfect." Stanley reached out and laid his hand on Nino's wrist, amazed at his own boldness. "Everything… is perfect."

The doorbell buzzed; Nino drew himself away. "That's Danny." He cocked his head. "We'd best get going."

"…AND then this dame says to me, she says, 'Don't get any on my dress!'" Danny burst into gales of laughter; the other men joined him. "On her dress! She was worried about her dress!"

"That's a dame for ya," Nino said. "Always thinking about the wrong thing."

He leaned forward and lit his cigarette from the candle on the table, puffing appreciatively. The meal had been excellent, the company convivial. Stanley had been slightly reticent at the beginning of the meal, no doubt thinking about his earlier outburst, but Danny had kept them entertained with funny stories about his and Nino's misspent youth and jokes at both of their expense, and pretty soon Stanley was chiming in with stories of his own—including one rather risqué tale involving a cow, a bottle of Coca-Cola, and Old Man Granger's pickup truck.

"I think we got you all wrong, kid." Danny clapped Stanley on the back as he lit the younger man's cigarette. "You're a real firecracker, ain't ya?" He leaned close. "I bet you were a real swell back home.... Spent a lotta weekends in the struggle buggy, didn't you?"

It was amazing, Nino thought. He had never seen anyone color so quickly or so completely before: a subtle staining of blood suffused Stanley's face to the hairline.

"Uh, n-no, I never... I mean, I uh...." He gulped, reached to adjust the knot of his necktie.

Danny, sensing live prey, moved in for the kill. "You mean to tell me...?" He was incredulous. "You never so much as...?"

Stanley shook his head. Even the tips of his ears were red.

"Aw, leave the kid alone," Nino said. "Just cause he ain't a champion skirt-chaser like you." Nino jabbed at the air with his cigar. "Leave him alone, Danny."

"Aw, close your head," the Irishman patted Stanley's shoulder. "I think we should be proud of him, showing so much restraint." He grinned at Stanley to show him there were no hard feelings. "Good-looking kid like you, I betcha gotta beat 'em off with a stick."

"No... n-no, not really." Stanley darted a glance at Nino and saw the gangster's watch was in his hand. "My goodness, is that the time?"

Nino examined the timepiece in his usual shortsighted manner. "Yeah," he drawled. "I reckon we should get back. I've been having such a good time, I hate to leave."

"Ain't you forgettin' something?" Danny asked with a pointed look in Nino's direction. "You said you were gonna."

THE base of Stanley's belly clenched. Now they would turn him out. Now they would abandon him, or worse, they would devise some horribly submissive role for him in Nino's organization, something as bad as what Big Frank had done. He wasn't stupid; he knew the way things worked. He knew gifts had to be bought and paid for, and kindness from men like Nino must be earned.

"Oh yeah," Nino said. He drew on his cigar. "Listen, kid, Danny and me have been talkin'."

Here it comes, Stanley thought. Was there any point in hoping Nino would be gentle with him? "I see." *Breathe*, he thought. *Keep breathing*. He drew hard on his cigarette; underneath the table, his free hand clenched into a fist.

"Well, we think you'd be a cinch to join our organization." Danny nodded at him. "You got a lotta brains, kid, and we like to make you an offer."

"An offer." He sounded idiotic, even to himself.

"I know you did the books for Big Frank," Nino said. He slid over on the banquette so he was closer to Stanley and spoke confidentially to the younger man. "Big Frank's mob never could hold onto nothin'— then you blow into town a few years back. Suddenly he's showing a profit—even his little penny-ante numbers rackets up in the Bronx and in Harlem are making money. And he's keeping all his dough. That sort of thing impresses me."

"Yeah, it impressed everybody. Big Frank is as dumb as they come," Danny said, "and suddenly he's making money hand over fist and keeping himself and his palookas bankrolled. People notice things."

"I d-don't understand." Stanley was completely at sea. What, exactly, were they asking him?

"Listen, Stanley…." Nino stubbed out his cigar in the ashtray. "I could use someone like you—"

Get in here, gunsel! Get in here and let me show ya what punks like you was made for!

"—to do the books in my main office. It ain't much. I got a club downtown, called The Two Aces—"

"—after me and Nino, see?" Danny chimed in, grinning. "We usta call ourselves that when we was kids."

"I'm afraid the books are a mess. It'll take somebody with your kinda gifts to straighten 'em out, put things to rights." Nino sounded apologetic. "I'll pay you three hundred a week to start." He twirled the pinky ring around his little finger. "I like to spread my money around, but we keep a low profile, Danny and me, so the cops don't get wise." He didn't need to add that The Two Aces was a front for his bootlegging operation, because everybody in the city knew it, and Stanley was too polite to say such things out loud.

Three hundred dollars a week... most bookkeepers, most honest-to-God accountants, made little over two thousand a year. Stanley's hand crept to the knot of his tie again. "What would... what would I have to do to earn that sort of money?" he asked. It came out rather more shakily than he had intended.

Nino glanced at Danny with worried eyes. "Uh, just keep the books... you know, money in and money out, profits and losses, the usual stuff."

Stanley suspected there was more—much more, in fact—but Nino was keeping it low-key to avoid scaring him away. Nino probably wanted to break Stanley in gradually, and he certainly wouldn't get Stanley to do any wet work—but make no mistake, Stanley was useful to Nino, and not merely for what he knew about Big Frank's organization. As for Stanley, he would be protected by Nino as long as he was loyal to Nino's cause. If he stepped over the line.... "Money in and money out, huh?"

Danny suddenly found the tabletop more interesting than seemed possible. "Nino," he said quietly. "Big Frank."

"No," Nino said sharply, "you don't never gotta do that no more! The only thing you do for me is the books, savvy? The only thing." He gestured with his thumb. "You'll have your own office, your name on the door, all that stuff. I'll put you in charge of these other bozos I got in my office, keep 'em in line. Even get ya a secretary, some dame to answer the phone and sharpen your pencils. You don't answer to nobody but Nino, see?" He traced the edge of the table with his forefinger. "That sound like something you could do?"

"Why?" Stanley asked, suspicious. "Why should I?"

Nino narrowed his eyes. "Why not?" he asked. "You need a job, and you need my protection. I need a guy what can work for me." He wasn't quite crass enough to point out that Stanley's life wasn't worth a plug nickel without Nino's protection. "We got a deal?"

"Uh…." Stanley swiped at his face with his sleeve. He felt foolish to be crying, but he couldn't seem to stop himself. The more he tried to stay the tears, the harder they fell. It was ridiculous. What was he, a schoolgirl?

"Here, kid." A square of silk with Danny's scent on it.

Stanley mopped his face. "Okay," he whispered.

Nino smiled. "That's great, kid. You make me very happy."

"And Nino better get home," Danny said, "because Nino's enemies are probably out looking for Nino, *capisce*?"

"Listen to him," Nino said. "Spoilsport."

Danny balled up a fist and pretended to hit Nino on the chin. "Why, I oughta…."

They collected their hats and coats and Nino paid the bill. It had begun to rain outside, a gentle, drizzling mist that collected on their clothes and on the tips of their brows and lashes. "I always liked walking in the rain," Stanley mused, "when I was a kid."

"Yeah, well, get in the car," Danny said. He took a quick look around before shoving Stanley into the backseat, Nino following after. "I ain't layin' no bets on Big Frank's goodwill. He's probably got his goons out looking for you. Not," he amended, "like we're afraid of 'em."

He hopped into the car himself and started the engine. Danny selected a succession of side streets, taking the main routes only when absolutely necessary and, once, cutting through an alley with the lights off. By the time they reached Nino's apartment, Stanley's nerves were a mess.

"Sure you don't wanna come in?" Nino asked. "Have a cuppa joe with us and celebrate?"

"Naw, I better not." Danny squeezed Nino's arm. "See you tomorrow."

"Tomorrow," Nino agreed. He put the key in the door and closed it quickly behind Stanley and himself. "Did you have a good time, kid? You like the food? It's a nice place. I like that place."

"It was great," Stanley agreed. He hung his new overcoat up carefully and laid his hat on the shelf.

"Tomorrow I'll take ya down to the office, get ya all set up," Nino said. He stifled a yawn. "That Danny, he sure can talk! That boy can chew the rag for hours. Now listen, tomorrow'll be your first day and I think you and me should—"

"Would it be alright if I went to bed?" Stanley asked. "I'm pretty tired out."

"Yeah, sure…. Whatever you want, kid." Nino was visibly disappointed. "No need to, uh, stand on ceremony. I might read for a bit, then turn in myself." He sat down with the newspaper. "Good night."

Stanley turned to go but stopped halfway. He turned around and looked at Nino. "Why?" he asked.

Nino looked up. "Why what?"

"Why are you doing this for me? What… what do you want?" For a moment the cornfields and wide blue skies of Kansas were in his mind—and then the city rose up, swarming with blackness, and blotted everything out.

"Nothing," Nino said. He turned back to his newspaper. "I don't want nothing."

NINO was dreaming. He was all alone in the dark, in some vast, cavernous space, slowly ascending a flight of stairs past giant mullioned windows through which shone a pale and scabrous moon. He was cold—he had left his coat in the carriage and his luggage was gone, and for all he knew he was being lured here to his death. No one would tell him anything… no one had come to meet him, and he would die here. He would die here, all alone and far from home….

"Hey, Nino…." A voice against his ear, a warm body at his back, curling into him. "It's just me. Shhh, don't get up. It's me."

Nino stiffened, instantly awake. His hand stole under his pillow and came out holding his gun. "Get out," Nino snarled, "Or I'll blow ya into little bits!"

IN HIS room next door, Stanley was dreaming too. He was alone in the dark, in some vast and cavernous space, walking up an endless flight of stone steps. There was a noise somewhere like water dripping, and he became aware he was no longer asleep. There were voices, people talking in Nino's room. Big Frank—Big Frank had sent his goons to Nino's place. They had seen Stanley getting out of Danny's car, coming up here with Nino, and now they knew... now they knew where to find him, where to find Nino and maybe they would bump him off, bump both of them off—

He dived for the door and yanked it open, stumbled down the hallway and into Nino's bedroom, his terrified cold fingers fumbling for the light. "Nino, I heard—"

THE light came on, and Nino realized two things rather more abruptly than was good for him.

A man had come into his room while he was sleeping.

The man wasn't Stanley.

"What'd I tell you, huh?" Nino reared up in bed, laying his palm against the palooka's face and pushing him onto the floor. "I told you we was through! Why'd you think you could just come in here, huh? I coulda shot you dead!"

The palooka stared at Nino as if he'd just sprouted horns. "Aw, Nino! You gave me a key, dontcha remember? You said for me to let myself in. You said—"

"I know what I said," Nino snarled. He kicked the covers aside and started toward the man, his pajama jacket unbuttoned and hanging open to the waist, his hair disheveled as though someone had run their hands through it. "I know I also told you we was through. Gimme that key!" He grabbed the palooka's pants from the bedroom floor and delved into the pockets, found the key, and threw the trousers in the man's face. "Get out! Unless you want me to fill you fulla lead!"

The man staggered back, bumped into Stanley, and for several seconds the two did a strange, impromptu dance. Then the palooka was gone. A moment later, the front door slammed.

Nino's alarm clock ticked off several uncomfortable seconds.

"Your pajamas are unbuttoned," Stanley said. He turned and fled.

"Kid, come on! Aw, don't be like that!" Nino grabbed his dressing gown and flung it on over his pajamas. Stanley was in the kitchen, drinking a glass of water. He drank it slowly, then refilled it from the tap, and drank that one too. He seemed to be quite angry—this was something new.

"Kid, I'm sorry you had to see that," Nino said.

"Sorry I had to walk in on you, you mean?" Stanley set the water glass down with a thump. "Sorry that I walked in and interrupted your little necking session with—" His cheeks flamed. "Does he have a name?"

"Uh, yeah, I think it's Charlie." Nino approached him, hands raised in surrender. "Kid—Stanley—it was a stupid mistake. Nothing happened. He had a key and figured he'd use it. There ain't nothin' between us! I can't stand that mug! Do you think I let just anybody come waltzing into my bedroom?"

"I don't know," Stanley said quietly. "Do you?"

"Aw, kid! You must think I'm a real heel," Nino said weakly. Stanley brushed past him on his way into the sitting room, slamming into Nino with his shoulder.

It was suddenly very, very quiet. There was a crackle of static as Stanley turned on the radio in the sitting room. He twirled the dial, looking for a station.

They're writing songs of love, but not for me

"I'm sorry I scared ya." Nino hovered in the doorway. "I didn't invite him here. He came in without asking me. I gotta protect my interests. I can't let some nitwit come in and stick me up."

"Yeah," Stanley said. He was standing by the fireplace, picking at a hangnail on his thumb, his face a study in abject misery. "I'll move out in the morning."

"What?" Nino moved closer but didn't touch the younger man. "What for? You ain't gotta do that."

"I've made a mess of things."

"So we had a little incident," Nino said. "Stuff happens. Danny and me been snipin' at each other for years." He leaned forward. "We jake, me 'n' you?"

Stanley raised his eyes. "We're jake," he said miserably. "I should... g-go to bed." He hunched up his shoulders and let them drop. "I'll just...." He turned on his heel and disappeared down the hall. Nino heard the bedroom door close softly behind him.

"Shit." Nino slumped against the back of the couch and rubbed his eyes. What a sap he was. And that damn palooka, tripping in here like he owned the joint. What was his racket, anyway? Couldn't he see Nino was...

Yeah. Nino was all wet. He rubbed his eyes again, blinked, got up, and roamed around the room. The city was strangely quiet beyond his windows—no sounds of sirens, not even ambient street noise. He spotted something on the carpet, bent, and picked it up: a curl of wood. So the kid had been carving. Probably making toothpicks for himself.

No. Not toothpicks. As his gaze fell upon it, Nino felt a sharp jab in his heart. A perfect wooden horse, tiny, exquisitely shaped... and another.... He twitched aside the newspaper covering the table and uncovered several more, each one unique, each one as beautiful as the last. The attention to detail was incredible: each miniature horse appeared to have been momentarily arrested in midflight, manes flying and hooves lifted. Nino's vision blurred and he sat down heavily.

I like to carve. If that's alright.

"Yeah," Nino spoke aloud. "Yeah, kid. That's alright."

CHAPTER THREE

"HEY, Nino said he was bringin' in a new guy." The girl was about twenty-five and exquisitely turned out, with what people usually called "a cheerful disposition." She snapped her gum and hummed and jiggled along to the radio; she executed a sort of complicated soft-shoe while standing in front of the filing cabinets. She was barely five feet tall, with light-brown hair, penciled eyebrows, and a disconcerting resemblance to the actress Joan Blondell, of which she was conscious and tried to play up with cosmetics and clothes. Her name was Delores, she was his secretary, and she must have decided she liked Stanley on sight. "Tell you what I'm gonna do, fish. I'm gonna take care of ya, see? You need anything, you just come to Mama Delores." She walked a slow circle around Stanley, looking him up and down. "Nice suit. And those wingtips are the cat's pajamas." She tweaked Stanley's cheek. "Oh, Daddy!"

Delores had his office ready when he came in: a huge space with oak filing cabinets, built-in bookshelves, and a big desk. His name, Stanley D. Zadwadzki, was on a brass nameplate on the door; a similar nameplate sat on his desk. The chair was upholstered in fine leather, soft as butter, and he had a modern adding machine all his own.

"Nino said you're gonna want to look at the books, so I brung some of 'em for ya." Delores tottered in, her slight frame swaying under a gargantuan stack of ledgers. "You can start with these."

Stanley relieved her of her burden. "I can fetch the rest," he said. "You'll get your dress all dusty."

"What a sweetheart you are!" She dimpled at him and snapped her gum. "This way."

Stanley followed her jiggling backside down the corridor to a narrow storage room where several more piles of ledgers were quietly moldering. He took a pair of reading glasses out of his pocket and put them on to examine the dates on the ledgers, selecting only certain years and leaving the rest behind. It wasn't strictly necessary he examine every single entry in every single ledger for every single year, but he wanted to get as clear as possible a financial picture of Nino's organization. By midmorning, he had examined the club's finances for the past five years and was able to form a temporary hypothesis: Nino's club was losing money and had been for a while because of certain inefficiencies in its operations. This was something Stanley understood, something he could sink his teeth into.

"Mr. Z, I brung ya a cuppa joe and a donut." Delores jiggled in and laid the aforementioned items on his desk. "Figured you might need a break."

"Thank you, Delores. I appreciate it." Stanley took off his glasses and rubbed his eyes. "Are these all the ledgers?"

"Yes, Mr. Z, that's it. There ain't no more. Once Mr. Nino told us you was comin', we dug 'em out for ya."

He sipped his coffee. It was delicious and he told her so, which appeared to please her. She fluttered and jiggled and smiled. "Aw, Mr. Z, me 'n' you is gonna get along just fine!"

He sipped the coffee and ate the donut while he worked through the ledgers systematically. By noon he had a hunch; by five that afternoon, he was certain.

He was equally certain he didn't want to be the one to break the news to Nino. But it had to be done. How would Nino react when he heard? He knew how Big Frank took such news....

Whatta ya mean? You tellin' me there's money missin'? Huh? That what you're tellin' me, gunsel? Get in here!

Stanley shuddered, drew himself forcibly back from his reverie. Maybe Nino would be more sanguine than Big Frank. Perhaps he wouldn't blame Stanley for the missing money... perhaps he'd understand Stanley was only the messenger.

You hope.

He lifted the intercom. "Delores, can you get Mr. Moretti on the phone for me?"

She snapped her gum. "Sure thing, boss. Hold the wire."

His gut tightened as he listened: one click, two, three, a moment of static. Maybe Nino wasn't there. Maybe the bad news would have to wait. "Call's connected, Mr. Z. You can go ahead anytime."

Stanley forced himself to swallow. "Mr. Moretti... it's... it's S-Stanley Zadwadzki. I... ah, found s-something I think you might want to see. When? Right now? Of c-course. Of course. I'll see you then." He laid the receiver back in its cradle with a shaking hand. His head was buzzing; he felt like he was going to pass out.

Luckily Delores picked that moment to enter the room. She reacted immediately with the same sort of response Stanley seemed to excite in all females. "Mr. Z! You look sick! You ain't eaten all day. Hold on. I'm going to fix you a sandwich in the kitchen. You just sit there and don't you move." Her heels clattered off down the hall, and within two minutes, she laid a plate at his elbow: a thick sandwich piled high with cold cuts and cheese, and a glass of milk. "You gotta eat something! I'm so sorry, Mr. Z. I shoulda told you to take your lunch break."

"It's not your fault, Delores." He tried to smile but contracting his facial muscles just made him feel sick.

"You poor baby," she crooned. "Eat your sandwich." She closed his office door and clattered away. Stanley regarded the sandwich with awe, and not a little nausea. Delores had gone to a lot of trouble to make it for him. He ought to at least try it. Maybe if he ate a little of it, he might feel better.

Ten minutes later, the plate was clean of even crumbs and the milk glass stood empty. Stanley polished his glasses with his handkerchief and was just putting them back on when Delores buzzed to tell him Nino had arrived. "Show him in, please, Delores." He checked that his shirt was tucked in and buttoned his waistcoat.

"Good morning." Nino shook his hand heartily and took a look around. "You get settled in okay? You like this place alright?"

"It's very nice." Stanley's palms were sweating. He didn't relish giving Nino the news. "Thank you so much. And Delores has been very helpful."

"Ain't she somethin'? Only the best for my boys, that's what I always say." Nino sat down and lit a fresh cigar. "What'd you have to tell me, kid? You find something important in these here books of mine?"

Stanley cleared his throat. "Nino," he began. It came out as a tortured squeak. "Nino," he said, "I don't know how to say this, but—"

Nino's dark eyes caught and held his gaze. "The club's losin' money, ain't that right?"

Stanley nodded miserably. "I'm afraid so. It has been for some time." He explained that, even though the books appeared fine on the surface, a closer examination revealed small amounts of money had been disappearing for close to five years, a little at a time. "Whoever has been skimming you has been very careful about it," Stanley said. He turned the ledger so Nino could see it. "Right here, in April of this year, someone placed an order for office supplies: file folders, notebooks, that sort of thing."

"Yeah," Nino said, "what's so weird about that?"

"When I checked the supply closet this morning, none of those things were there. I asked Delores and she said the order had never arrived—there was some mix-up with the supplier."

Nino clamped down on his cigar. "Mix-up with the supplier, eh?"

"Whoever ordered the materials did it in March, in February, January, and all the way back through last year. The amounts vary, and he was clever enough to bury the dates—"

"Wait a minute," Nino interjected. "Bury the dates? You're losin' me with the lingo, kid."

"He placed the fraudulent orders on wildly differing dates each month, and avoided any particular pattern of ordering—probably to deflect suspicion. Anyone examining your books would likely chalk it up to supplier problems and assume the supplies had eventually been delivered."

"But they ain't been." Nino regarded him with something approaching reverence. "You tellin' me someone's been cheating Nino?"

Stanley stood up, leaning over the desk to point to the ledger in Nino's hand. "I'm afraid so." He handed Nino his notations. "If you check the dates, you'll see something was ordered on each of these days, but nothing was ever delivered. My guess is your inside man was doing a split with his opposite number in the suppliers' office." He sat down. "I'm sorry," he said quietly, "I had to break this to you."

"No, kid!" Nino laid the ledger on the desk with a thump. "You're doing me a favor! You've just told me I'm losing money and you told me why." He glanced down at his hands. "You're playing square with me. I like that."

"Why wouldn't I?" Stanley asked. "This is why you hired me, isn't it?" He watched Nino carefully. "You aren't angry with me?"

"Angry?" Nino laughed gently. "Aw, Stanley, come on. We're jake, ain't we, me 'n' you? You did good." He took a slow breath. "So we got a rotten apple."

"Yes. In my experience it's probably someone who's been with you a while. These fraudulent purchases go back years. And it is most likely someone who has a grudge...."

"Say, kid, you eatin' enough?" Nino's dark brows knit. "You look kinda peaky."

"I wouldn't ask the staff directly," Stanley said, "but I would observe them... maybe plant a mole. And of course I'll keep an eye on things from my end." He clasped his shaking hands together underneath the desk. "I h-hope this is acceptable to you. I've tried to do my best."

There was silence from the other man and Stanley raised his eyes slowly. Nino was watching him, his face expressionless.

"What about supper?" Nino asked. "I think it's time we let you meet some of the boys."

"SO IF I got… let's call 'em investments…." Jake Giambi was tiny, a lean little ferret of a man with startling dimples and the neat figure of a professional dancer, which he had been before joining Nino's outfit. "…And I wanna make as much as possible from my investments, but I don't wanta end up behind the 8-ball with the G-men, you got me?"

"I think so," Stanley said. He leaned back against the lush banquette and gazed around him, a little in awe of his surroundings. They didn't have restaurants like this in Salina, Kansas, and Stanley had never in his life been inside a place as luxurious, as frankly opulent as this, with its rich wall paneling and a dozen sparkling mirrors reflecting beams of dancing light. It was, to be honest, rather dazzling, and he felt himself quite unsettled.

"Here, Stan, have one of these here cigars." Big Boy Floyd Roscoe leaned over, a naked flame dancing between his thick fingers. "Lemme light that for ya."

"So how do I keep the bulls from getting wind o' my nest egg?" Giambi asked.

"I would probably advise you to diversify your investments as much as possible," Stanley said. He puffed on the cigar and coughed a little, covered it by sipping from his water glass.

"He means spread it around, ya dumb schmoe!" Harry Bergen pretended to slap Giambi around the ears and a mock scuffle broke out at their end of the table.

"Hey, cut it out, you mugs!" Nino snarled at them. "I'm tryin' to drink my java here and you birds are achin' to break up the joint!"

"He's a smart kid, Nino!" Willie the Knife reached around to pat Stanley on the shoulder. "A very smart kid. You did right to take him away from Big Frank."

"Big Frank deserves whatever he gets," said a smaller man at the far end of the table. Stanley had been introduced to him earlier in the evening but had forgotten his name. The man was immensely old and was apparently the best safe cracker in the business. "He is no good. He was never no good. His father was no good, and his grandfather."

"Yeah, whyn't give us the whole rundown there, Ollie!" To the casual onlooker, Danny appeared relaxed and merry, even slightly tipsy; a glance at his eyes said otherwise. He had played along with the rest of them tonight, whistling at the floor show and patting the cigarette girl on the buttocks, but he stayed close by Nino's side and kept an eye on everything that went on around him. Stanley knew Danny was Nino's personal torpedo; most likely Danny never, ever forgot it.

"So, Stanley, tell me"—Giambi again. He appeared to have more than the usual number of accounting questions—"why do we gotta pay so much tax, huh? Me, I'm self-employed—"

"Self-employed," someone called out. "That's what he calls it?"

"Actually, Mr. Giambi, being self-employed means you could probably pay a lot less tax than you already do." Stanley pushed away his empty coffee cup and took a puff of his cigar. "I would be happy to explain it to you if you want to drop by the office sometime."

"What about me, Stan? Can you get me out of paying alimony?" Willie the Knife leaned in front of Floyd Roscoe. "It's hurtin' me awful bad in the wallet."

"How much alimony do you currently pay?" Stanley asked.

"About sixty a month," Willie said, "for each wife, and I got six of 'em."

The table erupted in laughter. Nino raised his hands. "Alright, you yaps, that's enough. I gotta get going. Maybe I shouldn't even be out here tonight. It's gettin' so I shouldn't be taking no chances, see?"

"Aw, Nino, you ain't afraid of Big Frank!" It was Big Boy Floyd who spoke, but the others joined in readily with various cries of what they'd do to Big Frank O'Hara when they caught him out.

"Now shut up!" Nino cried. "I'm gonna breeze, see? And you birds oughta do the same."

Danny touched Stanley's elbow and spoke into his ear. "Come on, kid. Time to go."

They collected their coats and slipped out into the darkness, Danny walking between Nino and Stanley. He held the car door while they climbed in, then got in and started up the car.

"You did real good tonight, kid." Nino patted Stanley's arm. "Real good. I'm awful proud of you."

"You sure had them mugs listening to ya," Danny said. "They were starin' at you like you were readin' 'em the gospels or something."

"Stanley here is a smart kid," Nino said. "I know quality, and kid, you're it." He smiled at Stanley. "How do you feel? Didn't have too much to drink, did you?"

Stanley shook his head. It felt strange to be so replete with warmth and ease, to have a full belly, to be wearing nice clothes and to be in the company of friends. "Just a couple glasses of wine." He felt quite dizzy, actually—as if, given half a chance, he could get up and dance. He had been with Nino for only a few days, but there was a certain comfort in the simple routine he'd managed to establish for himself, working at The Two Aces during the day and going out with Nino and Danny at night. He'd had wonderful meals, been introduced to the very best of New York nightlife, and Nino had promised to take him to all the latest shows on Broadway; Nino had even bought him a car to use, a late-model Stutz roadster with a shiny black body and lots of power under the hood. Nino had given him the keys at breakfast, grinning from ear to ear at Stanley's expression of disbelief. *My accountant can't ride no bus, see. You work for me, you gotta go in style.*

But Nino was like that. He delighted in leaving gifts for Stanley: a fine set of carving tools in an embossed leather pouch, a supply of tropical woods imported from South America, a handsome set of onyx cufflinks. And Stanley left some of his carvings for Nino, all beautifully shaped and polished to a satiny smoothness. He maintained that carving helped keep his hands and his mind steady, and he was rarely without a scrap of wood and his penknife. He carved horses and cows, dogs and rabbits, and exotic animals he'd seen in Nino's back issues of *National Geographic* magazine.

"Here you go, gents, have a safe night and don't do nothin' I wouldn't do." Danny pulled up to the curb and then turned around to bid them goodnight.

"Gives us a pretty wide berth, don't it?" Nino asked. He cuffed Danny affectionately on the shoulder. "Drive safe, now."

"You're the boss." Danny put the car into gear and drove away. Nino put a hand on Stanley's shoulder as they walked up the stairs and into Nino's apartment.

"So what'd you think, kid? You have a good time tonight?" Nino hung up his coat and slipped out of his jacket. "The boys were a bit rowdy. I hope they didn't ride you too hard."

"They were fine," Stanley said. He went to the radio. "Some music?" he asked.

"Sure," Nino said. "Music'd be fine. I'm just gonna get a glass of water."

Stanley shucked his jacket and switched on the radio. Nelson Eddy was singing "Rhythm of the Day," and despite himself, Stanley started tapping his feet to the music. He raised his hands to shoulder height and waved them like he'd seen bandleaders do, and shook his upper body like someone in the grip of an ague.

"Whatcha doin', kid?" Nino grinned at him. "You look like you're havin' a fit or something."

Stanley winked at him and continued his herky-jerky dancing.

"You like that music, huh?" Nino chuckled. "You look like you never heard music before." He laid his water glass down on an end table as Annette Hanshaw came on, singing "You Wouldn't Fool Me, Would You?" He reached out both hands. "Come here. You look like a chicken somebody just tried to butcher." To his amazement, Stanley came into his arms, still humming and waving and wiggling. "Whatcha' tryin' to do, huh? Here. Try and follow what I do." Nino paused for a moment, listening to the beat, then moved off at a rapid pace. Astonishingly, Stanley kept up with him. Nino danced him around and around the living room.

Gee how I wish that we could be alone
You wouldn't fool me, would you?

"Nicely done, kid!" Nino stood back and applauded. "You did real good!"

Stanley offered him an exaggerated bow, dipping forward stiffly from the waist. "Thank you," he said. He staggered a little on the way up, and Nino caught him.

"You okay?" Nino asked.

"Too much wine," Stanley said. He held up his hands and they danced some more, with very few mishaps but with a great deal of dizzy laughter. "Oh, dear me," Stanley said, laughing, "I am very afraid, Mr. Moretti, that I'll never make it as a hoofer."

"Aw, you don't need to worry about that stuff," Nino said. "You got everything you need, Stanley."

"I think—" Stanley stopped short. He leaned in to turn up the radio.

They're writing songs of love, but not for me

Stanley hesitated, looking to Nino for permission. "Could we…? Do you think…?"

Nino's voice was husky. "Come here, kid."

Stanley drifted into Nino's embrace, his arms around the other man's waist, his head on Nino's shoulder. There was no talking, no joking, nothing except the sound of their mingled breaths and their gently shuffling feet. Stanley's hands slid along Nino's back of their own accord and his body pressed closer to Nino's, seeking some stimulus he didn't understand and couldn't name. Nino smelled like tobacco smoke and good cologne; his back moved under Stanley's palm as he breathed, the strong shoulders moving up and down in an effortless rhythm.

A lucky star's above, but not for me

Stanley raised his head from Nino's shoulder and gazed into the other man's dark eyes. Slowly, wonderingly, as if seeing Nino for the first time, he brought his hand to Nino's face, smoothed his cheek and ran his fingertips lightly over Nino's lips. Nino's breath was warm and moist against his fingers and Stanley wanted to go on feeling it. Nino was looking at him and there was nothing hasty or strained in his looking, merely a quiet acceptance and an understanding that this had to proceed at its own pace—at a pace Stanley set.

"Would it be alright…?" Stanley asked. His own voice—husky, wholly sensual—surprised him.

"Yes," Nino whispered.

Stanley brushed Nino's lips with his own, gently and tentatively, and drew back. Nino's eyes were closed, his dark lashes resting on his cheeks. There was nothing here to be afraid of.

His kiss was fumbling, inexpert, clumsy, but Nino didn't seem to mind. He grunted softly as Stanley deepened the kiss, and after a moment, Stanley seemed to understand the necessary slide and rhythm, and was happily plundering Nino's mouth with a disconcerting thoroughness. He groaned as the tip of Nino's tongue slipped between his lips, gently probing, opening him to the caress.

Stanley slipped away from him, eyes shining. "Thank you," he murmured. "Good night."

He went into his bedroom and closed the door behind him.

STANLEY woke to the sound of Nino rattling around in the other rooms. He lay very still for several long moments, trying to remember, then smiled, his whole body suffused with a warm glow. *I kissed him.* This was followed by the less-than-salutary thought of, *Maybe he's mad because I kissed him.* Nino hadn't seemed mad: he had returned Stanley's caress warmly and eagerly. They had danced together; it was alright.

He got up and slipped into his dressing gown. Nino was sitting at the dining table, reading the newspaper and drinking coffee. His usual two slices of toast sat on a plate in front of him and the radio was playing in the background. Stanley moved at the edge of his vision and Nino looked up. "Good morning, Stanley. Come on over and have some coffee. You hungry?"

"Starving," Stanley confessed. As if in agreement, his stomach chose that moment to growl loudly.

"You sure are," Nino laughed. He pulled out a chair. "Come on, sit down over here and have some breakfast."

Stanley sat down, helped himself to toast and jam while Nino filled his coffee cup. "Have you been up long?" he asked.

"Aw, you know me, kid. I'm up puttin' the birds on the wires. Ain't nobody gonna get anything over on Nino." He folded the newspaper to the page he had open and passed it to Stanley. "Get a gander of that mug," he said.

SNAKE EYES JERRY GETS LIFE, the headline read. "There's something familiar about him," Stanley remarked. "I've seen him—"

Come out here! Big Frank wants ya! Stop yer snivellin' and get out here, okay? Don't make me come in there!

It was like a punch in the gut. He pushed the paper back across the table to Nino. "I—he used to—"

Nino laid a hand on his wrist. "He hurt you?" he asked. "Because if he did, I'll have him taken care of. Ain't nobody safe from me. I can always get at birds like him. Ain't no bird too smart for me. I'll get him."

Stanley shook his head. He wasn't eager to continue this conversation. It was better to think of other things, pleasant things. What good ever came of dwelling on the past? "He was one of Big Frank's... friends." He was suddenly cold all over. "I think he ran guns... something.... I don't want to talk about it. Please, let's talk about something else."

The sun was shining, the radio was playing a pleasant tune, and he was alive and above ground. Maybe that was something, after all.

"Kid...." Nino was smiling, but there was something else there, behind his eyes... something that looked an awful lot like pain. "Are you happy? Being here, working for me...." His hand tightened on Stanley's wrist. "I don't want you to think you owe me nothing... or I'm keeping you here." He stroked the back of Stanley's hand, his thumb moving in small circles. "You're free to go anytime you want to."

Stanley smiled. "And run to some rival mob and tell 'em everything." He glanced at Nino through his lashes. "Or do you trust me?"

Nino reached across, took Stanley's chin between thumb and finger, and raised his face. "Trust you?" His expression softened. "I picked you outta the crowd, baby."

Stanley felt the sting of tears against his lids. "Thank you," he whispered. It felt like his heart had broken open and was bleeding into his chest. "Thank you."

STANLEY arrived at his desk a little past nine and found Delores with a hot cup of coffee and a nervous smile. "Eli says he wants to meetya." She jiggled and snapped her gum. "He says he got something to tell ya."

"Eli?" Stanley put his reading glasses on and sat down at his desk. "Eli who?"

"Elisha McKenna," she said, like somebody announcing a bout, or a disease. "He's been with Nino a while now. Says he's got something to tell ya."

"Alright." Stanley pushed aside a pile of ledgers.

Delores reappeared, shoving a slender young man ahead of her. He was perhaps Stanley's own age, with round blue eyes, a snub nose, and a petulant mouth. He walked with a shuffle and there was something resentful in his attitude, as though he disliked being trotted in to meet Nino's newest trifle.

"Stanley Zadwadzki." Stanley stood up and stuck out his hand. "It's very nice to meet you, Mr. McKenna."

"Yeah." McKenna looked him up and down, then took Stanley's hand cautiously. "Likewise." He gazed around the office, his head moving slowly as though mounted on gimbals. "Pretty nice setup you got here, ain't it?"

Delores jiggled in carrying a coffee pot; she refilled Stanley's cup. "There ya go, Mr. Z. Anything else I can get for ya?" She patted her hair with her free hand and made cow eyes at Stanley. "Anything at all?"

It was incredible, Stanley thought, how quickly an amount of blood could suffuse a human face. McKenna turned a deep, violent red and his fists clenched. Stanley noticed his hands were shaking. "Anything like what?" he hissed. "Or maybe the two of you got some sorta arrangement?"

"Oh, close your head!" Delores snapped. "As if you'd even notice." She turned on her heel and flounced off.

"So you're doin' Nino's books." McKenna addressed himself to Stanley as if nothing at all had happened. "Must be good dough in that."

"What Mr. Moretti pays me is between myself and Mr. Moretti," Stanley said, his tone glacial.

"A wise guy, huh?" McKenna shifted on his feet. "Mind if I sit down?" His tone suggested Stanley had been remiss in his hospitality.

"Please," Stanley said. "Delores indicated you had something to tell me. Some information, she said."

"Uh-huh."

Stanley waited, growing more impatient as the seconds ticked by. McKenna didn't seem overly inclined to share what he knew; he appeared to be more interested in assessing Stanley and trying to figure out, via a series of hostile glances, whether Stanley was interested in usurping McKenna's position in the organization.

"Well?" Stanley asked.

"Someone's been running a racket behind Nino's back." McKenna nodded like a man privy to certain inalienable truths. "And you found out about it."

Beads of sweat popped out on Stanley's forehead. *Now he'll kill me. Now he'll take out a rod and finish me off, right here.* He'd seen it happen: once a minor button man had dared to question Big Frank in a meeting. Big Frank had whipped out his gun, taken careful aim on the center of the man's forehead, and calmly blew his brains all over the wall. "Yes," he said. He hid his shaking hands under the edge of the desk. Perhaps Delores might be outside the door... perhaps he would have time to shout for help, to lift the phone and dial....

"You're a pretty smart guy," McKenna said. "Maybe you're on our side, and maybe you ain't. I seen a lotta guys come through here. Some leave wishing they'd never been born." He struck a match off the sole of his shoe; Stanley jumped at the sudden noise. "Some don't ever leave." He inhaled and blew smoke in Stanley's general direction. "Which one are you, pal?"

Stanley's eyes narrowed. Deep inside his chest, his heartbeat slowed, thudding deep inside his ribcage like warning blows. "Listen," he hissed, "you can sit there striking matches off the soles of your shoes 'til the cows come home. If you don't have anything useful to tell me, you can leave. Don't waste my time." He picked up a ledger and flipped to a clean page, dipped his pen in the inkwell, and began entering the latest figures. His hands were no longer shaking.

Several moments passed. McKenna smoked quietly. The clock ticked. Stanley studiously ignored him.

"What kinda work you do before you came over to Nino?" McKenna asked, after about ten minutes.

Stanley didn't bother to look up. "I was with Big Frank."

"What'd ya do for Big Frank?"

"Anything he needed doing."

McKenna drew on his cigarette. "You do any wet work?"

Stanley glanced up. McKenna held his gaze. "Some," he said. "I don't generally brag about it."

Gunsel here is gonna learn a thing or two, ain't that right? Sonny, drive up there and stop. When Tiny comes out, gunsel here is gonna fog him.

The gun felt smooth, warmed to his palm. His index finger curled around the trigger. The smell of gun grease slid sinuously into his nostrils, acrid, enticing.

Wait 'til he's down the steps. Don't waste my time. Don't you waste my time. Big Frank sat next to him the whole way, his hand crushing Stanley's elbow, his breath hot against the side of Stanley's neck. *Don't you waste my time if you know what's good for ya.*

It was one of those curious things: once initiated, it could never be undone. Once his finger tightened on the trigger, once the first, fatal rounds erupted from the barrel and the man on the stairs threw up his hands and died, nothing Stanley could do or say could make it otherwise. Nothing could undo the thing that had been done. He had taken life. He would die with this blood upon his hands.

Later, he understood this was part of the mob's initiation: he had been required to kill, and killing, being made to kill, was a way to break him. Once broken, he could be more easily bent to Big Frank's will, to anybody's will. He was the perfect instrument—at least, that's what Big Frank and his goons thought. They hadn't reckoned on certain inalienable aspects of Stanley's character—his reluctance toward violence, his tendency to turn aggression inward, against himself. They hadn't planned on Stanley going off his trolley. The next time—there was a next time: some rival gangster's moll, coming out of a drugstore late on a Saturday night and Big Frank told Stanley to waste her—Stanley froze so completely it scared the shit out of Big Frank. His entire body went rigid, eyes bulging, the tendons in his neck standing out like leather cords. He slumped against the side of the car, and slowly, excruciatingly, his lips drew back over his teeth, forced into a savage rictus.

"Whatsa matter with him?" Vito, Big Frank's right-hand man, grabbed hold of Stanley's shoulder and shook him. There was no response. Zadwadzki's muscles felt as rigid as a corpse. "He having some kinda fit or somethin'?"

"Hey! Gunsel! Snap out of it!" Big Frank backhanded Stanley across the face. Stanley blinked, but the rigid posture didn't change, nor did his face relax.

"What's that noise?" It all but froze Vito's soul. It was like nothing he'd ever heard before. It came from the insane asylum, the aftermath of murder, the mouth of Hell.

"HHHHHNNNNGHHHH—hhhhhhhhhnnnnnnghhhh—hhhhnnnghhhh." The tendons in his neck stood out in sharp and violent relief; tears streamed down Zadwadzki's tortured face.

He was five years old the first time it happened, on a hot August day. He had gone with his father to watch some neighbor men try out a new, open-gear farm tractor, something big and unwieldy, with moving wheels and a noise like a thousand grinding teeth. He stood at the edge of the crowd, holding onto his father's arm, the sun in his eyes and heat bearing down through his straw hat into the crown of his head. Someone shouted and the world seemed to tumble sideways; there was a man on the ground, lying in a sticky, spreading pond of red, and there were loops and coils of intestine lying out beside him.

The boy is having a fit! He's having some kind of fit. Get him in out of the heat!

His father carried him to a shade tree and laid him down on the ground, and some of the other men fanned him with their hats but it didn't help. His face drew back into a rictus and his eyes bulged and he was grunting and drooling. He almost always knew when it would happen, could feel it coming on, but he was powerless to stop it.

"He's having a fit," Vito whispered. He blessed himself hurriedly.

Big Frank leaned forward and punched their driver on the shoulder. "Drive, you idiot! He's makin' too much noise! He's gonna give us away!"

Vito sneered. "We could shoot him. That'd shut him up."

It was the only thing that filtered through Stanley's delirium—the strange state he often found himself in under stressful circumstances. The words seeped in and stuck: *We could shoot him. That'd shut him up.*

Big Frank would never shoot him. He was Big Frank's favorite piece of tail.

"You okay?" McKenna's flat, expressionless voice snapped him back to the present. "You look kinda funny."

Stanley ignored the question. "Tell me everything you know," he said.

STANLEY debated with himself for a while after McKenna left his office. McKenna had mentioned three names to him—three names, and any or all of those men were bilking Nino out of a fortune, a nickel at a time. McKenna had quoted Stanley figures; delivery dates and times; the routes Nino's trucks took, ferrying merchandise to and fro; the numbers of foot soldiers, lieutenants, and ordinary goons who stood ready to rise up at Nino's bidding, as well as the potential trouble spots, places where a skimmer might have been putting his beak into the profits. *He isn't Joey Texas's hired gun anymore*, Stanley thought. *He's his own man now.* It was important Nino be sure there were no leaks in his organization, nothing left undone to jeopardize his plans.

It was more important than ever that Nino eliminate his enemies.

The thought made Stanley shudder. He wasn't naive; he had seen guys rubbed out, had even fogged a guy himself. He had been with Jimmy Two-Shots once when he and two more of Big Frank's boys had driven up to a soda shop and sprayed the front windows with gunfire, killing not only their intended target but three elderly sisters enjoying a malted milk. He understood the way things worked. He knew the sorts of things Nino would have done as a matter of course, as a means of advancing through the ranks or merely to survive. He knew, because Stanley had had to do some of the same things himself. He knew, too, a man could only do that sort of work for so long before it began to erode something in him, rob him of his humanity. And he'd seen guys who had spent long years doing the bidding of the mob, long years of rubbing guys out and smacking dames around, and long years, too, in and out of the stir and on the skids. He didn't want that to happen to Nino. He didn't want Nino to die in a hail of bullets like some other guys died. Nino was good to him, had rescued him from Big Frank, had given him a decent job and a place to live, had furnished him his dignity again… and it occurred to him: he didn't want Nino living this sort of life, being a wise guy and running with the pack. He suspected Nino could be better than that, if given half a chance, and so could he.

NINO called a meeting for eight that evening at Marcino's restaurant. Eddie Marcino had known Nino since he was a snot-nosed kid running through the streets of the Lower East Side with Danny Murphy and any number of Murphy's redheaded brothers. "Nino, so good to see you, how you been?" Eddie embraced him, patting Nino on the back. "Private room all ready for you in the back, go on in."

"You ain't pullin' something on me, are you, Eddie?" Nino glanced around the restaurant. "Maybe Big Frank and his boys are here and maybe you're letting 'em wait for me back there... give me a proper reception."

"Aww, Nino! You know I wouldn't do that. Ain't I always loved you like an uncle?"

"Yeahhh," Nino said, "some uncle." He peered over Eddie's shoulder. "The boys here?"

"They're all waiting for you, Nino." Eddie stood aside, executing a mock bow. "At your service, Mr. Moretti."

Nino followed Danny into the private rooms at the back.

Eli McKenna greeted them, rising from a plush red velvet banquette to shake Nino's hand. "I checked the place out, boss. It's clean." He looked Stanley up and down and sneered. "Why'd ya have to bring him?"

"You keep your nose out of it, McKenna," Nino said. He took off his coat and sat down; Eddie appeared with the coffee pot and cups and poured for them. "I don't want no bad blood between you boys."

"Oh, I don't mind if he stays," Stanley said primly.

McKenna bristled. "Hey, why don't you—"

"Sit down and shut up!" Nino barked—at both of them. Having to deal with this had put him in a bad temper; the knowledge there was a traitor in the organization irritated and annoyed him. He'd been square with these guys, every one of them, had treated them like his brothers, and the idea that someone was a wrong number—well, it didn't sit well. He gestured at Stanley. "Lay it out, kid."

For the next forty-five minutes, Stanley talked. He showed them ledger entries, receipts, delivery slips, invoices, bills of lading, and his own notations. Piece by piece, bit by bit, he built a case against the grifter in their midst. Where his evidence was lacking, McKenna put in, advising Nino of the things he had observed, things he had noted in his own quiet way, and supplementing Stanley's information with evidence of his own.

The more they talked, the darker Nino's expression became. He lit a cigar and listened, his gaze fastened on the tabletop. Now and then he would nod or gesture at one of the two men—a flick of the fingers that meant "go on," and Stanley or Eli would, albeit a little nervously.

Finally Stanley closed the folder and sat back. "That's everything I have," he said.

"You did good, kid." Danny offered him a cigarette and lit it for him. "You did real good."

"Hey, what about me?" McKenna asked. It wasn't quite a whine. "I did just as much work as he did!"

"You did good too," Danny said. "You want a bedtime story now? Glass of milk? Maybe I'll pat you on the bottom and send you up to bed?"

"Will youse guys close up your heads?" Nino snapped. "I'm trying to think here." He glanced at McKenna. "So we agree?" he asked.

Stanley's scalp prickled. Was he missing something here?

"I've been through 'em all," McKenna said. "Can't be nobody else." He glanced at his watch. "I asked him to meet us here. Should be along any minute now."

The outside door banged shut; Nino turned around in his chair. "Frankie," he said. "Good to see ya, baby!" Nino didn't get up, nor did he move to embrace Frankie or shake his hand.

Frankie Monaco: not exactly one of Nino's old-time pals, he was more or less an unknown quantity, transplanted from Chicago after (some said) a falling out with Al Capone. It was rumored Monaco had been playing around on the side with one of Capone's lesser molls, and three of Capone's meatheads had taken him to the South Side, parked the car, pulled his trousers down, and calmly relieved him of his scrotum. He had met Nino at some shindig a few years back and ingratiated himself into the organization. He was known among some of Nino's older soldiers as Daisy Frank, but nobody was ever dumb enough to say that to his face. Frankie carried the standard rod like everybody, supplemented with a straight razor he liked to take out and stroke with his thumb if he thought maybe you were getting on his nerves. Frankie was one of the best button men in the business, if you knew how to control him, which Nino did. Frankie specialized in slow deaths, painful deaths, deaths involving torture for information or for fun.

"How are you boys doing?" Frankie sat down at the table and lit a cigarette. "What's the meaning of this little gathering? You boys planning to bump someone off?" He laughed at his own joke.

"You're a real funny guy," McKenna said. Sometime between Frankie's entrance and the lighting of his cigarette, Eli McKenna had gotten to his feet and taken his hands out of his pockets. One of those hands held a gun, pointed at the middle button of Frankie's overcoat. "But save the jokes for later. You'll be needing a laugh."

Stanley started up. "Nino—"

Nino made a chopping motion with one hand; Stanley sat down. "How long you been skimming me, Frankie?"

Frankie's mouth opened, then closed. "Me? Skimming you, Nino? I wouldn't—"

"Keep talking," McKenna said quietly. "You're being fitted for a Chicago overcoat." His hand was shaking.

"Nino, you 'n' me is old pals! You wouldn't do that to me! I'm your buddy. Ain't I always been there for you?"

Nino's eyes were cold pools of empty black water. "In the past five years, you've taken nearly five Gs from me.... Nickel here, a dime there." He took the folder and turned it, flipped it open so the first page was lying face up. "Why'd you do it, Frankie? And why bother with these penny-ante schemes, anyway? You gettin' desperate? Is that it?"

Frankie's face was ashen, the color of wet putty. His eyes darted from Nino to the gun in McKenna's hand. "I needed money," he whispered.

"You needed money." Nino's mouth twisted. "You needed money?"

"Some guys—I got into a poker game with some guys in the Bronx. I lost bad, Nino—"

"Don't give me that!" Nino got to his feet, fists clenched. "You make me sick! I took you in, see? Took you under my wing! Ahhhhh! Poker game in the Bronx! You been playing poker with these guys for five solid years, is that it? Huh? You liar!" He lashed out and backhanded Frankie across the mouth. "You been sticking your beak in for five years. You been nickel and diming me to death!"

"I'm sorry, Nino!" Frankie wiped his mouth with a trembling hand. "I'll never do it again!"

"You shoulda never done it this time! I'd tell you to be a man but you ain't got the balls!"

Danny Murphy tittered into his hand. McKenna's hand was shaking so hard his gun actually swayed from side to side.

"Get outta here," Nino said. "And don't go nowhere. You try and leave town and I'll burn you. I mean it."

"Whatta ya gonna do, Nino?" Frankie sniveled like a child. "Whatta ya gonna do to me?"

"I ain't decided yet," Nino said. "When I figure it out, you'll be the first to know."

Frankie turned and fled; McKenna sat down heavily and drew a trembling hand over his face. The gun clattered as he laid it on the table. Stanley edged over to him. "Are you alright?" he whispered.

McKenna nodded wordlessly. He held his hands out in front of him and gazed at them as if he'd never seen them before. Stanley poured a glass of water from a jug on the table and passed it to McKenna, who grasped it and drank thirstily.

"Seems to me we got a decision to make," Danny said. "Conference?"

"Yeah," Nino said. He seemed to hardly hear Danny, so deep was he sunk in thought. "Yeah, come over to my place."

"Right." Danny stood up and settled his coat around his shoulders. "McKenna, you okay?"

"I'm fine," McKenna said. He shot a sideways look at Stanley, who seemed to be digging in his file folder. "Yeah, just fine, thanks for askin'."

Nino was uncharacteristically quiet on the drive home. He sat slumped against the side of the car, his head leaning on his hand. If Danny or Stanley spoke, he acknowledged them with a grunt before sinking back into his silence again. Danny parked the car and shepherded them up the stairs into Nino's apartment.

"Nino, you know what I think." Danny found Nino's percolator and set a pot of coffee to heat on the stove. "And it's none too good for Frankie. You know he ain't nothing but a mug."

"Yeah." Nino slumped in the easy chair, eyes faraway. "I wonder how long he's been doing it."

"As long as he could get away with it." Danny glanced at Stanley. "Ain't that right, kid?"

Stanley turned from hanging up his coat. "I… yes, I suppose."

"Five years or so, wasn't it, you said?" Danny wandered into the kitchen, checked the percolator. "Five years that mug has been skimming you, Nino. How much else he been gettin' away with? I say we take that big dumb palooka for a ride."

"I THINK—I'm g-going to take a shower," Stanley said. He slipped into his bedroom and undressed with shaking fingers. He was sweating and it felt like someone had dropped a stone into his stomach. He gazed at himself in the mirror over his dresser: he was pale, with dark circles under his eyes; his mouth was compressed and bracketed with lines of tension. He pulled his dressing gown on over his naked body and ran the shower hot, then stepped in. The steam rose around him, and for several long moments he simply stood there, letting the hot water beat on the back of his neck. He could hear the low murmur of Nino and Danny's voices from the other room, but he couldn't make out what they were saying exactly. It wasn't hard to imagine what they were talking about. His heart thumped in his chest, fluttering like a netted bird, and he leaned forward, laid his forehead against the tiles while the hot water streamed over him.

"...East River," Danny said.

"You think I wanna...." Nino's flat, nasal voice.

"...and another thing...." Danny again.

Stanley held his head under the water to drown out the inevitable conversation about Frankie's fate. Of course they were going to kill him—what choice did they have? If Nino didn't snuff Frankie, he'd be seen as weak, and that would spell the end of his career. He'd end up sleeping with the fishes or studying the view from some cellblock window upstate. He had to kill Frankie; it was as simple as that, except it wasn't simple at all, since it was Stanley who had discovered the missing money, Stanley who put the finger on Frankie in the first place. And McKenna, of course—poor, bewildered McKenna, trying to hold a gun on Frankie while his hands were shaking like a willow tree in a windstorm. Stanley wanted desperately to talk to Eli McKenna— needed to find out why his hands shook and what made him so scared. That had been beyond horrible. Sitting in that little room with Nino and Danny, watching and listening as Nino put Frankie on the spot, put him horribly on the spot in order to pin this on him so Frankie could take the fall.

We're gonna burn this mug and you're gonna watch. Ain't that right, kid? Big Frank's meaty hand around the back of his neck, slewing his head around, forcing him to watch. *Open your goddamned eyes! You're gonna see this, kid! You're gonna see it and like it!*

Stanley's fists clenched; he reached to turn off the water. Nino and Danny's voices came back with a rush. They were arguing.

"...can't sit there and tell me you're gonna just—"

"I ain't gonna just nothin', see? Ain't nobody skims from me! But this is murder! You think I just wanna drive off and waste a guy?"

"You ain't yellow, are you, Nino?"

A prolonged silence, then Nino's voice again, heavy and slow: "You remember who you're talkin' to."

"Yeah." Danny's footsteps moving toward the door. "Yeah, I just remembered."

The door closed behind him quietly. Danny never slammed a door; Danny didn't have to.

Stanley got out of the tub and rubbed himself angrily with a towel and then pulled his dressing gown on. He went out into the living room. Nino was still sitting in the easy chair, still wearing the same vacant look as before.

He saw Stanley and brightened a little. "Hiya, kid. You enjoy your shower?"

"You're gonna fog him, aren't you?" His voice sounded foreign to his own ears: lower than usual, with a pronounced throb. His heart sped up, banging away inside his ribcage, and his hands were shaking as hard as Eli McKenna's. "You and Danny. You're gonna kill Frankie."

"It ain't that simple," Nino said miserably. His face was pouchy, tired-looking, and his shoulders slumped. "You know it ain't that simple."

"Sure, it's simple." Stanley sneered at him. "Stick him in a car. Take him for a ride. Measure him up for a wooden kimono, what do you care?"

"Hey, come on, kid!" Nino stared at him as if he'd just landed from Mars. "Why are you talking like that? I ain't said I'm gonna—"

"You're gonna. You're gonna. You're gonna what, Nino?" He moved toward Nino, his gait unsteady. The room was dim around its edges; the light was going away. "Find out who was skimming, you said. Go through the books, you said. Yeah. And when the cops come sniffing around and Frankie's dead, who are they gonna look at, huh? It won't be you."

"Now wait just a minute!" Nino started up from the chair. "Somebody slip you a mickey or something? I don't wanna fog nobody! Sure, I'd do it—I'd do it in a minute, before—"

"Before what?" Stanley's fists clenched; he liked the way his anger felt, liked the way his blood was thumping in his head, in time with the beat of his heart. "Before you rescued me? I bet you think you're a good guy, huh? Yeah, a real good guy, because you took me away from Big Frank. You're the hero now. A real good guy."

"Wait just a second," Nino said, "I don't know why you're actin' like this! Are you sick or something?" He reached out, intending to touch Stanley's shoulder, but the younger man savagely knocked his hand aside.

"You keep your greasy mitts off me!" Stanley hissed, "Or I swear to God, I'll waste you! You think I left Big Frank so some dirty guinzo could put his paws all over me? Is that what you think?"

"I ain't thought nothin'!" Nino shouted. "I didn't want him beating on you like that—"

Stanley went into his room and began throwing on his clothes, sobbing with rage. The light was going away; the room was dim around the edges and things were small, much smaller than they ought to be, but it was alright. He couldn't feel his face, couldn't feel his lips or the tips of his fingers, but that was alright too. He went out into the other room and shrugged into his coat and drove his bare feet into his shoes.

"Where are you going?" Nino tried to get between him and the door, but Stanley shoved him aside. "Where ya going at this hour? Huh? Where are you going, kid?"

"Keep away from me," Stanley hissed, "or I'll gut you." He staggered down the steps and out into the street. It was better out here; he could breathe, and he could see things. There wasn't too much light, and things were easier on the eyes. It was too bright in Nino's apartment.

"You think I care?" Nino screamed after him. "You think I care what you do? You're nothing! You ain't never been nothing! Nothing but a cheap gunsel!"

Someone on the floor above opened a window and screamed at Nino to shut up; Nino picked up a rock and flung it wildly, and the windowsill went down with a thump. He went back inside and slammed the door.

It was 1:00 a.m.

NINO walked the floor for an hour, pacing his way from window to window, and still Stanley didn't come back. He wondered where the kid could have gone, what he might have done, whether he would ever come back. He remembered a conversation they'd had a few weeks prior, when Stanley asked if Nino trusted him. Nino's own answer rose up now to haunt him and torment him, swirling round and round inside his own head like mocking laughter. *Trust you? I picked you outta the crowd, baby.*

Stanley still hadn't returned by 2:00 a.m.; at half-past three, it began to rain. Nino pulled his coat on and went down to the car. For another half an hour, he drove up and down all the streets, watching, listening with the windows rolled down.

He found Stanley staggering down Canal Street near the intersection of Chinatown and Little Italy. He slowed the car and followed Stanley, always keeping well back so as not to startle him. Stanley stopped in front of a store and spent some long moments looking in the window; he was soaking wet and swaying on his feet. Nino killed the engine and got out, walking quietly but quickly toward Stanley.

"Stanley?" He kept his voice quiet. "Stanley, you should come home. You're getting wet, baby."

Stanley turned and looked at him, obviously seeing nothing. His pupils were enormously dilated, his eyes dazzled and full of protracted blinks. He reached toward Nino and took hold of his lapels. "They put me off the train," he whispered, "because I haven't got a ticket."

Nino's eyes filled with tears. "It's okay," he whispered. "I got a train of my own. You wanna ride the train with me, huh? I'll take you home."

"You seem like an awfully nice man," Stanley said. "Perhaps you can explain to them that I've lost my ticket. They don't seem to understand a word I say."

"Yeah, sure, I'll tell them." Nino led him to the car and put him in, got the lap rug from the back and wrapped it around him. *Ladies and gentlemen*, he thought, *mugs and clucks, the great Nino Moretti.*

"It has to be explained," Stanley said. He leaned his hot cheek against the window glass, eyes vacant. "Otherwise I'll never get where I'm going."

Nino helped Stanley up the stairs and into the apartment and locked the door behind him. He stripped off Stanley's wet coat and went in to fill the bath with warm water. The kid was freezing, and that's what he needed—he was wet and cold and he just needed to warm up. He needed to warm up and have a drink and get some sleep and he'd be just fine. It was too much, there was just so much the kid could take and maybe Big Frank knocked something loose in his head, and he was a bit funny, but that was okay because Nino was going to look after him and Nino was going to help him—

That noise. What was that noise? Nino shut off the taps and cocked his head to one side, listening. He'd never heard anything like that before; it sounded like a wounded animal, like something caught in a trap, something being slowly killed, tortured, torn apart—

"Mother of God." He stopped in the doorway. Stanley was on the floor, curled into a ball with his arms wrapped around his knees. Stanley was making the noise; that noise was coming from Stanley, a noise that sounded like dying.

"Hhhhhhhnnnghhhhh.... Hhhhhhhhnnnghhhh.... Hhhnnghhh...." He saw Nino and bared his teeth; the tendons in his neck stood out like cords of twisted leather. Tears were streaming down his face.

He looked like Ray. He looked like Nino's brother Ray after Pop had given him a going-over with the belt. He looked like Ray that time he opened up the window in Ma's bedroom and tried to throw himself out.

Stanley looked like that.

Nino dropped to the floor and crawled to where Stanley was. He sat in front of him, sat so Stanley could see him, hear him. He made no move to touch him, simply sat with him. "I'm here," he said. "Stanley? Baby? I'm right here, okay? Nino is right here. I ain't going nowhere."

He reached out slowly, his movements merely a suggestion, and took one of Stanley's hands in his. A long shudder ran through the younger man's body, but he didn't withdraw. "Nino's here, baby. It's okay. You're home now." He took the other hand and held them, held Stanley's hands and talked to him, talked nonsense like he used to do with Ray when Pop was beating on him. He talked and talked, and eventually Stanley stopped making that noise, stopped rocking, stopped keening.

He looked at Nino. "Where have I been?" he asked.

Nino's breath caught in his throat. "Away," he whispered. "But I brought you back."

"I NEVER really know," Stanley said. "It just happens." He sipped his whiskey and curled more closely into the warm blanket Nino had wrapped around him. He was naked underneath it, his wet clothes hung to dry over the shower rod in the bathroom. "It started when—"

Nino reached out a hand. "You don't have to say nothin'." He smiled gently. "You scared me, kid. Maybe you oughta save that for your party piece, huh? Don't be doing that every night." It reminded him of Ray, how Ray went funny in the head from being beat so much, and that bothered Nino. He didn't like somebody throwing fits or going off his trolley, least of all where he could see it. People got strange sometimes, they got stuff wrong in their heads, but Nino didn't like it. Maybe being queer in the head made a fellow weak, and weakness had to be avoided. He could never look at Ray when he started acting like that, when he started waving his hands around and making sounds and saying things.

"Why did you come after me?" Stanley asked. He extended his hands to the fire, warming himself. "After what I said to you... you could have let me... you could have—"

"You say something to me?" Nino pretended interest in his drink. "That's funny, because I don't remember."

Stanley smiled sadly. "Yes, you do." He sighed. "I understand about Frankie. I do. I know you've got to show that you—"

"—I ain't doing it," Nino said. He laid his glass down on the end table with a click. "That's what Danny and I were talking about." He stood up and stretched, then leaned against the mantelpiece. "Wasting Frankie wouldn't solve nothing. Mugs like Frankie are a dime a dozen." It was the truth: nothing could be gained by taking Frankie for a ride. He was pretty low on the totem pole, of no account, and Nino didn't like doing things halfway. Killing Frankie would only send a message to the other mobs that Nino couldn't control his guys. "Me and Danny, we'll run him outta town. Scare him a bit, rough him up. He won't come back. And once he's outta my territory, he's somebody else's problem." He rubbed his tired eyes. "I should hit the hay," he said. He closed his eyes, rested his head against his hand. "Frankie can be somebody else's problem. He don't need to be mine. And when it comes to bumping him off, Frankie ain't worth the bullet. I told Danny—" He opened his eyes; Stanley was standing in front of him.

"I wish," Stanley said quietly, "you'd hold me in your arms." The firelight made beautiful patterns on his pale, composed face; his blue eyes were lucid, shining. "I think I would really like that."

Nino sucked in his breath; Stanley opened the blanket and enfolded them both in it. "Kid, I—"

"Sh," Stanley said. "Please. Just hold me."

Nino did as he was asked.

CHAPTER
FOUR

"I DON'T get you, egghead."

Monday morning and Eli McKenna was standing in Stanley's doorway, looking distinctly put out. His baggy suit hung on his skinny frame like a scarecrow's; his round blue eyes were at once inquisitorial and petulant.

"Can I do something for you?" Stanley asked.

"You hear about Frankie?" McKenna came in and sat down, uninvited. He began going through a stack of forms on the desk, upsetting the neat pile Stanley had made.

"Could you not touch that?" Stanley took the papers out of reach of McKenna's fidgeting fingers.

"Ain't you jumpy today," McKenna said. He picked up a glass paperweight and started rolling it between his palms.

"What about Frankie?" Stanley's stomach jumped uncomfortably at the mere mention of his name. He didn't want to think or talk about Frankie; as far as he was concerned, Frankie was a closed chapter.

Are you sure? he had asked Nino as they lay chastely together the night before, wrapped in Stanley's blanket. *I need to know. I probably have no right to ask—*

You got every right. Nino's fingers traced the bridge of Stanley's nose. Stanley lay against him, his head on Nino's shoulder, eyes half-closed. Nino's shirt was open; Stanley drew his fingers through the dark hairs on Nino's chest, and every time he did this, a little thrill ran through him. His breathing was ragged, his body straining toward Nino. *You got a right to ask me anything you want.*

Why? Why do I have that right?

If you don't know by now....

"He's gone," McKenna said. He rolled the paperweight between his hands, faster and faster until the glass globe and his hands were merely a blur. The paperweight jumped out of his grasp and rolled under the desk.

Stanley suppressed the urge to curse out loud. "Where?" *Nino did it. He said he wouldn't, but he did.*

"Dunno." McKenna studied him as if he were a particularly interesting species of bug. "He just disappeared. Left a note saying he was going west."

Nino had said wasting Frankie wouldn't solve anything; he said he and Danny would run Frankie out of town, but what assurance did Stanley have that Nino had kept his word? When it came right down to it, what did Stanley even know about Nino, besides the obvious? "You came all the way over here"—McKenna worked in Shipping, which was located in another wing of the building—"to tell me this?"

"Thought you'd wanna know," McKenna said tonelessly. He ran his index finger back and forth across the desktop as if smoothing down a rough spot.

"What else?" Stanley asked. He had never met anyone who fidgeted as much as McKenna. The man was a bundle of nerves.

"You know, I used to live in Chicago." McKenna's tongue slid out and wet his bottom lip nervously. "Ever heard of a guy by the name of Nitti?"

Stanley had been chasing elusive paperclips through one of his desk drawers; he stopped. "Frank Nitti?" he asked.

"So you heard of him." McKenna's gaze was by now frankly unnerving; he seemed to be looking through the back of Stanley's head at something only he could see. "Used to work for him, back in the day."

Stanley's scalp prickled. Doing what, he could only imagine. "That how you got that twitch?"

"What twitch?" McKenna squinted. "I ain't got no twitch." He shifted his shoulders inside his suit. "You heard of Frankie Rio?" he asked. And when Stanley indicated he had not, he said, "I can't go back to Chicago no more, because of him." Then, apropos of nothing, "You after Delores? You trying to put the make on her?"

"No." Stanley resumed his hunt for paper clips.

"Me and Frankie once, we were riding with this guy. This guy, he was one of Nitti's boys." McKenna watched Stanley's foraging through the desk drawer with interest. "He was kinda twitchy. Frankie wanted me to take him into the woods and fix him up good. So I did." McKenna paused, waiting for Stanley's reaction and was disappointed when none came.

"You make me nervous," Stanley said. He couldn't figure out what McKenna wanted or why he was there.

"I make everybody nervous," McKenna said. "Got so I couldn't do it no more. Then one night Frankie wanted me to kill a woman. I don't do nothing to dames. This was worse. This dame, she lived in a walk-up over on the South Side, so I go over there, let myself in the kitchen window. She's sitting in the other room, listening to the radio. You know what? She gets up when I come in. She doesn't scream or nothing. She says, 'I know Frankie sent you,' and you know what? She's expecting. Yeah. Expecting a baby. That's what Frankie wanted me to do—he wanted me to put the drop on a pregnant dame. Can you imagine?"

Stanley sat up and looked at him. McKenna's flat voice, his petulant expression, his vacant eyes…. Yeah, he could imagine it.

"I ain't got no nerves left," McKenna said. "I wasn't gonna do it. I wasn't gonna do no pregnant dame. So I left. Came east." He stood up. "You didn't say nothing the other night, about me losing my nerve." He held his hands out in front of him; they were quivering ever so slightly, like trembling leaves in a slight wind. "That was white of ya." He paused. "You better lay off Delores. She's my girl."

"Listen," Stanley said. "I am not interested in Delores. Trust me. Delores is not—" He sighed. "She's all yours. Blow your wig, why dontcha."

McKenna turned to go. "How come you don't want her?" he asked. "She not good enough for you? You saying she ain't—"

Unfortunately for Stanley, Delores chose just that moment to jiggle into his office, bearing her customary cup of hot coffee. "I brung ya some coffee, Mr. Z, because you look like ya could use it." She straightened his tie, all but ignoring Eli. "Mr. Z, you sure are a handsome man. And you know how to treat a lady." She shot a poisonous glance at Eli. "Not like some people I could mention." She leaned in close to Stanley and pressed her generous bosom against his chest. "Such a gentleman and I would know. I've had my share of mugs." She turned and jiggled away, snapping her gum.

"You dirty—" McKenna balled up his fists and swung at Stanley, who stepped neatly aside. McKenna's fist hit the wall with a sickening crunch; he dropped into a chair and burst into tears.

"Oh, for crying out loud—" Stanley raised his voice and called for Delores, who came running. "Some ice from downstairs and a towel," he said, "and quickly!"

"I ain't got no nerves left," McKenna said, "My nerves are gone and you're tormenting me. I'm a sick man! You should be ashamed of yourself."

"You go around punching walls," Stanley said. "You sure are a sick man." He was grateful for the distraction and the opportunity to think about something besides Frankie. He turned McKenna's hand and looked at it; the knuckles were raw and bleeding but nothing seemed to be broken.

Delores appeared with some ice in a metal pan. "Here you are, Mr. Z, I got it out of the icebox in the lunchroom next door."

He took the ice from Delores and made a compress for McKenna's hand. The hit man stopped sniveling and allowed Stanley to attend to him, glaring at him with red-rimmed eyes. "Now, for once and for all," Stanley said, "I am not interested in Delores. The only reason she fusses over me is because she's trying to make you jealous."

"I don't believe you," McKenna said. "You're just saying that because you feel sorry for me. You think I'm some kinda weak sister—" He stood up, ready for a fight if Stanley wanted one.

"I don't like dames." It came out more sharply than he intended; he hoped the boys in the next room hadn't heard.

"You don't like dames?" McKenna stared at him. "What are you, some kinda—"

"Yes," Stanley replied, albeit a little hastily. "Yes, I am."

McKenna gazed at him in silence, his eyes playing over Stanley's face. He made as if to say something, turned on his heel, and left rather more quickly than he had come.

WHEN Stanley put his key in the door that evening, he was greeted with almost complete darkness and Nino in his shirtsleeves, lighting a barrage of candles. "Hey, baby, did you have a good day?"

"What's all this?" Stanley hung up his coat and hat and slipped out of his jacket. "Somebody's birthday?" It was unusual, to say the least, to see Nino like this. Was Nino feeling guilty about the other night? Maybe this was a prelude to Frankie, and Nino was softening him up before telling him the truth.

"No, I just felt like splashing out," Nino said. "Figured it was time we had a little treat. I called up Marcino's and got Eddie to do us up a meal in fine style. Yeah." He pulled out a chair. "Sit down—are you hungry?"

"Starving," Stanley said. The food smelled delicious. He wondered if it would be bad manners to roll up his sleeves—he wanted to dive into dinner and eat his way to the bottom. Nino was just as hungry as he was, and it was a while before their respective appetites were sated enough to allow conversation. "Eli McKenna found a new supplier in Jersey for our product," he told Nino. "He even got us a deal on the shipping."

"How are you two getting along?" Nino asked. He refilled Stanley's wine glass and topped up his own.

"Alright," Stanley said.

Nino laughed. "You're lying," he said. "He hates your guts. Thinks you're after his girl."

"No," Stanley said, "he doesn't think that anymore. Not after today. I… straightened out some things." *I don't like dames.*

"Set him straight, huh?" Nino sat back in his chair. "Well, that's good. I want you guys to get along." He picked up his wine glass. "Come on, let's go sit in the other room and put the radio on."

They sat for a while, talking in a desultory fashion of nothing in particular while the late-spring evening closed in around them. Nino sat on the sofa listening to the radio with his eyes closed; Stanley got up and went to sit next to him. He snuggled close to Nino's side when Nino put his arm around him, laying his head on Nino's shoulder. Nino stroked his face; Stanley leaned in and kissed Nino's mouth gently. Nino returned the caress, deepening the kiss, his eager tongue slipping between Stanley's parted lips.

"I want to touch you," Stanley whispered when next his mouth was free. "Can you take off your tie?"

"Sure, kid…." Nino did just that, unbuttoned his waistcoat and the top two buttons of his shirt. "That better?" He hissed through his teeth as Stanley slipped a hand inside his shirt, stroking his bare chest. "Aw, kid, you're killing me here…."

Time dissolved into nothing; there was nothing in the world for Stanley except this: Nino's mouth on his, the scent of Nino's cologne, the heat of Nino's body. Their kisses became deeper, more torrid, with long bouts of tongue play and periods of unendurable bliss when Nino's talented mouth licked and sucked at Stanley's slender neck. He drew back, gazed at Nino with passion-weighted eyes, and took hold of Nino's hand, pressed it against the bulge in his trousers.

"Oh baby…." Nino kissed him, licking and sucking at his top lip before taking the soft cushion of the lower between his teeth, nibbling it gently. Stanley whimpered, pushing into his hand, and Nino cooperated, rubbing him through his clothes. A pause, and Nino's hand went away; Stanley felt his flies being opened and then—

He groaned as Nino's hand closed over him, stroking him, handling him deftly, gently. He clung to Nino, shivering when Nino's thumb slipped over the head of his cock; sparks formed and burst behind his eyelids and he pushed himself harder into Nino's hand.

Harder and faster, driving himself forward, and Nino was with him, varying the speed and rhythm of his strokes, keeping him always on the ragged edge, near enough to coming to feel the first tantalizing shudders of his orgasm. If Nino didn't let him come, he would die. He would die of pleasure, right here; he would shudder himself to pieces, he would—

Sudden, shattering, brilliant, it ripped into him, it tore him to pieces and pulled him over the edge. He panted against Nino's neck, spilling himself into Nino's hand, groaning. He held Nino's wrist, trapping Nino's hand against his body as the aftershocks rippled through him, going out and out, obliterating him.

He came to rest against Nino's chest, his head on Nino's shoulder. He lay for a long time like that, held in Nino's arms, safe, protected. He felt Nino pulling a blanket around him, and then there was nothing. There were no bad dreams. There was only peace.

NINO lay awake in the dark, holding Stanley in his arms, his body taut with unspent desire. He shifted slightly, adjusting his erection in his trousers, suppressing a groan as his silk boxers slid enticingly over the head of his cock. It wouldn't take much. His fly was already undone, thanks to Stanley's wandering hands… he was hard and aching, and it had been ages, ages since that sandy-haired palooka had come into his bed.

He slipped his own hand inside his trousers, hardly daring to breathe for fear he'd disturb Stanley sleeping beside him, and began to touch himself. Within five or six strokes he was coming hard, panting, forcing himself silent. When it was over, he lay very still in the dark, listening to Stanley's quiet breath.

STANLEY was reconciling the club's bank statements when his phone rang. He picked it up and listened as Delores cracked her gum in his ear. "Eli wants ya," she said. "He got something to tell ya."

"Is that so?" What did McKenna want? Stanley glanced at the clock and decided he had time enough to finish his reconciliations before McKenna made it up from the loading dock.

"You gotta listen."

Stanley jumped. "How the—you—how'd you get—"

"I was in the outer office. I didn't want to waste time." McKenna leaned over Stanley's desk. "I need to know one thing," he said.

Stanley stared at him over the tops of his reading glasses. "Okay," he said. "Shoot."

"How tight are you and Nino?"

Stanley's hand strayed to the knot of his tie. "Uh, well...." He could hardly tell McKenna the truth. "Nino is a friend."

"Big Frank's making his move."

It was beyond McKenna's scope to make even the feeblest of jokes, Stanley thought, and right now McKenna looked as serious as a heart attack. "He is?"

"Yeah. I got a hot tip. Big Frank and some of his lieutenants are meeting tonight at Judy's, over in Little Italy. They're planning to take out Nino, and—" McKenna stopped as if he'd been punched.

"And what?"

"Nothing." McKenna lit a cigarette with shaking fingers.

Stanley was more able than most to put two and two together. "And me," he said quietly.

"I didn't say that," McKenna said. "I didn't say nothing about it." He didn't have to; it was written on his face like linotype.

"Thank you," Stanley said. "I'll tell him right away."

"Tell him I can be there if he needs me," McKenna said. "I owe Nino plenty and I ain't afraid to pay it back."

Stanley had seen McKenna's previous performance, trembling hands and all, and wondered what, if anything, McKenna might be able to do for Nino. "I'll tell him. Maybe you and him can...." He raked his gaze over McKenna's quaking digits. "... shake hands."

"Yeah," McKenna huffed, "pretty funny. You're a really funny guy."

"HEY, Eli, what do you think of this new dress?" Delores was standing near the full-length mirror in the reception area, examining herself critically. She wore a pale-pink summer frock with fluttery cap sleeves and a whole bunch of frilly bits hanging off of it. Was it supposed to be something like a costume, maybe?

"It's nice," Eli said. "I guess."

"That's the trouble with fellas. They don't know nothing about modern fashion." She turned from her contemplation of herself and gave a low whistle. "Well, lookee here! Where'd you get that suit, huh?"

He glanced down at himself. "Uh... Templeman's... I guess. I don't remember."

She hummed and stepped around him like some sort of exotic bird, examining him from all angles. "You look swell!" she said. "Like one of them movie stars!"

"Aw... I do not." But Eli was secretly pleased. "It's a real nice dress," he said. "I guess I ain't looked at it properly. You look real pretty today." He was amazed at himself, but also at her. What was going on, exactly? She'd never given him the time of day.

"You really think so?" She smiled, and Eli's heart, which had settled nicely in his chest, leapt up into his throat and started flipping around like a landed fish.

"I do," he murmured. "You sure do look pretty." He leaned close and nodded toward Stanley's door. "I just gave him some very important information. Guess I'm moving up in the organization, huh?"

"Did you?" She gazed at him. "Eli... is it dangerous?"

"It might be." He stood just a little taller. "I could be in a lot of danger. You never know."

"Oh, be careful!" She held onto his arm, squeezed. "I'd be awful sad if anything happened to you."

"Would you?" Her little white hand was lying on his wrist, so pretty with her fingernails painted pink to match her dress, and she was wearing pink bangles and a ring with a little pink stone.

The door opened; Stanley appeared, much to Eli's annoyance. "Delores, can you get Mr. Moretti on his private line?" He glanced at Eli. "You still here?"

Eli bristled, felt his face burning with hot color. "What's it to ya?"

Delores already had the receiver at her ear; she put her hand over the mouthpiece and hissed at them to behave themselves.

"You sure that's good information you gave me?" Stanley asked.

"It's good," Eli said. Did Zadwadzki think he was some kind of dumb bunny? Maybe the pencil pusher felt feisty this morning and wanted a dust-up.

"How do I know that?"

Eli gazed at him. "Because I said so."

Delores inserted herself between them, all business. "Mr. Moretti on the line for you, Mr. Z. You can take it in your office." She shoved him unceremoniously in the door and shut it behind him, returned, took Eli McKenna's elbow, and shoved him through the Reception door, then settled herself behind her desk with the air of a woman who has conquered. "Now then," she said to no one in particular, "let's get some work done around this joint."

She had scarcely turned to her typing when Boots Mahoney, one of Nino's lesser lieutenants, burst into the office. He was panting like he'd run all the way from Queens. "Where's Nino?"

"He's in his office," Delores said. Nino's office was located at the other end of the building, away from the noise of business. "Why? What are you doing here anyway, Boots? This ain't your end of the building."

"I gotta talk to Nino," he said. He was stuck in the same groove, like the needle on a record player. "I gotta talk to Nino."

"What about?" Eli hadn't gone much farther than the corridor, and he'd been listening. "What's happened?"

"It's Charley," he said. "They got Charley."

Eli looked to Delores, who had turned an awful ashen color. "Charley?"

She burst into tears.

THEY had hung him from a meat hook in an abandoned warehouse down by the docks with a sign around his neck. Stanley didn't need to read the sign to get the message: Charley's throat had been sliced savagely through and there was a stiletto sticking out of his eye. Nino read the sign, walked a few paces, and cursed an uninterrupted stream for several long moments.

Danny Murphy was standing nearby; Stanley moved to where he was. "Who was he?" he asked.

"Nino's office boy. He sort of... ran errands and stuff. Charley was from the old neighborhood. Me and him and Nino grew up together." Danny made a motion by his ear. "He wasn't right in the head... never grew up in his mind, you know? Nino looked out for him."

Stanley shuddered. He couldn't stop looking at the dead man's bloated face, the jagged tear in his throat, and the blackened blood that had congealed around the edges of the wound. There were longitudinal cuts on his fingers, and maybe he had put up a fight. Maybe he had tried to pull the knife away, to help himself.

Nino was standing with his back to them, shoulders heaving as he wept bitterly, and this moved Stanley more than even the sight of poor, butchered Charley. *I should go to him,* he thought, but he couldn't make his feet obey, and he watched woodenly as Danny drew Nino's head close to his own.

"We're gonna get them bastards," Danny murmured. "Those sons of bitches are gonna find out something. Oh yeah." He stroked Nino's hair, then pressed a kiss into the top of his head.

"Why'd they have to get Charley?" Nino asked. "Goddammit, he wasn't hurting nobody! He never hurt nobody in his life! He was just a kid in his mind."

"We're gonna go and find 'em," Danny said. "You and me."

Stanley wondered where this left him... or perhaps he didn't even figure in the equation. He couldn't blame them—he truly was the unknown quantity, and what reason did Nino or anybody have to trust him? For all they knew he was feeding information to Big Frank behind Nino's back, and maybe he—

Maybe he was to blame for this.

The expression in Nino's eyes was like nothing Stanley had ever seen. He moved toward Stanley as if seeing him for the first time, and when he spoke, his voice was echoing, sepulchral, a voice from the end of the world. Stanley forced himself to stand still and not run. He had nothing to feel bad about; he had done nothing wrong. He wouldn't be that stupid. He knew what happened to rats, to men who broke the code of silence, who spilled secrets to outsiders. He'd been with Big Frank the night they found Moosey Stein drinking in a speakeasy in Harlem—when they found him and dragged him out into the street and beat him with chains and broken bottles until he was just a smear of bloodied flesh, unrecognizable as a human being.

"Stanley," Nino said. He reached out and took hold of Stanley's arm, just above the elbow. Stanley could feel the grip of each individual finger, the pressure of Nino's hand. "You come with us."

He drew a shaky breath. "Okay," he said. "Okay."

LIKE any self-respecting hoodlum in this particular territory, Nino knew where Judy's was and could probably find it in the dark. Everybody said Judy's was Big Frank O'Hara's feeding trough of choice, and when Big Frank was in the joint, Judy herself did the cooking. "You should see him," Danny said, "like a prize hog or something, sitting up there and sucking it back. It's enough to make you puke up your breakfast."

The boys told stories about how Judy was a former good-time girl who had started off in burlesque, where she drew the attention of powerful men and soon found herself nicely bankrolled. She had bought a pretty townhouse with real lace curtains in the windows and salted enough away to keep her in her old age. The way the story went, she'd taught herself how to cook, bought the gutted shell of a burned-out flower shop on Mulberry Street, and pretty soon there was nobody but nobody in Manhattan who made a better meatball than Judy. "The best you ever tasted," Danny said. He punched Stanley's shoulder lightly. "Come on, buck up! Nothing very bad's gonna happen—least, not to us."

Judy's place was nice enough, with small tables set around a raised central dais meant to support a girl singer or maybe a small three-man combo. For Nino, however, it presented a logistical pain in the ass, being that it was smack in the middle of the floor and sure to slow down even the most determined race to the exits.

"Maybe he knows we're here and he decided not to show," Danny said. He sat next to Nino, his back to the wall, chewing gum with almost as much alacrity as Delores. None of Nino's boys were stupid; something very bad was going to happen here tonight, something very, very bad, and there was nothing they could do to stop it, nor was there anything they could do to hasten its arrival. "Here." Danny poured a glass of water and passed it to Stanley. "It'll be okay."

"Glad you're so certain," Stanley said.

"Don't be nervous," Danny said quietly. "This ain't got nothin' to do with you. This is between Nino and Big Frank."

"There he is," McKenna said quietly. He and Nino stood up.

"So, Nino, fancy seeing you here. This is a private meeting." Big Frank was fatter than ever, with diamonds twinkling on his fingers and from the depths of his necktie. He was accompanied by three of his lieutenants: Jimmy Two-Shots, Ricky "The Bench" Petrelli, and a third younger man who, for some reason, exchanged a nod with Nino. "So go on, breeze, mug."

"Ain't nobody leavin' 'til we get some things straightened out," Nino said. "You and me got business."

"You ain't nobody's boss here, Nino!" Big Frank waved one fat hand at him. "Maybe you better get outta here before you and that gunsel of yours get yourselves hurt." He nodded at Stanley. "How you likin' it with Nino, kid? Does he like it rough? You don't mind that so much, if the price is right!"

McKenna was a blur. He flew at Big Frank and backhanded him savagely with his gun hand. The big man's head snapped back and blood flew from his flapping jowls. Danny, incredulous, stepped back to avoid being splattered. McKenna reversed the gun so the butt was now nestled firmly in his palm. "Say it again," he said. "Go on. I wanna hear you say it again." His slight body quivered with rage, like a slender wire tuned to a frequency only he could hear.

Nino waved him back. "You took something from me, O'Hara. I ain't forgettin' it."

"You don't own this territory," Big Frank said. His voice was muffled, coming through his handkerchief like that, and it sounded as though he'd lost some teeth. "You think we're gonna let you march in and take what's ours?" His gaze flickered to Stanley. "That what you think, Nino?"

"You don't wanna know what I think," Nino sneered, "but you crossed the line with Charley. What'd you do it for? A kid like that, he ain't no threat to you. Maybe you wanted to send me a message, huh? Is that it?" Nino moved in so he was toe to toe with Big Frank. "I'm only gonna tell you this once: you try anything with me and you'll be picking lead outta your liver."

"You talk real big," Petrelli said, "but you ain't gonna do nothin', Nino."

"Is that right?" Danny edged around so he was behind Big Frank and his louts. Neither had noticed the gun in his hand. "Bright bunch of lugs you got, O'Hara. Now why don't yez start dancin' outta here?"

Nino stabbed the air with his thumb. "Everybody knows you can dish it out but you can't take it no more. You're through! Now why dontcha heel and toe before it gets messy?"

Three things happened at once: Big Frank dropped the handkerchief and delved into his coat; Petrelli dived for Nino; Danny's gun went off. The restaurant exploded in a hail of gunfire. Nino had his revolver and was blasting away while Big Frank tried to back out the front door. McKenna turned over a table, braced it against the rise in the center of the floor, and used it as a shelter while he fired repeated bursts at Ricky The Bench and Jimmy Two-Shots. McKenna's hands weren't shaking anymore.

There was sudden silence and the stink of cordite hanging in the air. Someone was cursing, a steady stream of oaths dripping like water. McKenna was lying on the floor, flat on his back, staring at the ceiling. Nino was near the door, struggling with the third man.

"No, don't—" Stanley stepped out and the third man brought the gun up, level with him.

A gun went off; the third man dropped to the floor, the back of his head blown away. Nino gazed down at him for a moment, then rushed for Stanley. "Kid, you okay? You alright?" He patted Stanley's arms, his chest. "Talk to me: you jake?"

"Yeah." Stanley stared at the dead man. Nino's coat was splattered with blood, but it didn't seem to be Nino's blood. "I'm oke," he said.

McKenna sat up and shook himself like a dog. "Everybody okay?" he asked. He got to his feet and surveyed the damage.

"He got away!" Nino spat. "The bastard got away!" Big Frank had taken Jimmy Two-Shots with him; the third man, the one nobody knew, would never go anywhere again. "Come on, let's get outta here," he said. He grabbed hold of Stanley's coat and pulled him toward the door, McKenna following behind and Danny in his accustomed place at Nino's side.

Once they gained the safety of the car, McKenna's hands had begun to shake, waving at the ends of his arms like storm ravaged leaves. "I guess we showed them," he said cheerfully. He leaned over Stanley and vomited out the opened door. "I guess we showed those guys." He wiped his mouth on his handkerchief and slumped against the seat.

"Thinks he's gonna show me! Me!" Nino cursed fluently and waved away Danny's hip flask. "That big dumb mug! Thinks he's gonna show me. He can dish it out but he can't take it, see? Me, I can take it. Nino can take it."

Stanley was swaying slightly in his seat, his gaze faraway, unfocused.

"Hey, kid, you alright?" Danny leaned close to him. "Ain't gonna throw a joe, are ya?"

"No," Stanley whispered. "I ain't gonna throw a joe."

"HERE—this'll help." Nino handed him a glass of scotch and then sat down heavily in the easy chair across from him. The night was warm and the windows were open, the curtains blowing in the breeze. Somewhere behind them, the radio played quietly in the dark:

They're playing songs of love, but not for me

"I'm fine, really I am." Stanley swirled the amber liquid in his glass. "You saved my life." He looked up, smiled at Nino. "Again...." He took a sip of scotch and shuddered. He knew he would never, ever forget the sight, that it was burned into his memory forever: looking down the barrel of a gun, counting the seconds until a bullet blew his life away, waiting for it, waiting. "Who was...?"

Nino shook his head sharply. "Don't ask," he said. "It's better if you don't ask." He rubbed his thumb around the rim of his glass over and over. "It's really better if you don't know." He stood up and walked to the window and stood to one side, gazing down at the street. "You start wondering, did he have somebody waiting for him at home? A girl? A wife?" He sipped his drink and gazed with sightless eyes over the darkened street. "A man who loved him? Maybe he was just like me, that's what you start thinking... maybe he was like me. Then you start feeling sorry for him... you wanna find his wife, his girl, his... moll." He reached up and loosened his tie and unbuttoned the top two buttons of his shirt. "Yeah... you starting wondering who was this guy, did anybody care about him, maybe I should send some flowers. You start getting strange ideas in your head."

Stanley understood; he saw it plain as day. "Did you know him?" he asked.

"Yeah." Nino was a shadow near the window, a solid shadow and a gray outline, a voice, a pair of gesturing hands. "Yeah, I knew him."

It hurt Stanley's heart to ask: "Who was he?"

"A kid. Kid I grew up with, back in the old neighborhood." A long pause; Nino was thinking, casting his memory back to the old days when he and Danny and any number of ragged gutter brats roamed the streets in packs like mongrel dogs. "We used to call him Fist. He wasn't much of a fighter... walking around with his fists balled up, like he was looking for it...."

"I'm sorry," Stanley whispered.

Nino whirled away from the window. "Don't you be sorry!" he said. "Don't you ever be sorry!" He came to Stanley and sat beside him on the sofa. "I'd do it again in a minute. In a minute, you hear?" He stroked Stanley's cheek. "I'd do it again in a minute for you. I'd do it a thousand times over."

And Nino, miraculously, started to weep. He dropped his head into his hands and cried, and Stanley reached his arms around him and held him close and kissed him and whispered sweet inanities. It was, Stanley knew, a horrible choice to have to make. It wasn't a choice he would ever want to make, and yet Nino had made it. Nino had decided, in the blink of the proverbial eye, to pull the trigger. How did a man like Nino make that sort of decision? How did anyone?

"You did the right thing," he whispered, holding Nino close. "You did the right thing. You did."

He would see it forever. He would go on seeing it until the day he died: the barrel of the gun, the blackness inside, the sudden flare, the man's exploding head.

"I never planned this, you know." Nino turned in his arms and gazed at him. "This whole thing. Me, I came from nothin'. Fought my way up from the gutter. I'll probably end up back there, who knows?" He rubbed a hand over his face. "My old man, he was vicious. Just vicious. He beat my brother to death. He beat my ma. I was planning to bump him off. Yeah, I was gonna do that, and then he drops dead one day. Drops dead on the subway." He sighed, leaned back against the couch. "I ain't never had nothin' handed to me, but I never figured on this. I was gonna go into business, you know? Do things, be somebody."

"You are in business," Stanley said. He wiped a stray tear from Nino's cheek. "You and Danny are in business together."

"Ahhhhhh!" Nino made a disgusted noise. "A front. You know that. Same kind of front me and every other wise guy made for himself as soon as the government turned off the taps." He sighed. His posture opened the line of his throat and exposed his jaw; Stanley enjoyed looking at him in profile, his nose and the curve of his lips. "I had dreams, same as any other mug." He picked at a hangnail on his thumb. "Only difference is, I couldn't make mine happen. I had to settle for what I could get." He turned his head and gazed at Stanley. "You know how I got started?"

"Tell me."

"I saw a story in the paper," Nino said, "about Joey Texas. Yeah, they were having some kind of big banquet for him, his boys were, and the newspaper printed a picture of it. Joey Texas, dressed up in a real swell suit and wearing a diamond ring, and I thought, yeah, that's what I want. I want to get some of that." He sighed. "I was nineteen the first time I killed someone. We did a robbery, me and—well, it don't matter what his name is—and I hadta plug a guy to get him to shut up." Nino took his watch out of his vest pocket and toyed with it, turning it over in his fingers so that the diamonds on its edge made glistening ice of the room's available light. "Yeah, we robbed a filling station. Wasn't but twenty dollars in the till, but when I did that… everything changed. I was somebody. I was getting other people to do what I said, making 'em dance to my tune—me, Giovaninni Moretti." He turned his head and gazed at Stanley. "It gets easier after the first one, and I started working for Joey Texas, taking care of guys, you know." He was silent for a moment. "Some stuff I ain't proud of. Some of it was just business. It ain't all roses. Some guys think it's all booze and pussy. Well, I don't drink very much and I ain't never been interested in pussy."

"Do you ever worry?" Stanley asked.

"About what?"

"The police, for one."

"That was self-defense," Nino said. "You think he wouldn't have fogged me? After he got through with you?" Nino sighed. "And the cops don't care. Far as they're concerned, the quicker we kill each other off down here, the better."

"Nino," Stanley said, "why don't you come away with me? For a couple of weeks, a month, until the heat dies down? The cops are going to be looking for you. Big Frank is gonna have his guys combing the city for you."

"Aww, kid, you're sweet. But where can I go, huh? Everybody knows me. There's nowhere I can go."

Stanley swallowed hard. "You can come home with me."

Nino smiled sadly. "We are home."

"No." His voice broke. He wet his lips, stumbled on. "No, we're not. Please," he begged. "Come home with me. Come to Kansas with me. We can lie low for a while, 'til the heat's off. I got a house out there, lots of land. It'd be safe."

"Well...." Nino thought about it. "No, it's... no. Maybe some other time. Maybe later, when—"

"When one of Big Frank's goons fills you full of lead?"

Nino sighed. "You know, you're the most persistent little gazabo I ever met. Once you get something in your mind, there's no getting rid of the idea." He cupped Stanley's chin in his hand. "I leave town now, it's gonna look like I'm running away. I can't do that."

"No," Stanley said, "Just... lie low for a week or two, 'til the heat's off."

Nino leaned in and kissed Stanley gently. "I'll think about it."

CHAPTER
FIVE

"WELL, now! Ain't this swell?" Nino stood in the middle of the Pullman car and looked around, thumbs tucked in the armholes of his waistcoat. "This is real class, ain't it?" He ran a hand along the back of the seat and whistled quietly. "Look at that upholstery. That'll set you back a bunch...." He was trying for the kid's sake to be cheerful, but Nino, like most men of his ilk, was uncomfortable when out of his native element.

Lie low for a few days, Danny had said. *Take the kid and go somewhere. It ain't a bad idea.*

You think I'm afraid of Big Frank? They were sitting in Nino's apartment, sharing a bottle of Scotch and listening to the radio. Stanley had already gone to bed. *You think I'm afraid of that big mug?*

It just makes good sense, Danny said. *You pop outta sight for a couple days, Big Frank wonders what you're up to. With you out of the picture, maybe he gets nervous, tips his mitt a little.*

Danny was right, of course. With Nino out of sight, Big Frank would wonder where he'd gone, wonder maybe what happened to him. It was the perfect way to put Big Frank off balance, and it was a trick Nino had used before, to good effect.

Alright, I'll go. I'll go to goddamn Kansas for a few days. But I won't enjoy myself.

"It sure is nice," Stanley said. Their compartment was a self-contained suite complete with a half bath and a separate sitting room.

"I've never travelled like this before." The last time he'd been on a train had been the tortuous trip to New York, five years before; it wasn't something he wanted to remember. "Are you sure we'll be okay? I mean, he's not—"

"Following us?" Nino shook his head. He sat down and lit a cigar. "Big Frank's lazy. He might send some of his boys after us but they won't go much past Chicago. Where we're going, Big Frank's boys would stick out like a sore thumb." He paused. "Naw, we got nothing to worry about. Relax, kid! You're with me. We're gonna have a swell time!"

There was a tap at the door; Nino stiffened like a hunting dog and his hand delved into his coat.

"Excuse me, sir, but do you want me to turn down your bed now?" The porter peered around the door; Nino relaxed.

"Why, sure!" he said. "That'd be fine! Come on, kid—let's give the man some room." He and Stanley stepped out into the corridor. "How do you feel, kid? You jake?"

Stanley smiled. He looked different—more relaxed, more open— and the furtive, hunted air that often haunted him was gone. Perhaps it was the fact that they were leaving the city behind, moving into open country. "I feel wonderful," he said. "Really wonderful."

"I'm glad, kid." Something welled up within Nino as he gazed at Stanley, something warm and tender, something he commonly felt whenever he looked at Stanley. "I really am." He shifted his feet to accommodate the train's rocking motion. "So, uh, what sorts of things they got to do out there in Kansas? You got any speakeasies?"

"I'm not sure... maybe I never went to... well, my family was... we went to church."

Nino's smile fell away. "Church?" he sneered. "What, like... Mass? Aw, kid, I ain't been in a church for years. Had to be... yeah, it was Louie the Goat's funeral. He got lippy, see, and some of the boys made him a pair of shoes."

Stanley gazed at him for a long moment. "We don't... I mean...."

The porter appeared, smiling. "All done, sir. All ready for bed."

"That's swell. Thanks, George!" Nino tipped the porter generously and they went back in. The berth had been made up into a large double bed with fluffy pillows and crisp white sheets; the porter had pulled down the window shades and turned on the reading light. The small compartment was cozy and inviting and wonderfully intimate.

"Just looking at that bed makes me feel sleepy," Stanley said. He shrugged out of his jacket and hung it on the hook, then went into the bathroom to make his preparations for sleep. He washed his face and hands and brushed his teeth, but hesitated at his pajamas. "Nino," he called to the other man. "Do you think it's too hot for pajamas?"

"It's pretty warm, kid." Nino paged through the newspaper; there was nothing in there about Big Frank or Fist's shooting, which was probably a good sign. It meant Big Frank's boys were lying low and nobody was saying anything much to the cops. Danny would keep an eye on Nino's business interests while he was away, and McKenna would have an avid ear to the ground, just in case.

STANLEY stripped to his boxers and climbed into bed. He sighed at the caress of cool cotton sheets against his hot skin, and Nino laughed.

"Are you comfortable, kid?"

"Nino, this bed is like a cloud."

"Aww, that's great, kid! Now I want you to relax and enjoy this trip. Just leave everything to me, okay?"

Stanley fluffed the pillow, rolled onto his side so he was facing Nino. The small reading light illuminated Nino's face and the upper half of his body and cast the rest of him into shadow; he looked happy, at ease, and relaxed. What would it be like, Stanley wondered, to be alone in his parents' house with Nino? What would his small town think of Stanley's friend, with his city ways and his New York accent and his flashy clothes? There were no illusions; Stanley wasn't stupid. Nino had clawed his way up from the gutter purely on the strength of his own nerve, his courage, and his daring. Stanley understood that to some people Nino might seem unrefined and even vulgar, a fast-talking swell—

—he'd punch anybody who said it, or anything like it, Stanley thought fiercely. He would.

Stanley had spent his childhood, his youth, in a state of indefinable yearning. He had always been a loner, existing in a world of his own making, a secret world that belonged to him alone, that had nothing to do with the small town where he lived. He had passed much of his life in a continual state of wanting—what, he didn't know. There was something missing, some vital part. Looking at Nino now, sitting in his chair in a circle of light, reading his paper, Stanley felt—it seemed silly to think it, much less say it aloud—as if he were really on his way home. He had never, ever felt this way about anyone before, and to some part of his mind, it seemed strange that it was Nino who made him feel this way.

He rolled onto his stomach and bunched the pillow under his cheek. Nino was so still, completely at repose, and that was something else Stanley admired about him. Nino always seemed entirely in control of any situation, never afraid. What made him so ferociously protective of Stanley, determined to shield him regardless of the cost to himself? Nino was, above all things, a practical man, and yet he repeatedly put himself in harm's way if anyone so much as blinked in Stanley's direction.

"What's the matter, kid? Can't sleep?" Nino laid aside the newspaper. "You're doin' a lot of movin' around there."

"I can't sleep." Stanley sighed. "It's so strange, going home, after all this time. It makes me feel a bit... lonely." He hesitated, wondering if he had the courage to ask for what he wanted. "Could you... lie next to me?"

"Lonely, huh?" Nino grinned. "Well, maybe it's time I turned in myself. I expect we'll be in Kansas soon enough."

He doused the reading light and undressed in the dark, laying his shoes side-by-side on the floor. Stanley could barely make out Nino's outline, just the momentary flash of white skin as he moved about, putting his clothes away; the mattress compressed with Nino's weight.

"Aw, this is real comfortable! Now this is what I call class! Ain't this a comfortable bed?" He pushed the blankets down to the foot, retaining only the sheet. "It's warm tonight, ain't it? Kid, you sure you're okay with this? I don't wanna crowd you."

"I'm fine," Stanley murmured. He moved closer, waited while Nino opened his arms, then settled into his embrace. "Mmmm... better."

They lay together for a while, Stanley's head on Nino's shoulder, his hand on Nino's bare chest as the train rocked them gently. Stanley nuzzled the underside of Nino's jaw and kissed his neck. He lifted his face and kissed Nino's mouth tenderly, a lingering kiss that quickly turned torrid, passionate, eager. The tip of Nino's tongue slipped between Stanley's lips, retreated; Stanley mirrored the action and smiled against Nino's lips when Nino whimpered. He held Nino's head, his long fingers in Nino's dark hair, and kissed and licked and suckled the other man's neck and the hollow of his throat.

"Aww, baby." Nino held him close. "Lie back. I want to do something for you. Just lie back." Nino stroked his face and kissed him. "You're the best thing that ever happened to me. You know that, dontcha? The best thing ever." He whispered in Stanley's ear: "Do you trust me?"

Stanley shivered, a series of long ripples that ran through the length of his body. "Yes."

Nino held his face and kissed him... kissed him 'til Stanley was a quivering, boneless mass floating in a darkness full of gentle sounds and exquisite pleasure. Nino kissed his way down Stanley's body, slowly, slowly... the line of his jaw... the sweet hollow at the base of his throat. He gently pushed Stanley's hands away and spent some time licking, sucking, gently nipping at Stanley's nipples while the younger man writhed and gasped, his hands clenching and unclenching at his sides. Nino kissed the center of his chest, his belly, each of his hipbones... he gently lifted the band of Stanley's underwear away from his skin.

"Alright?" he asked. "Kid, if you don't want—"

"Nnngh, do it—" Stanley clenched his fist and brought it down on the mattress. "P-please."

Nino licked the head of his cock. Stanley's back arched.

"Ahhhhhh—"

Nino took Stanley's cock into his mouth, suckling strongly, using his lips and hands to draw the younger man again and again to the ragged edge of his completion. His pleasure rose and rose, filling him up, tipping him over the edge, and he was shuddering, coming hard, panting and writhing back down to sanity again. He was dimly aware of himself, his body, his hands still clenched in Nino's hair, and he relaxed, allowed the aftershocks of his climax to ripple through him as Nino slid up to lie beside him. Nino lifted one of his hands, kissed the palm, then drew each of Stanley's fingers into his mouth, sucking. Stanley shuddered, suddenly weeping and not knowing why. And Nino—Nino was still unsatisfied, so Stanley reached for him but was gently stayed.

"You don't have to do that." Nino kissed him. "I told you: I ain't Big Frank. You're nobody's gunsel."

"It's hardly fair," Stanley protested. "You do this for me and you get nothing in return."

Nino smiled. "You think so? Don't be so sure, kid. I get plenty." He clasped Stanley in his arms and kissed his forehead. "Go to sleep and don't worry about it. We'll be there before you know it."

"There's something I should mention," Stanley said, just before sleep overtook him. "My cousin Wallace will be meeting us at the station. He's been taking care of the house for me."

"Oh, Cousin Wally, eh?" Nino chuckled. "Sounds great."

Stanley shuddered, thinking of his cousin: his utter disdain for Stanley, his cold blue eyes. "Not really... and I wouldn't call him Wally if I were you." He snuggled into Nino and was asleep in moments.

CHAPTER
SIX

THERE were very few people Eli McKenna liked: Nino, Danny, and, grudgingly, Stanley Zadwadzki—and then only sometimes. As a rule he despised the people he worked with because they were shallow and silly and talked about stupid things. Not many people knew McKenna had a college degree in the Humanities, that he read Shakespeare and Adorno and Proust (in French). Mostly McKenna kept to the glass box that served as his office and oversaw the shipping floor, and kept his accounts, his books, his bills of lading, and his papers in impeccable order. The guys who drove the trucks for Nino were all of a piece: big, thuggish, slow-moving, and generally ignorant; they would cross Eli if they thought it worth their while but few of them did. Eli's reputation as a gunman preceded him, and some of the boys had heard from other mobs what Eli had been doing back in Chicago for guys like Frank Nitti and Mitts Capella. The boys figured—rightly—that the best thing to do was to keep their mouths shut and their opinions to themselves and they would do just fine.

What nobody knew was how profoundly Eli's past had affected him. In short, his nerves were shot. He rarely slept at night and then only in intervals, waking to walk the floor and smoke, shaking like a man in the grip of a deathly fever. His dreams were horrible, haunted by phantasms and ghosts with shattered skulls and bloody eyes. He knew the things he had done and he relived them night after night in his dreams. He would never be free. It was for this reason he kept himself strictly to himself, avoiding emotional entanglements.

When the physical urge for sex became too great, he went to a certain house and was admitted by a solemn black man in a bow tie and shown to Miss Rosie's room. Miss Rosie had been taking care of Eli ever since he had arrived in New York City; she understood that Eli didn't want to talk, that he wanted his needs taken care of as expeditiously as possible. He always paid in cash before they started, and he always left the money neatly folded on the corner of the dresser, secured under one leg of her fancy clock. He didn't kiss, and the one time she had tried to kiss him, he'd turned his face away. "I don't do that," he had said—that was all he had said. So Rosie never tried to kiss him. She helped him undress; she led him by the hand to bed, and when he was finished, she handed him his hat and watched him leave. There was no romance in it; there was barely even feeling. It was like scratching an itch and always left him feeling faintly disgusted. He wondered what it would be like to have a steady girl—not some peroxided moll, like Nino's boys had, but a nice girl, a girl who would like him for himself. He had never had that. He doubted he ever would.

On this particular Tuesday afternoon, he was sitting at his desk in his glass box going over some delivery slips, attempting to reconcile them with his books. The loading dock was empty; most of the boys had gone to Jersey to drop off a completed shipment and pick up supplies.

"Hi there."

Eli jumped, trying too late to suppress it. It was only Delores. "Hello."

"I brought you a sandwich and a cuppa coffee." She laid the food on the desk. "Now that Mr. Z's away, I guess I'll have to take care of you instead." She smiled at him, perched herself on the edge of his desk, and glanced over his shoulder. "Whatcha doin'?"

"Nothing much." The coffee was strong and hot, just the way he liked it. "You didn't have to come all the way down here."

"Oh, I don't mind." She patted her skirt and then examined her fingernails. "It's been quiet. I keep waiting for Mr. Nino to call, but he doesn't. I'm getting worried. What if something happened to him and Mr. Z?"

"Aw, lay off. Nino can look after himself." It came out rather more harshly than he intended, and he was immediately sorry. "I mean... uh, they'll be fine. They'll be okay."

"Poor Mr. Z, I don't think he's well." She leaned back, laying her arm across his shoulders. "Hey, your hair curls around your neck back here... would you look at that?"

Her touch acted on Eli like a tonic, albeit a tonic calculated to cause acute embarrassment and severe blushing from his collar to his hairline. Delores stroked the back of his neck and a pleasant tremor ran through him; his hand shook, spilling his coffee.

"Oh, look at what I made you do!" She pulled his handkerchief out of his pocket and mopped his hand and wrist. "I'm sorry."

Eli caught her hand and held on. "Oh, I don't mind," he said. "I don't like this suit."

She stood back and gazed at him, obviously taking his measure with her eyes. "But it looks swell!"

"Do you think so?" He was blushing—dammit—again. Nobody made him blush. He had stood beside guys like Frank Nitti and Johnny the Fox, had done the nastiest of nasty work, things that made other guys throw up their guts. And here he was, blushing because a dame had touched him.

Delores came around to face him. She laid her palms on his shoulders and gazed into his eyes. "I think you're swell, Eli." She stroked his cheek and sighed. "I gotta get back to work. What if Mr. Nino comes back from Kansas and there ain't nothin' done?" She leaned in and pecked his cheek. "You behave yourself," she said, and she was gone. Eli watched her go, watched the undulation of her smooth, round buttocks underneath her dress, and felt a little faint.

Damn.

BY THE time the train pulled into the station, both Stanley and Nino were up and dressed and had had their breakfast in the dining car. The porter met them on the platform with their luggage and bid them farewell. "Welcome to Kansas, Mr. Moretti. I hope you like it here. It sure is flat, I'll say that about it."

Nino peeled off a fifty dollar bill and pressed it into his hand. "There you go, George. You were real swell to me." He gazed around him. "Yeah. Yeah, it sure is flat. They allergic to the vertical or something?"

"Well," Stanley said, "things are different here."

"Here" was the intersection of two long, flat roads extending seemingly without end toward the flat horizon. Even at this hour of the morning, it was already deathly hot and the slight wind twirled dust devils at the edge of the railway platform and into the road. Nino tilted his hat back on his head and look around. "Yeah. Kansas," he said. A man was hurrying toward them, albeit with the peculiar rolling gait of the Midwesterner in his own element; he was taller than both Nino and Stanley and dressed in a dark suit. He stopped in front of them and huffed out an annoyed breath.

"Hm." He had the same pale-blue eyes as Stanley, but where Stanley's eyes were warm, this man's eyes were glacial. "It's about time."

"Wallace." Stanley held out a hand. "It's so good to see you, after all this time." He started forward, obviously intending to hug the other man. Wallace stepped back abruptly, out of his reach. "Ah." Stanley seemed momentarily at a loss. "This is my friend, Mr. Moretti."

"Moretti...." Wallace looked him up and down. "Not an American name, is it?"

Nino bristled. "It certainly is! Why, my family—"

"—and Nino, this is my cousin Wallace," Stanley said hastily. "Why don't we get in out of the sun?"

Wallace's car was parked a short distance away; Stanley rode in the front while Nino occupied the back seat with the luggage. When Nino wondered aloud why Wallace couldn't let down the trunk rack, he was rebuked, told in no uncertain terms that he was a visitor, and as such, knew less than nothing about Midwestern customs.

"Customs?" Nino scoffed. "What's customary about makin' a guest ride with the luggage?"

Wallace turned around. "I could have made you walk," he said. "I'm only doing this as a favor." He appealed to Stanley. "All these years, Aunt Marjorie has been gone, and you left for Lord knows where." He sighed gustily. "It's not like I want to be thanked, oh no. But would a little consideration be too much to ask?" He stopped to let a group of schoolchildren pass, took out a handkerchief, and mopped his forehead. "I'm not well! I've never been well. You know this, Stanley, and still—"

"I'm sorry," Stanley put in quickly. "Please accept my apologies. We're very grateful. I'm very grateful. Nino is too. Aren't you, Nino?"

"Yeah," Nino said. "I'm so grateful I can hardly stand it."

They drove for perhaps ten minutes, turning off the main road onto a narrow dirt road that led up a small rise to a stand of willow trees and cottonwoods. At the top of the rise, a white Victorian sat in lonely majesty, surrounded by trees that had obviously been planted as a sort of wind break. There were flowers blooming in front of the house and a pair of wooden rocking chairs on the front porch.

"Oh my," Nino murmured. "Ain't that pretty...."

"As you can see, Stanley, I've been taking care of the old homestead." Wallace pulled up near the front door and turned off the car. The morning air filled with the hum of insects and the smell of blooming flowers. Nino took off his hat and fanned himself with it, and Stanley grinned.

"It's a different kind of heat," Stanley said, "but don't worry, there's a swimming hole right behind the house."

"Mmmm," Wallace intoned, "ask him about the time he tried to drown me in it when we were kids."

"I did not!" Stanley was trying to hide a smirk and failing. "That was an accident and you know it."

"Really?" Wallace sniffed. "Is that what they're calling it these days?"

Nino reached into the backseat to retrieve the luggage; Stanley took his own suitcase and one of Nino's and started toward the house.

"I suppose I should tell you...." Wallace fell into step beside Nino. "Cousin Stanley is of the same delicate disposition as I. I might even go so far as to say he's fragile... it's a family trait. He can't stand any overt excitement."

"That so?" Nino's mind was full of images from the night before: Stanley writhing in naked ecstasy in their bunk, fisting the bed sheets with his head thrown back and his mouth open in a silent scream. "I see what you mean." The idea of being left alone with Stanley in this house gave him a pleasant frisson. There was no limit to the things they could do.

"I've had Mrs. Murphy in to clean, Stanley. You know I'm allergic to washing soap." Wallace put the key in the door. "This way."

The door opened onto a spacious entrance hall with wide plank flooring polished to a gleaming shine. To the right, a set of pocket doors opened onto a sitting room with high, narrow windows and a fireplace with a walnut mantelpiece. Nino laid his suitcase down and whistled. "Wow."

"Come in," Stanley said. "Please, come in and make yourself comfortable."

"As you can see," Wallace said, following behind, "I've had the whole place turned out and cleaned from top to bottom." He trailed a fussy finger over the banister railing, glanced at it, and tutted. "Mrs. Murphy is slipping. I should have known."

"It's exactly as I remember," Stanley said. "Wallace, thank you. This is so kind of you."

"The least I could do," Wallace said, "considering how I cared about Aunt Marjorie." His expression said that Stanley, with all of his native virtues, would never live up to the memory of his mother, at least not in Wallace's estimation. He handed Stanley the key. "Here you go. You know where to find me." And with a searing glance at Nino, he was gone.

"IT'S wonderful… exactly as I remembered." Stanley floated on his back, naked except for a pool of moonlight. "Are you happy?" he asked.

Nino sat at the edge of the swimming hole, his trousers rolled up and his feet dangling in the water. "Happy?" He grinned. "You have to ask that? Sure, I'm happy." He glanced around him. "Kinda dark out here, ain't it?"

"Why don't you come in?" Stanley asked. "The water's fine."

"No, I'd—"

"What?" Stanley tilted his head. "Can't you swim?"

Nino was briefly ashamed. "No, kid. I never really learned."

"It's shallow here." He stood up; the water came to his armpits. "See? It's okay. Come on out."

Nino was deathly afraid of water. As a boy, he and his brother Tony had gone to swim at the local YMCA. Nino, misjudging the depth of the far end, had dived in. His cries for help had gone unheard in the churning mass of children, and he sank beneath the surface. By the time Tony noticed and alerted a lifeguard, Nino was unconscious; he was revived with great difficulty. He had never gone near a swimming pool since.

Nino came to the end of his tale.

"I'm so sorry." Stanley stood with his hands on Nino's knees. "I'm so sorry to hear that." He reached for one of Nino's hands, took it, and kissed the fingers and the palm. "I'll take care of you. I promise." He jerked his chin toward the dark expanse of moonlit water, holding out both hands. "Come on."

Nino stripped naked and slipped into the water, holding fast to Stanley. He gasped as the water touched his skin, but Stanley steadied him, held onto him and didn't let him go. Stanley walked backward with him until the water was up to their waists, then stopped. He wrapped his arms around Nino and cuddled him.

"Alright?"

"I think so." Nino was trembling like a leaf in a gale. All he could see was the dark water, the water that waited to pull him under.

"Hey, it's alright...." Stanley tilted his head back so he could look at Nino. "You're safe. You're with me." Their naked skins slid together under the warm water, and Nino grunted softly as Stanley leaned in and kissed him. Stanley held his head and plundered Nino's mouth slowly, deliberately. "Gee, I sure do like doing that."

Nino sighed with pleasure. "I'm trying to be a gentleman, kid. It ain't fair for you to tease me like this. You're making things hard."

One of Stanley's hands disappeared under water. "Am I?" He grinned. "Oh, yes," he said, "I certainly am."

Nino shivered as Stanley's hand closed around his cock. The kid was a first-rate, five-star, copper-bottomed tease! "Stanley," he whispered brokenly, "have mercy."

In answer, Stanley leaned in and kissed him again—a long, slow, hot, mind-blowing kiss.

"Is that supposed to keep me from being afraid of the water?" Nino asked.

"Come on."

Stanley took him by the hand and led him up onto the bank where they had spread out their towels. It was quiet here and dark, and they were utterly alone, because this entire stretch was Zadwadzki land and nobody would even think of trespassing. They lay down together and kissed for a while, and Stanley licked stray drops of water off Nino's skin, then straddled him and lay on top of him.

"You make me happy," he said. He laid a trail of kisses along Nino's neck. "I'm so glad you're here with me."

Nino sighed. "Baby, you're making it awful hard for me to keep being a gentleman...." He clasped Stanley's face between his palms and kissed him, parting Stanley's lips with the tip of his tongue, pulling the soft cushion of Stanley's lower lip into his mouth and sucking on it. "I don't want to hurt you. I never want to give you a minute's trouble." He sought Stanley's gaze. "You believe me, don't you?"

"Mmm-hmm." Stanley laid his head down on Nino's chest.

"Let's go back to the house," Nino said. "I want to make you happy."

The point of Stanley's chin rested on Nino's breastbone. "You do make me happy," he said.

"Really happy." Nino grinned.

"Oooh." Stanley slid off of him. "Now I'm interested."

IT WAS six o'clock that evening that it happened to Danny Murphy. He had just come out of Ernesto's on Bedlow Street after a sandwich and a cup of coffee and was feeling rather good about himself, his life, and the world in general. Big Frank O'Hara's boys had been quiet, and nobody was much bothered to find out what had happened to Fist. McKenna had positioned himself to hear everything worth hearing, and he reported back to Danny. So far there were faint rumblings that Big Frank was thinking up his next move, but since Big Frank's thinking generally took a really long time, Nino and the kid were safe.

What happened to Danny was that as he came out of Ernesto's he ran smack into Lloyd Funt.

"Danny Boy! Is that you?" Funt was a year or two older than Danny—a tall, thin flagpole of a man with arms of astonishing length and reach. "Are you still doing the Lindy?"

Danny embraced his old friend. "Lloyd, you dog! Whatcha doin' in this part of town, huh?"

"Auditions, old man—Jack Green's new thing, off-off-Broadway."

"Yeah, pretty far off if you ask me," Danny said. He smiled wistfully. "Still treadin' the boards, huh?"

"Yeah, you could say that. I been hoofin' it for the past six months in this thing up on Broadway. Just in the chorus, but it's a living." He glanced over Danny's clothes, his shoes. "What's tricks with you these days?"

"Working for a friend of mine," Danny said. "Sort of a... uh, business associate."

Lloyd nodded knowingly. "Uh-huh. Ain't got the legs no more?"

Danny drew himself up. "Sure I got the legs! Why, I could—" He sagged. "Naw, I guess I don't got the legs." He wasn't supposed to be interested in that sort of thing anymore, all that singing and dancing stuff. He'd left it behind. "What's the name of the show?"

"*My Gal Sal*—you've heard of it?" Lloyd couldn't help himself: he looked at over Danny's sharp suit, his striped silk shirt, and flamboyant tie. "What sort of business is your friend in?"

"He's uh... say, Lloyd, they looking for anybody for this Sal Gal thing?"

"Sorry, Danny... it's already been cast." Lloyd shrugged. "I can keep an ear to the ground for ya."

"Yeah... thanks. See ya around."

He left and walked back to his apartment, sunk deep in thought. Danny lived near Nino, mere streets away from where they had grown up on the Lower East Side. It was beautifully furnished, with such nice things as Danny could afford. He had excellent taste. The door opened onto a neat living room with fine Persian rugs on the floor, matching couches, and Tiffany lamps. Danny liked to read, and there were bookshelves filled with classic volumes, all bound in leather: *Don Quixote, Frankenstein, Silas Marner, The Scarlet Letter.* The fireplace mantel was maple, beautifully carved and stained, and the handsome antique mirror above had cost him a pretty penny. He regarded himself in it now: yep, there he was. Danny Murphy. Red hair, blue eyes— same old pan he'd been looking at for all these years. He stood back a ways, executed a quick little combination, and finished with a whirl.

"You still got it," he murmured. "You still got it."

At the age of eight, Danny had come to the attention of the local priest, a solemn, upright young man named Pat Driscoll. Driscoll had grown up on the Lower East Side himself and had specifically requested St. Mike's; he conducted the boys' choir and ran basketball games on weekdays after school, took the boys swimming, and in general did his damnedest to keep them off the streets. He had noticed Danny playing center court one day and had taken him aside.

You ever danced, young Murphy?

Aw, dancin's for saps. I ain't no sissy. I wanna be a boxer.

You know, some of the best boxers I've ever seen were good because of their footwork.

Footwork? I don't know from footwork.

So Driscoll had decided to teach him. He located a fellow priest in an adjacent parish and they worked out an exchange: Driscoll would teach his boys to box if he would come to St. Mike's and teach Danny how to dance.

"You think the boy's got something?" Driscoll's colleague was skeptical. His first look at the boy revealed nothing much in particular, just another snot-nosed little street punk, fast with his fists and with his mouth.

"I do," Driscoll said. "He can fight, but I want to show him there's more to life than fighting."

"Well, alright...."

Three times a week, Danny learned to dance. He started with basic tap, then moved rapidly upward, moving from the Paddle and Roll and the Shim Sham Shimmy to complicated time steps with some ballet thrown in, and from there to ballroom. He learned the Foxtrot and the Lindy Hop, the Viennese waltz, and the passionate, sensual Tango. At age twelve he was an accomplished dancer, as graceful and light on his feet as any professional. The boys quickly learned it was a grievous error to make fun of him: Bugs Muldoon had been dumb enough to laugh at Danny when he saw him coming out of the community center wearing tap shoes. Danny chased him down and gave him a split lip and a thrashing he'd remember for the rest of his life.

At thirteen Danny auditioned for and was accepted to a Manhattan dance company, and would have gone on to great things, except there wasn't any money and there wasn't any time. With nine brothers at home, most of Danny's efforts went to a part-time job, to running with Nino Moretti and, too soon, to stealing what he could to supplement the family income.

He still danced, and throughout his teenage years and young manhood he had even had a part or two in various productions, but he never made it to Broadway. He still danced—in his apartment, when he was alone, soft-shoe, in his stockinged feet so as to not disturb his neighbors. Late at night, when he was alone and when the day's bottle blonde had finally shrugged into her silken combinations for the taxi ride home, he imagined himself onstage, lighting up the night on Broadway, dancing and singing in some new hit show with the gleam of footlights in his eyes and the roar of applause in his ears. And if he cried a little bit, and if his hot tears ran into his ears and wet his pillow, it was nobody's business. Sometimes, if Nino gave a party for the boys, he'd say, "Danny, c'mon, give us a few steps," and Danny would wow them all.

He'd wow them all.

He hung his coat in the closet, took off his waistcoat, and rolled up his shirt sleeves. He pushed the coffee table back and turned on the phonograph.

Danny closed his eyes and danced. He danced as if he were on the stage, front and center with a full orchestra and the chorus behind him. He danced, romancing the music, anticipating the beat, always a half measure ahead. He danced with abandon, his hair falling into his eyes, sweat beading on his forehead, his arms floating at his sides.

"Hey!"

The banging on his door was approximately the speed and tempo of the music on his phonograph; annoyed, Danny switched off the music and opened the door. "Whatta you wa—"

She was little and dark, wholly beautiful; her head barely topped his shoulder and he knew the moment he looked into her dark-green eyes that he was gone, brother—but good. "Can I help you, miss?"

"Is that you banging on the floor? You sound like a herd of elephants. I'm trying to study so I'd appreciate it if you could keep it down to a dull roar."

"You're studying?" She had creamy pale skin with just the lightest spray of freckles across her nose and a perfect Cupid's bow mouth; her hair was wavy, bobbed, and in the humid heat, it curled against her neck. Danny's pulse speeded up 'til it was booming in his ears.

"I'm a student nurse, not that it's any of your business, and you're making too much noise with your... whatever it is you're doing up here."

"I was dancing. At least, that's what I thought I was doing."

She looked him up and down. "Dancing? Yes, well, do it quiet, won't you?"

Danny was cowed, despite himself. "Okay."

She turned on her heel.

"Wait!" he called after her. "Have a cup of coffee?"

"A cup of coffee?" She hadn't left, but she wasn't exactly rushing into his place, either. "Just one cup."

"Yes, ma'am."

"And no monkey business."

"No monkey business." He held the door wider. "Please, come in." He held out his hand. "Danny Murphy."

"Billie—Billie O'Caigne." She narrowed her eyes at him. "One cup."

"Yes, ma'am," Danny said. He executed a rapid time step. "Just one cup."

THE summer moon threw panes of silvery light across their naked bodies; Stanley's long fingers clenched Nino's back, released, clenched again as Nino nuzzled and sucked the side of his neck. Stanley's breath caught as Nino lightly bit his shoulder and laved the tiny hurt with his tongue. "Ohh-h-h—" Stanley's back arched; he wrapped one long leg around Nino's waist. "Mm, don't stop."

"Oh baby, I got no intention of stopping," Nino whispered. He grinned against Stanley's naked chest and tried to ignore his own burgeoning erection. "I wanna make you come like a freight train."

"Mmph." Stanley clutched Nino's head just as Nino's agile tongue swirled around the hard peak of his left nipple. "Oh God, that feels so good...." He sobbed with pleasure as Nino moved to the other nipple and captured it with his mouth. "Don't stop...."

Nino's cock throbbed. *Don't think about it. Think about the kid.* He didn't want to be just another Big Frank; that wasn't what this was about. He wanted this to be good for Stanley and eventually, with time, maybe good for both of them....

"Nino—" Stanley tapped on the other man's shoulder. "Mm... N-Nino... just...."

Nino laid a trail of burning kisses on Stanley's belly. "What is it, baby?"

"Come here."

"Is there something wrong? Am I going too fast for you? You want to take a break or something?" Nino cupped Stanley's chin in his hand and kissed his mouth.

"I want you to make love to me—I want us to make love—I want—I don't know what to do...." He didn't seem to have the words to tell Nino what he wanted. Had Stanley had been a virgin before Big Frank? Was that what this was about? "Together. I want that."

"Are you sure?" Nino held him tenderly, slipped his fingers through Stanley's soft hair. "Because we don't gotta do—"

"I'm not made of glass!" Stanley snapped. "He didn't break me—the things he did—"

"Shhh...." Nino laid a hand over his mouth. "Stay here."

"Where are you going?" Stanley sat up on his elbow. "Nino, don't leave, I won't—"

"I'm not leaving." He opened his suitcase, took out a small bottle, and brought it back to bed with him. "I ain't never gonna leave you. You know that, right?"

"What's this?" Stanley took the small bottle from him and opened it, then rubbed some of the contents between his fingertips. "It's slippery. Come here."

Nino groaned as Stanley's long fingers slid over the head of his cock. He lay back, eyes closed, as Stanley went to work on him, spreading the oil over his erection, leaning in now and then to tease Nino with his lips and tongue. "Kid, you're killing me here...."

Stanley lay back and pulled Nino on top of him, closing his thighs around Nino's cock. "I want you to do this," he said. He trembled. "Please."

It was sensual, blissful, heated; it was lips and tongues and Nino's hard cock between his thighs, rubbing, rubbing. Stanley's cock trapped between their bellies, everything warm and safe and oh so good, so good—

"Oh, baby...." Nino's eyes were closed and his face was slack, expressionless, his whole being turned inward. "Oh God... fuck." He trembled when Stanley drew his face down and kissed him, groaned as the kiss deepened. Stanley thrust up against him strongly and Nino came, shuddering; he dropped his head to Stanley's shoulder and cried out hoarsely, "Oh God, I love you."

THAT was enough for Stanley. His desire peaked and spread, dragging him over the edge. He came so hard bright sparks formed and burst behind his vision. Someone was crying out and he dimly recognized his own voice, shouting his release. He clung to Nino as the climax spun him back to earth again.

"You love me," he whispered. Nino's face was close to his; Nino's eyes were closed, his dark lashes lying on his cheeks. "You love me."

They woke at intervals throughout the night to make love and drift back to sleep again. Stanley learned where Nino liked to be touched and how, and which things made him keen with pleasure. He teased Nino with mouth and hands, touching him with long, artistic fingers, drawing him again and again to the brink of release, then finally nudging him over. Stanley, too, was pleasured by Nino, who delighted in their isolation and who took full advantage of their solitude to bring Stanley yelling into his climax.

"You're killing me," Stanley whispered. He collapsed across Nino's chest, his hair plastered to his sweating forehead. "I'm going to ooze right out of my skin."

"You ain't complainin'," Nino said. He lifted one of Stanley's hands and kissed the palm. "You're beautiful. You know that, right?"

"But?" Stanley propped his chin on Nino's chest and gazed at him. The dawn was coming; there was just enough light to make out Nino's features. "You're going to tell me that I'm beautiful, but—"

"But nothing." Nino's forehead creased. "Look, kid… this is hard for me. Maybe I ain't real good with words. And maybe sometimes I don't say things the way I oughta."

Here it comes, Stanley thought. *Here comes the part where he tells me that it's been fun, but there's no future for us. This is where he breaks my heart.*

"I never been in love but once in my life," Nino said. "I ain't gone lookin' for it. I figured, guy in my line of work, he gets to meet some strange birds and maybe strange things happen to him. You can't never tell, from one day to the next, what kinds of things might be waitin' around the corner." He stroked Stanley's cheek. "I never made no plans for the future." His eyes filled with tears, something so uncharacteristic of Nino that Stanley was alarmed. "No, kid, I'm alright. Let me finish." He took a breath. "I ain't never made no plans. But I'd think about making plans with you."

Stanley stared at him and blinked, and two tears slid down his face. "With me?" He was suddenly trembling all over, weeping, coming apart at the seams.

"Oh, baby, don't cry." Nino held him tight. "Don't cry, baby… shhh…." He kissed the young man's face and his hair and rocked him gently. "Maybe I'm going too fast for you? You want me to back off a bit?"

Stanley raised his head. "Don't ever back off," he said fiercely. "Don't ever leave me." He clutched at Nino almost desperately. "Promise me. Promise me you'll never leave me."

J.S. Cook

CHAPTER
SEVEN

"THIS is no good." Eli McKenna threw the stack of invoices down on the desk. "I've been over it a dozen times and I am telling you, no dice."

"I don't get you." Jake, one of Nino's drivers, stood easily a head taller than Eli. He sneered down at the smaller man. "Maybe you need to learn to add."

"Maybe you need to mind your mouth or you might be talking out of an extra hole in your head." Eli sat down behind his desk. "There's three hundred clams still owing on the Johnson account. Have it on my desk by lunchtime."

Jake cracked his hairy knuckles with a sound like cannons going off. "Or what?"

Eli smiled. It wasn't a pleasant smile. It wasn't a nice smile. It was the sort of smile that hinted at horrors to come. "Or I'll take it out of your hide."

Jake moved, but Eli was quicker: he popped up out of his chair like something strung on wires and his gun was out and pressed against Jake's temple. "Go on," Eli said, "Try it. I'd love for you to try it."

"One of these days," Jake said, "you'll get what's coming to you." He backed away and out the door.

Eli stowed his piece and sat down. He crushed his hands together in his lap to quell their shaking and forced himself to breathe. Three hundred dollars missing from the payout for a shipment, and if Nino were here, he'd be screaming bloody blue murder. Eli had no proof that

Jake was crooked—it could have been an error in arithmetic—but he had no proof that he wasn't either. Some of the guys, they figured that Nino was away, so maybe nobody would miss it if they put their fingers in the pie a little bit.

He wished Nino were here. The boss was good at handling these sorts of things—all Nino had to do was bark and the boys would jump—but Eli... everybody knew he was nothing, just some Chicago nobody. They weren't inclined to listen to a word he said, and with Nino gone, they knew his orders had no teeth.

"Hi, sweetheart. How's tricks?" Delores appeared and laid a steaming cup of coffee at his elbow. "Aw, sweetie, you look awful!" She lifted his chin and gazed into his eyes. "Whatsa matter? You sick or something?"

"It's nothing. Just one of the guys kickin' up." He smiled at her. "You don't hafta bring me coffee every day." He tasted it, sighed blissfully. "It sure is good, though."

Delores dimpled. "Not every gal would do that, but I'd do it for you, Eli."

"Why're you so nice to me, huh? Always bringing me stuff...."

Delores sighed and reached to straighten the knot in his tie. "Maybe I'm sweet on ya," she said. She snapped her gum twice, for emphasis. She leaned closer. "That's some nice aftershave lotion you got on. You smell good." She touched his cheek. "You look good, too... but you always do."

Eli felt a blush starting up his neck. "Aw, Delores—"

Delores leaned in and kissed him. For once in his life, Eli didn't pull away. His eyes fell shut as he leaned into the caress; he cupped her face in his hands and deepened the kiss.

"You sweet on me?" he asked quietly.

Delores smiled. "What do you think?" she asked.

He laughed gently. "I think you're a gal who knows what she wants."

Delores snapped her gum. "Now you're gettin' it," she said. She straightened up and patted her hair. "I gotta go. I'm sure the phone's ringing. Everything goes haywire when Mr. Nino ain't here. Hey, you think him and Mr. Z are having a good time?"

Eli smirked. "I think they are." He wasn't stupid, and maybe nobody else in Nino's organization understood certain salient facts about their boss, but Eli did. Sure as shooting, Nino was screwing Stanley, or maybe the other way around, but what the hell. He had no reason to resent Nino: the boss had always been good to him. And maybe Stanley wasn't who he'd have picked as Nino's ideal type, but nobody was asking him.

"You think Mr. Nino likes Mr. Stanley?"

Eli nodded solemnly. "Yeah, I think he likes Mr. Stanley a lot."

IT WAS well past eleven when Stanley rolled onto his back and opened his eyes. Nino was still sleeping beside him, and Stanley smiled. Sleep took about ten years off Nino, made him childlike and peaceful, erased the tense lines at the corners of his mouth and smoothed his brow. His thick, wavy dark hair fell over his forehead, still mussed from the repeated intrusions of Stanley's long fingers, and his long lashes cast dark shadows on his cheeks. Stanley sighed, leaned in, and kissed the corner of Nino's mouth. "Nino...."

"Mmm." Nino snaked out an arm and pulled Stanley tight against him. "Trying to wake me up?"

Stanley nuzzled his neck. "I thought of a number of different ways I could wake you...." He slid his hand down and he wrapped his long fingers around Nino's cock. "But I figured you might not like that."

He giggled at Nino's frustrated growl.

"Kid," Nino said. "Sometimes I think you're gonna kill me off before my time." He squinted at the clock. "Jeez, would you look at that!" He stayed Stanley's roving hands. "Whatcha got for a shower bath in this place?"

"Oh, hot and cold running—" and Stanley said a word that Nino was surprised to hear. In fact, he didn't think Stanley even knew that word.

"Room for two?" Nino asked.

"Oh, baby…." If Midwesterners could purr, Stanley was doing it now. "Come with me…."

The bathroom was as spacious as the rest of the house, with a claw-foot tub and a shower and plenty of hot water, which was good. Stanley leaned into Nino and kissed him 'til he groaned, then stepped away.

"You're askin' for it," Nino growled. He doused his head under the spray. "You're definitely askin' for it."

"Am I?" Stanley moved into his arms again. "Are you gonna give it to me? Or has a guy gotta beg around here?"

Nino pressed Stanley back against the wall and slid to his knees. He felt Stanley's long fingers insinuate themselves into his hair as he took Stanley's cock into his mouth.

"Oh God—" Stanley whimpered, and the back of his head thumped against the wall. "Mmph. Yes."

His hands tightened on Nino's skull as the older man began suckling him gently, pulling Stanley deep into his mouth. Nino played with Stanley, drawing him close to his climax and then easing off, varying the strength and tempo of his mouth's careful ministrations until Stanley was nearly incoherent.

He bent forward, his wet hair falling into his face, and clutched the back of Nino's neck. "Please—" He groaned, shuddering. "Oh," he whimpered, "you're killing me."

"What a way to go," Nino murmured, getting to his feet. "You want me to send for a priest?"

Stanley folded himself into Nino's embrace. "You do realize tomorrow is Sunday."

"So what?"

Stanley made a prim face—rather, he made a face that tried its best to be prim and was something more salacious. "Wallace will be by at ten to pick us up for church."

Nino blinked. "Church?"

"Yes, church."

"Christ."

"Nino."

"I'm sorry. It's just been a while since I've been inside a church." Nino stepped away and doused himself under the hot water. "What kind of a church is it?"

Stanley leveled a look at him. "Oh, there are pews and hymn books and a window or two."

"You're a pain in the ass," Nino said. He reached for the soap.

"Here," Stanley said, "let me help you wash that...."

IT WAS after four o'clock when Eli squared away the last of the day's scheduled shipments and reached for his jacket. He smiled to himself, thinking about Delores, that kiss, the way she had touched him. She was a real nice girl, just the kind of girl that he could really go for too. Maybe he'd ask her out and they could get to know each other. Perhaps she'd like to get a cup of coffee after work, if she was done for the day. That wasn't too much, was it? Girls liked to start slow and get to know a fella before committing themselves to something more. A cup of coffee—there was a nice place around the corner.

"Delores?"

She wasn't at her desk. She had left a pencil lying across her blotter and a stack of undelivered telephone message slips were stuck on their usual nail next to the telephone, but Delores was nowhere in sight. Eli tried in vain to quash the nervous quiver in his stomach that sixth sense that told him something bad had happened.

"Delores? You here?"

"You're Mr. McKenna, ain't ya?" A boy appeared, a snotty-nosed street ruffian with the knees out of his trousers and a dirty skimmer on his head. "Gotta message for ya." He thrust a scrap of paper into Eli's hand.

"Who's it from?" Eli darted toward him but the kid was too quick; he vanished down the hall and out the door. Eli ran to the window but he was too late. The kid had already disappeared into the milling mass of pedestrian traffic on the sidewalk below. "Goddammit." He unfolded the piece of paper and read it with a growing sense of unreality:

FIVE HUNDRED DOLLARS OR I KILL THE GIRL.

"YOU'RE holding it upside down," Stanley whispered. He took the hymnal out of Nino's hands and turned it up the right way, and tried to ignore the friendly smiles and the many faces turned their way. Here was Marjorie and Dick Zadwadzki's boy back home, and he'd brought a friend with him, all the way from New York City! Who would have ever thought it? Of course Stanley was such a nice boy, always so very helpful and so smart! He took that course, remember, something to do with bookkeeping... or was that beekeeping? He went East after his mother died, bless her sainted heart.

"Congratulations," Wallace said dryly. "You two have created quite the sensation."

"Maybe they ain't seen nobody from New York before," Nino said. "Sure is a lot of 'em," he said. "Everybody in this town go to church?"

"Yes," Wallace said primly, "everybody goes to church. We aren't like you godless New Yorkers."

"Please," Stanley whispered. "Please stop it."

"I didn't start it," Wallace snipped. "Mr. Macaroni here—"

"Moretti," Nino hissed.

A side door opened and the minister appeared, a young man around Stanley's age with warm brown eyes and a ready smile. He felt Wallace tense at his side, and Stanley turned to look at him. Wallace's whole being was concentrated in watching the man behind the pulpit, like a pointer stiffened before a covey of quail. What was it? Not anger, Stanley thought, but something else, something just as powerful. Wallace's posture, the tension in his body, and the intensity of his gaze, all this ought to have surprised Stanley but didn't. There were a lot of things about Wallace that didn't quite add up: his refusal to leave Kansas, the fact that he had never married, not to mention his continual bad mood. He reminded Stanley of a fast horse that, instead of being turned loose on the racetrack, had spent his life tethered to a plow.

"Good morning, everyone. And I'm so glad to see Stanley home again. We thought you'd been eaten by the city," the minister said.

Stanley grinned and stood up. "Thanks, Jim, and it's good to be home. I've brought a friend with me—this is Mr. Nino Moretti, my employer. He's visiting from New York City."

The congregation murmured their welcome and Nino nodded at them all. "Real swell welcome," he said. "Nice folks." He turned to Stanley: "What are we singing? We're supposed to be singing something."

"Number 435," Wallace said. "'Lead, Kindly Light'."

His eyes never left the pulpit. It was as if, Stanley reflected, he saw nothing but Jim.

"I'M SO glad to meet you, Mr. Moretti. You know, I was in New York once. Back in 1919 it was. It was my sister Beatrice's birthday and Mother decided she just had to have a dress from... oh, what was the name of that department store? You know, the big one on Fifth Avenue... there used to be a toy soldier in the window...."

"Sorry, ma'am, I don't recall." Nino tried to find Stanley in the milling mass of churchgoers but couldn't see the younger man for Mrs. Pimley's large hat.

"At any rate, it was a very big store, and I remember I got lost on the fifth floor. Now, let me see... what did they sell on the fifth floor? Was it gentlemen's hosiery? No, I mistake myself. Perhaps it was notions."

I got a notion, Nino thought, *that I'm gonna shoot myself in the head if Stanley doesn't come back here very soon.* "That's nice," he replied, completely unaware of anything the old dame had said. "Lovely, lovely."

Mrs. Pimley was staring at him. "I don't think it's lovely at all, Mr. Manicotti! Mother was in the hospital for three weeks after that episode!" She drew up her considerable bulk and flounced off in a huff.

"Talked your ear off, did she?" Wallace appeared with a rolled-up tablecloth and a picnic basket. "Good old Doris Pimley. You know she's been married five times. That"—Wallace gestured in her direction with the middle finger of one hand—"*woman* has killed more men than John Dillinger."

"Yeah?" Nino watched her go with renewed interest. "She doesn't look so tough."

Wallace made a face. "I was speaking metaphorically."

Nino glared at him. "I ain't speakin' no metaphorical," he said. "Where's Stanley?"

"He went to the little boys' room." Wallace spread the tablecloth on the grass and sat down. He opened the picnic basket and began laying out plates and silverware.

"Funny kind of a church," Nino said. "How come everybody's out here eating on the lawn, like?"

"Today is the annual church picnic and the beginning of the pastor's summer vacation." Wallace slapped Nino's hand away as he reached for an apple. "Please. Don't touch the food."

"I'm hungry," Nino snapped, "and I don't see what food's for if it ain't for eatin'."

"We haven't said grace yet," Wallace replied. And under his breath, "Heathen."

"Sorry, I didn't mean to take so long." Stanley folded his long legs under him, anchoring one corner of the tablecloth. "You two are getting along?"

"Oh, just swell," Nino muttered. "He won't let me eat anything."

"I explained to Mr. Moretti that out here, unlike the godless denizens of New York, we say grace before our meals, to give thanks to God for our food." Wallace arranged a platter of devilled eggs inside several concentric rings of lightly buttered toast points.

"God knows everything, don't he?" Nino asked.

"I think so," Stanley replied. He undid the top button of his collar and loosened his tie.

"Then he knows I'm hungry. Let's eat." Nino reached for a devilled egg.

"*No!*" both Zadwadzkis chorused.

Nino sighed and sat back, and ripped out some handfuls of grass and shredded them.

"So where is he going for vacation this year?" Stanley asked.

"Oh, I don't really know." Wallace's voice was just the tiniest bit unsteady.

"He didn't ask you to go on his fishing trip?" Stanley leaned forward far enough to hold Wallace's gaze. "But you two always—"

"No, we don't!" Wallace snapped. "And I'd prefer it if you just dropped the subject."

He was in a bad way, Nino thought. "Say, what's up between you and this priest fella, anyway? He some kind of special friend of yours?"

Wallace stared at him like he hated him—which at that moment he probably did. He was saved from having to answer by the general call to grace, but Nino couldn't resist sneaking a glance at him through his eyelashes.

Wallace looked positively miserable.

"AH, YOU know, kid, I could get used to this." Nino slipped out of his jacket and loosened his tie. "Although I think all this good country living is eventually gonna show up on my waist, you know what I mean?" He patted his stomach ruefully, stretched his legs in front of him, and laid his head against the back of the sofa.

"Never," Stanley said. He took off his jacket and waistcoat and sat next to Nino. The front room was deliciously cool and shaded from the midafternoon sun. "You made quite an impression. They'll be talking about you for months." Nino opened his arms and Stanley went into them. "Make that years."

"Aw, you're flattering me now." Nino sighed blissfully. He went quiet as Stanley leaned close and kissed him. "Oh, baby," he said, "I think I know the perfect way for us to work off that picnic lunch...." He returned the kiss, holding Stanley's face between his palms as he deepened the caress. The younger man groaned and pulled Nino closer, wrapped one leg around his waist.

"I'm sorry. I don't mean to interrupt, but—"

Nino leapt away from Stanley as if he'd been electrocuted. "What the hell are you doin'?" he snapped. "Just walkin' in here like you own the goddamn place? You're lucky I didn't pull a gat on you!"

"Wallace." Stanley wiped his mouth in the back of his hand, a hand that trembled. "It isn't what it looks like."

"Yes," the elder Zadwadzki said, "it is. And we need to talk." He walked several short, choppy steps back and forth, then folded himself down into the easy chair. "This has to be said."

"Now, see here—" Nino started up, but was gently stayed by Stanley.

"No, Nino," Stanley said, "Let him finish."

Wallace stared at them. "I don't know what to do!" He was on his feet again, walking. He went to the large window that overlooked the garden and stood gazing out for a moment. "When you wired to say you were coming, I wasn't sure... I didn't know if I wanted you here. We never were close—"

Stanley protested. "That's not entirely true."

Wallace waved him off. "Listen—please. Just... just listen." He drew a shuddering breath and turned to face them. The afternoon sun haloed his head and shoulders, picking up the early gray in his hair. "We never were close, not like cousins are, but I knew... I knew you were... different. Like me."

Nino got up and went to where Wallace was. "You don't like dames," he said. "Is that what I'm hearing, or are you just giving me static?"

Wallace nodded miserably. "I... figured I could go for years... maybe... you know, I can't be the only one who...." He gaze beseeched them. "Men like this... they live their lives... I could have hobbies and maybe I wouldn't...." He buried his face in his hands.

"You're in a bad way, Kansas." Nino reached up and laid a hand on the taller man's shoulder. "You really got yourself tied up in knots, ain't ya?"

"I had hoped... I mean, when I saw you guys getting off the train I thought maybe...." He huffed out an exasperated breath. "I knew. I could tell."

Nino gazed at him and made a decision. "Sit down, Kansas." He drew Wallace over to the sofa. "Something tells me you need to talk."

"'NOTHER one?" Nino held the whisky bottle poised over the lip of Wallace's glass.

"Sure." Wallace waited while Nino refilled his glass, then took a healthy slug. "Here's to you. And to me. And whatever the hell it is I'm still doing in this shit-kicking town." His eyes were red-rimmed from crying and he looked absolutely dreadful—torn up inside and hurt and wrung out but good.

Stanley stood behind him, just as he had during Wallace's confession, his palm smoothing gentle circles on his cousin's back. "You don't have to stay," he said.

"Oh, I've got to stay," Wallace replied. He gazed into his whisky. "Where else am I gonna go?"

"You could always come back to New York with—" Stanley caught Nino's eye and stopped short. He was doing it again, just like Big Frank always said he did: sticking his foot in, opening his big goddamn mouth.

"With us," Nino said.

Nino smiled at Wallace, and Stanley's heart was suddenly very, very full.

"Thank you," Wallace said quietly. "It's very nice of you."

"I could find a place for you in my organization," Nino said.

"Your… organization?"

"Yeah, it's a business." Nino coughed. "Sort of."

Wallace raised his head. "Are you a gangster?" he asked quietly.

Stanley moved quickly to interject. "Wallace, how long have you known that you felt this way about Jim?"

Months, he told them, years, as long as he'd been alive, as long as Jim had been the pastor of their church, had been his friend and fishing buddy, forever, since yesterday and just this minute. "When I saw you two—"

"We're sorry about that," Stanley said. "We didn't think—"

"No, it's good." Wallace drained the last of his drink and stood up. "It's good that I saw you. I needed to… come clean. I'm glad…."—this last was addressed to Stanley—"I'm glad you found someone to love." He held out a hand to Nino. "Thank you for… your invitation. It's very kind of you."

Nino took out a pen and wrote something on the back of one of his visiting cards. "Here," he said, handing it to Wallace. "If you're ever in the city, look me up."

Wallace read aloud: "Nino Moretti, Imports and Exports." He looked at Nino. "You really are a…."

"Businessman," Stanley smiled wryly. "Let's leave it at that."

Stanley saw Wallace to the door, then locked it for good measure. He watched his cousin drive off down the road. "It's sad." Nino came to stand behind Stanley, wrapped his arms around the younger man from behind. "He's so goddamn lonely." He bent his head and kissed the side of Stanley's neck and smiled when Stanley shivered.

Stanley turned in his arms and kissed him. "Take me to bed," he said, his voice low and urgent, his blue eyes blazing. "Take me upstairs and—"

And Stanley said that word again—that word Nino didn't think he knew.

ELI MCKENNA was way past frantic. In fact, he had left frantic several stops behind. He paced the floor of Danny Murphy's apartment, arms folded on his chest. "That's all it said: five hundred clams."

"Hm." Danny picked up the phone. "Long distance." He listened to the clicks and tried to ignore McKenna's pacing. "Guys like that won't do nothing to Delores," he said while he waited for his connection. "They're all talk. They're just in it for the money." He listened. "I want a number in Salina, Kansas. Yeah, Main 2757."

IT HAD begun to rain: a fierce, spattering cloudburst on the heels of an incoming thunderstorm. Nino lay on his back in bed, his fingers clenched in Stanley's hair, his body shuddering. He spoke constantly, a low, rumbling murmur broken at intervals by gasps. Stanley moved to lie on top of Nino, pinning his hands to the bed and riding him fiercely. Stanley's hair was in his face, his features shadowed, and he seemed to Nino like some savage, sexual stranger.

"Yes," Stanley panted, "yes, ohGod ohGod ohGod, yes—" His fingers dug painfully into Nino's shoulders and his breath was hot against Nino's neck.

He's coming, Nino thought, and he was there himself, falling over the edge, his body bent into a rictus of pleasure.

The phone rang; Stanley groaned and forced himself upright, away from Nino. "Hello?"

It was never good, Nino thought, when the phone rang in the middle of the night.

CHAPTER
EIGHT

LILAH'S was another of those tiny Italian restaurants that seemed to crop up everywhere, with checkered tablecloths, a pianola, and candles dripping slowly in Chianti bottles. There should have been people at the tables and the pianola should have been cranking out "O Sole Mio," and the waiters ought to be passing out baskets of bread and pouring ice water, but there was none of that. At this hour, the restaurant was empty, the Closed sign was in the window, and Nino was holding an ad hoc council of war with his lieutenants.

"This ain't good. Now, whoever took that girl made me cut my vacation short and come all the way back here from Kansas." Nino sat back in the chair and puffed on his cigar. "That sort of thing makes Nino angry." He had sketched a makeshift map of the office on a sheet of paper; he turned it so the rest of the boys could see it. "McKenna's in the back talking to the girl, but later on, when he goes up front, she's gone and some little gazabo's in the front door with a note."

"It was just after four o'clock," Eli said. He looked terrible: pale to the lips with dark circles under his eyes. "I ain't slept." He coughed, as if to ease his discomfort. "I keep wondering where they took Delores. I gotta get her back." He dropped his eyes, aware that he had said too much.

"You'll get her back." Stanley touched McKenna's shoulder briefly. He stood behind Nino, shoulder-to-shoulder with Danny, who looked grim, and one of Nino's chief button men, Junior "The Axe"

Spicoli, and Nino's brother Tony, fresh from an after-hours fracas at a chop suey house in Chinatown. "Nino will find her."

"I want you boys out on the street." Nino poked a finger at each of them in turn: "Vito, you and Tony go to Jake's place. If he's there, bring him here. Don't hurt the girl. Danny, you and the kid are with me." Nino stood up and shrugged into his coat.

"What about me?" McKenna started forward. "I ain't gonna sit around twiddling my thumbs! I want to help you find Delores!"

"You go back to the office," Nino said, "and stay there."

"You think I'm some kind of chump? You think I can't take it?" McKenna's hand delved into his coat—in the space of time it took to blink, Danny stepped forward and slapped him in the face and then shoved him back against the wall.

For a moment, tears stood in the rims of Eli's eyes and he looked like he was going to bawl. He took a deep, shivery breath. "I ain't yellow," he said slowly.

"Ain't nobody said you were," Danny replied quietly. "Ain't nobody said you were."

Nino picked up the phone and dialed. "Yeah, gimme Willie the Knife." A beat. "Willie—Jake took the girl, Delores. Yeah, he's gone off his nut. What's that? Five hundred clams. I want you to take Turkey Joe and Little Dopey and start checking out the warehouse district. You know the places he goes. Grab a coupla torpedoes, just in case. I don't want anybody eatin' lead over this."

"—LOUIE the Lug," Nino said. "I want him and his boys spread out on the Lower East Side. We gotta find this smack-off." He hung up, took out a handkerchief, and mopped his forehead. The night was hot and the atmosphere inside the restaurant close.

You gotta let me handle things my own way. It had been a different Nino, then, who had stroked Stanley's face and kissed him as the train sped east. *This is Nino's turf, and Nino's gotta defend it. You understand what I'm saying to you?*

I'm worried. Stanley had gone into his arms, hugged him close in the narrow Pullman bed. *I'm worried about Delores and I'm worried about you.*

Don't be worried about me. I can take care of myself, and I can take care of what's mine.

Am I yours?

Sure, kid. I picked you outta the crowd, remember?

Their bodies moved together, almost as if their joining was a reflex, and they had made love in silence, intently, pleasuring each other as if this would be the very last time.

He could get killed, Stanley thought, looking at Nino's dark expression and his intense and predatory eyes. *And so could I.* It so rarely occurred to him these days, and yet, the possibility of death was as near now as it had ever been during his time with Big Frank. Fist was dead; Nino had killed him that awful night in Judy's restaurant, had shot him at point-blank range. It could have just as easily been Stanley, and would have been, if Nino hadn't saved him—saved them both, really, because sure as shooting, Fist would have done Nino right after he'd finished doing Stanley.

Kansas seemed like a far-off daydream, something Stanley had conjured in the privacy of his mind. Perhaps he'd only imagined the swimming hole, the church picnic, and making love with Nino in the big bed that once belonged to Stanley's parents.

You sure you don't mind, kid? Nino had said, sitting on the edge of the bed, his suspenders around his hips, his shirt undone. *I don't want to disrespect your mother. I would never do that.*

My mother wouldn't mind, Stanley had thought. *She would be glad to know that someone loved me.* He remembered the expression of awe on Nino's face when he'd shown him what had been his childhood room: shelves and display cases filled with his early attempts at carving— animals and flowers and nature scenes. His father had kept them all, displaying them proudly.

My old man never gave me nothing but the back of his hand, Nino had said. *Yeah, he never said he was proud of me for nothing.* He held one of Stanley's early carvings: a charmingly childish representation of a horse, mute and clunky.

You don't want that one, Stanley had said when Nino asked if he could have it. *It isn't very good. I was just a kid when I made it.*

No, seriously, kid. Nino handled it lovingly. *This is the one I want.*

He had tucked it into Nino's suitcase the night they left Kansas.

"Alright, let's get this done. I want that mug in my office." Nino took up his hat and motioned to Stanley and Eli. They went outside where a touring sedan had been parked at the curb, the keys left inside. Nino got in and started up the car; it was the first time Stanley had ever seen Nino drive.

"Where's Danny?" he asked. "Isn't he coming with us?"

"Danny might need to do some wet work," Eli said from the backseat. His voice sounded like it was coming from down a well. Stanley turned around to look at him but half his face was in shadow. "They might need to take somebody out, quiet like." He drew a finger across his throat. "A shiv comes in real handy in a situation like that."

"You're making me nervous," Stanley said. He was suddenly glad they were leaving Eli at the office.

"I make everybody nervous." Eli looked out the window.

"And Jake says something to you after you told him about the money, right?" Nino pulled out into the street. At this hour there was very little traffic, but he drove at a steady rate of speed. It was pointless to attract police attention and get himself pulled over and possibly incarcerated for carrying a piece.

"He said I made a mistake... said he didn't have the dough. He musta seen me talking to Delores." Eli picked absently at a hangnail on his middle finger. "I shoulda fogged him."

"He riding you?" Nino glanced at him in the rear-view mirror. "That what this is about? Because if that's all it is, and you're wasting my time—"

"I ain't wastin' your time! He stole from you. I know it."

Nino said nothing. The other men were silent as Nino navigated the city's dark streets; he stopped at The Two Aces, where the night's entertainment was still in full swing. The club's front doors open to admit two girls in sparkly evening gowns, giggling and obviously the worse for wine; "Ain't We Got Fun" blared briefly into the street before the doors swung shut.

Nino turned to Eli. "Go in the back way," he said, "and wait by the phone in my office. You hear anything from that mug, you write it down. I'll check in with you every half hour."

"Okay." Eli got out of the car and stood for a moment, his hands hanging down forlornly. "I guess I'll go in and wait." He could have been going anywhere, Stanley thought: to the grocery store or to the gallows.

"Good luck," Stanley said quietly. He could think of nothing better to say. Nino pulled away from the curb, maneuvering the big sedan into traffic again. "Where are we going?" Stanley asked.

"There's an after-hours club—Jake goes there. It's a long shot."

"What are you going to do if you find him?" Stanley asked; Nino turned and stared at him.

"Whatta ya mean, what am I gonna do?" He stomped on the brakes in time to avoid a fat man steering a gaudily dressed girl across the street, yelled out the window. "Hey, watch where you're going, old man!"

"We should turn him over to the police," Stanley said.

"What?" Nino looked at him as if he'd just sprouted a second head. "You been shooting smack or something? Whatta I want with cops? I don't need no cops."

"I suppose not," Stanley said. The tight knot in his stomach was growing; he twisted his hands together in his lap and tried to breathe normally. He didn't like Nino when he was like this. Nino like this frightened him; he was no one Stanley knew, no one he wanted to know. This Nino was a killer, a man who took life without remorse because he believed it was his due. Stanley wasn't stupid: he had been with Big Frank O'Hara for five years, and when it came to the blood of his enemies, his own hands were hardly what he'd call clean. "Do you think he'll hurt Delores?"

"Naw. Jake ain't got no guts. He's all talk."

Stanley watched the light of passing streetlamps briefly illuminate Nino's features. "Did you like being in Kansas?"

"Yeah, sure, kid." Nino gestured at him. "There's a gat in the glove box there. Get it out, willya? I don't want him catchin' us flat-footed."

Stanley took out the gun, a .38, and put it in his pocket. "Do you think we'll find him tonight?"

"Sure," Nino said. "Jake's like a big, dumb dog—he always goes to the same places and does the same things." He squinted at a street sign and turned left, pulling the car smoothly in to the curb and killed the engine. "Come on," he said. "Quick and quiet. Stay behind me. Don't do nothin' 'til I tell you."

Stanley swallowed hard, trying to force back the taste of rising bile. "Okay."

Nino stopped, glanced at him. "You jake, kid?"

No, Stanley thought, *I'm not jake at all. I don't want to do this. I don't want to go in there and blow a hole in some guy.* "Yeah, sure." There was a foul taste in his mouth and his hands were shaking as bad as McKenna's. He wondered, briefly, about Eli, how Eli was faring back at the office, and wished himself there as well.

Nino knocked on the door; a smaller window opened and a man's face appeared. "That you, Nino?"

"Yeah, Manny, it's me. You gonna let me in?"

"I dunno, Nino. The boss might not like it." The eyes swerved left, lighting on Stanley. "Who's the gunsel?"

"Hey, watch your mouth!" Nino snarled. "He ain't nobody's punk, you hear me?"

"No need to get hot," Manny said. He stood back to let them in. He was tall and skinny, about Nino's age, with a pockmarked face and long, thin hands. "Kinda late for you to be in these parts, Nino. Most everybody left hours ago." He scratched his beard stubble and struck a match off the sole of his shoe. "You lookin' for someone in particular?"

"Yeah, looking for one of my boys. I been paying the boys their summer bonus and he forgot to pick his up, see?" Nino glanced past Manny into the main room of the club, which was deserted except for a blonde sitting at the bar trying not to fall asleep in her champagne cocktail. "Name of Jake—kind of a big guy, one of my drivers. You seen 'im?"

"Naw, Nino." Manny grinned around his cigarette. "We ain't seen nobody in here."

"You wouldn't lie to me, would you?" Nino moved closer, 'til he was gazing up at Manny with an expression of frank interest. "Because that'd make me real unhappy." He reached out and smoothed the placket of Manny's shirt. "When Nino gets unhappy, things start happening—all kinds of things. It might get unpleasant."

"I swear to ya, Nino, he ain't here!" Manny was visibly shaken. "I'm on the level! If I knew where he was, I'd give him to ya!"

"Can I use your phone?" Nino asked. "Just want to make a local call."

"Sure," Manny said. "It's on the bar."

"Why don't you show me?" Nino said. His gun had appeared in his hand, the muzzle pointing at Manny. "That'd be real nice of ya."

"Okay, Nino, anything you want."

They followed Manny into the bar, a dimly lit narrow space with tables set along the walls and a pianola in the corner grinding out "Ave Maria." The blonde at the bar raised her head and giggled at them, then put her head down on her folded arms and appeared to be instantly asleep.

"Get rid of the dame," Nino said. Manny hurried over to the girl and shook her, hissing at her to get up. "Put her in a cab," Nino said. Then to Stanley, "Go with him. Make sure the girl gets in a cab."

Stanley followed Manny to the door and hailed a cab for him. The driver was half-asleep, surly, and seemed the worse for drink; the girl stumbled as she got into the car and he yelled at her.

"I ain't messing with you," Manny said. "Jake ain't here. You gotta tell Nino. It's the truth. I ain't lying to him." He was clearly terrified, his eyes rolling like a frightened animal's. "I wouldn't lie to Nino. I swear. I'm on Nino's side."

"You can tell it to Nino," Stanley said. He wanted nothing to do with it. He followed Manny back inside where Nino was just hanging up the phone.

"See, what'd I tell you?" Manny said. "I'm on the level, Nino. I ain't lying to ya."

"Yeah." Nino reached behind the bar and, in one smooth, sharp movement, yanked the phone out of the wall. "That's so you can't call nobody. Can't have you giving in to temptation." He jerked his chin at Stanley. "Come on."

"Eli ain't heard nothing," he said when they were back in the car. "Jake ain't come by and nobody ain't called." Nino huffed out an irritated breath. "He can't be that far. Ain't nobody—" He stopped short—so suddenly, in fact, that Stanley was alarmed. "Of course."

The knot in Stanley's stomach twisted itself tighter. "What?"

"Nothing," Nino said. "A hunch."

THEY drove for some time in silence, passing through the Lower East Side and up Manhattan's long flank to the Bronx. Stanley watched out the window, marking street names and various landmarks just in case something happened and he had to find his way home on his own. He couldn't shake the feeling that Nino was heading into a bad situation, but he wasn't about to say anything. Nino was bossing this job; it was Nino's call. But Stanley was convinced Nino was making a huge—a colossal—mistake.

They stopped in front of a boarded-up candy store and got out. Nino lit a cigarette and leaned against the car, looking for all the world like a man completely at ease with himself and his environment. Stanley kept his hands in his pockets and his thoughts to himself; the street was narrow, dirty, and mostly deserted, but there was music coming from somewhere up above, and now and then peals of female laughter erupted from a building across the street.

"See that place?" Nino spoke quietly, feigning interest in his fingernails. "Across from the fireplug there, and up."

Stanley followed the directions with his gaze. "Yeah."

"Big Frank ever take you there?"

Stanley shook his head. "No."

"That's one of Lili Wacker's places. You heard of Lili Wacker?"

"No. I've never…. I don't know who that is."

"She's a pretty smart dame," Nino said. "One of them bulldaggers, you know?"

Stanley didn't know, but he wasn't about to say so. "Yeah?"

"Lili keeps a stable of molls there." Nino grinned. "That's probably why he didn't take you there. One look at you, and them janes'd be falling all over themselves."

The idea of molls—or any raddled, drunken whore—batting her eyes at Stanley made his skin crawl. He changed the subject. "Can I ask you something?"

"Sure, kid. Anything you like." Most of the windows sported heavy roller blinds, but Nino's eyes never left the thin gleam of light from the building opposite.

"You ever think about getting out?"

"Getting out?" Nino drew on his cigarette. "Out of where?"

"Out of the life," Stanley said. "Out of this. You know."

"Yeah, sometimes," Nino said, and hope flared—briefly—in Stanley's chest. "And then I think about living like my mother, God rest her soul. Hand to mouth, never knowing where the next meal was coming from." He shook his head. "That ain't for Nino."

"Don't you worry that—"

"What?" Nino squinted at him. "That I'll get hosed some time? Sure. I think about it all the time." He took a final drag on his cigarette and tossed it away. It bounced on the pavement and died in a shower of sparks. "I'd be lying to you if I said I didn't." He leaned closer. "You worried something's gonna happen to Nino? Is that it?"

"Look," Stanley said. "Someone's coming out."

The thin gleam of light from the building opposite widened into the crack of a door and a woman stepped through onto the sidewalk. She looked around, glancing up and down the street, then set off in the opposite direction, none too steadily.

"Well," Nino said to no one in particular, "ain't that nice. Rita's come out for some fresh air."

He set off after her at a trot, Stanley racing to catch up. When he drew level with her, Nino doffed his hat and sketched an exaggerated bow. "Rita, don't you remember your old pal anymore?"

She stopped and turned around. The woman was easily forty-five, heavily made up, and wearing the sort of clothes that would look better on someone half her age. Her hands were cluttered with cheap, gaudy rings, and several strands of fake pearls clanked and clattered around her neck. "Nino, baby!" She wobbled to him and threw her arms around his neck. "I missed you! How come you don't visit me no more?"

Stanley couldn't imagine Nino with her; it would be like stuffing his dong in a sewer.

"Aw, Nino ain't got time these days! Nino's a very busy boy." Nino took hold of her hand, caressing her red-tipped talons. "You know Nino'd be over to see you if he could."

They walked with her for a time, Nino flattering her and deftly avoiding her reaching, rubbing hands while he questioned her about Jake's whereabouts and if Jake had entertained any new—or old—friends lately.

"You wanna know about that big dumb palooka, dontcha?" Rita stopped in front of Nino, teetering in her high heels. "He keeps coming around. Tried to touch me and I gave him what for."

I'll just bet you did. Stanley grimaced. *Down on your knees with your can in the air.*

"You seen him lately?" Nino asked. "Because if he's been bothering you, Nino wants to know. I'll take care of that big mug for you."

It occurred to Stanley that nobody, including Rita, could be that stupid.

"Oh yeah," Rita caroled, "he was here tonight! Lying on the couch like he owned the place!"

Dear God, Stanley thought, *is she even a nitwit?*

"Yeah? Just laying there and dishing it out, huh?" Nino leaned closer and caressed her cheek. "Did he say anything nasty to you, baby? You can tell Nino anything, you know that. Anything at all."

"THAT'S all he said." Eli handed a slip of paper to Danny.

"You tell Nino?"

"He ain't checked in since Manny's place."

"Hm." Danny laid the piece of paper against his lips. "And nobody else called?"

"No. Look, are you guys gonna find Delores before it's too late? I don't get you guys, all this running around. How is this doing any good?"

"You're an educated guy," Danny said. "Right?"

"Sure," Eli replied. "What's that got to do—"

"Stick your nose in one of them books of yours and keep it there 'til Nino calls," Danny said, making for the door.

"Where are you going?"

"To check this out." Danny waved the slip of paper at him. "See if it's anything, or if it's nothing."

"AND that's where he said he was going?" Nino asked her. Rita was leaning heavily on his arm, giggling up into his face like a schoolgirl with a crush.

"Are you sure?" Nino asked.

"Sure I'm sure!" Rita ran her fingers up his arm, then squeezed his bicep. "Mmm," she said. "Such a muscle!"

"None of that, now." Nino disengaged her arm. "Nino's got business. You run along like a good girl."

"Aw, Nino." She made a face. "You don't love me no more." She glanced at Stanley. "What about this one? He looks like he might like to have a good time with a girl who knows her stuff...." Her gaze traveled up Stanley's body, stopping at all the obvious places.

"He's with me," Nino said. He took out his billfold, counted out a hundred dollars in twenties, and shoved it into her hand. "Here. Go buy yourself something nice."

"Aw, you're so good to me, Nino!" She stuffed the bills between her sagging breasts and teetered away down the street.

Nino watched her go with an expression of profound distaste. "Did you hear what that hag said?"

"Yeah." Stanley nodded as Rita passed a clothing store, staggering a little as she turned the corner. "So he was lying."

"I think we should pay him a call," Nino said. "Maybe some of the boys got the same idea. You never know. I just feel lucky about this one."

Yeah, Stanley thought, *that's just what I feel: lucky.*

DANNY and Louie the Lug were already there, standing around smoking on the sidewalk, when Nino and Stanley pulled up in front of Manny's speakeasy. Tony hopped out of a car that had been parked on the corner with Vito close behind him.

"We do this my way," Nino said. "We're going in and he's gonna tell us where that lug is. First thing we do is get the girl. Tony, when we get her, you take her home, make sure she's safe."

Nino's brother nodded. "You got it, Nino."

"—Tony, Vito, and Danny, with me. Louie, I want you and the rest of the boys outside. He might give us some trouble, and I'm betting he's got a coupla guys in there." Nino's guts were full of lead: he'd done this more times than he could reasonably count. Why was it bothering him? Was he getting yellow in his old age? He went up to the door and knocked.

"Nino!" Manny's face appeared in the slot. "You're back! Come in, my friend! Come right in!"

Nino pushed past him and walked through to the bar. "Where is he?"

"Nino, I told you—" Manny stopped in midsentence as Nino's gun came up and leveled itself on the middle of his forehead.

"No more lies, mug." Nino nodded toward the end of the bar. "Where is he? And the girl. And she better not be hurt."

"Okay." Manny led them through a hidden door at the far end of the bar and into a separate room; Jake was sitting at a scuffed deal table with a scrawny youth known to Nino and the others as Nuts Mahoney. When he saw Nino, Nuts leapt to his feet and reached for his gun, but was too slow.

"None of that," Nino said, "or I'll blow a hole in you, see." He grinned at Jake, a nasty smile with nothing friendly in it. "Two-timing me, Jake? That's pretty dumb, even for you. And then you take the girl." He gestured at Nuts Mahoney. "I know you got a back room here. I been here before. Now go in and get her. She better be okay."

Delores emerged from the other room, blinking sleepily and obviously unhurt. She gasped when she saw Nino and rushed toward him. "Oh, Mr. Nino! What are you doing here?"

Nino ushered the girl toward Tony on the other side of the room.

"We came to get you," Nino said. "Are you okay?" He spoke to Delores over his shoulder. "Anybody hurt you, honey?"

"No, Mr. M. I'm fine." But she shuddered against Tony's side like a leaf in a sudden storm. Nino jerked his chin at Tony. "Take her home, huh? I want her to go with someone I can trust."

"You got it, Nino." Tony shrugged out of his overcoat and draped it around the girl's shoulders. He guided her out the door to the waiting car.

"That's good," Nino said. "Danny." His bodyguard came to stand behind Manny, arms dangling at his sides. "You lied to me, Manny. I came here tonight, came to you in friendship. I didn't ask you for nothing, just a little information. And you lied to me. That hurts Nino's feelings."

"I'm s-sorry," Manny stuttered. "It won't happen no more."

"No," Nino said quietly. "No, you ain't gonna do that no more."

Danny had a knife; he took it out of his sleeve and held it delicately between finger and thumb. He took hold of Manny's chin and tilted his head back, like a barber preparing to give another man a shave, and Nino remembered that was Danny's nickname, Danny the

Barber, only he'd forgotten it until just now, and why was he remembering things like this? Why was he— Nino spoke: "Okay, Danny."

Danny's hand moved, soft and smooth and slow—a man drawing the bow across a violin—and hot blood spurted out of the wound in Manny's throat, driven by the hard pulse of his terrified heart. A jet of dark-red liquid lurched through space and splattered, thickly wet and horrible, against Louie's coat. Nino barked some orders, and Danny was stepping over Manny's body, and Louie the Lug had Nuts Mahoney by the back of the neck and was dragging him out the door, while two of Nino's boys frog-marched Jake between them.

"You know what to do," Nino said. "You know where to do it." He took out his handkerchief and wiped a little of Manny's blood from his face. "I don't want no mistakes."

CHAPTER
NINE

THE room was white, and the ceiling was white, and his bed was white as well. He lay immobile, arms pinned to his sides, and he was crying. He had been crying now for years, and he had to keep on crying because that was the only thing that would help. Nothing else would do except the sacrifice of Stanley's tears.

"Shhhh, baby… don't cry. Don't cry." A man's face loomed over him: dark hair, kindly dark eyes, and a familiar smile. "Don't cry, sweetheart. Nino's here. Nino loves you." The man stroked his face. "You want something to eat? Huh?"

Blood, Stanley thought, there was too much blood on Nino's hands. Maybe Nino shouldn't touch him with those hands; there was so much blood. He blinked himself into existence. "Your clothes," he said. His voice sounded strange and hoarse. "Burn your clothes."

"Don't you worry nothing about that," Nino said. He reached for Stanley but the younger man jerked away.

"Don't touch me," Stanley whispered.

"Okay, baby, whatever makes you happy." It was daylight; Nino was dressed except for his jacket. "I'm just going over to the club to see how things are going. Delores here is gonna stay with you."

Delores stepped into sight, bright-eyed and pretty, dressed in a frothy pink blouse and a heather tweed skirt, her dark curls confined by a pink velvet ribbon. "Hiya, Mr. Z. I'm gonna take good care of ya while Mr. Nino's at work."

"Oh," Stanley breathed, "you're alright."

"Aw, I sure am, Mr. Z. Thanks to you and Mr. Nino." She adjusted his covers. "You feel hungry? You want a cuppa coffee or a shave or something? Get you a warm glass of Horlicks?"

Stanley scratched his stubble. "I could use a shave," he admitted, "but I could probably do it myself if I had a basin and a mirror." He felt as weak as a newborn kitten. "How long have I been asleep?"

"You slept for a while, Mr. Z." Delores helped him sit up and adjusted the pillow behind his back. "I'm gonna go get some hot water and then we'll get you all shaved and cleaned up."

"What... what happened?" Stanley couldn't look at Nino; he concentrated on pleating the edge of the sheet between his fingers. "You guys got Manny, didn't you." It wasn't a question.

"Yeah." Nino frowned. "We had to croak Manny." He shrugged. "But don't you worry none about that, okay? That's for me to take care of." He laid a hand on Stanley's wrist. "You're gonna be okay. I got Eli coming over later. He'll make sure you're oke."

Stanley slid his hand out from under Nino's and suppressed a shudder. "Thanks."

Nino was looking at him queerly. "Yeah, I'll see you later, kid."

Stanley hugged himself and shivered. So much blood. The whole time he had been asleep, his dreams had been full of blood, and he tried to wash it off, but it wouldn't come out. He supposed that was symbolic, and maybe some doctor with a head full of psychiatry would tell him he needed to relax, but that wasn't what Stanley needed. "I should have stayed in Kansas."

"What's that, Mr. Z?" Delores positioned a lap desk across Stanley's middle and laid a basin of steaming water on it, along with his razor and soap. "You want some help?"

"You could hold the mirror," he said. The first sight of his own face astonished him: he looked like a man who'd risen from the dead. Even his lips were pale, and the dark circles around his eyes looked like they'd been hammered into his skin. He stropped the razor and soaped his face, but his hands were shaking so much he was afraid he'd cut his own throat.

"Here," a different voice said—Eli McKenna. "Let me do that."

Stanley was inordinately glad to see him, and told him so. For some reason, the sight of McKenna nearly made him weep. He wanted to throw his arms around the other man and hug him.

"Quite a show the other night at Manny's," Eli said. He dipped the razor in hot water and cut a long, precise swath through the soap. "Too bad you missed it."

"Yeah," Stanley said. "I heard about it."

"You betcha Big Frank ain't gonna take this lying down. Manny was one of his boys."

"War?" It came out as a strangled gasp. Stanley cleared his throat. "It's gonna be war, isn't it?"

"Looks that way." Eli gazed at him for several long moments. "I don't get you," he said. "I don't get you at all."

"What?"

"What's a guy like you doing, involved in the rackets? You should be teaching Sunday school or something." He tilted Stanley's head to the side. "I don't get why you're even here." He dipped the razor, then stroked it along Stanley's face.

"Life's funny." Stanley suppressed a shudder. "I don't really remember how I got here—to New York, I mean." It seemed so long ago, before his apprenticeship with Big Frank, before Nino and all the rest of it.

"Kinda surprised you didn't want to be there." Eli's touch was that of a professional, and Stanley found himself wondering whether the gangster had ever attempted the tonsorial trade. "Nino usually insists. It's a thing with him."

"I have fits."

"My uncle used to have fits. He'd fall down on the floor and everything. It was pretty scary. Nothing you can do about them, of course." Eli wiped the razor and handed Stanley a towel. "Bet that feels better."

"Thank you." Stanley rubbed a hand against his skin. "It does. Thank you." Something occurred to him. "They didn't... do anything to Delores, did they?"

"Nope. Just stuck her in another room and told her to shut up. Manny slapped her around a bit, but he didn't hurt her." Eli gazed at him. "You're trying to balance it out, ain't ya?"

"Balance it out?"

"Trying to make it okay, what happened to Manny—what happened to Jake and Nuts Mahoney." Eli took the lap desk away, laying it on a table by the door. "Nino and Danny killed Manny. The boys took Jake and Mahoney for a ride. You're trying to"—he made a balancing motion with his hands—"make it come out right."

"I guess I am."

Eli shook his head. "Don't."

"What?"

"Don't do it. Don't spend your time trying to figure out if the ones who got whacked deserved it. Don't drive yourself crazy adding it all up." He hovered near Stanley's bed for a moment. "Leave it be. Stuff like that ain't for you to worry about."

NINO had spared no expense in decorating The Two Aces for a party: Delores and Billie, Danny Murphy's latest girl, had gone over earlier in the day to supervise the hanging of streamers and the spreading about of balloons, and to direct the seemingly endless supply of food and drink that came through the service entrance. By ten that evening, the party was well underway, and everybody—including Delores—was having a great time.

"Aw, Mr. M, you ain't gotta do all this for me," Delores had said. She leaned in and kissed Nino on the cheek. "So I got myself kidnapped. It ain't no big deal." Delores was as pretty as always, and tonight saw her dressed in a short, sequined number festooned at strategic places with floating bits of marabou. Her brunette curls were pinned up and she wore a fresh gardenia in her hair.

"No big deal, she says." Danny faked a punch at Delores's jaw. "We call out the entire mob to find her, but she thinks it ain't no big deal. Why, I oughta—"

Delores winked at Billie. "Real pussycat, ain't he?"

Billie grinned. "Oh he's alright—now that he's been tamed." Billie was as resplendent as Delores, but where Delores' dress was pink, Billie's was a deep, gas blue with shimmering beads on the bodice. She clung to Danny's arm as if he might vanish any moment in a puff of smoke.

"You deserve it, baby." Nino returned the kiss. "No way I was gonna let Big Frank take something of mine." He glanced over the heads of several dozen revelers. "Where's Stanley?"

"Aw, he went to the Gents'," Danny said. "You want me to go in there and get him?"

"Excuse me, Mr. Moretti." A tall young man appeared at Nino's elbow. He was perhaps a year or two older than Stanley, with wavy dark hair and laughing blue eyes and a handsome, vaguely triangular face. Like the other men, he was dressed in a tuxedo with the requisite black tie, but unlike Nino and Danny, he carried a napkin over one arm.

"Ah, Richard! How's tricks, baby?" Nino grinned and clapped him on the shoulder.

"Wonderful. I couldn't complain if I tried."

Nino introduced him to the group. "Ladies and gentlemen, this is Richard Kelly. Richard manages the joint for me, makes sure everything is jake around here. I'd be lost without him."

"I'm sure Mr. Moretti exaggerates just a bit," Richard said. "Mr. Moretti, the champagne you ordered earlier—shall I bring it to your table, or would you prefer to wait?"

"Ain't he something?" Nino asked, "Always lookin' out for me. Come on, boys and girls—the good stuff's this way." He led his party past the bandstand to a table set against the wall. Like most men of his profession, Nino preferred always to sit with his back to the wall and a full view of the front door. "Sit down, sit down, plenty of room for everybody." Nino pulled out a chair as McKenna appeared, swallowing nervously and touching his tie. "You alright, McKenna? You look like you swallowed an elephant."

"Oh, I'm oke," McKenna replied. He sat down next to Delores and laid an arm across the back of her chair. "Just taking a look around the place."

Danny bristled slightly. "You don't need to do that. I told ya, I done that already."

"No rule against making sure, is there?"

"Why don't you mugs button up?" Nino looked up as Richard appeared with the bottle of champagne. "Ahhh, yeah, that's the stuff. This didn't come from nobody's bathtub, that's for sure. Nothing but the best for Nino." He glanced around. "Say, where's Stanley?" he asked, again. "Anybody seen Stanley?"

"I believe he's in the restroom," Richard said quietly. The words were intended for Nino's ears alone. "He's been in there for some time."

Nino frowned. "Yeah?"

"Yes, sir."

"Huh." What was he doing hiding in the bathroom? Stanley had been perfectly fine earlier that evening while they'd gotten dressed at home, chatting amiably with Nino, asking for opinions on his outfit, cufflinks, and tiepin: *The emerald or the diamond? What a choice! I never saw this in Kansas!* Stanley had his own room in Nino's apartment, but the two had shared a bed for a while now, ever since they'd first become intimate; Stanley still slept with Nino, but when Nino reached for him early that morning, Stanley had rebuffed him.

I'm tired.

Okay. Nino had sought to hide his disappointment in his usual cheerful bluster. *That's jake with me, kid.*

But it wasn't, not really. Why was Stanley suddenly so strange around him? Why was he refusing Nino's lovemaking? His smiles seemed brittle and he was forever on the edge of tears or anger, his moods flashing restlessly from one distraught state to the next. They'd driven to The Two Aces together in Nino's car, but Stanley had hovered near the bar for most of the evening, offering only the most perfunctory of greetings to anyone who spoke to him. Danny said Stanley had seemed morose and depressed, and when Delores reached in to hug him, he'd fled to the men's room and stayed for twenty minutes or more. When he finally emerged his clothes were disheveled, his eyes red from weeping.

"Are you okay, baby?" Nino took him aside quietly and offered him a handkerchief. "If you ain't feelin' well, we can go home. I'll take you home if you want."

"I'm fine."

No, Nino thought, *you're not. You're not fine at all. There's something really wrong and I can't help you because you won't tell me.*

And now Stanley had disappeared again.

"Richard." Nino spoke confidentially to the manager. "Could you have a look in the Gents'? I think Mr. Zadwadzki is sick or something."

"Of course." Richard laid the bottle of champagne in the ice bucket. "I'll be back directly." He bowed to the ladies and vanished into the milling throng.

"Something wrong with the kid?" Danny asked.

"I dunno." Nino sipped his champagne. "Hey, that's good stuff! Nothing like that fizz-water, huh? Drink up!"

"Did he say anything to you? Is he sick, or...?"

"Naw. He's not... he ain't been himself lately." Nino pulled out his watch and squinted at it. "Say, where the hell is Tony? He shoulda been here by now!"

He's starting to leave you, his mind whispered. *Stanley's leaving you, like everybody leaves you.*

RICHARD KELLY was the soul of consideration and a gentleman to the tips of his fingers—which was why Nino had hired him in the first place. Nino had wanted someone who was not only a capable manager, but who could, upon seeing a problem, know immediately how to deal with it in a private manner, without attracting attention. Richard kept an eye on everything that went on in The Two Aces, from the number of drinks the bartender mixed over the course of an evening, to how long certain gentlemen spent chatting up the hat check girls. A certain amount of chat was necessary, Richard knew—he was the product of a very old Connecticut family, and certain cultural subtleties ran freely in his blood—but too much chat might well border on harassment, and that was something Nino wouldn't stand for. "They ain't whores, these girls. I ain't hired 'em to be chippies. Make sure none of these mugs bother 'em, see?" And Richard knew to have Nino's favorite champagne chilling when his boss was expected—a very fine Bollinger, imported especially for Nino and his friends—and to wait upon Nino's every need with the utmost skill and courtesy.

Richard was the perfect gentleman's gentleman, with a mind for business and a sparkling wit. Everyone liked him and he liked everyone—indeed, he had no need to dislike anyone. Nino paid him well; he liked his job and got along with the other employees and the patrons equally. He was a sort of father figure to the younger waiters and a big brother to the girls, and with Richard on the premises, The Two Aces ran like the proverbial well-oiled machine, and if Mr. Richard's private life was the topic of much backroom speculation, well... nobody would dare utter the word "fairy" in his presence, much less to his face. Everyone remembered the New Year's Eve when three toughs had decided to take exception to an older homosexual couple at the bar. Mr. Richard had thrown them out like so much trash.

IT WAS safe in here and so much quieter than outside, Stanley reflected. He could sit and think, or at least sit and wait for his anguished heart to stop thumping in his chest. He wasn't actually sitting, not at the moment; right now he was leaning over the wash basin, gazing at himself in the mirror. He looked awful. It was obvious to anyone with any sense at all that he'd spent the evening crying, closeted away in here all by himself.

You have to straighten up, he told himself. *Pull yourself together and go out there. You're making a fool of yourself. You're making a fool out of Nino.* But ever since Nino's boys did Manny, Stanley had stayed as far away as possible.

He straightened as the bathroom door opened, reached reflexively inside his jacket.

"Whoa." Richard Kelly raised his hands to shoulder height. "I won't shoot if you don't."

Stanley laughed in spite of himself. "Sorry, I'm sorry.... I thought—"

"Yeah, I get that a lot." Richard dusted down the napkin he carried across his arm. "I guess I just look like a wholesale dealer of death."

Stanley laughed—then abruptly burst into noisy tears. He bowed his head over the wash basin and cried and cried. "I'm sorry," he choked out. "I'm so sorry. I don't usually do this."

"It's alright." Richard offered him a handkerchief. "I'd give you the napkin but it's probably got butter on it." He waited while Stanley wiped his eyes. "What would be ideal about now is a shot of brandy." He reached into his hip pocket. "Fortunately, I come equipped for every eventuality." He offered the flask to Stanley, who took a healthy slug.

"Thank you," Stanley said, choking a little on the strong drink. "I'm sorry to have been such a bother."

Richard gazed at him for a moment, his whole manner concerned and kindly. "You're Mr. Moretti's accountant, aren't you? You work in the office."

"Yeah, that's me."

Richard grinned. "Don't be so excited. You're making me nervous."

Stanley managed a smile. "I'm sorry—"

"You just said that," Richard interjected. He glanced around the room. "This is hardly the place for a civil discussion. Why don't we take a walk outside? I bet you could use some fresh air about now."

Stanley followed Richard out of the men's room and through the kitchen, where three Oriental chefs were chopping vegetables with wicked-looking knives and loudly arguing with one another in some unknown language. Richard led him around the side of the club and into a little walled garden which the building's original owner had had installed for the pleasure of his little daughter.

"She died of tuberculosis," Richard said. He gently touched a small brass plaque that was set into the wall. "Or consumption, as they used to call it in those days. It's very peaceful here." He took out a cigarette case. "Smoke?"

"Thank you." Stanley waited while Richard lit it for him. "How come I haven't seen you before?"

"You work in the office during the day. I work in the club at night." Richard took a drag and grinned. "Never the twain shall meet."

"I'm sorry I made a fool of myself back there." He'd actually broken down in front of a complete stranger. It was inconceivable.

"Come on—let's sit down." Richard led him to a small stone bench set against a wall. A veritable forest of willows grew around it and slender beeches formed a sort of natural gazebo. "Your name is Stanley, isn't it?"

"Stanley Zadwadzki—forgive me. I seem to have forgotten my manners." He offered his hand to Richard.

"Richard Kelly. So why so sad, Stanley Zadw—" Richard looked so utterly puzzled that Stanley couldn't help but laugh.

"Zadwadzkee," he said. "It takes some practice. And, a certain amount of Polish blood, or so I'm told."

"Are you Polish, Stanley Zadwadzki?" Richard asked. "Is that where you get those beautiful eyes?"

Somewhere inside the club, the band was playing; the music filtered gently into the garden, and everything seemed surreal and faraway. They might have been on some other planet, Stanley thought, and suddenly the stars were very near.

"You're actually blushing," Richard said. "It's been ages since I've seen that. Here I thought it had gone out of fashion." He leaned closer. "Why are you always apologizing, beautiful Polish Stanley?" He took his handkerchief and very gently cleaned the last traces of Stanley's tears from his cheeks. "Have you done something bad?"

Stanley shook his head. "Not exactly."

Richard pressed the silk handkerchief into his hand. "I'm thinking you might need this, Stanley. But I'm hoping you don't. I think you've cried too much already." Richard made as if to say something else, but shook his head. "We should go back inside. I suppose—" He reached out and touched Stanley's cheek. "You are so beautiful," he said, "and I wish I knew why you're so unhappy."

Stanley laughed mirthlessly. "I wish I knew that, myself."

"You're lying," Richard said quietly. "You know exactly why you're unhappy… but you don't feel you have the right to be sad. But you are sad—and a little bit angry, I think, Polish Stanley."

"Are you always going to call me Polish Stanley?"

Richard winked. "It can be our little secret. I was just thinking, the other day—" He was interrupted by the sound of a car door slamming out front, and men shouting, and running feet.

The short hairs on the back of Stanley's neck bristled and he reached instinctively for his gun. "Are they in the club?"

"I think so." Richard stepped aside to let him pass.

The inside of The Two Aces was a study in chaos: the band had scattered, leaving overturned instruments in their wake; Nino was standing on a chair shouting instructions to the boys; and Delores and Billie had taken shelter in a booth with some of the other women and were clinging to each other. Danny intercepted Stanley as he came in the door. "Where the hell have you been?"

"I w-went outside for a—"

"Give it to me later." Danny's hand was on his pocket, no doubt resting on his gun. McKenna had taken up position next to Nino, and Tony was behind him. Louie the Lug and Big Johnny, two of Nino's lesser soldiers, were stationed at the entrances.

"You mighta got in," Nino shouted, "but you mugs ain't gettin' out." Nino was red-faced and furious; he had obviously been in a scuffle, because his dark hair had fallen over his forehead and someone had torn off the top two buttons of his shirt. "Not unless you shoot your way out. And these boys of mine are ready to let ya have it, soon's I say the word."

"Well, that's why we came here, Nino." Big Frank O'Hara's bulky presence was unmistakable—he seemed to take up half the room. He swung his big body forward, and immediately Danny and Eli closed ranks around Nino.

"Get down off that goddamned chair," Danny hissed at Nino, *sotto voce*. "You tryin' to be a target?" He grabbed hold of Nino's sleeve, supporting him as Nino climbed down.

"You got something of mine, Nino." Big Frank's blubbery lips closed around his cigar, and Stanley shuddered, remembering.

You get down on your goddamned knees and give it to me like you mean it!

Big Frank pointed at Stanley. "The gunsel's mine," he said. "I told you before and I'm telling you now."

"You better keep away from him." McKenna's finger moved to lie on the trigger of his .38. "Something might happen to you. You might get hurt."

Big Frank nodded at Stanley. "Why don't you come on back where you belong, you whore?"

Eli's knuckles were white. Obviously he was struggling to control himself. "He ain't your whore," he said. "Keep riding him and you'll be spitting out lead."

"You ain't got no business here," Nino said. He walked up to Big Frank and stared at him, his dark eyes blazing. "You got business with me, we do things business-like. You don't come in here with your heavies and start breaking up the joint." He poked his thumb into Big Frank's chest; the fat man slapped his hand away.

"This is your last warning, mug." Big Frank sucked on his cigar and blew a plume of smoke into Nino's face. "From now on it's war. You been moving in on me, Nino. You're getting too big for your boots. It's time you learned what's what in this business."

"Is that right?" Nino sneered. "Who told ya that? That dumb yap, Ameche?" Giorgiano "Fingers" Ameche was a small-time hood and a friend of Big Frank's; underworld buzz had it that he was itching to move up in the world. Big Frank was encouraging him to start by horning in on Nino's piece of the action. "You give him a message for me."

Suddenly something flashed silver in Nino's hand, and Big Frank backed away, roaring like a wounded elephant. The tip of Big Frank's nose was gone; blood fountained down onto his white shirt front and through the fingers of his hands, held closely clasped over his injury. He waved at his boys and they backed away. "This ain't the time or the place, Nino, but I'll make sure you get yours." Big Frank's voluminous white handkerchief was insufficient to stem the flow of blood. "You and everybody close to you's gonna pay."

CHAPTER
TEN

NINO raged around the apartment, stalking up and down, heedlessly passing in front of the opened windows, oblivious to Big Frank's blood on his clothes. Stanley sat slumped in the easy chair, Danny standing behind him, fists dangling at his sides. The radio played softly, a song nobody knew.

"I shoulda cut off his goddamn head." Nino stopped, gestured at Danny. "Never mind his nose. I shoulda cut off his head."

"You shoulda climbed down off that goddamn chair and used your brains," Danny said, "instead of shooting off your mouth. What the hell were you thinking?" He unbuttoned his jacket and loosened his tie. "And now it's gonna be war. You know this is gonna be ugly, Nino. Why'd you have to—" He rubbed his forehead. "You shoulda waited. You shoulda waited 'til it was time. We could have planned it out, me and you and the boys, but no. You had to go and shoot off your big mouth!"

"Don't be ridin' me!" Nino snapped. His hand strayed to the knot of his tie. "I ain't gonna let Big Frank come into my club and try and stick me up!"

"It doesn't matter now," Stanley said, dully. Both men looked at him. "It doesn't matter now," he repeated. "Either way, it's gonna be war."

Danny pulled out his watch and looked at it. "I gotta go check on Billie. She doesn't know what the hell is going on."

"Yeah, you do that," Nino said.

Danny's expression hardened. "Don't, Nino. You ain't got no cause."

Nino waved in his direction. "Yeah, yeah. Go see about your jane."

"I'll check in with you later." Danny nodded at Stanley. "You gonna be okay, kid?"

"Fine," Stanley replied. His face felt numb, as if his entire head were encased in glass. He didn't want Danny to leave him here with Nino. He didn't want to be where Nino was.

"Well, that's that," Nino said when the door closed behind Danny. "I can see why he's sore." He rubbed tired eyes. "It's gotta come down to this. It was gonna, sooner or later, be me and Frank. And after Manny...." He slumped onto the couch and dropped his head into his hands. "It's gotta be done," he repeated.

Stanley watched him for a few moments. Nino was bent so far forward that the back of his neck showed above the collar of his shirt. It looked vulnerable, exposed. He went and sat beside Nino and laid his arm across Nino's shoulders. "I think a lot of this is my fault."

"No." Nino shook his head but didn't look up. "No, this has been brewing for a long time."

Stanley caressed the nape of Nino's neck, sifting his fingers through the other man's dark hair. "You're tired," he said. He leaned his cheek against Nino's shoulder and reflected on how all his desire for Nino had drained away, leaving nothing in its wake but a vague fondness. "How about a bath?"

"Mmm. Probably just take a shower and go to bed." Nino sat up and glanced down at his clothes. "Might as well throw these out." His shirt and waistcoat were spattered with Frank's blood; Nino sighed heavily. "Why the hell do you put up with me, kid?"

Stanley didn't answer. "I think I'll go to bed," he said. He felt a hundred years old; it seemed like eons had passed since he'd gotten up that morning. He passed Nino's bedroom door and stopped. "Would you mind if I slept alone tonight?" He deliberately kept his voice light. "I just... because the weather's so hot... you know, outside."

Nino gazed at him, and his look was unfathomable. "If that's what you want."

Stanley started forward.

"Stanley."

"Yes?" His heart paused, then made an anguished leap in his chest. "What is it?"

"You okay?"

"I'm fine." The lie came easy to him; he didn't even have to think about it. "I'm fine, Nino."

"Okay."

NINO went into the bathroom and stripped off his soiled clothes. He gazed at himself in the mirror. He looked haggard, empty, a man whose options had entirely run out. He saw Big Frank O'Hara whenever he closed his eyes: Big Frank, roaring like a wounded bull as blood splattered down onto his white shirt front. Big Frank's blood and Manny's blood, and still more blood, a red river running through the whole of Nino's life like an evil thread. *Do you ever think of getting out?* Stanley had asked. Out where? Where would Nino go? His life was the mob; you didn't go back on a gang. The idea of doing it—of doing anything at all—made him extremely tired.

He opened the medicine cabinet and took out a bottle of aspirin, read the label, and swallowed a handful with some rusty-tasting water from the bathroom tap. He peered in his short-sighted way at the label again, and swallowed another handful for good measure. Then he ran the shower cold and stood under it, letting the chilly water pelt down on his head and neck. There was a knot in his gut the size of a fist; the world had tilted the wrong side up and was sliding away from him, or he was sliding off it. He was sliding away.

He hit the bathtub hard as he fell, thumping his knees against the cold porcelain; his forehead slammed into the ledge. His surprised gasp drew in a mouthful of water and he choked, sputtering and struggling to breathe. "Stan—"

Hands under his armpits, hands pulling him upright. Stanley's long arm reached out and turned off the tap and then wiped Nino's wet hair away from his forehead. "What happened?"

"Slipped." He was numb. He tried to stand, tried to climb out of the tub, but he couldn't seem to find his feet. He sank down onto the floor and huddled there, arms wrapped around himself. "I'm so tired," he muttered. "Just want to sleep." He tried to lie down but the kid wouldn't let him. The kid had his hands around Nino's upper arms and was pulling him. The kid was making him walk. "I just want to sleep."

"How many did you take?" Stanley had the bottle in his hand, shaking it in Nino's face. "Huh? How many aspirin did you take, Nino?"

"Dunno." His eyes focused on Stanley, but barely; already his words were becoming slurred. "Couple handfuls."

"A couple handfuls?" Stanley's fingers tightened on his arm, hurting him. "What the hell did you think you were doing?"

"I never do what he tells me." Nino staggered a little as he and Stanley turned the corner into the living room. "That's why he hates me." *Why don't you do what I tell you to, you stupid little shit? Why're you always talking back to me, huh?* His father towered over him, over him and Tony and Ray, and Nino was trying to keep the old man off them, keep the old man from hurting Ray and Tony. *You wanna be the big man, huh? Is that what you want?* His father had gone to the cupboard and brought out his .38, had loaded it and laid it in Nino's ten-year-old hand. *You wanna be the big man? Yeah, you be the big man, Nino! Go ahead!*

His father had knelt on the floor in front of him. His father had crept forward until he and Nino were eye to eye, until the barrel of the .38 was pointing at his own forehead. He leaned in, leaned in close so the mouth of the gun pressed against his skin. *Go on, big man. Pull the trigger.*

No, I don't want to. Don't make me. No, Pop, I swear, I'll be good. I'll be good from now on!

Go on, shoot your old man! That's what you want, ain't it? Pull the trigger, why don't you? Are you afraid? Hard slaps, falling on the sides of his head, rattling his teeth. *Are you afraid, you fucking little pussy?*

"I just want to rest," Nino whispered. "Don't let him hurt Ray and Tony. I gotta keep it together. I gotta be the man."

"How about we walk a little bit more?" Stanley asked. "Just a few more. Just walk around a bit more, me and you."

"I won't do it no more," Nino said. "I promise. Honest. I'll be good from now on."

"I know," Stanley said. "You'll be good."

"I just wanna rest," Nino said. He made to go into the bedroom but Stanley stopped him and steered him back toward the corridor.

"Let's walk a bit more," Stanley said. He held Nino up, one arm around the other man's waist.

"No, I don't wanna walk. I wanna go to sleep," Nino said. "Just let me lie down somewhere.... I gotta get somewhere I can lie down."

Stanley walked him until daylight was showing through the windows. Nino was hoarse from talking, and by the time he finally fell silent, Stanley had his entire life's history, including the way Nino expected it to end.

"They'll fry me," Nino said. "You can bet on it. I'll end up on the hotsquat, just like all these other mugs. Just you wait and see."

"Come on." Stanley walked Nino into the bedroom and pulled the covers down, then helped Nino into bed.

"You're so good to me," Nino said. "So much better than I deserve." He reached out for Stanley and embraced him.

"Go to sleep," Stanley whispered, smoothing the covers over Nino's bare chest. "You need to rest."

STANLEY was sitting in the easy chair, sipping at a glass of whiskey, when he heard a tentative knock at the door. He switched off the radio and reached for his gun, tiptoed to the door, and peered out through the fisheye.

Dear God.

"Stanley. Thank God. I didn't know if you'd be home, I—" Wallace Zadwadzki looked distinctly out of place, standing on the doorstep of Nino's New York townhouse. "He said to come. Nino said—"

"You better come in." Stanley held open the door. "Hurry up. This isn't a good time to be standing around on doorsteps."

Wallace had one suitcase, a rather battered-looking valise Stanley suspected had belonged to some Zadwadzki ancestor down on his luck. "Why? What's going on?"

"Nino cut off the top of Big Frank's nose."

Wallace gaped. "He cut off—who's Big Frank?—where's Nino?"

"He's sleeping. He's... not feeling well." Stanley wished violently for a steadier personality—someone like Richard Kelly—who could step in and lend a hand. All he needed right now was a bitchy flit like Wallace gumming up the works.

"Wh—d-did he get—gassed?" Wallace laid his suitcase down and gazed, blinking, around Nino's home. "I read about that in a book." He moved to open his case. "I got it right here." He extracted a copy of Burnett's *Little Caesar*. "He dies in the end."

"You probably mean, did he get fogged," Stanley replied, "and no, he didn't. He just.... I'll explain later." He looked Wallace up and down. "Burnett, huh? I heard it's good. Are you hungry?"

"I ate on the train," Wallace replied. "Hey, you don't look so good yourself...."

"We were at The Two Aces earlier. There was... an incident."

I was in Kansas, Stanley thought wistfully, *skinny-dipping in the swimming hole, going to church picnics, and making love in the rain.*

"What sort of an incident?" Wallace hissed.

"Keep your voice down," Stanley said. "Nino is trying to rest." He took Wallace by the elbow and steered him into the kitchen. "Nino and Big Frank threw the gloves down." He hunted under the sink for the percolator, filled it with coffee from the canister, and set it on the stove to heat. "Nino got mad and... cut off the tip of Frank's nose."

"He cut off the tip of his nose."

"Right there in the club."

Wallace made as if to say something, then changed his mind. "Nino's a...."

"...businessman," Stanley said.

"You were never a very good liar, you know." Wallace's tone was withering. "Just like the time Aunt Marjorie had an apple pie cooling on the windowsill and you decided she wouldn't notice if you just stuck your finger in...." He grinned. "It was still hot and you burned yourself. And then you told Aunt Marjorie that Joey Pitcher had caught your hand on fire."

Stanley fought in vain against a smile. "She gave me such a walloping," he remembered. He was suddenly very, very glad to see his cousin; he reached out and embraced Wallace, hugging him tight. "I'm so glad you're here," he whispered. "Oh Lord, it's awful... it's just awful...." To his surprise, Wallace returned the embrace.

"Hey... are you bawling, you big crybaby?" Wallace swiped at Stanley's cheek with his fingers. It was about as playful and affectionate as Wallace ever got. "What's the matter?"

Stanley glanced over Wallace's shoulder; there was no sound from Nino's bedroom. "Let me get your room ready and we'll have a cuppa joe and talk."

"He's not—" Wallace jerked his chin toward the other room. "—treating you bad or anything?"

As if Nino has ever been anything but kind. "No, he's... no. It's not him."

It isn't him. Not exactly.

STANLEY lay awake for a long time, his mind and body wound into intractable knots by the events of the past few hours. The party had been Nino's idea, a celebration welcoming Delores home; it was supposed to have been a joyous occasion, but like most people, Stanley knew instinctively what the road to Hell was paved with.

And Richard Kelly... what about him? It gave Stanley a pleasant tingle, thinking about the handsome maître d'. Was it wrong to be attracted to Richard at the same time as he experienced an enormous antipathy to Nino?

And Nino.... What the hell was that all about? Nino hardly seemed the sort of guy to knock himself off. Seeing Nino from the outside, anyone could be forgiven for thinking of him as an impenetrable colossus, a man of unimpeachable self-confidence, but Stanley knew it simply wasn't true. Nino was a damaged soul, and nobody really knew how deep the damage went.

He's damaged, Stanley thought, *but so am I.* He drifted to sleep and dreamt he was in a walled garden with Nino and they were conversing with the ghosts of dead children.

NINO rose late the next morning and went into the office around eleven. His sleep had been troubled with nightmares, and around three in the morning he awoke to find Stanley sleeping peacefully beside him, and Stanley's cousin Wallace ensconced in the spare bedroom. He hadn't heard Wallace arrive, and Stanley hadn't woken him to mention it; indeed, Nino hadn't even heard Stanley come to bed. Wallace made Nino some coffee when he woke and advised him Stanley had left "really early" to go to work.

Probably so he doesn't have to talk to me, Nino thought.

He unlocked his office and had just sat down when Delores appeared with a fresh cup of coffee. "Here you are, Mr. Nino, and if you don't mind my saying so, you look awful."

"Didn't sleep," Nino mumbled. He rubbed his temples with his thumbs; the headache had moved to sit behind his eyes, which he knew from experience meant it would stick with him for most of the day.

"Aw, Mr. Nino!" Delores came around behind him and took his head into her hands, gently massaging his forehead. "You got all this worry. That's what it is. You do all the work and the rest of us—" She broke off as there was a knock at the door.

"Come in!" Nino called.

Eli McKenna stepped through, gazed at Nino and Delores, then shook his head slightly. "I got a final tally on those cases, Nino." He laid the sheet on the desk, stepped back, and tilted his head. "You don't look so good."

"He's got a headache," Delores said. She resumed rubbing Nino's forehead.

"Anything I can do?" Eli asked. "You know I'm here whenever you need me, Nino. I hope I don't have to tell ya."

Nino waved a hand. "It's fine. I'll be needing you later when Big Frank decides to take as big a piece outta me as I took outta him...."

"That's something else I wanted to talk to you about," Eli said.

"Oh?"

"It's got to do with Fingers Ameche," Eli said.

Delores picked up a stack of filing. "I'll be out here if anybody wants me," she said.

"So tell me about it," Nino said. He sat back and put his feet up on the desk.

STANLEY was reconciling Nino's bank statements when his telephone rang; he set aside his ledger with a muffled curse and picked up the phone.

"Are you working yourself to death? You know, I imagine you there at your desk, wearing a green eyeshade, with your sleeves rolled up. I bet you make a pretty cute picture, don't you?"

Stanley blinked. "Who is this?"

"I'm cut to the heart." A beat. "No more midnight tête-à-tête in the garden for you, my boy."

"Richard!" He was flooded with an unreasonable glee but sought to contain it lest he appear a fool. "I thought you would still be in bed at this hour! What's the matter? The night life not keeping you up like it used to?"

Richard laughed. "You're a real sharp guy; I can see why Nino keeps you around. You'll find that I'm an early riser, although I don't see why that would bother you since you seem the type that likes to get to bed early."

There was nothing even remotely salacious in this, but Stanley found himself blushing madly. He was grateful no one could see him—Delores was at her desk out front, and Nino was safely stowed away in his office. "Maybe I do," he said. He lit a cigarette and leaned back in his chair. "So why are you calling me at this early hour of the morning?"

"Can't I call just to say hello?" Richard laughed. "I was wondering if you're up for a lunch date—with me, of course, unless you've already got your own personal chorus line of gorgeous men waiting outside your door?"

"No chorus line," Stanley replied, "and I'd love to go to lunch. Can we make it early? About half an hour?"

"Perfect," Richard said. "But I want to take you somewhere really nice and impress you with my urbanity and my wealth…. Maybe a secluded table in the Garden Room at Max?"

Stanley had never been to Max, had never even heard of it, and where he came from, the only garden rooms were strictly seasonal arrangements located out of doors. "It sounds marvelous," he said.

"I'll fetch you, will I?"

It would, Stanley reflected, cause a minor sensation if he was seen exiting the building with Richard Kelly—especially since most of Nino's employees assumed Stanley and Nino were, if not an exclusive item, at least an item. "Meet me out front at five 'til."

"Oh." Richard was obviously doing his best to sound forlorn. "Ashamed of me, are you?" He sniffled. "I see no future in our love, if you're going to act this way."

Stanley giggled, then looked around, terrified that someone might have heard. "You're going to get me into trouble."

"Yes please," Richard said, "and plenty of it, or I miss my guess. Five 'til, then, my beautiful Polish Stanley. I'll try not to count the minutes."

He rang off, and Stanley found he was grinning. Some small part of his mind was shrieking at him, saying things about how Nino had been so good to him, had rescued him from Big Frank's clutches, and wasn't he really cheating on Nino with Richard?

Yes, but Nino's so busy now.... You're doing him a favor, not bothering him... he has so much to do.

It was only lunch. He was only going to lunch with Richard. It wasn't like they were sneaking off to couple in a motel bedroom.

It wasn't like that at all.

CHAPTER
ELEVEN

"...SO AMECHE thinks that if he throws in with Big Frank, then Big Frank'll give him a piece of territory." Eli traced a rough rectangle on the map. "This here, and his interests in the Bronx, of course. And that ain't all—Mugs Mackey and Little George saw Big Frank over on Mulberry Street night before last. He was comin' outta Lili Wacker's place."

"Lili Wacker?" Nino sneered. "What's he want with that dame?"

"Word has it he's throwin' in with her," Eli said. "Oh yeah, him and Wacker are real tight these days." He paused to light a cigarette. "Real tight."

Nino swore floridly, a long stream of oaths mostly concerned with the various names of God. "I'm interested in the Bronx!" Nino said. "As far as the booze rackets go, anyhow. He wants to run numbers out of some penny-ante candy store, let him. But he better not get up my nose. I can't stand it when mugs get—" The telephone rang at Nino's elbow. "Yeah?"

"I very much need your advice."

For a moment Nino didn't know who was on the other end; then the night's memories flooded back. "What do you want, Kansas?"

"I'm trying—trying—to make a sauce for the chicken, but if you have capers anywhere in this—ridiculous dump of a kitchen, I can't find them!" Wallace sounded on the edge of hysterics. "I'm trying to make a decent meal, and God knows, it's hard enough—"

"Wait a minute," Nino interrupted. "You're cookin'? We only just had breakfast."

"If the chicken is to be properly marinated for tonight's dinner, it must be sauced within the next half hour." He huffed out an irritated breath. "That's all there is to it!"

You're sounding pretty sauced yourself, Nino thought. "Say, why don't you go do something else, huh? I'll buy dinner. We can get all dressed up and go out. You'll like that, since you ain't never been nowhere."

"Well, I—"

"Naw, it's fine. We'll go out, the three of us, somewhere really nice, huh? Now stop bothering me. I got work to do." He hung up with a grimace.

"House guests?" Eli asked.

"Nnn. The kid's cousin is here from Kansas." Nino peered at the map. "So he's thinkin' of moving in, huh? Ameche gets the territory if he takes care of me. You know, that's just like Big Frank. He ain't never fought his own battles—always sending his mugs out to do it for him. I ain't got no respect for the man." Nino waved his cigar. "He sits in that big office of his, eating like he's got two assholes"—Nino made an offensive gesture—"and getting mugs to do the wet work." He waved away Eli's protest before he could make it. "Yeah, I know, it ain't the way it's done no more, but can I help it if I'm a hands-on kind of guy?"

"So you're saying we go after Ameche before he goes after you?" Eli lit a cigarette. "Is that it?"

"Yeah, but I wanna hit him when he don't expect it. Show him that Nino's still in town. Yeah."

"You run any of this past Danny?"

"Murphy? Naw. I ain't had time. He's off somewhere with that dame of his—"

The door of Nino's office opened and Danny was there, almost as if he'd been summoned. He stopped short when he saw Nino and Eli staring at him. "I got something on my face?"

"No," Nino said. "Come here. Eli wants to explain something."

Eli and Nino explained Big Frank's plans to move into new territory by using Fingers Ameche to do his dirty work. Nino wondered aloud if it were better to wait for Ameche to make his move or to take the fight to him.

"We need to ask the rest of the boys," Danny said. "I ain't committed to nothing, Nino, unless the rest of the boys are in on it."

Nino narrowed his eyes. "You saying you don't trust my judgment no more?"

"I ain't saying nothin' of the kind—but we were supposed to be having a nice, quiet little celebration at the club the other night, and you climb on a chair and cut off Big Frank's nose."

"Hey!" Nino stood up. "You sayin' I had to climb on a chair to cut off his nose? I wasn't standin' on no chair when I did Big Frank, and I won't be standin' on no chair when the time comes—"

Eli got between them. "You guys are making me nervous," he said.

"Aw, go suck your mother," Danny said.

Eli turned his bland, baby face toward him. "That's a dirty crack, brother." He shifted his shoulders under his coat. "Maybe instead of ragging on each other we should be figuring out how to fight Big Frank—and how to keep Ameche from hornin' in on Nino's territory. You think?"

Nino sat down and stabbed his cigar out viciously in the ashtray. "Yeah, alright," he said grudgingly. He pointed a finger at Danny. "I don't like the way you been talkin' lately! That dame of yours ain't no good! What's she been sayin' to you, huh? Trying to get you to quit the rackets?"

Danny narrowed his eyes. "Billie's worried about me."

"Worried about you?" Nino hissed. "What is she, your goddamn mother?"

"You leave her out of it!" Danny leaned over the desk. It would have been a threatening gesture if anyone else had done it, but Danny and Nino had known each other too long.

"What's she been sayin' to you, huh? She been trying to get you to quit the rackets? Is that it?"

"Billie would never do that!" Danny said. "She's on the level. She ain't got nothing against you."

Nino's dark brows knit. "You ain't around when I need you. You're always off canoodling with that dame!"

Eli started laughing. Eli laughed and laughed. He looked at Nino and he looked at Danny and he laughed. He gazed at the floor and the ceiling and he laughed.

Finally, it got on Danny's nerves. "What's so goddamn funny?"

Eli gazed at him blandly. "Nothing's funny." He fished in his pocket and drew out a small bundle wrapped in tissue paper. "What do you think of this?" He unwrapped it carefully, reverently, and laid it on the desk for their inspection.

"You're gonna fight Ameche with...." Danny leaned in and peered at it. "... an antique silver bracelet?"

"No!" Eli snatched it back. "It's for Delores." He turned it around in his hands. "It belonged to my mother. I wanted to... I wanted to give her something. Do you think she'll like it?"

Danny shrugged. "Who knows what women like? Billie keeps telling me not to wear this tie—" He lifted it up and flapped it; the tie was dark green with small white dots. "—because it makes me look sick or something."

"Hey...." Nino looked at it. "Ain't that tie mine?"

Danny winked. "Maybe that's why she don't want me wearing it."

"It's a nice bracelet," Nino said. "Now put it away."

Eli stowed the gift in his pocket. "I want to take her out to dinner, somewhere nice.... You know, somewhere classy. And give her this. Only I'll get it wrapped up, professional-like, so it looks nice."

"Or you could roll it up in your underwear and play Go Fetch," Danny said.

"Danny!" Nino tutted his disapproval. "You want someone talking about your dame like that?"

"Aw, close your head." Danny waved it off. "I was just joking. It's a nice gift, Eli. Take her out and give it to her. Tell her whatever you want. Dames like that stuff." He pulled out his watch and glanced at it. "Half past twelve! And I told Billie I'd meet her at the drugstore for a sandwich."

"You're really getting serious about that jane, aren't you?" Nino asked. "Yeah, I see she's got the cuffs on you alright."

"What about you, Nino?" Eli asked. "Any dame ever gonna put the cuffs on you?"

Danny laid an arm across Eli's shoulder and pretended to whisper into his ear. "There ain't a dame invented that can catch Nino." He stepped back and indicated by an elaborate pantomime what he meant.

Eli blinked at him. "Oh," he said. "Really?"

Danny shrugged. "More for us, ain't it?"

"Huh. Yeah, I guess so."

Nino, uncomfortable with the turn the conversation was taking, shooed them out. "Go on, you mugs. I got business to do here. I'll let you know when we're meeting to suss this thing out."

"Don't wait too long," Danny said. "Ameche's got his eye on you."

"Yeah," Nino drawled, "and I got both eyes on him. Ain't nobody messes with Nino." When the door closed behind them, he picked up the phone. "Agnes"—he summoned his personal secretary—"can you get Mr. Zadwadzki on the telephone? Tell him it's important." She spoke, and his heart thundered in his ears. "Whatta ya mean, gone to lunch? With who? Oh. Okay. Sure."

He laid the heavy receiver gently back in its cradle.

He's leaving you, his mind whispered. Nino felt sick.

BY THREE o'clock Stanley still hadn't returned, and Nino sat alone in his office getting angrier and angrier and trying to convince himself he wasn't angry. He snapped at Agnes when she brought in a stack of phone messages and there was nothing from Stanley. "Have you seen him?"

"I ain't seen him, Mr. Moretti, sure as I'm standing here talking to you." Agnes was a cute redhead with large breasts and a tiny waist; a man of different sexual persuasion would have been all over her. As it was, Nino had hired her because of her ability to type a mind-numbing one hundred words per minute and answer three phones at once.

"Well, where the hell is he?" he roared. "He goes off to lunch and he stays away all day? Is that it?"

"Is what it?"

"Oh, so you're back."

Stanley lingered in the doorway, waiting for Agnes to leave so he could speak to Nino alone. He had one hand stuffed into his trouser pocket. "I'm sorry. I'm afraid I lost track of time."

"Yeah, well." Nino found he just couldn't sustain his anger. "It's jake. I just wondered where you were. I was gonna take you out to lunch but I guess you ate already."

"Yes, Mr. Kelly was kind enough to treat me to a very nice lunch at Max."

And you don't look the least bit sorry about that, Nino thought. *He's leaving you*, his mind whispered. He barked at it to shut the hell up. "I'm glad you and Richard are getting along."

"Oh, we're getting along fine," Stanley said. "He's been very kind to me, explaining the nightclub aspects of the business." Stanley's simple statement sounded almost accusatory, as if Nino had been remiss in certain aspects of Stanley's corporate education.

"Is that so?"

"Anyway." Stanley shifted uncomfortably on his feet. "I wanted to let you know that—"

"Your cousin's in town? That he came in late last night and you didn't bother to wake me up?"

"Nino." Stanley sighed. "Perhaps I should go out and we can start all over?"

Nino rubbed his forehead. "I'm sorry, kid. It's this damn heat." It was indeed very hot in the office; even with all the windows open there was scarcely a breeze to dent the New York City heat. "I didn't know where you were. I was worried." *Worried you and Richard Kelly were getting friendly in some cozy little motel room.* "I don't hear from ya, you don't call to check in, I got Big Frank and his mob loose and on the lookout for anybody what can be connected to me." Nino's telephone rang. "Hello? Tony. I thought you was—"

The intimation of sudden disaster hung in the room like a bad smell. Stanley took an inadvertent step backward; Nino's face was like a thundercloud.

"What is it?" Stanley whispered, but Nino wasn't listening to him.

"Which hospital?" Nino's knuckles tightened on the receiver 'til the bone showed through the skin. "Uh-huh. Meet me there. Okay." He hung up the receiver and sat motionless in his chair for a moment.

"Nino, what is it?" Stanley was spooked; Nino was way too quiet. "What's going on?"

"They got Danny."

IT FELT to Danny Murphy—during his mercifully brief periods of lucidity—that someone had crushed both his feet with a steamroller. He was able, despite being under the thrall of a significant amount of morphine, to swim up to consciousness for a moment or two at a time, and so gleaned information from the conversations taking place around his bed.

"…tarsals and metatarsals quite crushed. Need to be pinned. Not entirely…."

"…that's not possible! My God, he's a dancer!"

"…specialist from Vienna… in the city for a conference. Oh no, a very odd duck indeed…."

He sensed Billie near him and reached out for her through his haze of pain and drugs. She smoothed his forehead and kissed him, begged him to tell her how it happened, but Danny wouldn't. Instead he pretended not to remember. There was only one person he would tell— one person who knew what to do about it and upon whom he could lay the responsibility for vengeance.

"It's okay, baby… don't cry. Don't… want you to… cry." Danny rested one hand on top of her pretty head, stroking her soft, dark hair. "You're… so pretty." The pain in his feet was intense and unrelenting;

it throbbed up into the sockets of his hips and pulsed, sickeningly, in the bottom of his belly. He had vomited on the way to the hospital, retching painfully until his empty stomach contracted and recoiled; the pain was bad enough, but worse was the knowledge he most probably would never dance again.

Ever.

He needed to talk to Nino, but every time he tried to sit up, someone pushed him back down on the bed and stuck a needle in his arm; it was starting to piss him off. This was important; Nino needed to know about it, know Big Frank had struck what was arguably the first blow. "Need to talk to Nino." He had pleaded with Billie before the morphine took hold, nearly crushing her hand in his insistence that he talk to Nino right now. Finally she had gone out into the corridor to telephone Tony from the nurses' station, and Danny had relaxed a little.

"Hey doc, whatcha gonna do about these hoofs of mine, huh?" He didn't really want to know, and yet he had to ask. He'd heard the doctors talking, had heard the whispers of "amputation" and decided to nerve himself for what was coming. "I'm gonna look pretty funny walking around on my knees." He was trying to be brave—Danny was always brave—but the pain and fear were getting the better of him. He wished everybody would get out of the room so he could just put his head down and cry, get it over with—but the doctors were there and Billie was there and now they had sent for some other guy, some specialist from Vienna, some fancy foreign surgeon who was going to do what, exactly? Sew on a new pair of feet?

You should have known, boyo. You were getting ahead of yourself. Danny Murphy, dancing on the stage on Broadway! Getting too big for your boots, so you were.

He could almost hear Grandfather's voice in his head now, the thick Waterford brogue that gave his words their rolling, lilting quality—still there, despite all these many years in America. Funny how Danny could hear the dead man's voice, but the Murphys were all a little bit fey.

You got a bit o' the Gentry blood, you do. Danny laughed aloud.

"It's just the drugs," the doctor reassured Billie. "He doesn't feel any pain at all." Danny's feet had been bandaged and stuck out the bottom of the bed at incongruous angles. He knew feet didn't bend that way, that no human foot was capable of that degree of abduction; Danny knew, too, the implications of a foot that had been forced to bend beyond its normal radius.

"Where's Nino?" Danny asked again, fighting the pull of the morphine. "I gotta talk to Nino."

Tony shouldered his way to the bedside. "He's on his way, Danny. I called him. He's coming right over."

"Oh, that's good," Danny murmured. "That's real good. Think I'll sleep a little."

THE doctor drew Tony out into the corridor. "Does he have any family?"

"Yeah, he does," Tony said, "but I don't have a telephone number. Mr. Moretti, he might know."

"Mr. Moretti is—"

"Yeah, Mr. Moretti is his employer," Tony put in. "My brother, Nino. Danny works for him."

The doctor peered at Tony narrowly, no doubt taking in the flashy suit and the surfeit of diamond jewelry. "What sort of work does Mr. Murphy do for Mr. Moretti?"

"He's a driver," Tony said. "More than that, you don't need to know."

The doctor nodded sagely. "Ah," he said. "I see." He turned at the sound of shouting down the other end of the hall; the double doors that closed off this section flew open as if struck by something hard, and Nino Moretti came through at a run.

Nino was furious; his face was a snarling mask of hatred and his dark eyes were twin pools of rage. He bore down on the doctor. "Where is he? Where are you keepin' Danny, huh?" He caught hold of the doctor's coat and twisted it. "Speak up, you mug, or I swear to God, I'll—"

Stanley Zadwadzki laid a hand on Nino's shoulder. "Nino, I think he's probably in here." He kept his hand on Nino until the other man released the doctor's coat and stepped away.

"Yeah." Nino straightened his tie. "Let's go in and see him, kid. I wanna see what these mugs have been doing to him."

The doctor started forward. "Mr. Murphy has sustained serious—" He stopped, brought up against Tony, as broad and unyielding as a stone wall.

"You might wanna let Nino see him," Tony said. "It's healthier for Nino, and it's healthier for all of us."

"Danny." Nino approached, trembling, twisting his hat brim between his hands. "Danny, it's me, it's Nino. I come to see ya. Aw, whatcha done to yourself, Danny?"

"Hey, Nino." Danny's eyelids seemed heavy, as though he'd been drugged. "Where you been? We were in the old neighborhood, we were playing stickball, you and me—" He paused. "No... I was dreaming that. I was only dreaming it."

"Who did this?" Nino's eyes were suddenly full of tears. "Was it him? Huh? Was it Big Frank's goons?"

"Yeah. Fingers Ameche's boys, too. Tall Tony and Vinnie Meatballs, and some torpedo I didn't recognize."

Nino held tight to Danny's hand. "What—how'd they—"

"Aw, with a hammer." Danny pressed a hand against his eyes. "Yeah, they got me good, Nino."

Nino ground his teeth together. "And I'm gonna get them good," he said. "I'm gonna send him a message he ain't never gonna forget."

WALLACE was sitting by the window reading a novel when Nino and Stanley arrived home. He'd showered, because his hair was still wet, and a small cut on his chin proclaimed he'd shaved as well.

"...I don't care what he thinks. Nobody pushes Nino around!"

"Yes, but don't you think—" Stanley shut and locked the door behind them. "Oh, hello, Wallace. I trust you weren't too bored today?"

"No." Wallace glanced around the apartment, which was spotless. "It took most of today to clean this place up. Really." He looked pointedly at Nino. "I'm sure a city this size boasts any number of fine cleaning women you could hire—even a part-time butler, if absolutely necessary. Did you know you have mold in the bathroom? Under the sink. I scrubbed it with bleach. It's gone now. And I reorganized the cupboards. It's impossible to find anything in this place. I don't know how you manage to live like this."

Nino frowned. "Live like what?" he asked. "There something wrong with the way Nino lives?"

Wallace arched an eyebrow. "The way Nino lives—"

"Enough!" Stanley's eyes were practically bulging from his head. "Shut up! Both of you!" He stormed into the bathroom and slammed the door. After a moment, Nino and Wallace heard the shower running.

"Well," Wallace said.

"Hmph," said Nino. "Drink?"

"Love one." Wallace accepted a glass of scotch. "What's gotten under his skin, I wonder?"

"Yeah...." Nino flopped into the armchair and loosened his collar and tie. "I wonder...."

"You look like a man with something on his mind," Wallace said.

"Yeah, it ain't nothing," Nino replied. He wasn't ready to trust Wallace to the point of unburdening himself. He did fill Wallace in on what had happened to Danny, but kept his suspicions about Stanley's behavior to himself.

"So explain to me how this works, exactly." Wallace accepted a refill from Nino but declined a cigarette. "This Big Frank person. How did you...?"

Nino took a deep breath, and told Wallace—briefly—how he had rescued Stanley from Big Frank O'Hara, and what that meant. Wallace listened carefully, his eyes never leaving Nino's face until he'd finished speaking.

"So this... O'Hara." His jaw was set and there was a vein jumping in his temple. "He... you're telling me...." He swallowed hard. "This man raped my cousin."

"More than once." Nino drew on his cigarette. "Stanley was with him for nearly five years. From the things he's told me—" He stopped. "I'm sorry. I can't—"

"There's no need to tell me any more," Wallace said. He drained his glass and thumped it down on the small table at his elbow. "That son of a bitch...." His fists clenched. "Stanley, he—" He glanced toward the bathroom door, reassuring himself that the shower was still running. "His parents died kind of close together. His father had a heart attack one afternoon. He came home from work, sat down in his favorite chair, opened the newspaper and... died." A callus on the heel of Wallace's palm seemed suddenly very interesting to him. "It hit Stanley really hard. He was close to his father. His father taught Stanley how to carve—I guess you know about the carving?"

Nino nodded. "Yeah. He's really good."

"After Uncle Dick died, Stanley...." Wallace sighed. "He stopped talking."

"He stopped talking?"

"Yes. He didn't speak for... maybe six months. Aunt Marjorie thought there was something wrong with him. She took him to the doctor—" Wallace made a face. "—who said there was nothing wrong with him that a good whipping wouldn't fix."

Nino's heart pounded painfully in his chest. "So what did she do?"

"Thankfully, Aunt Marjorie didn't listen. She figured Stanley would talk when he had something to say." Wallace shrugged. "He did, of course. Aunt Marjorie was right—but Stanley scared us. He's always been like that... he's always been... fragile."

"And his ma died soon after?"

Wallace nodded. "Yes. She'd had a heart condition that she was hell-bent on keeping from everybody. Our religion—" He rubbed the callus on his hand. "—the religion we were brought up in—"

Nino stubbed out his cigarette. "You don't go to doctors."

"Well… yes and no."

"But she didn't go."

"No. She died in the kitchen, making a sandwich for Stanley's lunch."

"Jesus."

The shower cut off; Nino and Wallace turned as the bathroom door opened. Stanley's footsteps went down the hall and into the bedroom and closed the door behind him.

"So you're going to war with Big Frank," Wallace said.

"Yeah."

"Count me in."

"Now see here, Kansas—"

"Count me in, I said."

Nino threw up his hands. "Damn stubborn goddamn country hick!" he said, exasperated. "So what happens if you get the top of your head shot off, huh? What happens then?" He stood up. "Forget about it."

Wallace stood up too. "He's my cousin," he said in a tense, angry whisper, "and somebody hurt him. I have the right—my family—"

This struck a chord with Nino. "Your family, huh?" He punched Wallace lightly on the arm. "Sure you ain't got any Italian blood?" He sighed. "Alright. You get yourself killed, it ain't none of Nino's business."

STANLEY was sitting on the end of the bed wearing a towel around his waist when Nino stuck his head around the door. "Safe to come in here?" he asked.

Stanley nodded wordlessly. Nino sat beside him; Stanley picked up a comb and began combing his wet hair back over his head.

"Pretty mad at me, aren't ya?"

Stanley kept his gaze fixed on the mirror opposite. "Yep."

"Wanna tell me?"

"Nope."

Nino lapsed into silence. Stanley combed his hair. They could hear Wallace rummaging around in the bathroom. Nino turned to Stanley and took the younger man's chin between his thumb and finger. "You hate me because of what happened to Danny."

Stanley's lower lip quivered. "No."

"Then what is it?"

He shook his head.

Nino sighed. "Get dressed for dinner," he said. He patted Stanley's cheek. "I'm taking you and Wallace out for a night on the town."

"A night on the town," Stanley said dully, "when Danny's in the hospital?"

"It's because of Danny that I'm taking you out. Nino's going to be seen, because Nino ain't scared of Big Frank O'Hara, nor none of his mugs, neither. I'm taking you to 21."

"Are you sure that's a good idea?" Stanley asked.

"Kid…." Nino gazed at him. "It's the only idea."

"21" WAS crowded, and many heads turned when Nino, Wallace, and Stanley arrived, resplendent in white ties and tails, freshly washed and shaved and smelling collectively of several sharp and masculine scents. Nino had made reservations for a late dinner at nine since the three men intended to visit a nearby speakeasy after they dined.

"I still don't think it's a good idea," Stanley said once the maître d' had appeared and shepherded them to their table. In keeping with Nino's habits, it was in a corner of the dining room with a clear view of the front door. "Why, Big Frank could come in here—"

"He ain't gonna come into 21 and start shooting," Nino said. He glanced up at the sommelier, a tall, thin man with an unfortunately purple nose. "Oh, right, we wanna get drinks and stuff. So what's good to drink in this joint?"

"In this joint, sir?" The sommelier ran a manicured thumb down the wine list. "I would suggest—"

"Bring me that Bollinger," Nino replied, nearly closing the leather folder on the man's thumb. "That'll be good."

"As sir wishes." The man disappeared as though blown by a strong wind.

"Yeah, now this is class!" Nino tried to tuck his thumbs into the armholes of his waistcoat, but his stiff, boiled shirt did not allow for much flexion of the fabric. He ran a thumb under his collar. "Glad I don't gotta wear this monkey suit every night of the week." He ran an approving eye over Stanley. "You look real nice, kid. And you too, Kansas."

"Why thank you," Wallace replied coolly. He really wasn't at all like his cousin, Nino thought. "And here I thought I had escaped your eagle eye." Wallace was cool where Stanley was warm, prickly where Stanley was gentle and embracing.

Rather, had been gentle and embracing. These days it seemed like Stanley spent most of his time fending off Nino's advances. Nino had tried to kiss him while they were dressing for dinner; Stanley had offered his cheek instead of his lips. When Nino crept up behind him and wrapped his arms around Stanley's waist, the younger man had slipped out of his embrace, pretending to have an itchy spot on his back. And the long lunch with Richard Kelly. That still bothered him. In fact, it stuck in Nino's craw.

"Well, what are we gonna eat, huh?"

"Oh look," Wallace said, "they have oysters." He canted a look at Stanley. "I've heard they're quite the aphrodisiac."

"I don't like oysters," Stanley said. "I've never liked oysters."

"Get what you like, kid. Nino's paying for this."

Stanley's gaze was fixed on the far corner of the restaurant; he hadn't heard a word.

"Stanley, Mr. Moretti is talking. God knows, the rest of the room heard him loud and clear."

"Huh?" Stanley turned guileless blue eyes on his cousin. "I'm sorry, what?"

Nino's stomach churned. "Nothing," he said. "It ain't nothing."

"I saw someone I know," Stanley said. "Sitting over there."

"Nino, I think I'll join you in some oysters," Wallace said. "I haven't had them in ages and they certainly do sound lovely. You know, the first time I ever had oysters was in Chicago… it's the only trip I've ever taken. I went with one of the men from my college… must be years ago now."

"Chicago, huh? One of my guys used to run with the Chicago mob—yeah, Frank Nitti and the boys." Nino was watching Stanley; Stanley was watching something across the room.

"So, Nino, tell me—has your family always lived in New York?" Wallace glanced up as the sommelier appeared and poured their wine.

"Huh? Uh, yeah, yeah, I guess so, Kansas."

"I think that's Richard Kelly over there." Stanley dropped his napkin onto the table and slipped out of his chair. "If you gentlemen will excuse me, I won't be a minute, just…." And he was gone. Nino followed him with his eyes until Stanley disappeared into a crowd of departing diners on the other side of the room.

"This may be hard to believe." Wallace leaned in. "But I really am a very good listener."

Nino frowned. "So?"

Wallace tilted his head in the direction Stanley had gone. "You're wondering what's between him and this Richard Kelly. You have an idea but you don't want to admit that it might be more than just an idea to him… that maybe he acted on it."

Nino stared at him but Wallace would not be cowed. "I don't know nothin' about that," he said.

"See, I think you do." Wallace touched Nino's wrist lightly, rested his hand there for just a moment. "You're in love with him, aren't you?"

"So what if I am?" Across the room, Stanley was chatting to Richard Kelly in an animated fashion, laughing now and then, wholly engaged in the man in front of him—as if Nino didn't even exist.

"He's behaving like an ass. He doesn't mean to." Wallace sighed. "Sometimes the people we fall in love with don't realize how deep those feelings go."

"Feelings?" Nino sneered. "Are you tight, or something?"

Wallace ignored the jab. "He doesn't understand. Stanley— Stanley has led a very sheltered life. His parents doted on him. Uncle Dick and Aunt Marjorie married late in life. They didn't expect to have any children and so, when Stanley came along... well. He was the center of their world. Then, when they died...."

"Yeah." Nino couldn't imagine being doted on by either of his parents—his father was too busy beating them to a pulp and his mother was too distracted. "Yeah, I guess."

"He doesn't mean to hurt you. He probably doesn't even realize that he is hurting you."

"You're a real fountain of wisdom, ain't ya?"

"No, Nino, I really am not. I've spent my life in a town that's little more than a wide spot in the road, pining after a man who doesn't even know I exist."

Nino's pulse thudded in his wrists and throat. "He's leaving me," he whispered. "I don't know what to do." The confession left him feeling sick to his stomach.

Wallace sighed. "He doesn't know what he wants." He brightened. "I suppose," he said wryly, "if it came to it, you could just have this Kelly man killed."

Nino burst out laughing in spite of himself. "Kansas, you said a mouthful!"

Wallace pretended to buff his fingernails on his lapel. "Mmm. Didn't I?" The waiter appeared with their oysters; Wallace waited 'til the man had set their plates down and left. "Amazing thing, the oyster." He picked one up and squinted at it, quivering on its half shell. "One little grain of sand gets in and what the oyster can't get rid of...." He tilted his head back and tipped the raw shellfish down his throat.

"If you're gonna crack wise about oysters—" Nino followed suit and then sipped his wine.

"What?"

"I dunno." Nino grinned. "I was gonna say something and then it just went outta my head."

"That happen to you a lot?" Wallace smirked.

Nino was laughing in spite of himself. "I swear, it never does."

"Such a shame," Wallace sighed. "Such a pretty head too." He winked at Nino and tipped another oyster down his throat.

"You think I'm—"

Wallace was immediately serious. "Oh yes," he said. "Good Lord, yes. Don't you ever look in the mirror?"

"Yeah," Nino admitted, "but I try not to. I don't much like what I see."

"That's a shame," Wallace said quietly. "I think it's awfully nice." He reached for another oyster. "Forgive me if I'm too forward. I don't bother with tact and I think being subtle is a waste of time. I always think people should be honest with one another whenever possible."

"You do, huh?"

"You are—" Wallace sipped his wine. "—magnetic. You know, everybody back in Salina was talking about you when you were there. They'd never seen anything like you before." He gazed at the other man speculatively. "I wonder if you know how much of a ripple you cause wherever you go."

Nino was actually blushing. This was a novel sensation—how many years had it been since he'd actually blushed? "Aw, you're kidding me."

"No." Wallace laid his hand on Nino's arm and squeezed gently. "I'm not." He gazed at Nino for several long moments, then smiled gently. "I'm just sorry Stanley got there first." He nodded to where Stanley was still talking to Richard Kelly. "Do you think he's coming back?" He realized what he had said and scrambled to amend it. "To the table, I meant."

"I dunno." Nino pushed away the rest of his oysters. "To the table or anywhere else."

"MOVE outta the way—come on, clear a path there!" Nino shouldered past several larger men, opening a way in the crowd of bodies. The music was loud, and over in a corner, the band was in full swing, throwing themselves into the very useful pursuit of making a great deal of very fine jazz. "Come on—I see a table over by the wall."

Stanley and Wallace followed Nino, ducking their heads to avoid some low-hanging streamers that appeared to have been strung around the place before the last war. They disposed themselves around a tiny table and peered through the haze of cigarette smoke, searching in vain for a waiter. "How the hell do you get any juice in this joint?" Nino wondered.

"This is certainly... unusual," Wallace remarked. "What do you call this?"

"It's a speakeasy," Stanley said. "One of the places you can always get a little something in your ginger ale, if you know what I mean." He seemed in good spirits, and there were spots of color burning high up on each of his cheekbones. Nino wondered what he and Richard Kelly had been talking about at 21, and if they had made an appointment to meet later. It wouldn't surprise him to see Kelly here, except Nino hadn't told Stanley where they were going.

"No, it's not just that...." Wallace peered around. "Ah."

"Figured it out?" Nino asked, smirking.

"There are no women here," Wallace said.

"You ain't as dumb as you look, Kansas."

"I thought...." Wallace blinked. "Is this sort of thing...."

"We keep it quiet," Nino said. "Sort of a private club. Anybody who knows about it generally keeps it to himself—and a few of his friends."

There were men dancing with men, men holding hands on top of the tables, men cuddling and petting in the corners. A handful of bemused waiters prowled the premises, each with a tray and the requisite napkin over his arm. "You should have invited Richard Kelly," Nino said to Stanley. "He'd love this place."

The muscles of Stanley's face flattened out; he looked like a cat cornered in an alley. "I don't see why he would," he said.

"Really? Seems to me like you and him were having a great time back at the restaurant." Nino was spoiling for a fight; he wanted to have this out in the open and get it over with.

"We were discussing business matters," Stanley said tightly. "He was concerned about some cost overruns. I helped clear up the matter." He glanced around the room, ostensibly looking for the waiter. "My, but this really is an interesting place."

"You sure took a long lunch break the other day," Nino said. "You and Mr. Kelly must have found a lot to talk about."

"We were discussing business. I guess time just got away from us." He shrugged.

"Time got away from you." Nino stared at him for a moment and shook his head. Stanley pretended interest in an argument that had broken out between two men at the edge of the dance floor. "Yeah. It got away from you."

"You know, I would really like to dance," Wallace interjected. "Nino, would you do me the honor…?"

"Huh? Oh, you wanna dance with me. Sure, Kansas. I'll dance with you. After all, I ain't got nothing better to do."

Nino drifted into Wallace's arms and tried not to think about Stanley, Richard Kelly, or the rest of this whole mess. He couldn't keep himself from worrying about Danny, however—what were they going to do with Danny? Could the doctors save his feet or was he doomed to be a cripple?

"Tense up any further and you'll crush my hand." Wallace pulled away for a second. "Jeez, do you mind?"

"I'm sorry," Nino replied absently. "Got a lot on my mind."

"Yes… not the least of which is my horrible little cousin." Wallace glanced over Nino's shoulder. "He looks like he's a million miles away, if you care, and I know you do." He tilted a look at Nino. "How is Danny?"

"Not good." For a moment Nino wavered, tears wobbling on the rims of his dark eyes. "They, ah… they might have to… you know, amputate."

"I'm so sorry." Wallace's hand was warm against Nino's waist. "I'm a very good listener, you know, like I said. And you should talk to somebody… even if that somebody is me."

Nino grinned in spite of himself. "You sure got a way with words, Kansas." He dropped his head, overcome with emotion. "He's leaving me," he whispered. He freed his hand from Wallace's and scrubbed angrily at his face. "Dammit, would you look at me? I'm like a little goddamn girl."

"Sometimes you have to loosen up a little," Wallace said. "Stanley has never been in love—with anyone."

"Yeah, well, he ain't in love with me no more, either."

"Are you sure?" Wallace squeezed Nino's hand. "Maybe he's scared. Maybe he needs to have a fling—"

"Yeah, and maybe he's leaving me for good!" Nino tore himself away from Wallace. "You ever think of that, Kansas?"

He turned and forced his way through the mass of bodies on the packed dance floor, shoving men aside with impunity. Anyone watching knew Nino was putting up one hell of a fight with his emotions. Nino was huddled in a stall in the men's room, his head in his hands, when Wallace found him.

He wedged himself into the narrow space and pulled out his handkerchief. "I'm reasonably sure this is an effective seduction ploy," Wallace said gently, "offering someone your handkerchief and using it to get close to him." He took Nino's chin between thumb and finger and lifted the other man's face. "There." He assessed Nino with his cool blue eyes, and smiled. "It hardly shows that you've been in here sobbing your guts out."

"I ain't been sobbing my guts out," Nino snuffled angrily.

"You know," Wallace said, "you could talk to him and tell him how you feel."

"I ain't good at talkin'! Okay? Nino don't talk. I get in a tight spot, I shoot my way out."

"Well," Wallace smirked, "maybe shooting him might actually do some good in this case." He drew a deep breath. "I am so sorry you have to go through this. Really." He reached out and stroked away an errant tear that was drying on Nino's face. "And I'm sorry Stanley got to you first. The little bastard always gets… the good stuff." On the last word, his mouth closed over Nino's in a gentle kiss. The gangster responded eagerly, reaching to hold Wallace's face between his palms. The kiss turned torrid, and Nino groaned under his breath as he felt the warm intrusion of the other man's tongue—

"—no, we gotta stop." Nino pulled away. "Don't get me wrong—" His forehead rested against Wallace's, eyes closed. "—if I was lookin', you're absolutely what I could go for."

"But you're not," Wallace finished. He smiled, straightened up and tucked his handkerchief away. "That's just my rotten luck, isn't it?" He touched Nino's shoulder. "Talk to him," he said. "Please. Before it really is too late."

The bathroom door swished shut behind him, and Nino was alone.

DANNY was sleeping and dreaming a curious dream: he was lying on a cloud while a bald gnome massaged his feet with ice cubes and sang songs to him in German.

"The structure of the feet has been quite crushed, quite crushed."

"I agree, Doctor Groer—but isn't there something that can be done?"

Danny opened his eyes slowly. A very short, very bald man—that must be the German accent—was gently lifting and turning Danny's feet while conversing with a very tall, dark-haired man with a lean face and a hungry, haunted expression. He reminded Danny of a mad scientist, someone shut up alone in a tower while lightning bolts crackled and sizzled above him.

"What's this?" Danny asked. "Somebody having a party?"

"Hardly, young man." The bald German peered at him balefully. "How on earth did you manage to smash your feet so? Perhaps you were dancing with the devil?"

"Something like that," Danny said. "I was talking to some guys. They disagreed with me."

"Hm," the bald man said, "one only hopes you were not persuading them to sell you a pair of shoes." He smirked at the taller man, who did not return the gesture.

"Mr. Murphy, I'm Dr. Henry Franks, and this gentleman is Dr. Groer. We've been consulted in connection with your case."

Danny nodded. "Nino... yeah, he's always spreading his dough around." He sighed. "So, doc—any hope of fixing these feet of mine?"

Groer conferred with Franks by a look. "What do you think, Dr. Franks? Can we do something for him?"

Franks looked uncertain, and if possible, more haunted than ever. "Well, there is always the possibility of amputation. That doesn't change in these cases, and there isn't anything I can do to remove that risk. However...." He raised his shoulders and let them drop. "If the circulation is as good as you say it is, Dr. Groer, well... we might attempt a surgical intervention."

"Good!" Groer clapped his hands and his round face split in a grin. "Then I think we should start as soon as possible!"

"Alright by me," Franks replied. He flexed his long fingers. "I'll tell the nurses to prepare."

"Good," Groer replied. "I should like him completely unconscious when I arrive...."

"I don't understand why you insist on that condition...."

They left the room together, their voices trailing out into the hallway. Danny was left alone. He stared at the ceiling and tried to pretend he wasn't crying. He knew how dangerous hope could be and he wasn't about to succumb to it. He'd been here before—most notably in his dancing career, when he'd seen promising parts go to less-able dancers—and he knew enough to guard against premature optimism. But he knew Nino, and he knew that Nino, whatever else he might be, was no piker—if there was help available for Danny, Nino would find it and would pay whatever it cost to get it for him. Nino was good that way; he'd do just about anything for his friends.

There was a tap on the door, so slight that Danny wondered if he'd merely imagined it. Stanley poked his head around the door: "Are you asleep? Because…."

"No, kid, it's fine. Come on in." Danny scooted up on his pillows. "I'm sick of sleeping. I'm getting so I don't never want to sleep again." He grinned at Stanley. "How are you doing, huh? Things going okay?"

"Can I…." Stanley sat down in the chair by Danny's bed. "Can I talk to you about something?"

"Why sure, kid. You can talk to me about anything."

Stanley's lower lip trembled. "I'm in trouble," he whispered, "and I don't know what to do."

"What's on your mind, kid?" Danny reached out and clasped Stanley's hand. "Been worrying about Big Frank's mob, have you?"

"No… not really."

"Nino done somethin' stupid?" Danny grinned. "Let me guess— he said something dumb to ya. Nino's all talk. Don't let him get to ya. Give him a day or two—"

"I cheated on Nino."

Danny wasn't sure he'd heard right. "Cheated?"

"With Richard Kelly. W-well, n-not—we didn't g-go to bed together, well, it was like, lunch and I had—crying, I was crying and Richard—" Stanley was stumbling all over himself, stuttering, losing the thread of what he was trying to say. It had been a long time since Danny had seen him in quite so wrought a state.

"You and Richard Kelly?" Danny whistled softly. "Kid—you scored a big fish there. Richard Kelly's the real deal—you know that, right? Comes from the Connecticut Kellys, the ones who own all those mines and stuff. His family's got more money than Fort Knox. How'd you—" He blinked. "You cheated on Nino, huh? I can't say I'm surprised."

"What? You aren't—you aren't surprised?"

"No. No, I'm not surprised. Nino's like strong drink—you take a sip and it's nice, it's bracing, you like it, so you take a couple more sips. Then you notice it's kind of taking your breath away. Before you know it, you're drunk on the stuff and you don't want it anymore—at least not right away."

"But Nino's been so good to me."

Danny knew it was more than merely good: Nino had rescued Stanley, Nino had saved his life. To all appearances, Nino was nuts about the kid.

"Do you love him?" Danny asked, seriously. "Because if you don't, then you better get out now. Don't stick around because you're afraid of hurting him. You'll hurt him a lot more if you stay when you'd be better off gone. You hearing me, kid?"

"Sure, Danny." Stanley looked at his hands. "I hear ya."

"Do you love him? I mean, are you in love with him?" Danny reached for the water jug on his bedside table and poured himself a glass. "Because if you ain't—"

"I don't know," Stanley replied. "I really, really don't know."

CHAPTER
TWELVE

THE sun was warm, pouring heat into his bones, melting him blissfully into the soft grass. The book he was reading held little interest for him, and from his vantage point under a spreading shade tree, he could see one of Stanley's bare feet where it protruded from the hammock, swinging gently to and fro.

There was no need to go anywhere, no need to do anything or say anything at all. They were here, together, comfortable with one another and easy in themselves. Nino raised his left hand to turn the pages of his book and smiled to himself as the sun shot brilliant sparkles across the gold ring on his finger. *This is just perfect*, he thought. *It's good that we're alone together. I know he loves me now.*

He was standing in waist-deep water, black and cold; the light was gone. "Stanley?" The stars twinkled cruelly above him and there was no moon. "Stanley?" He turned in a circle, calling out like a frightened child. "Stanley? Baby? Where are you?"

Nino woke with a shout, bolting up. The flat gray of false dawn tinted the windows; he was shivering. Stanley was sleeping beside him, lying on his belly, one arm wrapped around his spare pillow. Nino wanted to shake him, to wake him up, to make him pay attention, but he couldn't bring himself to interrupt the younger man's slumber. Sleep was precious, and Nino had spent too much of his own life battling his nighttime demons. He got up and pulled his dressing gown on, then padded out to the kitchen.

"You too, huh?" Wallace sat at the table, playing solitaire and drinking something from a cup. "Whisky, with a little milk in it," he said when Nino bent to smell it. "Nerving myself for the battle. Kind of like Napoleon, when you think of it."

"Napoleon." Nino opened the refrigerator and took the milk out. "He was just a little guy, wasn't he?"

"Napoleon was five feet six and a half inches tall—the average height for a Frenchman of that era." Wallace turned up a card and hissed between his teeth. He watched Nino pour milk into a saucepan and turn on the gas. "Why the sudden interest in Bonaparte? Are you planning something Napoleonic?"

"Had a bad dream," Nino replied shortly.

Wallace laid aside his cards. "About Big Frank's mob?"

Nino made a noncommittal noise and stirred his milk, careful not to let it burn.

"You don't have to do this, you know," Wallace said. "Although, knowing what this jerk did to my cousin...." He glanced toward the hallway. "Where is the little bastard, anyway?"

"Sleeping," Nino sighed. "Sleeping the sleep of the just."

"Oh, the sleep of the just?" Wallace made a face. "Tell me another one."

Nino shook his head as he sat down across from Wallace. "It ain't his fault. I figured he could love me, you know?" He watched Wallace turn over several of the cards. "My mother, she used to read cards... like those, what you call 'em, telling your fortune...."

"Tarot cards?" Wallace asked.

"Yeah." Nino sipped his hot milk. "She could tell your fortune by looking at plain old cards."

"Did she ever tell yours?"

"No. She wouldn't read for us kids. She said if there was something bad, she wouldn't want to know." Nino rubbed tired eyes. "Too bad. Maybe she coulda kept my old man from killing my brother."

Wallace's skin prickled. "He killed your brother? Jesus."

"Yeah, my old man, he... beat my brother 'til he died." There were certain things that never failed to bring it back for him: a scrap of red, anything the color of blood or the blunt, wet noise of fists hitting a human head. His father kept on hitting Ray, long after Ray had fallen silent; he dragged Ray's unprotesting corpse over to the settee in the kitchen and propped him up. Nino had waited 'til the old man had fallen asleep, then he crept over to where his brother was, sitting lifeless in a pool of blood.

Ray? You awake? Come on, Ray, wake up.

His brother's eyes were half-open, staring; there was blood around Ray's nose and mouth, blood trickling out of one ear. Then the old man came back, saw Nino sitting on the floor and told him to get up. *Get your pansy ass to bed. Whatcha sittin' on the floor for? You gone screwy or something?* He went and crawled in next to Tony and lay there, straining his ears into the darkness, desperate to hear a sound, any sound at all, but when he went out into the kitchen the next morning, Ray was still and had already begun to stiffen.

Wallace was white to the lips. "Did... did she... did your mother call the police?"

"Naw...." Nino looked at his hands, his expression unreadable. "She was afraid... one of the neighbors heard the racket and he, uh, called the police. The bulls came to question the old man, but he had a story ready." Nino laughed sourly. "Yeah, he said that Ray had been beaten by some older boys in the alley, and he crawled home and died on the settee." No one bothered to investigate it further; the Church gave Ray a cheap funeral and a burial on Hart Island.

"Did he... I mean, did your father ever... do anything to you?" Wallace asked.

Nino shook his head. "No. After he killed Ray, I took off. Bunked in where I could, lived how you might expect, getting whatever I needed on the run." He had lived like an animal, shacking in burned-out buildings and under bridges until he could earn or steal enough to pay for a flop in the Bowery. He met Joey Texas one cold February morning, coming out of a diner on Orchard Street, red-cheeked and well-fed.

Mr. Texas, I read about you in the papers. I wanna be like you some day. I wanna be just like you.

Joey Texas had reached into his pocket and given Nino a silver dollar. *Here ya go, kid. See how far you can get on that.*

It was a picture of Joey Texas, years later, that Nino saw in the newspaper—a photograph and a caption, *Underworld Toasts Texas,* that made up his mind as to his vocation. *I wanna be like that,* he told Danny. *I wanna be somebody, do things, make stuff happen.* "You had a nice life," Nino said, "out there in Kansas, with your cows and corn... a nice life."

"I'm sorry...." Wallace shook his head. "So what are you going to do to Big Frank?"

"I know you wanna help," Nino said. "I'm just not sure—"

"Don't try and talk me out of it." Wallace shrugged. "Stanley was with him for... what? Five years? Can you imagine how many times you can rape someone in five years?" His face hardened. "Personally, I'd like to gut him like a catfish, if nobody minds."

"I keep going over it," Nino said quietly. "The things he did to Stanley... what he did to Danny. I keep asking myself if I wanna do this... if I wanna... take him out." He sipped in silence for a moment. "Big Frank and that Wacker dame... they're two of the same kind. Both of 'em are no good."

"You don't like her, huh?" Wallace got up and went to the stove, inquiring with a look if Nino wanted any more of the hot milk. "I take it she did something to you? Back in the day?"

Nino laughed. "Yeah, you could say that." He took up the deck of cards, shuffled, and began to lay out a game of solitaire. "When I wanted to get started, years ago, I needed some capital. A little something, you know, to cover expenses." He frowned at the cards in front of him. "Well, Lili Wacker fronted me the money. You might say we had an understanding. Signed a paper and everything."

Wallace sat down opposite Nino and tried his hot milk. "What kind of an understanding?"

Nino looked up. "She'd give me the money if I spent a weekend at the Ritz with her."

Wallace uttered a low whistle. "I'm thinking the two of you weren't playing pinochle," he said.

"Nope." Nino turned over a Jack. "I showed her a good time." He turned over a Queen. "Yeah. Then she tried to go back on our arrangement. She said she never gave me no permission for nothing, that she never signed no paper. I was just about to close escrow on The Two Aces and she called the bank and said I didn't have the capital to make the payments."

Wallace allowed that this might have been annoying.

"Yeah," Nino said, "and that ain't all. That same piece of paper? She agreed in writing that she'd stick to her own territory and not go trying any funny business. Next thing I know, she's runnin' girls and numbers right across the street from me. I went to see her—real friendly, like, trying to do business—dame completely blows her wig. Started accusing me of stealing from her. Said I was too busy making opportunities for myself and not leavin' any for her. She even asked me for a list of places I went and who I talked to—figured I had the bulge, you know?" He shook his head. "That dame is screwy."

"She sounds more than screwy," Wallace said. "She sounds dangerous."

"Oh, she's got bite," Nino replied. "She ain't shy about putting the bleed on anybody who'll listen to her. But I got that piece of paper that we signed. It's in my safe at The Two Aces."

"What are you going to do?" Wallace asked. He stifled a yawn. "To Big Frank, I mean."

"I'm gonna take care of him," Nino said grimly.

"Can I say something?" Wallace laid aside his cup. "Maybe you're doing this for Stanley, but you're wondering if it even matters because you aren't so sure Stanley loves you."

Nino's eyes were fathomless and deep, his expression inscrutable. "You said a mouthful, Kansas."

"So don't do it." Wallace laid a hand on Nino's wrist. "Walk away. Take Stanley and Danny and Eli and the rest of your boys and leave town. Go somewhere quiet and live out your life in peace."

"What?" Nino stared at him as if he were insane. "Turn yellow? Run away? Nino don't do things like that. Ain't nobody gonna call Nino yellow!"

"Ain't nobody gonna call Nino yellow," Wallace said, "until some day someone calls Nino deader than a doornail." He squeezed Nino's arm. "I don't want to see that happen to you. And I certainly don't want to see it happen to Stanley." He released Nino and sat back. "You love him. Anybody with eyes can see that. And I think—in his own stupid, immature way—he loves you, too. Do you know what any other man would give for that sort of love? D-do you—" He caught a breath and stumbled on, "Do you know what I'd do if someone loved me like you love Stanley?" He got up quickly and walked to the window.

"Great view from those closed blinds, ain't it, Kansas?" Nino had come up behind him quietly. "What did he do to you, this preacher man?"

"He didn't do anything to me." His voice sounded strangled, choked off at the source. "That's the joke. He didn't do a damn thing."

"You ever tell him?" Nino asked. "Stanley said something about fishing trips together—"

"Stanley should learn to keep his mouth shut!" Wallace sounded tired, defeated, like a man who knows the truth and wishes he could unknow it; Nino could sympathize. "We were friends," Wallace said. "We went fishing whenever he took his summer vacation. He had a cabin up in the woods, on a nice little lake and we'd go up there, just the two of us." He turned around. "It was nice. It was really nice. He thought we were just two pals, you know? Getting together for a good time. Except I… got the wrong idea." His voice sounded brittle, was undergirded with patent misery.

Nino nodded. "Yeah, I get that."

Nino, it ain't about you kissing me or me kissing you… I ain't into fellows… men just don't do it for me, and you gotta understand that. Danny's voice, as clear as a bell in his memory. He would never know how he'd broken Nino's heart that night.

"I'm an idiot. I should have known. We were always close, you know? He'd put his arm on my shoulder, we were always wrestling, kidding around...." He shook his head, as if to rid himself of a bad memory. "He gave me a proper talking to... sat me down in his office and assumed a pastorly air... said he was worried that a valued member of his flock was heading down the road to perdition!" Wallace waved his arms, an evangelical gesture. "He's engaged to be married. Can you get that?" His mouth twisted. "Miss Rosie Lee Summers, all buttons and bows."

"I been there," Nino said. "It hurts like a sonofabitch."

"Does it ever stop hurting?"

"No."

"Then there's no hope for me," Wallace said, smiling wryly. "I might as well throw in the towel."

"Wish I had better news for ya, Kansas." Nino drained the last of his milk and laid the cup down. "So, Big Frank."

"Big Frank."

"He's got a warehouse in the Bronx—a big warehouse. It's where he keeps all his hooch. There's two watchmen, but Eli can take care of them." Nino led him over to the table and fetched a sheet of paper and a pencil. "The first watchman is always in this guardhouse, here...."

"If we send Eli and his boys out there first, on the quiet, then we can probably get in and out pretty quickly," Wallace said.

Nino looked up and grinned at him. "You catch on quick, Kansas. Yeah, I like your style!"

DANNY swam up from the anesthetic, woozy and slightly nauseous. The first thing he saw upon opening his eyes was the bald man, now clad in surgical whites and with a little white cap on his head. "You look like my Uncle Dermot," he said.

"I very much doubt, Mr. Murphy, that your Uncle Dermot was as skilled a surgeon as I."

"Quite right, Dr. Groer." Henry Franks's tall frame dwarfed the German. "A success, Mr. Murphy."

"Then I can dance?"

"I would suggest you start with walking," Groer replied. "It is going to take much time. There will be a great deal of pain. You will want to give up. You will decide to give up, and then you will decide to try again." He shrugged. "Only time will tell. I have given you back a perfectly functional pair of feet."

"What he means is, don't get your hopes up too high just yet," Franks said. "The surgery is only the very first step. You've a lengthy rehabilitation ahead of you, young man. It's going to take a lot of courage on your end to see it through." He laid a hand on Danny's shoulder. "I won't lie to you: we don't know if you will ever dance again. The human foot is… a complex instrument, so very delicate, and yet so suited to its purpose. My advice is, see how things go."

"Thank you," Danny said. His throat felt raspy and raw. "Can I have a drink?"

"A few sips of water only," Groer instructed. A nurse came with a glass and a straw, and Danny drank thirstily until she took the water away. "Young man, I will come and see you tomorrow, and then the day after, before I return to Vienna. We will have a talk, and I must give instruction to the hospital about your rehabilitation." He turned away, paused, and turned back. "Your friend, this Mr. Moretti—he must care for you very much. My fees are quite expensive, as are Dr. Franks's. You are very lucky to have such a friend."

Billie wasn't allowed to see Danny until he had been moved to his room; she was waiting there for him when the orderly wheeled his bed in. She was dressed all in pink and carrying a bouquet of rosebuds. "Darling… I've been here the entire time. I was sick with worry…."

"I was in good hands," Danny rasped. "Can't think but they took something outta my throat to fix my feet with, though."

Billie grinned. "You had a tube down your throat," she said. "To help you breathe."

"What?" Danny blinked sleepily. "What's the big idea? I can't breathe on my own now?"

She leaned over and kissed him on the mouth. "There's someone else here to see you too."

"Nino!" Danny reached out and Nino hugged him. "They did something to my feet, huh?"

"They sure did," Nino said. He seemed relieved to see Danny was okay. "Does it hurt?"

"Not so much," Danny said, "but they gave me something. I guess it'll hurt later on."

"I can guarantee it'll hurt later on," Billie said wryly. She stayed close beside Danny, hovering protectively with her arm around his shoulders. "I'm sure the attending will give you something for it. You'll want it."

Stanley moved into the room, his hat held between his hands. "Danny. It's good to see you." He clapped Danny on the shoulder, smiling, but was obviously ill at ease with being in the hospital. Perhaps Big Frank had sent him here a time or two, Danny thought—it wasn't unreasonable to expect. God only knew what Big Frank had done to him, what injuries he had sustained in his time, and whether the gangster had inflicted lasting physical wounds to match the psychological damage he'd done. "I'm glad you came through okay."

"Thanks, kid. That's white of ya." Drugged he might be, but it didn't take a genius, Danny thought, to see Stanley was keeping his distance from Nino. What was going on there? And Stanley's cousin, what was his name? The guy from Kansas... he was like Nino's shadow. It was weird.

"We're gonna get Big Frank," Nino said. "For good, this time."

The hairs on Danny's arms stood up. "Nino, you ain't seriously thinking about—"

"It's all settled," Nino interrupted. "It's high time somebody got rid of him."

Stanley started forward, suddenly pale. "W-what? Y-you didn't tell me anything about—what? When?"

Nino raised an eyebrow. "Tonight. We're gonna get Big Frank tonight. And it won't be no tidy affair, neither."

"Wait a minute—" Danny struggled to sit up. "Nino, think about what you're doing!" He gestured at his feet. "You think this is the end of it? Look at what Big Frank's torpedoes did to me. Maybe you should leave things for a while, wait 'til the heat's off—"

Nino was scornful. "You think I'm gonna let Big Frank dish it out to me like that?" He glanced around the hospital room. "We hit him tonight, and we hit him hard. Ain't gonna be nobody left standing after this, except Nino."

ELI stood on tiptoes just outside the guardhouse. The man inside was on the telephone, having a protracted argument with some dame. It was important Eli wait for the right time—if he tried to silence the man too soon, he'd reach for his whistle and alert the other guy, and that would ruin the whole thing.

"Yeah, but Susie, you know me, I don't care about that dame! I ain't been near her all week!"

Eli rolled his eyes. Come on, already. How long did it take to break up with some jane?

"Aw, Susie, don't be like that! Wait—Susie! Come on!" He hung up the phone with a muttered curse and turned around to see Eli framed in the doorway. "Hey! Where'd you come from, mac?"

"Nowhere," Eli said, right before he hit him.

The man dropped like a rock. Eli slipped into the shadows and was joined by Nino's brother Tony and his friend Al. The three men ran around the long side of the warehouse, the part that faced the river, and met the second watchman standing by the wall, lost in thought. Eli thumped him on the head and lowered him noiselessly to the ground.

"You hit him too hard!" Tony hissed. "You don't hafta crack their skulls! Just a tap is good enough."

"Shut up," Eli said, "You ain't runnin' this operation. I am." He looked left and right, then broke the lock on the door and let them in. The warehouse was cavernous, dark, and empty. "It ain't gonna take much to set this alight," he said. He grinned. "It should go up like a Roman candle."

CHAPTER
THIRTEEN

STANLEY stayed close behind Nino as the older man crept along in the shadows, hugging the side of the building. He could feel the tension radiating off him, an almost palpable presence. Nino's shoulders were hunched up and he bent forward from the waist, like a hunting hound on the scent of something he'd been chasing for a very long time. Even though Wallace was most capably bringing up the rear, Stanley felt safer next to Nino. He exuded that invisible aura of confidence and power, and Stanley wanted to be near it, especially since they were bearding the lion in his den, as it were.

Nino hadn't wanted him along, not at first.

I don't want you anywhere near that son of a bitch. Me and Kansas here, we'll take him down. He'd argued Stanley's current state of mind was fragile, and seeing Big Frank get knocked off probably wasn't a good idea. *You ain't gonna miss much.*

I want to go. Even Stanley didn't know why he insisted on this, but it was important to him. *Maybe I want to make sure he's dead. Why are you taking Wallace? He's just as green as me.*

This ain't gonna be pretty, kid. Both Nino and Wallace wore black leather gloves and dark overcoats buttoned to the neck. *Sometimes it don't go easy. Sometimes they make a scene. You sure you're up for that?*

You think I'm gonna have a fit.

Nino looked guilty. *Kid, I don't want you to get hurt.*

This man owned me. Stanley made sure to look Nino in the eye when he said it so there'd be no mistake. *For five years he owned me, and the things he did to me, you don't wanna know.*

Maybe you're giving me a wrong steer. Nino checked his Luger, then stowed the gun in his pocket. *You know what's gonna happen if you wig out while we're in Big Frank's place? It's not just you to think about, here. It's me and Kansas.*

I won't wig out.

Nino exchanged a look with Wallace and sighed. *Alright, kid. It's all our necks if somebody drops a dime.*

BIG FRANK'S private apartments were located on the penthouse floor of a very swank and very expensive building of white granite that rose over the East River like a colossus. Almost nobody knew Big Frank's address, not even those closest to him—but before his accident, Danny had charmed one of Big Frank's distant female relatives, who, under the thrall of his Irish blue eyes (and a bottle of wine), had disclosed the mob leader's location. A lot of guys kept three or four places and moved around a lot, just in case someone was looking for them. Big Frank, however, was a creature of habit—once accustomed to a particular set of walls, he couldn't be persuaded to live anywhere else. He was certain no one in his right mind would even think of disturbing him in his lair, and made it known to the other mobs that anyone who tried would get a face full of lead.

"Alright." Nino pressed his back flat against the building. "This is gonna be quick and it's gonna be quiet. Kansas, you're with me. Kid, I don't want you in until me 'n' Kansas here get in the door." Nino pulled out his watch and squinted at it.

He needs glasses, Stanley thought. He had a sudden image of Nino twenty years from now: still dignified, still piss-and-vinegar, with a touch of gray at the temples and wire-rimmed reading glasses. He'd look like a genial college professor or a bank cashier.

"I'm gonna take him out—two shots, quick and clean. If my information's right, he's in the bathtub." Danny's informant had told him Big Frank took a bath every night at exactly 11:00 p.m., unless otherwise occupied.

Get your rube ass in here, kid! I'm nice and wet and slippery.

Stanley shuddered, willing the memory away. He had been little more than Big Frank's sex slave, and Nino had saved him from all that. Nino had made sure Stanley would never, ever have to submit to anyone again.

Suddenly Richard Kelly seemed a lot less interesting, and Stanley was vaguely ashamed of himself.

"I don't want you anywhere near Big Frank," Nino told Stanley. "Your job is guard the door. You got your chopper?"

Stanley hefted his violin case. "Right here."

"Good. Nobody comes in or out. Anybody comes in, you give us the high sign, but don't start firing guns. Me 'n' Kansas slip into the bathroom and get it done. Then we all three of us leave by the service stairway at the back. You got me?"

Stanley nodded.

"What about you, Kansas?"

Wallace looked like he was going to either throw up or pass out. "S-sure. I'm good. Let me have it."

Nino made as if to say something, but decided against it. "Come on."

The door to Big Frank O'Hara's private penthouse was breached by means of an ingenious wire loop Wallace had constructed and brought with him. "Where'd you learn to do that?" Stanley hissed.

"None of your business," Wallace replied.

Nino laid a gloved finger against his lips. "I said shut up," he whispered. Wallace slid the loop into the lock and twisted; the door popped open with a gentle click. Nino jerked his head toward the door; Wallace stepped lightly through and Nino followed. Stanley, tommy gun braced against his hip, straddled the entrance so he could see both the apartment and the corridor.

NINO reached into his jacket and removed his silenced Luger. He stopped, standing stock-still in the middle of the floor, all his senses straining to gather and process vital information. The icebox was humming in the kitchen and somewhere in the apartment a radio played quietly—a dance tune. The wind had risen and a light rain tapped gently against the windowpanes, a noise easily separable from the sound of someone splashing and grunting in the bathroom. Wallace nodded and Nino turned and went toward the bathroom.

Big Frank sat in all his blubbery glory, completely naked and surrounded by bubbles. A glass of brandy sat on the rim of the tub; a cigar protruded from his lips. His fat knees rose from the ocean of bubbles like twin islands.

I should at least look him in the face, Nino thought, but he had no stomach for it. He raised the Luger, sighted along its barrel, and squeezed off two shots. Big Frank sank into his bubbles without so much as a sound, and Nino was suddenly weak in the knees. He stumbled backward and crashed into Wallace, who caught him.

"Okay," Wallace murmured, "I've got you."

Nino couldn't stop looking at the spreading pool of blood, staining the bubbles pink. "Yeah. That's Big Frank taken out of the game."

Stanley was in the doorway, his gun held level between badly shaking hands. He watched Big Frank's lifeless face slip below the water, turned, and vomited violently on the floor.

"Come on...." Nino recovered, grabbed Stanley's arm, and motioned to Wallace. "Let's get the hell outta here already." He wrapped an arm around Stanley's shoulders and herded him toward the service stairs. "You jake, kid?"

Stanley nodded, wiping his mouth on his sleeve. "Yeah, I'm jake," he said. "I'm jake."

Behind them, Wallace was silent and pale. Nino hurried them down the stairs and outside; the street was relatively empty of pedestrian traffic and nobody driving by in a car would think to question three men coming out of an apartment building.

Nino pulled Stanley and Wallace into a doorway and waited. At a quarter past eleven, a dark sedan pulled up and blew its horn once. Nino shoved Stanley and Wallace ahead of him into the backseat. "Drive," he said. The car pulled out.

It had taken less than ten minutes for them to gain entry to the apartment, kill Big Frank, and escape. Stanley laid his head in his hands and shook; Wallace, sitting on the other side of Nino, stared out the window at the passing city, seeing nothing. The car was being driven by one of Nino's employees, another faceless soldier in the seemingly eternal gangland wars. Big Frank was dead. He was dead and gone forever; he would never hurt anybody ever again. Nino had shot him dead and Big Frank had slipped underneath the water, like a dead whale. The water, dyed pink from the spreading pool of blood. Nino hugged himself and shivered, his body vibrating in his clothes. Some impulse made him raise his head; Stanley was looking at him and there were tears standing in the rims of his blue eyes. Wordlessly, Nino reached out and pulled Stanley into his arms and hugged him close.

"It's okay, baby." Nino held him, and as he did so, he reached out a hand to Wallace on the other side and clasped it, held on. "It's gonna be okay now," Nino said, but he knew better. By killing off Big Frank, Nino had struck an irrevocable blow against Big Frank's gang, and they would be compelled to strike back. Anything was fair game now— anything and anybody. They would come after Nino, they would come after Eli and Stanley, Wallace and Tony and Delores. They wouldn't stop until everyone was dead.

IT WAS very late. Danny lay under the thrall of strong drugs, his dreams a series of disconnected images: in one episode, he and Nino were eight years old, playing in the vacant lot behind their tenement while Nino's brother Tony sat watching, picking at the scabs on his bare knees. Then the scene changed: Danny was dancing on stage with Billie, twirling her around and around in ever-widening circles while she mounted higher and higher, seemingly lifted into the air until she was flying over his head. He was running on the playground, running after Nino, but he tripped and fell because his new feet were too big, too clumsy and too big and his legs were too skinny, and something stuck up out of the ground and dug into his neck just underneath his ear.

"Wake up." The voice was harsh, not part of his dream. Danny lifted his eyelids with an effort and tried to turn his head on the pillow, but found he was immobilized by the gun barrel pressed into his neck. "You listenin' to me, mug?"

Danny forced himself to breathe. "Yeah. I'm listening." He wondered if he'd have time to yell before they plugged him. Somebody else would hear a gun go off. They'd have to. You couldn't just walk into a hospital in the middle of the night and shoot a guy.

"Your pal Nino made a big mistake tonight. And now we're gonna put one in him. Maybe we'll put one in you too. What do you think about that, mug?"

His vocal cords almost wouldn't work. "I wouldn't like that."

"You wouldn't like that." A second man came around the bed and leaned down, grinning at him. He had a skinny face and ears that stuck out and a shiny red carbuncle on his chin. Danny forced himself to remember the face. "How're your feet feeling?"

"Oh, you guys did a great job on 'em. I don't expect I'll ever dance on 'em again," Danny said.

"Didja hear that, Joe?" The first man pushed the gun harder into Danny's neck. "He ain't never gonna dance again."

"Breaking my heart," Carbuncle—Joe—said.

"Listen, boys, is there something you wanted?" Danny asked. "Because they're kinda strict about visiting hours in this joint. I don't want you birds to get into trouble, see."

"Give me a reason why I shouldn't put one in ya," the first man said. Carbuncle laughed, a harsh wheezing noise.

"Aw, come on. You guys got me already. It ain't fair."

"Whatta ya think, Joe?" The gun barrel pressed hard into his neck, and Danny started to pray The Act of Contrition: *Oh my God, I am heartily sorry for having offended Thee.* "Should I put one in him?"

He would never see Billie again. He would never see Billie in her wedding dress or dance with her at their wedding, would never hold her in his arms again.

"Aw, leave him alone." Carbuncle straightened up, took a toothpick he'd been chewing out of his mouth, and dropped it on the floor.

"We're gonna put one in Nino," the first man said, "and maybe we'll be back to put one in you." He leaned in and kissed Danny's cheek, a loud, smacking kiss, then backed away. Danny heard the door fall shut. He emptied his bladder into the bed.

"So HOW does this work?" Wallace asked quietly. He was sitting by the window, watching the breeze lift the net curtains and smoking a rare cigarette.

"They'll come after me," Nino replied. He took his cigar out of his mouth and examined the end of it. "Now that I've taken out their boss, well...." He glanced behind him to where Stanley lay asleep on the couch, covered with a throw blanket. "He took it pretty hard," Nino said.

Wallace nodded. "I didn't think—I didn't think he'd have the balls for it. But he did." He rubbed his eyes with his free hand. "God! Didn't I used to live in Kansas? Wasn't I a nice, churchgoing boy?"

"Yeah," Nino drawled, "church. Pfft. What'd church ever do for anybody?" He drew on his cigar. The radio played softly in the background: Scrappy Lambert singing "Make Believe."

"Oh, I dunno," Wallace said, "maybe if the preacher's a fox...?" He grinned. He looked tired and about a thousand years old. Of the three of them, he had stood up the best during the hit on Big Frank—something which impressed Nino mightily.

"I like you, Kansas."

"Do you?" Wallace turned to stub his cigarette out in the ashtray. "That makes me feel so much better. You have no idea."

Nino laughed softly. "Bitch," he said.

"Yeah," Wallace concurred. "Well," he said, "Now what?"

"Now we wait for Eli and Tony to show. If they got it right, Big Frank's warehouse is burning nice and hot about now."

"So you kill him and burn down his warehouse? What's that supposed to accomplish?"

"It puts him outta business," Nino said. "His whole organization's gotta start from scratch now."

"So... I don't get it," Wallace said. "You bump him off because his boys beat on Danny—"

"—No," Nino said, "not just because of Danny. Danny's only a part of it. This started with your cousin, there."

"So it's... revenge. For Stanley." Wallace nodded. "Why did you wait so long? Is there a statute of limitations on revenge?"

Nino smiled, but it was a weary smile. "Not that I know of." There was a series of soft taps on the door; Nino drew his gun and nodded at Wallace to get behind him. Nino went up and looked through the fish-eye, then unlocked the door.

"Nino—where you been, huh?" Nino's brother Tony rushed at him and embraced him; Tony no longer had any eyebrows.

"Shhhhh!" Nino shushed him, gesturing at Stanley. "The kid's worn out." He patted Tony on the back and stood back to let Eli come in. "How'd it go?" he asked.

"Aw, Nino, it was beautiful." Eli shrugged off his coat. "You shoulda been there." The warehouse had burned with a ferocious rapidity, Eli told them, flaming up in a conflagration that was seen for miles. He had made sure the fire department boys were kept busy with a series of false alarms, and so nobody managed to get to Big Frank's warehouse 'til it was too late. "Like a Roman candle," Eli said. He accepted a cold beer and gulped it thirstily. His hands and face were black with soot and his hair was singed. "It was really very nice."

"Alright, get on outta here," Nino said. "Last thing we want is all of us in the same place. You guys lay low for a while. Don't go nowhere 'til I call for ya, you hear me?"

They left by the back door, creeping down the alley to where Tony had a car. Nino waited at the open door, straining his ears until he heard their car drive away.

"I'm going to bed," Wallace said. "If you hear me crying or throwing up, just ignore me." He waved a hand and staggered wearily into his bedroom.

Nino sat in the dark, listening to the radio. Stanley stirred in his sleep and Nino was instantly at his side. He took hold of Stanley's hand and drew him into gentle wakefulness. "Hey, baby... you were dreaming."

"Nino...?" Stanley rubbed his eyes. "I was in Kansas. We were swimming. I couldn't find you." The memory of the night's business came rushing back at him; he sat up. "Did—how come—"

"It's oke," Nino said. "Don't worry. Everything's jake." He took a deep breath. "Listen, you should go to bed. You wanna sleep by yourself, I understand. I can sleep out here on the sofa. I don't mind."

"I don't want to sleep by myself," Stanley seemed pretty adamant about it. "I want to sleep with you. I want to sleep next to you, in our bed." He reached up and cupped Nino's face in his palm. "I never want to be anywhere but near you. Ever again."

He led Nino into their bedroom and closed the door behind them, and reached to unbutton Nino's waistcoat. He moved very slowly and with infinite tenderness, stripping Nino naked and tucking him into bed, then undressing himself. He took Nino into his arms and held him and kissed his forehead and his face, and after a little while, he kissed Nino's mouth, and the kisses turned torrid, hungry. Nino's whole body throbbed and pulsed with his mounting desire; he didn't know how much longer he could hold off.

"I have something I need to tell you," Stanley whispered.

"No," Nino said, "no you don't, kid. I don't care what you did or who you did it with—"

"It's not about that," Stanley said.

"You're here with me now," Nino said, "and that's all I care about, okay? We're jake, kid. There's no more to it."

"Yes," Stanley said, "there is. I love you."

Nino flushed hot and cold. "What?"

"I love you," Stanley said. "Nino, I love you. I'm in love with you."

"You love me?" *Now I'm gonna make an idiot of myself,* Nino thought.

"I love you," Stanley repeated. "I've treated you very badly. And I'm sorry. I want to make it up to you."

"Make it up to me?" Nino asked. He pulled Stanley close and kissed him, a lingering caress. "How long is this gonna take?"

"Rest of my life," Stanley whispered. "And I—"

The phone rang. Nino cursed and reached for it. "What?" he snapped. *Can't you dumb mugs see I'm in bed with my guy?* "Who is it and what do you want?"

"Nino?" Danny's voice sounded weak and faraway. "Nino, what'd you do to them, huh? What'd you do to Big Frank?"

Nino was suddenly cold all over. "Why?"

Danny told him.

"Did they do anything to you?" Nino pulled Stanley close. He wrapped his arms around Stanley's waist and held on to him.

"I'll kill them all," Nino said. "I'll kill every one of those bastards if it's the last thing I ever do."

CHAPTER
FOURTEEN

STANLEY sat at his desk, his reading glasses sliding down his nose, his whole attention buried in his ledgers. It was all a show. He was trying not to think about the way things stood: the impending war between Nino's mob and the remnants of Big Frank O'Hara's gang, the threats made to Danny while he lay helpless in his hospital bed, and Stanley's own state of mind, which nowadays teetered close to hysterics. Nino, being Nino, had taken steps to curtail the damage: he'd sent two of his boys to infiltrate the hospital staff and he'd had Danny moved to a private room. The nurses and orderlies had explicit instructions not to let anyone in; Nino's boys kept the room under continual surveillance, just in case.

A missive had been sent to Louie the Dope, Frank O'Hara's right-hand man. Written in Nino's own hand and wrapped around a box of expensive cigars, it more or less detailed what would happen to the remainder of Big Frank's boys if they decided not to take the proffered olive branch. The answer had come this morning, by messenger, and explained why Nino had sequestered himself in his office with the door closed: a silver-handled dagger wrapped in black silk.

Stanley sighed, pushed his glasses up on his nose, and bent to his ledgers with renewed determination. It was 11:00 a.m., and the temperature was already well past 80 degrees and climbing. There was a small electric fan on his desk and he had allowed himself the luxury of working in his shirtsleeves, but a telltale wash of perspiration was already dampening his armpits and his forehead was beaded with sweat. He reached up to loosen his tie just as his intercom buzzed. "Yes?"

"Mr. Z, there's a man here to see you. It's Mr. Kelly! Ain't that nice of him, coming all the way back here to see you?" Delores snapped her gum happily; Stanley could practically hear her jiggling.

"Uh, yes. Send him in, please." He took off his glasses and rubbed the bridge of his nose. This wasn't going to be very nice. This was going to be... decidedly ugly. He hated scenes like this, and anyway, it wasn't like Richard had done anything to him—quite the contrary. He'd taken a shine to Stanley, thought him beautiful, took him out for expensive meals, flattered him, and late one afternoon, pleasured him—quite competently—in the back of an automobile. It had been exciting, for perhaps all of one week, and then Stanley's keen and merciless conscience reminded him of his prior obligations... and his love for Nino.

He did love Nino; he was certain of it now. Perhaps he had been certain of it all along and had denied it to himself because he was afraid... afraid of being kept and captured and forced to do the will of another. But Nino wasn't Big Frank O'Hara—Big Frank was dead, and Stanley would never have cause to fear him ever again.

A tap on the door. "Come in."

Richard Kelly was resplendent in a pale-gray suit of light summer wool; he carried a walking stick and held his hat balanced in front of him like a plate of eggs. "Hello, beautiful Polish Stanley."

"Good morning," Stanley replied, deliberately formal. "Please, sit down. I... we need to talk."

Richard made a sad face. "That doesn't sound so good," he replied. "Are you blowing me off, beautiful Stanley?" He took a seat and laid his hat on Stanley's desk. "Have I been replaced in your affections?"

Stanley rubbed his forehead. "Richard—"

"—Richard, I think we should see other people. Richard, I don't love you. Richard, there's someone else. Richard, I've decided to join the priesthood." He grinned. "Although I've never understood how that last would prevent an amorous liaison, personally, but that's just me."

"I can't—I'm afraid I can't see you anymore." Stanley picked up a pencil and examined it, twirled it between his fingers—anything to avoid looking Richard in the eye.

"Beautiful Stanley, won't you look at me? I don't bite, I promise." Richard ducked his head in an effort to find Stanley's gaze. "Ah—those baby blues. So tell me: is there someone else?"

Stanley nodded miserably.

"Are you in love with him?" Richard quirked an eyebrow. "It is a him, isn't it? Please God, don't tell me you've gone over to the other side!"

Stanley laughed gently. "It is a him... it's Nino."

"Ohhh...." Richard exhaled dramatically. "Trading up, are you?"

"I'm in love with him."

"And what about us?" Richard leaned forward. "I'm not angry. I would just like to know. Is it me? Was I not... enough?"

Stanley shook his head. "I love him," he whispered, "and I can't stop loving him. He's—"

"The one for you," Richard finished. He stood up and reclaimed his hat from Stanley's desk. "Ah, well," he said. "All's fair in love and war, I suppose." He looked Stanley over appreciatively. "I hope he knows how good he's got it."

"I know how good I've got it," Stanley said.

"And there's no chance you'll change your mind?" Richard asked.

"No. I'm sorry." Stanley stood up as the door opened; Nino stepped through, holding a sheaf of papers. "Nino!"

"Hiya, kid." Nino handed him the papers and turned to nod at Richard. "Funny to see you up and about so early, Richard. Everything oke with The Two Aces?"

"As jake as you please, Mr. Moretti... but I was just leaving. I'm afraid your accountant has just broken my heart."

Stanley's face felt frozen; he could barely speak. "What he means is—"

"What I mean is, he's in love with someone else," Richard said. "And I don't have a hope in hell, or so he tells me."

"Yeah?" Nino glanced from Richard to Stanley and back again, uncertain whether he was being kidded or not. "That so?"

"He tells me he's in love and that he intends to remain that way." Richard sighed again, even more gustily than before. "I asked him about us—"

"—And I told him there is no 'us'," Stanley finished. "There wasn't, and there isn't, and there's never going to be."

A fleeting gaze passed between Stanley and Richard, and the latter smiled gently. "I fear I am out of luck," Richard said—a gentleman to the tips of his fingers. "Good day."

And he was gone. Stanley's legs suddenly gave out, spilling him into his chair. He clasped his hands together, squeezing his fingers. "I didn't invite him here," he said, his eyes fixed on his desk blotter. "He just showed up. I didn't—" He stopped short as gentle fingers lifted his chin. Nino was sitting on the edge of his desk.

Nino was smiling. He stroked Stanley's cheek, his lower lip, then leaned in and kissed him. He drew back, slipped off of Stanley's desk, and opened the door. He paused, and the muscles in his back tensed, but then he decided—the door closed firmly behind him.

Stanley picked up the phone. "Delores, I want to send somebody some flowers."

"Oh, Mr. Z, you shouldn't have!"

Stanley rolled his eyes. "Not for you," he said. He relented. "Alright... and some roses for you."

"Aw, Mr. Z! You're the best!"

A moment or two of beauty, Stanley thought, *before the slaughter starts.*

RICHARD KELLY stepped into his office and carefully hung his hat on the peg, laid his gloves side by side on his desk, and dropped his walking stick into a large Chinese urn by the door. He had forced himself to smile all the way back from Nino's offices, lest someone see him. It was vitally important that he keep up appearances, and an overt show of emotion in front of strangers—or even friends—was to be avoided. Now, in the relative privacy of his own small office at the rear of The Two Aces, it was safe to unbend a little. He sat down behind his desk and opened his ledger, closed it again, squared a pen-and-pencil set, touched a box of paperclips.

There is no us. And of course Stanley had been as gentle as he could be, under the circumstances, and Richard had taken his refusal like a gentleman. *I'm in love with someone else.*

But, my God! How it hurt! It hurt to be refused, of course, but worse, this was Stanley, who had somehow managed to pry open Richard Kelly's shiny chrome heart and climb inside. Stanley was the first in a very long time—not since his college days, when Richard had been an upperclassman at Yale, had anyone gotten as close to him as Stanley had. There was just something about the man, something utterly vulnerable but completely masculine, something that drew you in and held you there, struggling gorgeously like a butterfly on a pin.

Christ. Richard pressed his palms into his eyes and took a series of deep breaths. This was utter nonsense. Stanley was just another man, a man who belonged to someone else, a man in love with Richard's boss.

What he needed was a facsimile of Stanley. Perhaps an older, slightly more used version, a Stanley with a bit more iron in his soul—a worthy sparring partner, dammit. Richard needed someone who could dish it out and take it, a man who would go toe to toe with him and not gainsay an inch of that blessed conflict.

Too bad he doesn't exist.

He reached into his desk drawer and took out a bottle of Scotch, splashed two fingers into a glass, and drank it off quickly, with hardly a grimace. Ah, well. Good-bye, beautiful Polish Stanley of the big blue eyes and the sweet smile and the Kansas naïveté.

"Is anyone in here, or should I keep knocking 'til my knuckles wear out?" The door to Richard's office opened, and a man peered around. By his expression, he was none too pleased. "I'm supposed to be touring this place but he ran away and left me."

Blue, blue eyes, heart-stoppingly blue, and there was something familiar, Richard thought, in the set of the mouth—that full lower lip, perhaps....

"Did he?" Richard stood up and offered his hand. "Richard Kelly. I run The Two Aces. I don't believe we've met."

"Wallace Zadwadzki."

Oh God. "Z-Zadwadzki? Are you—"

"Related to him? Yes. I'm his cousin, but don't hold that against me, will you?"

Richard clasped his hand. "I wouldn't think of it. A tour, you said?"

"Yes. Some sniveling dunderhead was supposed to show me how this place works, but he decided to vanish." Wallace looked Richard up and down, obviously liking what he saw. "Think you could do the honors?"

"I'd like nothing better." Richard held the door open. "This way."

BY FIVE that afternoon, Richard and Wallace were still at lunch, lingering over their private table at Max and nursing their highballs with no intention of going outside until absolutely necessary.

"They're going to kick us out on the street," Wallace said.

"No, they won't," Richard said. "We're still spending money, aren't we?" He gazed at Wallace across the table, lingering on each of his features in turn. "You aren't like him at all, and yet you are." Richard offered him a cigarette and lit it for him.

"Is that a problem?" Wallace asked. "Of course, if you're looking for a reasonable facsimile—"

"No." Richard faltered for a moment, regained his composure. "No, I'm not."

"Because if you are—"

"I'm not."

"Don't play with me," Wallace warned. "You won't like it. I'm not like Stanley. I'm not like him at all."

"I realize that," Richard replied. "I'm not a stupid man, or even unobservant." He allowed his hand to rest on the tablecloth, close enough to touch. "I'm sure you have enough... romantic experience to understand—"

"I don't, actually." Wallace peered through the cigarette smoke at him. "Have any romantic experience, I mean."

"None at all?"

"None. I was in love with someone who... wasn't in love with me."

"Ah." Richard smiled wryly. "You'll find that's a sensitive subject."

"Oh, really? Am I to understand my rotten little cousin broke your oh-so-noble heart?"

Richard burst out laughing. "My God!" he said, "You are a bitch, aren't you?"

Wallace blushed. "Well, I—if you're going to—I mean, you—"

Richard clasped his hand on the tabletop. "It's quite alright. Really. And, by the way...." His gaze grew heated. "You're adorable when you blush."

"I don't blush."

"Mmm."

"I don't."

Richard smirked at him. "Shut up, please."

"How dare you—?"

Richard leaned across the table and kissed him full on the mouth. Wallace, flustered, returned the caress; the kiss was over as soon as it had begun. "I'd like to do that again," Richard said quietly, "but not in public. In fact, I'd like to take my time and do it, possibly more than once."

Wallace shivered. "I'd like that too," he replied. "I should tell you—"

"If you tell me you're in love with someone else, I'll cry. I've done that once already today."

Wallace blinked. "I'm... I've never...." He laid his cigarette in the ashtray. "I've never—"

Richard took care to be exquisitely gentle. "Ever?"

Wallace shook his head, unable to meet the other man's eyes. "Never," he whispered.

"Then I'll have to be extra careful."

The waiter appeared, hovering over them. "Would the gentlemen care for another cocktail?"

"Nothing for me," Wallace said. Richard shook his head.

"Then if the gentlemen are finished, I might gently remind them that we have to be making up the dining room for dinner...." He clasped his hands together and made the mournful face that seemed to be the province of waiters everywhere.

"Wallace, my dear, I think we should let the man do his work and get out of his way." Richard held up a hand as Wallace reached for his wallet. "No—this one is on me." He tossed some bills onto the table and took Wallace's elbow, steering him through the restaurant's shady interior and out into the hot white light of the summer afternoon. "Shall we take a cab, or do you want to walk?"

"Let's walk," Wallace said. "I'm... enjoying myself."

"So am I," Richard said. "I'm enjoying you too." He looked at Wallace and they burst into gales of laughter. "Careful," Richard said. "We'll get arrested for being drunk. They aren't even supposed to serve us alcohol—they'll lose their license and I'll have to drink in my office like I usually do!"

STANLEY sighed and lay back in the warm water, smiling as Nino's arms went around him. "This is the life," he said.

"Ain't it just?" Nino asked. He nuzzled Stanley's neck, kissed him, and Stanley shivered as Nino's lips touched his wet skin. "Where's your cousin?" he asked.

Stanley frowned. "Out—somewhere. I think Eli's showing him around, actually." He caught hold of Nino's hand. "I think we should make the best use of our time while we're alone, don't you?"

"Let the water out," Nino said. He stood up, shedding water droplets around him, and reached for the huge bath sheet that was hanging on the hook by the door. "Come here," he said as he laughingly enfolded Stanley and himself in the towel.

"This is cozy," Stanley said. He leaned in close so they could kiss. "I could get used to this."

"Mmmm," Nino said, "and then we'd never make it to bed." He rubbed them both dry, then dropped the towel on the floor and walked naked to the bedroom, Stanley following behind.

Stanley closed the door and leaned against it, grinning. "You know something? You look real good in those sharp suits you wear, but, baby? You look even better naked…." He pulled Nino against him and kissed him.

"OH GOD…." Nino was incoherent except for periodic invocations of his personal deities. "Oh God…." He was naked, trembling like a leaf as wave upon wave of mounting pleasure rolled over him. He hovered perilously close to his peak, but every time his breathing quickened, Stanley stopped what he was doing and waited 'til Nino's pulse slowed. It was impossible to feel so much pleasure; Nino would die from it, die from the ministrations of Stanley's long fingers and his clever mouth. "Oh, dear God…." The waves grew higher, deeper, more intense, rose and crested, and Nino was shouting, fists clenched in the sheets— shouting like an idiot and he didn't care, he didn't give a damn because it felt so good, impossible, impossible to feel so good and live, Stanley was killing him.

Stanley cried out hoarsely, his body shuddering, his breath coming in harsh pants against Nino's shoulder. He thrust against Nino and whimpered, a deliciously satisfied sound, and collapsed, exhausted, on the rumpled sheets, chest heaving. He rested for a moment, then grappled blindly for his cigarettes and lit two, handed one to Nino. "You okay, baby?"

"Mmph." Nino drew on his cigarette and let the smoke out slowly. "I think I saw God that time."

Stanley reached out and stroked Nino's cheek with the back of his knuckles. "I love it when we're like this… it makes the rest of it just… disappear, somehow… all the bad things go away."

"You know this isn't gonna be no cakewalk," Nino said, suddenly serious. He snuffed his cigarette and turned onto his side, gazing at Stanley. "People are gonna get hurt…. Probably a lot of people. Big Frank's mob has to come after me now. They can put two and two together just as well as we can. They know it's us what did Big Frank."

"I know," Stanley said. His face contorted. "It's my fault, isn't it? All of this is me—this whole thing with Big Frank—" It would go on and on and on, revenge upon revenge, another eye for another eye until everyone was blind.

"I don't wanna hear you talking like that," Nino said. "Listen to me, okay? You listen. I love you. This ain't got nothing to do with you. Big Frank hadta be stopped. If it wasn't you, it woulda been someone else that gave me a reason—after his boys got to Danny, I hadta do something." He kissed Stanley gently. "Sweetheart, if I could do this some other way—"

"No." Stanley crushed his cigarette into the ashtray and went into Nino's arms. "Don't talk about it. Don't say anything." He snuggled into Nino's embrace. "Just be here with me," he pleaded. "Just be with me."

"There's something I wanna say," Nino said, "and I need you to listen 'til I'm done talking, okay?"

Stanley nodded; there was just enough light for him to see Nino's face. "Okay."

"If anything happens to me—" He saw Stanley's eyes grow wider, the pupils dilated with sudden fear. "—then you go to Tony, okay? I told Tony he's gotta look after ya."

"When—" Stanley's voice cut off suddenly; he swallowed and forced himself to go on. "When did you tell Tony to do this?"

"About a month after I met you, when I knew…." Nino couldn't look at him. "When I knew I was in love with you. I told Tony that if anything ever happened to me, he was to look after you. And I went and made it legal." Nino rolled over and pulled open the little drawer in his nightstand. "Here—" He handed Stanley a folded sheaf of paper. "It's all legal and everything. Whatever I got is yours."

"You—Nino, you—" Stanley took the paper with trembling fingers and unfolded it. "You don't have to do this."

"Hey." Nino took Stanley's face between his palms and kissed the younger man's cheeks, his lips. "I'm in love with you. There ain't nobody else, and there ain't never gonna be nobody else, *capisce*? This is it, baby—me and you, Nino and Stanley, forever." His brow furrowed. "Tony ain't too bright, but he'll do right by ya. You keep the business going, you and Tony. Danny'll be on his feet one of these days, and you and Danny and Tony—" Nino took a deep breath. "Anyway," he said, "I ain't trying to be morbid or nothing, but I wanted you to know." He traced the folds of the sheet, following each crease with his index finger. "Everything I got is yours. You promise me you'll keep the place going, okay?"

Stanley went into his arms and hugged him tight, his slender body vibrating with the force of his emotions. "I'm sorry," he whispered, "about Richard and all of that. I didn't—"

"Sh." Nino kissed his forehead and pulled the covers over them both. "Shut up, now, or I'll make ya sleep on the wet spot."

Stanley laughed, wiping his eyes. "Wet spot?" he scoffed, "Like there's only one."

They were quiet for a moment, Stanley dozing in Nino's arms.

"Helluva way to end out the summer, ain't it?" Nino's fingers drifted through Stanley's blond hair. "Let's hope it's over quick, and we can get back to business around here."

"You know the cops are gonna perk their ears up," Stanley said. "You up to doing a stretch in the joint?"

Nino laughed. "No," he confessed, "but you ain't gotta worry. Ain't nobody gonna put the cuffs on me."

"Mmmm... that's what they all say," Stanley smirked.

"Hey—you ain't gotta worry about me," Nino said. "I'm not planning on leaving you for a long time yet, kid."

Stanley gazed at him for a long moment, memorizing the softness in his lover's face, his open expression and consummate vulnerability at this moment. "Promise?"

Nino cupped Stanley's face and kissed him. "I promise."

THEY were asleep when it happened, which was probably why the dark sedan bearing two of the late Frank O'Hara's trusted lieutenants was able to roll up to Nino's building unnoticed. Nino was dreaming: he was shooting dice with Danny and Tony in a vacant lot beside their old apartment, and Ma was shouting at them to get in and eat something before it got too dark to see their food. Ma was mad; she was thumping on the floor with a broom handle, and the sound got louder and louder until it finally burst against Nino's eardrums like thunder.

"Stanley!" Nino sat bolt upright; the front of the building was already in flames. "Go get Wallace! Wake him up! We gotta get out of here!"

"What is it?" Stanley was still half-asleep, stupefied and staggering. "What's going on?"

"Cocktail," Nino answered. "Not surprised. Come on, get dressed. Go get Wallace." He dressed quickly and grabbed his pistol from the drawer. There was nothing in the apartment that couldn't be replaced; the main thing was to get out. "Come on!" Nino yelled. "Kansas, get your ass outta bed already!"

Stanley came toward him, coughing, holding his coat together. "He's not there," he said. "Didn't come home."

"You sure?" Nino threw a glance toward the kitchen. "Go on outside. Call the fire department from next door. I'm gonna check the other rooms."

"Nino, he's not there! You—"

"Get out, goddammit!" Nino shoved him toward the door. "Listena me when I'm talking, okay?"

Stanley nodded, coughing, and went outside. Nino threw a blanket over his head and shoulders and crouched as low as he could manage, trying to see through the smoke. He kicked open the bathroom door and checked the kitchen, but Stanley was right: Wallace wasn't in there, and probably hadn't come home. Nino turned, intending to go out the front door, but the entrance was already ablaze and to go that way would have been suicide. He darted into the spare bedroom, went down the fire escape, and found Stanley standing on the sidewalk by the deli on the corner, where the rest of the building's occupants had gathered.

"Was he in there?" Stanley asked.

"Nope." Nino turned aside and coughed. "He didn't come home." He spat out a gob of smoky phlegm and what felt like part of his lung. "Maybe he got lucky."

"Yeah," Stanley replied. He could hear the fire engines coming; several of their neighbors craned their necks to see. "I hope so. What do you think happened?"

"The cocktail?" Nino asked. "Big Frank's mugs. Count on it."

Stanley huddled into his blanket and shivered, even though the night was warm.

"ARE you sure you want to go home?" Richard checked his watch. "It's just a little after two. The shank of the evening, as my old grandfather used to say."

Wallace reached across for Richard's hand. "I'm sure. Nino is probably having a green hemorrhage."

"Do people still have those?" Richard turned onto Nino's street and slammed on the brakes. "Good God." The street was choked with fire engines, policemen, and people in their nightclothes milling around. "Wallace, no—stay in the car!"

"My cousin's out there!" Wallace tore open the door and took off down the street. Richard pulled the car into the curb and set the handbrake, cursing fluently in a way that would have made his wealthy Connecticut ancestors spin in their graves.

"Wallace, wait!" Richard followed at a trot, damning the hot night air and the fleeing man, after whom he was compelled to go for reasons he still didn't quite understand. "Oh my," he breathed. The entire front facade of Nino's building was engulfed in flames.

"Woulda look at that?" Nino gestured angrily at the fire. "Goddamn it! I'm gonna hunt every single one of those mugs down like dogs!" He tried to light a cigarette but it snapped in two; he threw it on the ground and stamped on it.

Half an hour later, sitting over cups of coffee in an all-night diner, Nino was only slightly less enraged. "Every goddamn thing I own! We coulda been burned to death in our beds!" His face twisted. "I'll kill those mugs. I swear." The door opened; Tony appeared with Frankie Meatballs, Louie the Lug and Georgie O'Mara in tow. "Tony! Where the hell you been?"

"Sorry, Nino. All the phones was out. I didn't know nothin'." Tony slid into the booth and looked Nino over. "You oke?" he asked.

"Fine," Nino waved it away. "Every goddamn thing we owned was in that apartment. Those fucking bastards—"

The soda jerk paused in his attentions to the counter and glared in their direction.

"Those bastards," Nino continued quietly, "are gonna get something."

"I was afraid they'd attack The Two Aces," Richard confided. "It makes sense to go after your place of business, but I suppose...." He paused to light a cigarette. "I suppose they wanted to drive the message home—literally."

"You been by the club?" Nino asked.

Richard nodded. "Everything's fine. I left Harry in charge. He'll close up and make sure everything's locked down good and tight."

"Tony, get a coupla guys on The Two Aces. I wanna make sure there's nothing else planned for tonight." Nino looked at the big clock over the counter. "I gotta get some sleep. I'm tired." He called to the soda jerk, "You gotta phone in this place?"

"Sure," the man said, "over there by the door."

Nino called the hospital and got Mickey Rubble, one of the guys he'd sent to watch Danny. "How's he doin'?" Nino asked, after he'd told Mickey about the fire. "He oke?"

"Sleepin'," Mickey said. "Ain't nobody been in or out except that doctor, the little bald guy."

"He's jake," Nino said. "Don't let nobody else in. We can't take no chances. I'll call yez in the morning, as soon as I know who done this and what I'm gonna do about it, okay?" He hung up, rubbed tired eyes. "Tony," he called to his brother, "Call a meeting, you know where, for noon tomorrow—I mean today. Make sure everybody's there." He beckoned to Stanley. "Come on, kid. Let's find us somewhere to sleep. Kansas, you coming?"

Wallace threw down his napkin and dropped a quarter on the counter. "Yeah, I'm with you." He whispered something to Richard and hurried to keep up. "Nino, what's going on? What are you going to do?"

Nino turned at the cross street and hailed a cab. "I'm gonna wipe out the rest of Big Frank's mob, supposing it kills me. I'm gonna end this shit for once and for all. I'm gonna end it. Ain't nobody makes a monkey outta me."

CHAPTER
FIFTEEN

"TELL me you ain't gonna do this." Danny was sitting up in bed, looking better than he had since the attack. It was a little after eight on a Thursday night, and Nino had come to visit him, bringing Stanley and a bunch of violets. "Tell me all this ended when you fogged Big Frank, wouldya?"

"I wish I could tell you that." Nino was apologetic and a little shamefaced. "But it's gotta be done."

"Like hell it's gotta be done!" Danny appealed to Stanley. "Kid, can't you talk no sense into him?"

"They set my place on fire. Some of Big Frank's boys poured me a cocktail," Nino said. "You think I can let somebody do that to me?"

Danny was incredulous. "Nino, listen to me—I been laid up here forever and I've had a chance to do a lot of thinking. These pins of mine are probably finished—oh, I know that doctor is good, more than good, but there's only so much he can do and either way, I'm gonna be a cripple—"

"No you ain't!" Nino surged toward him, grabbing hold of Danny's arm. "You ain't gonna be no cripple. Don't even say that." His expression said he was fighting with himself, trying not to give into despair. Danny was his oldest and dearest friend. It was intolerable, after everything they'd been through together, that he should end up like this.

"If I ever walk again—if, Nino—I ain't gonna be no good. You think I can ever go back to the life we been leading, you and me?"

Danny swore softly. "Nino, I got news for ya: I get outta here. I'm gonna marry Billie and make a life for myself… somewhere away from here."

Nino's face closed up. "So that's it, huh? You're gonna leave me. After everything we been through—"

"This ain't about you!" Danny was furious, on the verge of tears. "It ain't about Big Frank and it ain't about you! I want to have a life, Nino—not running from the cops all the time or some other mob—a real life, with peace and quiet."

"Peace and quiet!" Nino sneered. "I got your peace and quiet right here!"

"Even you might want something different someday, Nino… even you. Don't you want to make a life for yourself, away from all this? Do yourself a favor. Take the kid and buy a house in the country or something."

"House in the country! That's a great idea," Nino said. "You got any more great ideas?"

Danny pressed his palms against his eyes. "I ain't doing it no more, Nino. I'm out."

"It's that dame of yours, ain't it? She's the one who turned you off all this. Yeah, well…."

"You leave her outta this. This ain't got nothing to do with her."

"Whatsa matter with you anyhow?" Nino asked. "You turnin' yellow or something?"

"Nino!" Stanley's pale face was flushed red with anger. "You're going too far!"

"Yeahhhh—" Nino made a disgusted noise, turned on his heel and stormed out of the hospital room, leaving Stanley alone with Danny.

"I'm sorry," Stanley said. "He didn't mean that."

Danny appealed to Stanley. "Kid, can't you talk to him? He'll listen to you, won't he?"

Stanley shook his head miserably. "No. No, he won't. He's got it in his head to do this. You know what he's like."

Danny sighed. "Yeah, sure, I know what he's like." He shook his head. "I'm tired... I'm so damn tired of all this crap. One of these days he's gonna walk into something that he won't be able to get out of...."

"I know." It haunted Stanley night and day. "I'm gonna lose him like that. I know I am."

"Ahhh, maybe I'm wrong." Danny made an effort to cheer up. "Maybe Nino can pull it off, huh? Maybe me and you are just a coupla old women, worrying about him so much. He's Nino. He's been in tough spots before, right?"

"Right."

"You wish you were back in Kansas, don't you?"

Stanley smiled. "Yep. Cows and corn and... Nino."

Danny peered at him. "You in love with him, kid?"

Stanley nodded, not trusting himself to speak.

"Then talk him out of this," Danny said. "For God's sake. I got an awful feeling. I think Nino's gonna get himself in trouble... bad trouble."

"WHO'S he think I am?" Nino raged and fumed all during the taxi ride back to their hotel. "Some kinda dumb kid? Some schmuck who don't know nothing?"

Stanley tried in vain to calm him down. "He's worried about you. I'm worried about you."

"Don't be," Nino said. "There ain't no need." He puffed savagely on his cigar and pretended to look out the window at the passing vista. "I know what I'm doing."

I'm not so sure, Stanley thought—but he didn't dare say it out loud. "I'm just afraid I'm going to lose you," he murmured. "That something might happen to you...."

"Ain't nothing going to happen to Nino."

That's what you always say.

Eli was waiting in Stanley and Nino's suite when they got upstairs; he'd brought some of the boys along with him, just like Nino had asked.

"Now here's how it's gonna go," Nino said. He pulled out a sheet of paper and spread it on the table. "We ain't gonna worry about retaliation because there ain't gonna be any. There ain't gonna be any time for that because we're gonna hit these goons hard and fast."

"That's the only way I like it." Georgie laughed. "Hard and fast, different dame every night."

"This ain't funny!" Nino swore at them. "Listen up, you mugs. We ain't getting no second chance here. We gotta do it right the first time. I'm aimin' to put these lugs outta business for good."

"So that's how we're gonna play it," Eli said.

"Yeah, that's how I figure it," Nino replied. "Here, here, and here—I want guys at the warehouse, the hotel, and the speakeasy, the three joints what make up the most of Big Frank's business. And I don't want no little tap on the shoulder, see—I want you to take 'em out. Bust 'em up good and set fire to what's left. I want 'em burned to the ground. This ain't no time for half measures. Hit 'em hard."

Stanley hung his coat in the closet and mixed himself a drink from the bar. The sick feeling in his stomach was back, mixing nicely with the butterflies and knots. "When's all this gonna happen?" he asked.

"Tomorrow night," Nino said. "I ain't wastin' time." He pulled out a cigar and lit it. "Besides," he said, "tomorrow's my birthday." He grinned. "Gonna make it a little present to myself. Sure."

Stanley waited 'til the others had left, then locked the door behind him. The briefing had taken most of the evening; it was now just past midnight. Nino sat on the sofa, smoking quietly, contemplating his fingernails. "Happy Birthday," Stanley said. He sat beside Nino and took the older man's hand. "How old are you? I forget."

Nino turned and gazed at him, something unfathomable in his eyes. "I'm thirty-nine, kid." He turned so he could look squarely at Stanley. "My brother, Ray, he woulda been thirty-six... if he lived. Yeah, he... he woulda been... no, I lie... he woulda been thirty-five. I was four when he was born. Ray, he wasn't never strong, right from the get-go. I guess Ma tried to protect him a bit more than me and Tony...

she had Ray right after she lost our sister... I had a little sister... she didn't live much past a week... pretty little thing...."

"Nino." Stanley's eyes burned with unshed tears. "You don't have to do this. It's not too late to pull out." Stanley clasped Nino's hand, squeezed. "Come back to Kansas with me. We can make lives for ourselves, you and me. Nobody'll care if you leave. Big Frank's dead and that's all over with—"

"Can't do it, kid." Nino reached out with his free hand and brushed Stanley's soft blond hair off his forehead. "This gotta be done. I gotta finish what I started, see. I ain't one to leave things undone. You know, the first night I saw you, at Big Frank's party, I thought you was the most beautiful thing I ever saw. I'll never forget it. And that song was playing, what's it called? That song you like."

"'But Not For Me'," Stanley whispered. "I remember it too. You were with Danny. You were wearing that black suit, and you looked—" He couldn't go on.

"Come here." Nino laid his cigar down and pulled Stanley into his arms and hugged him tight. "You're the best thing ever happened to me, kid. Don't you ever forget it." He drew Stanley's face to his and kissed him fiercely, kissed him again and again. Stanley clung to him, wanting him; he unbuttoned Nino's waistcoat and his shirt and wriggled a hand inside and nuzzled Nino's neck, but Nino pushed him gently away.

"Naw, kid. I can't never do nothin' when I got things on my mind." Nino stroked his cheek. "You don't mind too much, do you?"

"I just love you," Stanley murmured. "I just love you, Nino. That's all."

He took Nino's hand and led him to bed with a terrible sense of foreboding he couldn't shake. He lay awake for hours, watching the play of light and shadow on the ceiling and listening to the hum and rattle of passing traffic. Nino, for his part, didn't seem to be sleeping either, and around 4:00 a.m. he sat up and wrenched off his pajama jacket. "Too hot in here," he said. He flipped his pillow over and lay down and fussed with the sheet a bit, then huffed out an irritated breath and turned onto his side, facing Stanley. "It's gotta be done."

"Nino," Stanley said, "I'm afraid you're going to die. I'm afraid if you die, then I'll die, too, because I don't think I can go on without you." It was the longest, most emotional speech he'd ever made, and perhaps he was a fool for making it.

"Don't think that way, kid."

"I can't help it. I've got this awful feeling—"

"Come here." Nino opened his arms and Stanley moved over and laid his head on Nino's shoulder. "You don't got nothing to worry about, see? Nothing's gonna happen to me. Bullets just bounce off me." He tilted Stanley's face up and kissed him tenderly. "Tell you what: I'll make a promise to ya. After we get it all done, I'll take you out for breakfast, huh? Stand you to a real feed, just me 'n' you."

Something occurred to Stanley. "The apartment—it's all gone, isn't it?"

"Yeah, although I won't know 'til I get the report from the insurance guy." Nino sighed. "It looked pretty gutted to me. I'm thinking it's all gone." He kissed the top of Stanley's head. "Why're you worried about that? I can get you whatever you want. We'll replace all your clothes—I'll buy you new ones."

"It's not that." Stanley was going to cry. He was going to cry over something stupid and then Nino would think he was soft. "My horses...."

It was dark; he couldn't see Nino's face. "Your horses... oh God... oh, kid... I'm so sorry.... Lookit, right after we have our big breakfast, I'll take you over to that hobby shop over there on Orchard Street, okay, and we'll get you some nice wood and a whole new set of carving tools."

"That's very kind," Stanley said. "Thank you so much." It felt stiff and formal, the words awkward in his mouth. It was like one of those dreams where he was trying to say something, only it wouldn't come out right and he had to hurry up and say it before time ran out. "Nino, I wish—"

"Go to sleep, kid." Nino kissed his forehead, and Stanley knew the conversation was over.

He lay awake until dawn began to stain the windows and then drifted into a strange, twilight state where he dreamt he and Nino were partners in a failing brewery that would be repossessed by the bank unless Nino could find a doctor bag full of thousand-dollar bills someone had hidden underneath a bed.

He woke to the sound of Nino humming in the bathroom and the smell of coffee percolating in the suite's small kitchenette. He pulled on his bathrobe and went out to find Wallace sitting at the table, reading a newspaper.

"Huh," Stanley said.

"Good morning to you too," Wallace replied. "Coffee?"

"Yeah." Stanley accepted a cup from Wallace and gulped it black. "Ever wake up feeling like this is the last day of the rest of your life?" he asked.

"Yes," Wallace replied. "You know, if you're worried about him, you should probably say something."

"Oh, I've already tried that," Stanley said. "It's like talking to a shoe."

"Huh." Wallace turned up a new section of the newspaper. "But you are trying to talk him out of it."

"Nino doesn't listen to me on matters of business," Stanley said. "He does what he wants to do. The rest of us just... fall into line."

"Did you get any sleep at all last night?" Wallace asked. "You were pretty quiet, so I'm thinking you weren't making any whoopee."

Stanley goggled at him, shocked. "Making—excuse me?" He sat down at the table. "Were you?"

"Ah, no." Wallace lifted one eyebrow. "Please. I hardly know him."

"But I'll bet you were getting to know him," Stanley said. "Anyway, maybe we're quiet, Nino and me."

Wallace leaned across the table and regarded his younger cousin with concern. "If you love him—"

"I do."

"—then for God's sake, talk some sense into him."

The bathroom door opened, emitting a cloud of steam and Nino, smelling of soap and shaving lotion. He was wearing one of the hotel's toweling bathrobes and his dark hair was wet; he carried his toothbrush and had a towel slung around his neck. "Big conference in here?" he asked.

"We were talking about you," Wallace said.

"Yeah?" Nino helped himself to a cup of coffee. "Say, kid, I got an insurance adjuster gonna call around today about the apartment. I made a list of what was in there. Can you take care of it? You're better at that sorta thing than I am. I still got some planning I wanna do."

"Sure," Stanley said. He wondered if this was Nino's solution to Stanley's misgivings: keep him busy with the insurance company and thus keep him out of the way.

"So exactly what am I supposed to do," Wallace asked, "while you're off... wreaking havoc and Stanley is committing insurance fraud?"

"Hey!" Stanley objected. "I never said—"

"I think it's better if you stay here tonight, Kansas." Nino spooned sugar into his coffee. "It's gonna get nasty."

"Nasty like Big Frank?" Wallace asked. "Or maybe you think I'm gonna cause trouble? Lose my nerve at the last minute."

"Naw, you got a good nerve," Nino said. He gazed at Wallace for several long moments, measuring some ineffable aspect of his character. "Yeah, okay. You and the kid are with me."

"Where?" Stanley asked.

"We hit Big Frank's nightclub," Nino said. "Eli'll show you boys how to make cocktails."

"Believe it or not, we do learn how to mix drinks in Kansas," Wallace sneered.

"Molotov cocktails," Stanley said. "Fire bombs."

"Yeah," Nino said, "and I've already got a coupla guys in there, stuffing the place. It oughta go up like a Roman candle."

"But the people will be out," Stanley said. "Long before we hit the place—right, Nino?" He gripped his coffee cup so hard that his knuckles showed white against his skin. "There won't be anybody there. Isn't that right?"

"Yeah, sure, kid. Whatever you say." Nino picked up the room service menu off the table. "Now—who's ready for breakfast, huh?"

THE insurance adjuster had come and gone and Stanley prowled the hotel room like a restless animal while Nino stood smoking at one of the darkened windows. All the lights had been extinguished save for a small lamp on the writing desk in the corner.

"Nino—"

"Yeah."

"Are you sure?"

"Yep."

Stanley went to him and wrapped his arms around Nino's waist, laid his cheek against Nino's back. He didn't say anything; he didn't need to.

"Maybe I'll get outta all this," Nino said. "Your cousin's right—" Wallace had gone with McKenna earlier in the evening. "—And I should forget about the rackets." He studied the end of his cigarette for a moment, then crushed it out on the windowsill. "I got a bad feeling."

Stanley came around to face him. "Yeah?"

"Like someone's walkin' over my grave, you know?" Nino's eyes were huge, and he was paler than Stanley had ever seen him. "I ain't never been one for talking—it ain't my kind of thing. I gotta do something about things. I can't just stand around chewing the rag." He sighed, his shoulders drooping. "The people who give a damn about me, I can count 'em on the fingers of one hand—" He saw Stanley's mouth opening. "No, don't argue, kid. It's true. There's you, and my ma, God rest her soul, and my brother Tony, and Danny. And Danny... he's probably ruined for life because of this racket... laid up in hospital there.... We always drunk outta the same bottle, Danny and me, and what does he get for it?" He grimaced. "I might as well have done the job myself—it might as well have been me in there, swinging the hammer." He gazed out the window for a moment, looking over the city, his hands in his pockets. "Yeah, I gotta give this up. It ain't doing me no good. It ain't doing nobody no good." He reached out and caressed Stanley's cheek. "It ain't fair to you, neither. This ain't what you signed on for."

"Nino, I—"

"Remember what I told you: if something happens to me, them papers been drawn up by my lawyer, okay? Tony's got a copy and there's a copy in my gray coat that's hung in the closet there."

"Nino, I don't think—"

"Kid, don't be arguing with me!" Nino held him by the shoulders and shook him gently. "I ain't stupid. I know Big Frank's mob is gunning for me. This is how it's gotta be. If something happens to me—"

"Nothing's going to happen to you," Stanley said. Something very cold swelled inside his belly and spread throughout his body. "I will kill anyone who tries."

There was a tap on the door; Nino stiffened like a hunting dog and reached for his gun. "Who's there?"

Stanley peered through the fisheye. "It's Tony," he said.

"Alright, let him in."

Nino's brother stepped through, nodded to Stanley, and accepted a cigar from the box.

"Everything jake?" Nino asked.

"Yeah," Tony said, puffing appreciatively.

"That's us, kid." Nino pulled a shoulder holster on over his waistcoat and slipped into his jacket. "You oke?"

Stanley nodded. "Sure. Let's get this done."

TONY cut the lights on the car before they even turned the corner and rolled soundlessly up to the front of Big Frank's speakeasy. The place was deserted and silent and no lights were showing in the windows, but Nino was taking no chances. They had to stand up in the car in order to lob the cocktails into the building, and Nino knew this made them a target for anybody with a yen to throw shots at them. He held Stanley's arm until the last possible moment. "Okay, kid. Let 'em go."

Nino had learned to make a Molotov cocktail almost as soon as he could walk. He knew, too, there were only a few seconds between lighting the fuse and throwing the gasoline-filled bottle through some convenient window. He prided himself on his aim, which was almost always right on the nose. The bombs smashed through windows, landing their cargo of burning juice deep inside the structure. The front of the building exploded outward with violent force, knocking Stanley backward and showering the three men with debris.

Nino slapped Tony on the shoulder. "Go on, drive!" But for some reason the gears wouldn't engage. Nino cursed loudly and climbed into the front seat, then began yanking at the gearshift.

That was when it happened.

"Nino—"

Too late—a single man, running out of the ruin, raised his gun and sighted along the barrel. A flash erupted from the muzzle and Nino fell back, bleeding from the head

"Nino!" Stanley reached for him, cradling Nino in his arms. "Nino...?" He began to shake, the tremors starting in his knees and shuddering up his body, rattling his teeth and the bony ladder of his spine. His temples throbbed and it seemed as if a great weight was pressing down on the top of his head, crushing him. He had to stay awake; Nino needed him to stay awake. Nino needed.

STANLEY had frozen in place, one hand on the door latch of the open door, the other clenched in front of his face. His lips were drawn back over his teeth and his eyes stared ahead, seeing nothing. "Goddammit!" Tony grabbed the tail of Stanley's coat and tried to pull him back, but Stanley resisted.

"What's wrong with him?" Carl, a friend of Tony's and the replacement wheelman for the getaway car, bent and stared into Stanley's face. "He sick or something?"

"He's having a fit." Tony tried to pry Stanley's fingers off the door. "That smack-off with the gun? Where'd he get to?" A shot ricocheted off the hood of the car and another flew past Tony's ear. Obviously the smack-off had stuck around, and maybe he had friends. "We gotta get him to a hospital…. Nino, he needs a doctor."

He tugged Stanley backward, pushing him down on the backseat. "Here, take care of him. I gotta get this bucket out of here." He glanced at Nino, lying unconscious near the steering wheel, his hair matted with his own dark blood. Maybe there wasn't any point in getting Nino to the hospital… maybe he was dead already and the doctor would only confirm what Tony already suspected.

"Hey, Nino." He reached down and touched Nino's face; his fingers came away wet with his brother's blood. Tony slammed the car into drive and slewed the vehicle around, turning a wide circle in the middle of the street. The big Packard bumped the sidewalk, groaning as Tony crashed through its gears in quick succession, then roared away, leaving nothing in her wake but death and flames.

CHAPTER
SIXTEEN

"YOUNG man, you must get out of the way!" The attending physician stuck out an arm and forcibly pushed Stanley away from Nino's side.

"Please—you have to help him." Stanley was on the verge of tears, wringing his hands, trying desperately to contain himself and failing miserably. He was lucid now; his earlier fit had passed off, leaving him more or less untouched.

"I can't help him if I can't see him." The doctor was perhaps fifty-five, tall and thin, disgruntled and unshaven, as if he'd been awakened from a good night's sleep quite against his will. He peered at Stanley with bright blue eyes that took in everything, examined it, and dismissed it as not worth his interest.

"Please—he can't die."

"I don't know anything about that," the doctor snapped. "All I know is he's got a bullet in his brain."

Nino's face was utterly still and completely without expression. He might have been sleeping except for the blood that had run down and dried in his eyebrows and gummed his dark lashes together.

"Come over here, Stan—you 'n' me can get a cuppa coffee or something." Nino's brother, Tony, took hold of Stanley's elbow and guided him out into the waiting area. "Can't be getting in the doctor's way there. He needs to take care of Nino."

"I knew this was going to happen." Stanley clenched his fists so hard that his nails dug into his palms. "I begged him not to go. I told him there was no need. I didn't want him to go."

"He'll be okay," Tony said—but his staring eyes and pale face belied his attempt at cheer. Nino was going to die—Stanley knew it. It was only a matter of when. "They'll put him under and take the bullet out," Tony said. "He'll be oke."

Stanley's legs gave way and he fell into a chair; Tony rushed to his side and wrapped a brotherly arm around his shoulders. "Hey, hey, kid, don't take it so hard! Nino's tough. He'll make it."

"No, he won't." Stanley buried his face in his hands. "He won't make it this time."

He began to shake, and Tony rubbed his back and arms, trying in vain to soothe him. "Let me get you a cuppa coffee, huh?"

"I don't want any coffee."

"Kid—please." Tony gazed at him, and Stanley realized for the first time that Tony and Nino had the same dark-brown eyes, the same long lashes. "Let me do something. I'm liable to go off my nut sitting here."

"I'm sorry," Stanley whispered. "Of course—he's your brother. I'd love a cup of coffee." He sat with his hands between his knees while Tony fetched coffee from a machine and brought it back to him. "I keep forgetting… you and Nino…."

Tony nodded, not trusting himself to speak. "After Ray died, and our sister… there was just me and Nino left." He gazed at the opposite wall, tears standing in his eyes. "He looked out for me, and we both looked out for Ma. It's always been that way." He dropped his head, suddenly overcome; Stanley slid over and hugged him. "He's all I got left… I don't wanna lose him…."

They sat huddled together as the big clock above their heads ticked away the hours. Around midnight a nurse came out and told them that Nino had gone into "exploratory" surgery.

"What's that mean?" Tony demanded. "Exploratory. What's the doc gonna do?"

"I'm afraid I can't give you any more information," she replied. "You'll have to wait for the doctor."

"Hey!" Tony started after her, but by then the door had swung shut. "Don't you know who my brother is? Huh? Don't you know?"

Stanley put an arm around Tony's shoulders and led him to a chair. "We just have to wait," he said.

Eli arrived with Delores in tow; Wallace showed up on Richard's arm, and Agnes, Nino's private secretary, brought coffee and sandwiches, although nobody felt very much like eating. A group of the boys came shuffling in and sat in a huddle near the door, talking quietly among themselves and sipping coffee.

At three in the morning, the doctor came out, his clothes spattered with blood. "There's a bullet in his brain and I don't know if I can remove it," he said. "It's sitting in the longitudinal fissure between the two hemispheres."

"Can't you just reach in and pluck it out?" Stanley asked. "If it's just there—"

"It isn't that simple," the doctor said. "X-rays show the bullet is there, but it's migrated so deeply into the fissure that we can't actually see it. I'm not about to go in there and start digging around blindly."

"What are you gonna do?" Tony asked. "You can't leave it in there!"

The doctor peered at him narrowly. "That's exactly what I'm going to do," he said. "And if he regains consciousness—well, we'll see."

"What do you mean, if—" Stanley bit off the rest of the question. He didn't want an answer—at least, not the answer that was forthcoming. "Can I see him?"

"Are you family?" The doctor looked him up and down. "Oh, right," he said, not quite sneering. "All of you are his 'family'."

Eli straightened his back and glared. "That's a dirty crack, brother."

"Yeah, sure, go on in," the doctor said. "One at a time." He pointed at Stanley. "You can go in first. No more than five minutes."

Stanley slipped out of the group before anyone else could make a move, and went into Nino's room. Nino's head had been shaved and the wound in his scalp cleaned and bandaged; he was unconscious and might have been sleeping except for the incongruous cap of white gauze.

"Nino." Stanley sat down and took his hand, turned it over, and kissed the palm. "I know all about needing a rest but this is going too far." He stroked Nino's cheek, his full lower lip, the bridge of his nose. "You can't leave us like this. Tony won't make a good boss, you know that. He's not too bright and he's not you." He scrubbed his face angrily in his sleeve. "Nobody's going to listen to a word he says." He kissed Nino's cheek; his skin was warm and smooth. He still smelled like aftershave lotion. It might have been any ordinary night. They might have been in their bed at home, lying in each other's arms and talking quietly while waiting for sleep, or lounging together in their dressing gowns. Nino was self-conscious when it came to his looks and thought himself unhandsome, but Stanley loved it when Nino was naked or close to it.

Let me look at you.

Aw, kid, you don't wanna look at me. I ain't pretty like you are.

You're beautiful, Nino.

Yeah? You think so?

"You can't leave me," Stanley whispered. "I love you." Someone touched his shoulder and he looked up; Tony was standing behind him.

"I never approved of the way Nino lived his life," Tony said. "I always told him the best thing for him was to meet some nice dame and get married…. This was back in the day, when he was running after Danny." Tony sighed. "I was ashamed of Nino… ashamed of him being…." He stammered over the word, had trouble getting it out. "A finocchio."

"What's a finocchio?" Stanley asked.

Tony's mouth opened and closed a few times. "You know." He coughed. "A homo."

Stanley clenched his jaw. "He's your brother," he said quietly.

"He's all I got left." Tony turned to Stanley, looking frightened. "If he dies, I got nobody. Nino—"

Stanley hugged him fiercely, marveling to himself how like Nino he was when you got right down to it. "He won't die," he said. "Nino's tough. He's been through worse than this."

"I always knew somebody'd put one in him," Tony said bitterly.

"Do you want to be left alone with him?" Stanley asked. Tony nodded wordlessly, and Stanley stepped out into the corridor and shut the door behind him. McKenna was waiting for him. "How is he?"

Stanley shook his head.

"That bad?"

"Yeah." The desire for revenge was so strong he could taste it, a bitterness at the back of his throat. "I wanna find the mugs who did this."

"This ain't like you," Eli observed. He offered Stanley a cigarette and lit it for him. "Ain't you a nice, peace-lovin' kinda guy?"

"Am I?" Stanley snapped, the cigarette bouncing between his lips. "Nice and peace loving? Yeah." He snorted. "See how far that got me."

Eli did something uncharacteristic—he reached out and laid his hand on Stanley's shoulder. "It got you Nino," he said. He made as if to say something else but changed his mind. He nodded at Stanley as if the two of them shared a secret, and ambled back over to where Delores sat napping in a chair.

The door to Nino's room clicked open quietly and Tony came out, red-eyed and sniffling. He sat down next to Stanley, very much undone. "We had a nice talk, Nino 'n' me." He stared at a spot on the floor. "I told him how it was gonna be from now on. I told him."

Wallace left Richard's side and went to sit with Stanley and Tony. "How is he?"

Stanley shrugged. "Unconscious. I don't know. He looks like he's sleeping...." Something occurred to him. "Has anyone told Danny about this?"

"Maybe we should wait," Wallace said. "Danny isn't—"

"He'd want to know," Stanley said quietly.

"I'll tell him," Tony said. He got up and went to the public telephone, and in a moment, was heard speaking quietly to someone on the other end.

"So what happens now?" Wallace asked.

"To whom?" Stanley examined his hands, picking at a loose piece of cuticle on his left index finger.

"You... me... Nino... the business."

"I don't know." Stanley was suddenly and violently glad of Wallace's presence. "Can I tell you something?"

"Sure," Wallace replied, albeit a little hesitantly.

"I'm really glad you're my family," Stanley said, gripping Wallace by the arm. "You're all I have left."

Wallace looked anywhere but at Stanley. "Thank you," he said quietly. "That means a lot to me."

Stanley sighed gustily. He felt about a thousand years old. "The problem is—if I were a girl—if I were a girl and he asked me to marry him—well, I wouldn't wait for him to ask." He caught and held Wallace's gaze. "I'd just marry him."

Wallace reached for Stanley's hand and held on. "He had better be alright," he said. "He's been kind to me… took me in… I came out here after Jim. I mean, I know Nino's not a walking advertisement for your average law-abiding citizen. I knew when I came here that he was a g—"

"—businessman." Stanley finished it for him; they both burst into laughter so loud it drew Richard near.

"How is he?" The manager of Nino's nightclub was as dapper as ever, beautifully dressed in a dark suit and carrying his cane and gloves with his habitual aplomb.

"They… stitched him up," Stanley said, "but the bullet is still in there. It's lodged in the…." He couldn't go on. He stood up abruptly and fled down the corridor and through the double doors that led to the elevator. Stanley was outside the hospital, bent double and sobbing, when Tony caught up with him. He reached for Tony and held onto him, his long fingers digging into Tony's arms. "I'm going to find him," he hissed. "I'm going to find who did it and I'm gonna put one in him."

"I'll help you do it," Tony said, "but right now, you should be with Nino. He'd want that."

"Do you think he's gonna die?" Stanley asked.

"I dunno," Tony said. "Nino's tough… I mean, he's really tough, but…." He shrugged. "This time somebody really put one in him." He wrapped his arm around Stanley's shoulders. "Come on. Let's go back upstairs."

CHAPTER
SEVENTEEN

THE ambulance driver took his time on the many turns in this narrow country road, and Stanley was glad. He was glad, too, they'd hired an ambulance to take them out of state, because it meant everything Nino needed would be right at hand. Tony had arranged for the hiring of a nurse—a wide-awake blonde named Joan who wore her nurse's hat with the authority of an army helmet—to accompany them to Connecticut as soon as Nino's doctor judged him well enough to be moved. It was essential to get Nino out of New York just in case the remnants of Big Frank's old gang came looking for him. At first Tony and Stanley had wondered about a private hospital—until Richard had stepped in and suggested an unusual solution.

"He needs to recuperate somewhere quiet," the manager had said, "with lots of fresh air, and around-the-clock attendance, am I right? Well, what about my place?"

"Your place?" Tony was puzzled. "How's that gonna solve anything? You live in Manhattan. Last I checked, that was still part of New York."

"My family home in Connecticut has been nearly empty since my parents died. My older brother lives there now, but he teaches at the university and isn't home except on weekends. It's quiet and it's certainly secluded."

"You'd let Nino recover at your home?" Stanley realized, not for the first time, that there were untold depths in Richard Kelly, depths hardly hinted at by his placid exterior. "That's... incredibly kind of you."

"Nino's my employer," Richard replied—and he seemed a little embarrassed. "And he's also someone I admire and appreciate a great deal. More than that...." He trailed off. "I like Nino. I want to help him get well."

All of which had led to their ambulance driver taking the turns quite slowly and Stanley's cautious optimism on this sunny, late-August morning.

"You can talk to him, you know." Joan looked up from her book to smile at Stanley. "He may be able to hear you. And I'm sure he's wondering what's going on. It will do him good to hear a friendly voice." She handed Stanley a newspaper. "Here—get him caught up on the latest news. But nothing upsetting." She grinned, and Stanley suddenly liked her enormously. "Better stick to the Society pages."

Tony and Wallace were following in Richard's car; Eli and Delores had opted to stay behind in the city just in case something broke that Stanley or Tony needed to know about. Eli had gone to ground in Delores's apartment; the two of them were enjoying a private lovers' weekend while Delores's younger brother, Casey, acted as both lookout and errand boy. Nino had always trusted Eli and Tony trusted him just as much; Eli had instructions to contact Tony at Richard's house if any of Big Frank's old cronies surfaced.

"You really care about him, don't you?" Joan regarded Stanley with affection.

"Yes...." He couldn't meet her gaze. "Yes, I do. I l-love him."

"He's a relative of yours?"

"No." Stanley smiled to himself. "No, he's no relation to me at all." *Here it comes*, he thought. Now the girl would look puzzled, then it would occur to her what Stanley meant, and if she was like every other woman nowadays, she'd blush red and stammer and Stanley would have to reassure her it was all right, but yes, he and Nino were a couple, and maybe she'd rat him out to the cops.

She surprised him. "How long have you been together?" she asked.

"Uh...." Stanley blinked, but recovered. "Just a few months."

"You're very lucky. What a handsome man he is." She laid her hand on Nino's arm for a moment. "I'm so sorry this happened. I hope we can all help him to recover."

Her unexpected kindness brought Stanley to the brink of tears, or maybe it was the unmitigated strain he'd been under the past few months. "Thank you," he whispered.

"Keep the faith, Mr. Zadwadzki—I have a good feeling about this one."

He nodded, not trusting himself to speak; Joan reached out and clasped his hand. "Don't cry," she said, "or I'll start crying too. I'm such a sucker for a love story."

Stanley laughed gently through his tears. "I couldn't bear to lose him. He's all I've got." He wiped his eyes and tried to marshal himself. "I'm curious," he said, once he'd regained his faculties. "Most people are shocked when they realize that Nino and I are... a couple. But you aren't shocked at all."

"My brother," Joan said. "My younger brother loves a wonderful man named Donald. They live in San Francisco together."

"Oh," Stanley said quietly. "So you knew... Nino and me...."

"No, not outright," she said. "But you were definitely concerned with his well-being. That's why I asked if you two were related."

"Most people make that assumption," Stanley said. "I don't correct them. It's generally safer that way."

Joan lifted Nino's wrist to take his pulse.

"It's too bad everyone doesn't think like you," Stanley said. He glanced up as the ambulance took the final turn leading to the Kellys' private drive. "Looks like we're here."

"Oh yes," Joan said. "That's old Dr. Kelly's place. I'd know it in the dark."

"Doctor Kelly?"

"The Kelly family patriarch. I'm from these parts. Yes, old Doctor Kelly, now there was a character." She smiled. "But listen to me, telling tales out of school!" She adjusted the covers over Nino's chest. "Here we are, Mr. Moretti—your personal, private hospital.

You're here for the duration. Now how about you open up your eyes and talk to us, huh?"

But Nino remained in his coma just as he had since the night he'd been shot. Perhaps, Stanley thought bleakly, he'd never come out of it. Perhaps he'd be this way for the rest of his life, in a lingering state, or whatever they called it. Perhaps he'd never wake up again.

The ambulance stopped neatly in front of a large Colonial mansion. Stanley whistled quietly. "Would you look at this place?"

"Come on," Joan said. "You can help me get him settled."

RICHARD had instructed the servants to set aside a large, sunny room on the main floor for Nino's sickroom. Tony had worked with Nino's doctor and Joan to determine the patient's needs, and had such things as Nino might require already installed in his room. And Richard, in his own inimitable fashion, had filled the room with flowers. Under Joan's guidance, the ambulance attendant and Stanley soon had Nino installed in bed, with the windows open to let in the summer breeze.

"Well," Stanley said. "This sure is a nice place you got."

"Thanks," Richard said. "We like it just fine."

"It's really nice of you to let Nino recover here," Stanley said. He wished Wallace would hurry back from the bathroom; he was running out of things to talk about and the conversation was rapidly becoming awkward. "Listen, I meant to say, about you and me—"

"There's no need to say anything," Richard replied. He moved closer to Stanley, close enough to touch his arm. "Really, I mean it. You and I might have lasted a week, maybe a month. We're too different. You belong with someone like Nino." He squeezed Stanley's arm and let his hand drop. "If you hadn't... dumped me—" He grinned to take the sting out of the words. "—I would have never met Wallace." He glanced around, satisfying himself that Wallace was nowhere near. "He may be The One, you know."

"Oh?" Stanley couldn't help grinning. "That bad, huh?"

"Horrible," Richard replied. "He's so dreadfully chaste and proper. Won't let me stay the night, insists on keeping himself pure until we're married—you know the sort of girl."

"Mmmm." Stanley had a sudden urge to giggle. "Let me guess: you're just dying to pry apart his dimpled knees and... make free with the goods." He offered Richard a cigarette, then lit it for him.

"That's about it," Richard said. "It's killing me," he confessed. "I've no idea what to do!"

"My heart bleeds for you," Stanley said.

"Hey!" Joan bore down on them with the ferocity of a harpy. "No smoking in the sickroom! Get out!"

Richard attempted conciliation. "We were just—"

"I don't care, Richard Kelly! Get out of here!" She gestured at Stanley with her chin. "I'm going to give the patient his bed bath in a minute. You can help if you want to—but finish that smoke before you come back in here."

"Yes ma'am," Stanley said. Five minutes in Nino's new home and she had already taken charge of everything. He stepped back just as she closed the door in his and Richard's face.

"Fierce little thing," Richard said. "Come on—I'll show you the grounds and we can finish our smoke in peace."

TONY hung around long enough to see that Nino was safely installed and then went to unpack his things in the room Richard's butler had indicated was to be his for the duration. The room was a very spacious and well-appointed suite, like something out of the Waldorf, and Tony felt more than a little conscious of his plebeian roots as he hung his shirts and trousers in the spacious closet. He opened all the drawers in the dresser, more out of habit than from curiosity, and tried all the windows to see how they opened and closed. The window nearest his bed looked out over the Kelly estate's manicured acres and was shaded by a large sycamore tree—it probably scraped against the roof and made a helluva racket, Tony thought. There hadn't been any trees shading the windows of his and Nino's old bedroom back in New

York, and the only thing that made a helluva racket at night was his father, beating the hell outta Ray or their ma.

He left the room and went down the stairs, finding himself in the wide entrance hall. *Now what?* Nino was being looked after by the nurse dame, and Stanley and Richard had disappeared. Maybe he shouldn't wander around in a place like this, just in case someone thought he was gonna take something. *Yeah, that'd make 'em really blow their wigs,* he thought—*there's some mug from New York wandering around and touching our stuff.*

There was a door off the main foyer. He pushed it open and found himself suddenly in a room full of books. Maybe he oughtn't to be in here either, but he couldn't help himself. Since he was a kid, Tony had loved books and read as many as he could lay hands on. Their ma had never had any money for college, and even if he could get in, Tony wasn't exactly university material. Then Nino got into the rackets and it was only natural Tony follow him, so thus was the pattern of his life.

But he loved books... and this room, this fancy-pants library... this was like one of Tony's wet dreams. He glanced over his shoulder, but nobody was around.

He forced himself to go slowly, because this was a library that encouraged one to indulge the senses: more fine books than he had ever seen, bound in leather and their titles stamped in gold. All the classics were here, and a great many modern novels. He chose a volume of Dashiell Hammett and settled into a leather chair. He was deep into the adventures of Sam Spade and the black bird when he became aware he was being watched. He raised his head and met a bemused, blue-eyed gaze from a slightly older man in silver-rimmed glasses.

"Enjoying yourself?" the man asked.

Tony stood up. "Yeah, maybe I am," he said. "As long as nobody minds."

"Oh, I've no problem with you..." The man was trying hard not to smile. "...appropriating my library."

"Your library?"

Oh shit.

"Just as long," the man continued, "as you're enjoying yourself." He read the title of the book Tony had abandoned. "Hammett, eh? He's one of my personal favorites."

"I wasn't touchin' nothin'," Tony said. "I swear to God, I didn't touch nothin' except this book. I'm—Mr. Kelly, he—my brother is—"

"It's fine," the man said, laughing. "Please, don't trouble yourself. It's perfectly fine. I'm Henry Kelly, by the way—" He extended his hand. "—The other Mr. Kelly, you could say."

"Nice to meetcha," Tony said. He couldn't let go of Henry Kelly's hand; there was something compelling, something magnetic, in the other man's blue eyes. He'd never gone in for men—he'd only ever been interested in women, and few enough of those. Since his sixteenth birthday, Tony had had exactly one "serious" girlfriend. He'd just never had the time or the inclination, and the guys he'd seen who had steadies of their own had nothing but trouble. If he wanted sex, he'd pay for it like any other self-respecting mug—or boff it, like he usually did.

He'd been boffing it a while.

"Most people call me Hank," Henry said. "And you are…?"

"Oh! Uh, Tony… Anthony… Moretti."

"Giovaninni's brother, right?"

Tony blinked at him. "Who?"

"Giovaninni Moretti. Your brother."

"Oh, right! Yeah, Nino's my brother. Yeah, we're real tight, me and Nino. Real tight. Listen, I'm sorry I barged in here. I'll just be going."

"Wait." Henry—Hank—caught Tony's wrist. "It's perfectly alright. You're welcome to read anything in here. I guess I was surprised to see someone in here. Someone besides me, that is."

He smiled, and Tony's heart paused, literally, then restarted itself with a god-awful thump.

"Are you alright?" Henry asked. He stepped a little closer and took hold of Tony's arm. "You've gone rather an alarming shade of pale…."

"I think I'm sick or somethin'," Tony whispered. He staggered a little, suddenly light-headed, and was caught in the other man's arms. "Maybe it's the heat," he said... and fainted dead away.

"WHAT just happened?" Tony opened his eyes to an unfamiliar interior landscape and the face of a vaguely familiar man wearing wire-rimmed glasses.

"I'm afraid you fainted. Here—" The stranger passed him a glass of cold water. "—You might want to drink some of this."

Dr. Kelly—Tony remembered now. Richard Kelly's older brother was some kind of professor. "I've never fainted in my life," he protested.

"Well, you did, I'm sorry to say." Kelly sat on the edge of the sofa. "When's the last time you ate a decent meal, by the way?"

Tony thought back. "It musta been... I dunno... day before yesterday?"

Hank made a rueful face. "You poor man! No wonder you fainted. Your blood sugar is probably around your ankles."

Tony glanced toward his feet; someone had removed his shoes. His tie was loosened as well and his collar undone. "Huh?"

"I'll ask Mabel to make you some breakfast." Hank Kelly rose from the sofa. "How do you like your eggs?"

"Aw, I ain't fussy," Tony said. "And some coffee?" He hoped he wasn't coming across too bold—if Ma were still alive, she'd knock his ears down. "I mean, some coffee please."

"Some coffee please?" Hank Kelly smiled at him in a way that made Tony's empty stomach turn somersaults. "I'll see if we have any coffee please. You take it black or...."

"Cream and sugar," Tony replied, "and thank you."

"You're very welcome, Anthony."

The way he said "Anthony" made Tony's unshod toes curl. He hoped Dr. Kelly didn't notice.

"Dr. Kelly?"

Hank turned at the doorway. "Yes?"

Tony struggled for a moment then mastered himself. "How's my brother?"

"He's going to be just fine, son."

Tony allowed himself to exhale. "Okay."

"You love your brother a lot, don't you?"

"Yeah. Nino's all I got."

Hank nodded. "I know just what you mean. It's just Ricky and I in the world… I wouldn't know what to do without him. He really will be just fine, you know."

"I'm not sure. Nino and me, we ain't… we come in this world outta luck, ya know? I ain't so sure."

"I am." Hank squeezed his shoulder. "Breakfast?"

"Please." Tony nodded, ashamed of the tears standing in his eyes. "Thank you."

CHAPTER
EIGHTEEN

THE long summer days wound slowly down to the cooler, shorter days of autumn, and the magnificent old trees on the Kelly estate turned from green to orange and gold. Stanley spent much of his time at Nino's bedside, reading to him, talking to him, massaging his hands and his head, and playing the radio for him. Joan was insistent the patient be given as much positive stimulation as possible.

"Positive stimulation," she said. "Positive. I want none of that New York gangster talk, no loud noises, no quarrelling." She guarded Nino's sickroom like a terrier with a bone; the only one who had carte blanche was Stanley, and then only if he behaved himself. A day or two into Nino's convalescence, Joan had reprimanded Stanley for sobbing by Nino's bed. "He might be able to hear you," she chided, "and what's he going to think? That you've given up on him? You want to snivel, go somewhere else."

Tony spent much of his time with Hank, sitting in on his university lectures, organizing his papers for him, and retrieving research materials from the library. Nino's brother seemed to revel in the chance to be Dr. Kelly's unofficial research assistant, and if he and Hank sometimes disappeared for an hour or two after dinner, well, nobody would begrudge them their time alone. Maybe they were friends, and maybe they were feeling their way slowly forward into something else, but no one—least of all Stanley—had any intention of interfering with it. Tony looked in on his brother several times a day, always inquiring after Nino's condition, anxious for Nino's return to consciousness, but apart from his brief, hovering visits to the unconscious man's bedside, he occupied himself elsewhere.

Wallace, too, came to see Nino, mostly standing over him and gazing down at him with rapt attention. "He doesn't move?" he asked.

"No," Stanley replied. He was careful to keep his tone light: it wouldn't do to betray the desperation that was the companion of his hours. "No, he doesn't move. He just sleeps."

"He's so still," Wallace observed. He didn't touch Nino like the others did—like Tony did, holding Nino's hands or stroking his face or, once, when he forgot Stanley was in the room, kissing his brother's forehead gently. Even Willard Joyce, the family gardener, came to pay his respects to Nino, leaning down to speak to him or standing quietly, one hand pressed palm down against the blankets over Nino's heart. "His hair's grown back."

"Yeah. If this keeps up, we'll have to get a barber," Stanley replied. But Nino's rich black hair was dull and lusterless and ragged.

"Do you shave him?" Wallace asked.

"Joan—Joan shaves him," Stanley said. He didn't say that touching Nino's skin disturbed him, that it was distasteful to him and smacked of disrespect. "I'm too clumsy."

Stanley sat beside Nino's bed one warm October evening, reading aloud to him while the radio played softly in the background. The sickroom windows were open to the gentle breeze, and the sounds of crickets and birdsong could be heard from the garden just beyond. Stanley was reading F. Scott Fitzgerald's *The Great Gatsby*—more for himself than for Nino. Despite Joan's protestations that Nino was, at some level, aware of him and even eager for his presence, Stanley doubted anything he said or did had any impact on Nino whatsoever. He knew it, in his most secret heart of hearts, just as he knew whatever personality Nino possessed, whatever made him irrevocably himself, was elsewhere.

"Our eyes lifted over the rose-beds and the hot lawn and the weedy refuse of the dog-days along-shore. Slowly the white wings of the boat moved against the blue cool limit of the sky. Ahead lay the scalloped ocean and the abounding blessed isles," said Stanley. He paused in his reading and looked at the still, placid face in the bed. "Maybe when you're well, we can take a trip, huh? That sure would be nice." He turned the page and then stopped suddenly.

Nino was awake.

"Oh my God." The book slid from Stanley's nerveless fingers and hit the floor with a muffled plop. He was shaking as if he'd been suddenly taken with a catastrophic illness. "Nino. Joan—Joan!" He bolted from the room, his heart hammering in his chest, and so great was his excitement he felt it might well tear him in half. "He's awake—call the doctor. Nino's awake."

"Are you sure?" She reached for her stethoscope and followed Stanley into the sickroom. "Sometimes comatose patients open their eyes but it's just an involuntary—"

"Miss." Nino's voice was weak and raspy from his long silence, but it was Nino's voice. "I'm afraid I don't understand. Where am I? What's this place?"

"Nino." Stanley tried to keep his voice level and not upset Nino. "You're awake... oh my... this is... amazing. I'm so glad."

"Mr. Zadwadzki, really, you're in my way—" Joan pushed past him with a glare. "I need to check the patient's vitals, if you don't mind."

Stanley took up Nino's hand and held it, gently stroking the backs of Nino's fingers. "I'm so glad... you had us so worried... but you're better now and we can... well, we can go wherever we want to, can't we? And do whatever we want."

Nino's brow furrowed. "I been sick?" he asked.

Stanley nodded. "Yeah. You been sick for a while. But you're okay now—"

"What's the date? What day is it?"

"It's October seventeenth," Stanley said. "You're all better now, and we can—"

"And where are we?" Nino asked. "I mean, what's this place?"

"You're at Richard Kelly's house... in Connecticut."

Joan looked across at him. "Try not to excite yourself." She patted Nino's chest. "I'll send for the doctor."

"Nino." Stanley clasped his hand, eyes shining. "Nino, we can have our own lives now. We don't have to run anymore. Big Frank's mob—they think you're dead! Don't you see, Nino? It's wide open. We can go anywhere we like and do anything we want to do."

Nino tilted his head and regarded Stanley, and something about that look froze Stanley's soul. "There's just one thing," Nino said. "Who are you?"

TONY was in the library when Nino's nurse tapped on the door. "Mr. Moretti!" She seemed flushed and out of breath. "He's awake—your brother is awake!"

Tony raced along the corridor, stopped suddenly in the doorway of Nino's sickroom, and stared at the dark-haired man sitting up in bed. "Nino?"

"Hey. Get in here."

Tony stood motionless, as if rooted to the floor. "Nino?"

"Get in here, I said! Whassa matter? Don't you listen to direct orders no more?" Nino reached out and grasped Tony's hand as his brother came near. "How are ya?"

"Aw, Nino." He hugged Nino gingerly. "You sure had us scared there for a while. Don't do that no more, okay?" He turned, aware that Stanley was sitting quietly on a hard wooden chair in the corner of the room. "Nino's awake, huh? Ain't that good? That's good, ain't it?"

Stanley nodded. "Yeah, it's great. I'm glad." He got up and walked out.

"You know," Nino said. "That young fella—he seems like a pretty good sort... bit down in the mouth, though. Maybe we could get him to work in our organization. Whatta ya think?"

Tony stared at him. "Nino, don't you... don't you know who he is?"

NINO was sitting up in bed, freshly washed and shaved and eating a bowl of soup. Joan hovered nearby and attempted to help him, but Nino waved her off. "I can still feed myself," he snapped. "I ain't so far gone." He saw Tony standing there and motioned him over. "Listen, we're going back to the city as soon's I finish up here. I got a lot of work to do. I want you to get on the horn to Sammy. Tell him I need three—no, five—more trucks. No reason why we can't expand toward Jersey, Long Island. What's the climate like in Westchester? That's Big Joey's territory, ain't it? Call him and tell him I wanna chew the rag."

Stanley's stomach felt as if he'd swallowed a lump of lead. "Nino, you can't be serious! You just woke up from a coma!"

Nino squinted at him—the sort of look Stanley had seen him direct at his sworn enemies. "Yeah, and I'm awake now and I feel fine." He pointed his soup spoon at Stanley. "Stay out of it, kid. This is business. You think I'm gonna let what's left of Big Frank's mob take over our territory? No, we take 'em." One hand strayed to the site of his wound and hovered there, close but not touching. "We can rip the rug right out from underneath 'em. They won't even see it coming."

Stanley turned, ready to bolt, but was gently stayed by Tony. "He doesn't know what he's saying," Tony murmured. "Stay here."

"He doesn't know me," Stanley replied, miserable. "It's like I don't even exist."

"He's got a bullet in his head," Tony replied quietly. "That's gotta be messing with his brains. Give it time."

Stanley, suddenly voiceless, shook his head.

"Yeah, we're gonna smash whatever's left of that mob, grind 'em into the dust. Easy pickings, if you ask me." Nino dropped his spoon, letting it clatter into the bowl. "Tony, get my suitcase packed. We're getting outta here. It's time to finish what I started."

CHAPTER
NINETEEN

TONY stuck close to Stanley during the train ride into the city; he seemed to sense that recent events had thrown Stanley for more than merely a loop. Nino had taken up residence in an empty commuter car and was holding court, planning how to best strike at the remainder of Big Frank's mob. He'd telephoned Eli before leaving for New York, and instructed Eli to advise Danny of Nino's return.

"Sure you don't want a cuppa joe, kid?" Tony shuffled a deck of cards aimlessly. His thoughts were with Hank, back in Connecticut. He hadn't wanted to leave, would have preferred to stay on with the Kellys for a little longer, but Nino had other ideas and Tony went where Nino went.

"A good, stiff drink might do wonders," Tony said. "There's a bar on the train, you know."

"Nothing, thank you." Stanley was haggard, and to Tony's unpracticed eye, he looked like he was worn out with sorrow, numb through and through. There was something wrong with Nino—something worse than being shot. Tony figured maybe it was worse than being in a coma. Nino had gone back to the way he was before....

"It'll come back to him, kid." Tony tried to be reassuring. "He'll remember you. It's just a side effect. Remember what the doc said?"

Stanley nodded, his eyes bright with tears. "Yeah."

"It'll come back to him," Tony said. "You'll come back to him."

"I wonder," Stanley said, "if he'll ever come back to me."

"NOW here's what we're gonna do, see?" Nino stalked back and forth across the floor, gesturing broadly with his hands, his cigar bobbing from hand to mouth and back again. "There's three of Big Frank's guys what are holed up in the Lower East Side... some warehouse belonging to Little Monty Spinelli.... Yeah, well, we're gonna go in there and take 'em out."

"Nino, would you listen to what you're sayin'?" Danny, balanced on crutches, started forward. "Don't you think this thing has gone on long enough, huh? Big Frank's dead. You nearly got yourself bumped off. What the hell are you thinkin'? You tryin' to get croaked?"

Stanley sat in the easy chair near the door, feeling like a nonentity. Nino hardly looked at him and never spoke to him; it was as if Stanley didn't exist.

"If I leave any of them guys standing, you know what'll happen. I gotta wipe 'em all out. All of 'em." Nino stopped and stared at Stanley. "Do I know you? You look...." His forehead creased. "You look kinda familiar...." He shrugged. "Eli, I want you to take a couple of torpedoes and go find Big Frank's boys. Do whatever you gotta do. This town needs to know that I'm back!"

Danny shook his head. He lowered himself slowly and painfully to the couch. "You can count me out," he said. "I told you before, I ain't doin' this no more. I've had it."

Nino turned and stared. "What?" He chewed his cigar. "Whatcha mean?"

"He's right, Nino." Eli, standing by the entrance to the kitchen, hadn't spoken 'til now. "Big Frank's boys think you're dead. You got a chance to go away somewhere, start over. Why don't you take it?"

"Don't you tell me what I oughta do!" Nino snarled. "I'm still head of this mob, ain't I?"

"You ain't talkin' sense!" Danny snapped. "You almost died, or don't you remember?"

"What the hell are you talkin' about?" Nino asked. "They can't kill me. I'm Nino Moretti! You off your nut or something? We were plannin' to take out Big Frank's mob, and then I went to Big Frank's place and whacked him, yeah, just me... I did that... and then...." He paused, staring into the middle distance. "I went to... there was...." His mouth opened and closed. "I went to Big Frank's place... there was... he was in the bathtub... and then I went to a dance.... Yeah, me and Danny went to a dance!"

"You're dingy," Danny grumbled, "I ain't danced in months and you know it."

Nino turned pale. "What?"

Stanley clenched his fists. "You were shot in the head by one of Big Frank's gang when we firebombed one of his nightclubs. You spent months in a coma and you just woke up the day before yesterday. Don't you remember?"

Nino looked from Stanley to Tony, then to Danny, as if hoping that someone could help him understand. "No," he said quietly. "No, I don't... I don't remember...."

"You don't remember me either," Stanley said. "You don't remember us. You don't remember how Danny was nearly killed. You don't remember how Wallace and I went with you to kill Big Frank. All you remember—" He ground his teeth, forced himself to go on. "—is killing."

Nino pressed a hand to his forehead. "I don't feel very well," he murmured. "Is it hot in here?"

Stanley caught him as he fell.

CHAPTER
TWENTY

"THERE'S no question." The doctor frowned. "The bullet has to come out. I've got no other choice. I can't believe the previous doctor didn't think it necessary." He gestured at the X-ray films: anyone with eyes could see the bullet in Nino's head, clear as day. "The sooner I can operate, the better." He glanced at Tony over the tops of his reading glasses. "I'll need your consent."

Tony nodded. "Okay. I'll... whatever you gotta do. Just—" He nodded at Stanley and hurried out of the room.

Stanley drifted closer to the lighted boxes where Nino's X-rays were displayed. "It's bad, isn't it?"

"He will die if I don't remove that bullet immediately."

Stanley forced himself to breathe: in, out, gently and calmly. "Okay." He wiped his sweating hands on his pants. "I guess that would be okay." He was talking to himself. "Yeah, okay. Do that."

He waited with Tony and Wallace in a narrow little anteroom that felt no bigger than a closet. He paced and smoked and drank seemingly endless cups of lukewarm coffee that Wallace brought from the hospital coffee shop. The operation seemed to be taking a long time: Stanley dragged his eyes reluctantly from the wall clock and tried to think of something else.

At length, a door opened and the surgeon went by, still clad in his operating clothes. A short, bald man was hurried down the corridor between two nurses who were stripping off his heavy overcoat and yanking the rings from his fingers. Stanley started up, but they ignored him, and the double doors closed on the remnants of their conversation.

"... So glad you could come, Doctor... really, a case that requires your unique skill...."

"That's him," Tony murmured. "That doctor that operated on Danny."

"Yes," Stanley said. He wondered if the little man's appearance was a harbinger of good fortune—or a sign that an ordinary surgeon's skill was no longer equal to the task. He didn't dare allow himself to hope. It was too much. He'd already exhausted himself in Connecticut, sitting by Nino's bed day after day, praying for him to awaken and finding, when Nino did, that he, Stanley, was little better than a stranger to him.

He didn't know if he could take that sort of pain—again. He didn't know if he could stand being rejected all over again by a man who didn't remember him—who couldn't remember him.

Selfish, his mind whispered, *Nino is fighting for his life in there and you're worried about yourself. Shame on you.* He examined his hands, with their bitten fingernails, and smiled wryly—much more strain and he'd have chewed them off to the elbows. That would make a pretty picture, for sure. "I wonder what he'll be like when he wakes up," Stanley said. He was suddenly close to tears. "You know, it might be better for everybody if I just went back to Kansas. I mean, I can hardly—"

Wallace, standing quietly near the window, turned. "Go back to Kansas?" He laughed mirthlessly. "And do what? Pretend he doesn't exist?" He shook his head. "You just don't get it, do you?"

Stanley blinked at him. "What?"

"Sure, go back to Kansas. Turn your back on him. Act like you never met him, like he never rescued you from that lunatic O'Hara. Sure." Wallace was worked up: twin spots of color burned high up on his normally pale cheeks; his hands were shaking. "Just run off and forget about the best damn thing that ever happened to you!"

"Wallace." Richard approached and took Wallace's arm gently. "Give the kid a break, huh?" He smiled affectionately at Stanley and led Wallace to a chair. "Everybody's on edge," he said to the room in general, "but we aren't helping Nino by acting this way. He's going to need all our prayers and good wishes. Agreed?"

"Yeah," Tony said. "Yeah, he's right. Stop raising Cain, you mugs. This ain't doing us no good."

I would raise a bushel's worth of Cain, Stanley thought, *if I could make Nino well again....*

If I could make him well, and make him remember.

GROER came out some hours later, white-faced and exhausted, wiping his hands on a towel. "I have managed to remove the bullet," he said, "but it was difficult. I cannot say whether there will be brain damage or not. Only time will tell." He spread his hands, an expansive gesture that might have conveyed anything at all. "In these cases, the surgeon's skill is not always equal to the problem. I have done the best I could, but I will not lie to you. There may be certain changes.... Things I cannot predict might crop up. It is difficult to tell, and even the best surgeon cannot be entirely assured of the outcome."

"What sorts of changes?" Tony asked. He made to speak, broke down, then struggled to marshal his emotions. "What... will he be different? He'll still be Nino, won't he?"

"Any surgery in which the brain is breached carries with it the possibility of alterations in personality." Groer drew a deep breath. "You will want to prepare yourselves." He held out a hand toward Tony and Stanley. "Come—I will take you to him."

They found Nino bandaged and silent in a private room, still sleeping under the anesthetic. "He will sleep for perhaps several more hours," Groer said. "The longer he sleeps, it is better for him. Sleeping will help him to heal, hm?"

"Can I...." Stanley swallowed hard. "Is it okay if I talk to him?"

Groer nodded. "Of course. He will register your presence as a... fantasy or a dream. It is alright. But be careful not to overtax him. He must rest as much as possible, or all my best efforts will be undone."

"Nino." Stanley crept near and laid his hand on Nino's chest. "Nino, it's okay, I'm here. It's Stanley. I'm here." He trembled uncontrollably, his body racked with spasms... and he was sobbing, tears streaming down his face. "Nino, it's me, it's Stanley, I'm here, I'm right here—"

"Listen," Tony approached quietly and laid a hand on Stanley's back. "Why don't I take you home? You need some rest. Nino ain't gonna be awake for a while. You heard what that doctor said: the longer he sleeps, the better, huh? Why don't we go get you something to eat, and then maybe a little rest—you can come right back here to see Nino." Maybe helping Stanley would give him an outlet for the things he was feeling. *Be useful*, his mother always said. *If you can't be anything else, be useful to somebody.*

"Promise?" Stanley's face was bleak; it hurt Tony to look at him.

"I promise," Tony said. "I'll bring you back here myself."

Stanley nodded. "Okay," he whispered. "Yeah, let's do that. Let's go home."

HE OPENED his eyes to whiteness and the tentative rays of the late-autumn sun. He felt slightly nauseous, but apart from that, there was no pain. He wiggled his fingers and his toes, turned his head. He was alone in the room, and it was very early in the morning.

My name is Nino, he thought. He said it aloud, testing his voice. *My name is Nino and the year is 1931.*

"I'm awake... would you credit that? I ain't dreamin'." He reached up to touch the bandage on his head, and it all came back to him: *Tell me you ain't gonna do this. Ain't nothin' gonna happen to Nino. Napoleon... he was just a little guy, wasn't he?* Ray was dead; the old man beat him to death and left him on the settee. Ray, buried on Hart Island. *I wanna be somebody, do stuff, make things happen....*

They're writing songs of love, but not for me

"Stanley." He grabbed the bed rails and hauled himself upright. "Where's Stanley? Hey!" Nino shouted. "I gotta find Stanley! I gotta tell him. I'm done with all that stuff." Nino wasn't a stupid man; he understood he had been given a second chance to live differently, to make things right. It was important he not waste it. It was important he use what had been given to him, use it for something besides the things he'd been doing. All of this was very clear to him now, clearer than it had ever been before. "I'm done with all that stuff."

"What stuff is that, Mr. Moretti?" A pretty blonde nurse leaned across and took his wrist. "Or were you talking to yourself?"

"Aw, it's nothin'," Nino said. "Hey, you look familiar. Do I know you?"

"Of course you do. We met during your first convalescence. Promise me this one will go a little better?" She fell silent, counting his pulse. "Well, your heart is nice and strong."

"Say—" Nino barely restrained himself from reaching out and yanking at her clothes like a child. "Look here, am I gonna be okay? I ain't gonna be screwy or nothin', am I?"

The nurse's generous mouth quirked at the corners, but to her credit, she did not give in to her mirth. "No screwier than usual," she murmured.

"What's that mean?"

"I'm assured you'll make a full recovery." She pressed her stethoscope to the center of his naked chest and listened. "Breathe."

"Yeah, but what I wanna know is—"

"Breathe."

Nino breathed. "Listen, sister, I can make it worth your while. Don't you know who I am? I'm—"

"—You're the idiot who got up out of his sickbed and decided to start a gang war." She took the stethoscope away. "Yes, I know who you are." She bent a look on him. "Now, we aren't going to have any of that silliness this time, are we?"

Nino swallowed. "No, ma'am."

"I'm going to get the doctor." She twitched the covers up over him. "If you get out of bed, I'll hurt you."

"I won't get out of bed." He clutched at her wrist. "Please—can you tell Stanley—Mr. Zadwadzki—to come in here."

"You won't get out of bed?" She fixed him with a basilisk stare.

"I won't get out of bed."

"Darn right you won't."

Nino listened to her footsteps disappearing down the hallway. He pushed back the covers and sat up; a wave of dizziness made him sway and he hastily lay back down again. The room was spinning in lazy circles around him and the pit of his stomach throbbed sickeningly. He took long, slow breaths until the urge to vomit passed.

The door opened, and Stanley was there, and he looked the same as he had that first day when Nino saw him at Big Frank's party—when Nino saw him there and fell in love. "Come on in, kid." Nino reached out a hand. "Whatcha waitin' for? You scared of somethin'?"

Stanley's lips moved, but there was no sound. He cleared his throat and tried again. "You… you know who I am?"

"Come over here," Nino said again. He waited 'til Stanley was close enough, then reached out and pulled him into an embrace. "Don't you never go away," Nino murmured, kissing Stanley's cheek, his mouth, his hair. "Don't you never go away from me, you hear me? Promise."

"I promise." Stanley laid his head on Nino's chest and tried unsuccessfully to hide the hot tears sliding down his face. "I will never leave you again." He pressed something into Nino's palm: a tiny, beautifully carved wooden horse.

Six months later

"I DUNNO, Danny." Nino fished his watch out of his vest pocket for the fifth time in as many minutes and peered at it myopically. "I got a bad feeling."

"You worry too much." Danny, leaning on a gorgeously carved ebony walking stick, gazed around the room. Every inch of space in The Two Aces was occupied, and the line at the bar was easily five deep. The orchestra had been blasting away for over an hour—Bix Biederbecke, Benny Goodman, Duke Ellington, Artie Shaw, the Dorsey Brothers—and the spacious dance floor had become a sea of marcelled heads and thrusting elbows. A veritable platoon of waiters, all in formal dress, ferried trays laden with teapots and china cups to patrons seated around the room's perimeter, while leggy cigarette girls slipped through the assembled crowd like a school of sequined eels. "He'll be here." He offered Nino a salacious wink. "I'm so excited. There's no telling what I might do."

Nino stubbed out his cigar in a potted plant. "Aw, close yer head," he said. "It's a wonder my heart's still beating. Wasn't too long ago they were digging lead outta me, remember?" His hands clenched and unclenched at his side and there was a slight sheen of perspiration on his pale forehead. "Say, Danny."

"Skip it, Nino."

"But he said he was coming, right? When you asked him, he said he'd be here." Nino caught hold of Danny's sleeve, crumpling the fine fabric between his nervous fingers. "You asked him, and he said he'd be here. Right?"

Danny scanned the heaving mass of bodies twisting and pulsing on the dance floor and tried not to smirk. "He'll be here."

The song ended with a crash of cymbals and a flurry of applause from the floor. There was a general rush toward the powder rooms or the bar, and the white-jacketed bandleader raised his baton.

They're writing songs of love, but not for me

A lucky star's above, but not for me

Nino couldn't breathe.

Eyes... pale-blue eyes... that face... that long-limbed youth, moving effortlessly in a gorgeous bespoke suit, his body drifting. In the space between heartbeats, something slammed into Nino's chest like a freight train.

Danny's face swam into his vision. "You okay?" And when Nino nodded, "You look like you seen a ghost. You sick or something?"

"He's here." He couldn't stop looking at Stanley. If he did, Stanley would disappear and Nino would never find him again, not ever, and that would be... he'd die.

"I'll die," Nino whispered.

And then Stanley was in front of him, reaching out to take his hand—discreetly, as if he were merely going to shake it—and holding on. "I made a promise." Stanley swayed as close to Nino as propriety would allow. "Your first night back in The Two Aces, was I going to miss that?"

"But you went away," Nino pointed out. "You been gone two weeks, Stanley. What's a fella to think?"

"He went to Kansas, Nino," Danny interjected. "Not the moon."

Nino wasn't going to let it go so easily. "You said two days, maybe three. What kept you?"

Stanley brought a sheaf of folded papers out of his inside pocket. "This took a little longer than I thought it would. Daddy's lawyer, Mr. Parker, was out of town, so I decided to wait until he got back."

"It would be a real shame to go all the way to Kansas," Danny said, "and not get what you came for."

Stanley unfolded the document and held it out so Nino could see it. "Exactly."

"What am I looking at?" Nino squinted at the paper. "I don't see what I'm supposed to be looking at."

"Right here." Stanley pointed. "This indenture witnesses that Stanley Dwight Zadwadzki, an unmarried man of the town of Salina, Saline County, Kansas, does hereby—"

"Yeah, what's it all mean?" Nino cut in impatiently. "You know I ain't no lawyer. Come on!" He looked from Stanley to Danny and back again, beseeching.

"It means you own half of everything I have." Stanley grinned. "In Kansas, I mean. I figure you got plenty of property here in New York. But… if I die before you do." He transferred his gaze to a point just over Nino's left shoulder. "You inherit my property, and nobody can take it from you."

"It's a home… in Kansas, like." Nino grinned. "A home for us."

"For both of us," Stanley said.

Nino reached out, not caring who was watching, and cupped Stanley's cheek in his hand. "You're aces, kid." Tears trembled in his dark eyes, tears he was too proud to let fall. "You're aces."

J.S. COOK was born and raised on the island of Newfoundland. She holds a B.A. and an M.A. in English Language and Literature and a B.Ed in postsecondary education. She makes her home in St. John's, Newfoundland, with her husband Paul and their two spoiled rotten dog-children, Lola and Sheppie.

J.S. Cook also writes as JoAnne Soper-Cook.

Facebook: https://www.facebook.com/AuthorJSCook

Twitter: https://twitter.com/jsopercook

LiveJournal: http://joannesopercook.livejournal.com

Website: http://joannesopercook.net

Also from JOANNE SOPER-COOK

JOANNE SOPER-COOK

The Eye of Heaven

http://www.dreamspinnerpress.com

Also from DREAMSPINNER PRESS

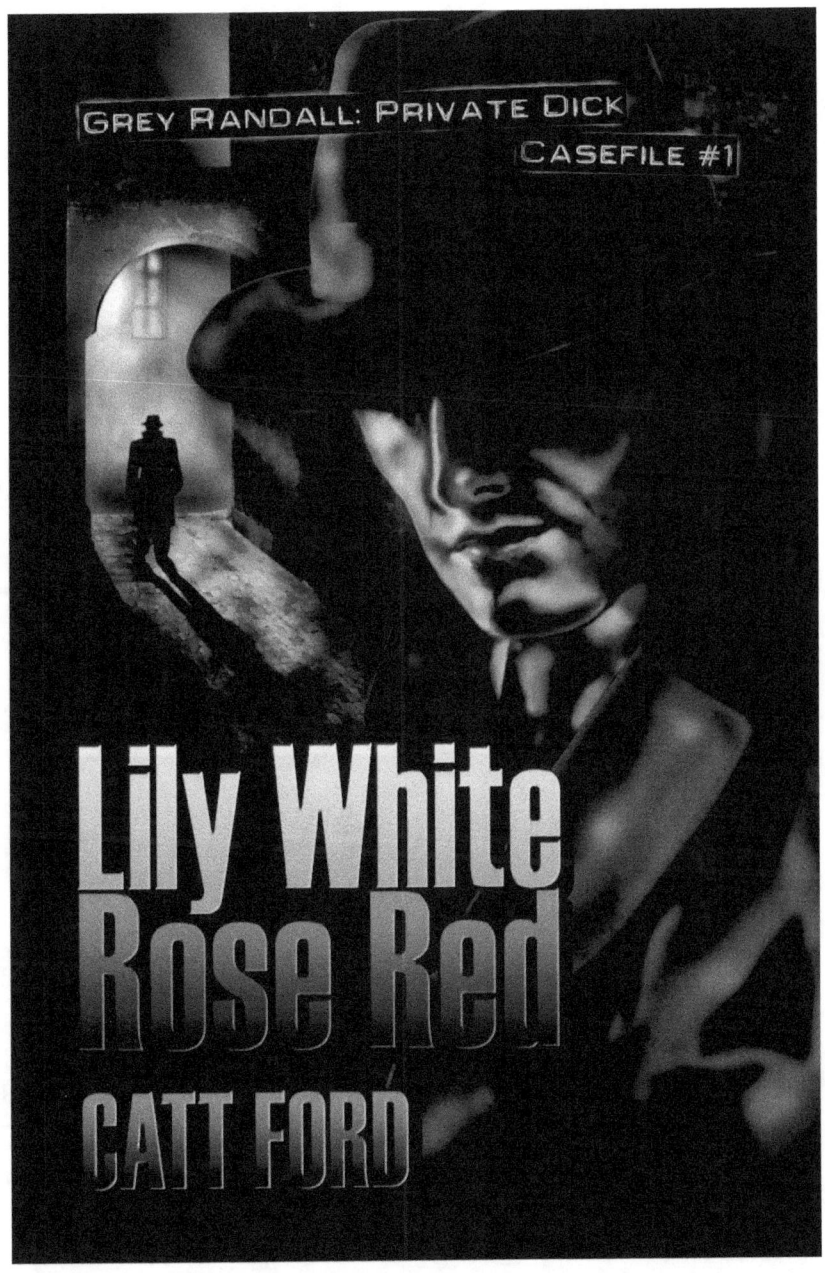

GREY RANDALL: PRIVATE DICK

CASEFILE #1

Lily White
Rose Red

CATT FORD

http://www.dreamspinnerpress.com

Also from DREAMSPINNER PRESS

Windows in Time

M. JULES AEDIN

http://www.dreamspinnerpress.com

Also from DREAMSPINNER PRESS

Summer Song

LOUISE BLAYDON

http://www.dreamspinnerpress.com

Also from DREAMSPINNER PRESS

http://www.dreamspinnerpress.com

Also from DREAMSPINNER PRESS

WHISTLE
PASS

KevaD

http://www.dreamspinnerpress.com

For more of the
best M/M romance,
visit

Dreamspinner Press

www.dreamspinnerpress.com

www.ingramcontent.com/pod-product-compliance
Lightning Source LLC
Chambersburg PA
CBHW070051030726
47506CB00002B/432